Praise for
SHADOW OF HONOR

"Ronie Kendig embodies the very heart of speculative fiction, taking important human issues and exploring them against a backdrop of the most extraordinary circumstances. Kendig's talent as a writer shines not only in her worldbuilding skills, but also in her ability to craft characters I can connect with on a deep level."

— LANI FORBES, award-winning author of The Age of The Seventh Sun series

Praise for
THE DROSERAN SAGA

"Kendig weaves suspenseful intergalactic intrigue in the entertaining . . . space opera in the Droseran Saga series."

— PUBLISHERS WEEKLY

"This Christian science fiction series is an epic story in the making . . . Readers will eagerly await future books after becoming engaged in Kersei's redemptive arc."

— BOOKLIST

SHADOW OF HONOR

Books by Ronie Kendig

SHADOW OF HONOR

THE DROSERAN SAGA
BOOK 3

RONIE KENDIG

T O
BECKY MINOR

The realm of speculative fiction is as beautiful as it is weird, and it takes a very special type of Creative to not only understand this genre, but to also be so wholly passionate about it and its writers that you make it your life's work to provide a safe haven for those who find joy and freedom in writing these stories. A million thanks to *Rebecca "Becky" Minor* for heroically stepping out and starting Realm Makers, one of the most fantastic and inclusive organizations for speculative fiction authors. You are beautiful and amazing! You've created an environment where writers of speculative fiction have found community, encouragement, laughter, instruction, safety, freedom, recognition, camaraderie, beauty . . . There simply is no adequate way to thank you for the many sacrifices you and your family have made to make Realm Makers possible. Becky, thank you from the bottom of my heart and my own created universes. You are an out-of-this-world hero!

Iaizon
Ice Island
Arilamet Ocean
SHAU'LI
Vaqar's Bay
LAMPROS CITY
Bay of Kalonica
Kardia
River Callista
Lampros River
Altas Silvas
XANTHUS
STRATIOS
KALONICA
ı'Una Issi Desert
Kalonican Sea
CRAGSHEAD
Trachys
MOIDIA
Prokopios
JHERAKO
Avrolis
Vantharq Ocean
Forgelight
N
W
E
S
Ironesse Island

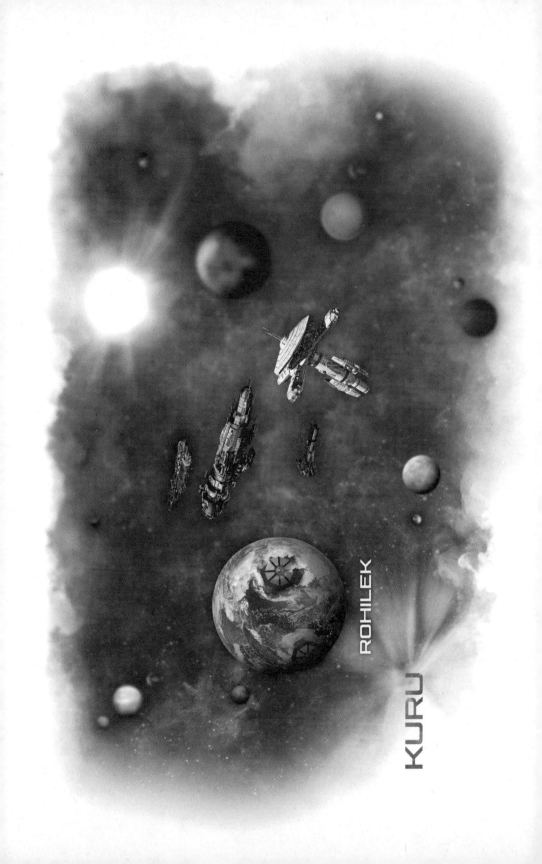

The disorienting, terrible pull on his body only increased the agony pulsing through his veins. One wrong twitch, one hesitation would send them hurtling into the nothingness of space. But at least they'd take the Draegis with them—even now he felt that the other ship hadn't undocked, making the *Prevenire* shudder as it gave its all to thrust them toward their destruction.

Marco Dusan had jettisoned the crew's drop pods, then initiated the jump. That's when he'd realized two pods had malfunctioned, leaving Eija Zacdari and Reef Jadon at the mercy of the beasts and victims to this suicide mission to nail the rings of Kuru System's Sentinel, thereby destroying both the *Prev* and the Sentinel.

One beast with a blue mark on its cheek had the girl in its grip. Others looked on with glowing red stares, sentrylike in the way they stood by, waiting for orders.

Marco Dusan tapped into the tethers that synced him with the hyperjump ship and dipped the port side down, back up, then again so he rocked the *Prev*, hoping to dislodge the Draegis strangling the girl—at least the thing hadn't charbroiled her. While the maneuver drew the creature's attention, the powerfully built beast with its cracked-lava skin didn't yield its captive. Incredibly, it seemed magnetized in place. The feet—hooves?—remained fixed to the deck, though its torso swayed like grass bending under a strong wind. The thing chortled, either in objection to Marco's attempt or as a victory yell for not losing the girl.

But that beast wasn't his only worry. If he was too distracted by what would be an ultimately futile attempt to save the girl, he'd miss the spot at which to leave the jumpstream and hit the right Sentinel. Which meant he'd fail. And that meant these beasts could jump back to Kedalion and kill everyone he knew and loved.

Focus, Marco.

He closed his eyes. Rolled his shoulders back, his neck forward. Traced the scent of that Sentinel. The Signature—seemed wrong to apply that term to an inanimate object—was just as unique as a person's, except sheathed in a familiar waft of burnt air and metal, spent fuel, and . . . death.

Exactly what he'd bring to these creatures. They would not get to the Quadrants. He wouldn't let them kill his people, Isaura . . .

My daughter.

Emotion rocked him at the thought of the babe—his child and heir. And here he was, weeks after being snatched from Isaura's arms, trapped on a ship an inconceivable distance away. He strained his receptors across the universe, searching, aching for them. Where were they? What he wouldn't give to see Isa again.

He moaned, startling himself. "No," he growled.

Focus. Trust Vaqar in all his wisdom to guide and protect.

Two Draegis lurched away from the pods and toward him. Had they finally figured out what he intended to do?

Vibrating with effort, Marco trained every molecule of his body, every thought, every ounce of willpower and desire into accelerating the jumpship toward the Sentinel. Yes, that—

Black, tarlike hands surged at him. Closed around his head.

"Augh!" Gritting his teeth against the vise grip, he harnessed his strength. Refused to be distracted or stopped. Mentally guided the *Prev.* Felt the engines smooth out in their continual acceleration, though they strained against the added mass of the Draegis ship.

The beast trilled, squeezing harder.

A burst of sweet, coppery blood spurted through Marco's mouth—he'd bitten his tongue trying to brace against the beast's crushing hold.

"*Siz quorbonliklaringiz uchun ko'llarga yuborilgansiz,*" came an ear-splitting noise—*words?*—from the Draegis trying to kill him. The beast's eye slits burned near a silver mark on its cheek, yet it remained unfazed by the hard-g pull toward the Sentinel.

Trembling from the force of pressure against his head, Marco had no idea what it'd said. And didn't care. Just had to get the ship to the Sentinel. Destroy both. Strand these monsters. Prevent them from reaching the Quadrants.

Pain tore at his focus. "Augh!" He struggled to lift a hand to stop the beast from cracking his skull. The agony, the heat from the lavalike skin . . .

Crimson slits expanded. "*Xatrimaza belgilangan! Xatrimaza belgilangan!*" It thudded back a step. The eye slits seemed to pulse with anger as it chortled, stirring a commotion among the other Draegis.

The blue-marked one released Eija and turned to them.

Whatever Silvermark was shouting, at least it wasn't trying to kill him anymore. Marco could work with that. Use whatever time he had to keep the ship on course. He reassessed the trajectory. How much farther to the Kuru Sentinel? Could he hang on?

"*Uchuvchi Xatrimaza belgilangan.*" The beast sounded calmer as he repeated the words, drawing over another Draegis, who yanked up Marco's arm, then thrust it down again, howling as if burned by acid.

Marco's brand was glowing bright blue. With all the other sensory pain, he hadn't even noticed.

Chortles and screams echoed through the ship, but Marco couldn't afford the distraction. *Think only about the mission—taking them out, the ship, and the Sentinel.* He sensed its proximity. A few light-years and it'd be done.

A mangled cry snapped his gaze sideways. The first blue-marked Draegis had thudded back to the girl and hauled her from the deck. Her panic spiraled out and assaulted Marco's receptors, making his own ratchet. Tense, he wanted to react. But what could he do? Tethered to the ship, synced to its systems, he could only concentrate on piloting the *Prev* toward destruction. If he unplugged or unfocused . . .

Something slammed his receptors. Sucked the breath from his lungs. His gaze shot to the girl and Blue. He was crushing her. Eyes wild, she shoved a hand against his chest. Suddenly, a glow—no, not a glow . . . a hue or aura—swelled around the two.

Mint saturated the air.

The scent made Marco falter. There'd only been one other time he'd detected *that* efflux. On Iereania. In the Temple with Kersei. What the reek?

With a howl, the beast thrust the girl back. She landed, stumbling, trying to break her fall. Caught the edge of the pod and held on as she stared at Blue, who collapsed in a heap before her.

What . . .?

Shock and fear coated her Signature. Gaping, she looked to Marco, then at the creature, who had yet to rise from where he'd fallen.

No. Not fallen.

Knelt. The beast was *kneeling*!

Shaken, Eija touched her temple, head still pounding from the oxygen deprivation she'd suffered beneath the beast's attempt to crush the life from her—that and the minutes stuck in an oxygen-deprived pod. Until she figured out what had prompted the creature to release her and crouch before her, she didn't dare move.

Insane! The docuvids of the Lavabeasts had not exaggerated. These monsters were fast, lethal, vicious. Yet . . . twice she'd been in its grip, and it'd held back from actually turning her into a dusty pile. Why?

Yeah, maybe don't ask. Just . . .

What? *What* could she do against beasts that reduced people to ash with their arms?

Keening filled the ship. With bewildering speed, the other three Draegis bolted out of the bay, their thudding steps fading down the passage as they headed to the aft port, where their ship clung to the *Prevenire* like a remora on a shark.

Nerves thrumming, Eija glanced at Marco, whose chin was tucked to his chest again. Unconscious? Twitches of his head and hands alleviated that fear. Probably super focused on piloting the ship to the Sentinel.

So we can all die.

Right. So much for the relief she'd felt. Her gaze slid down to the immobilized Lavabeast at her feet. What was wrong with it—him? Was he more AI than biological? Had he powered down or something? Fried his neural net? What was she supposed to do?

She discarded each question as it arose. Assessed her precarious situation. The crackling and swelling of his strange skin said he was still breathing. So alive, not dead.

I can help with that.

He was also awake—glowing eye slits proved that.

Reef shifted on the deck where he'd landed after being tossed by one of the monsters, his arm hanging at an odd angle. Gray eyes came to hers, asking what neither of them could actually voice—*What just happened?* Why had the other Lavabeasts fled? Why had this one not killed her or left?

"Why isn't it moving?" Reef hissed as he slowly climbed to his feet.

She shook her head, still terrified of arousing the beast's anger.

Locked on the Draegis, Reef inched closer and angled toward her. "You okay?"

"Yeah. Sure." Again, she again checked on Marco, who still had his head down. Maybe the other Draegis had done something to him. "Marco?" she called quietly at the same time she heard Reef suck in a breath.

In front of her, the mountain of lava erupted with a piercing howl, terrorizing her as it lunged. Like a lightning strike—a very large, fat, black bolt—it shot forward.

Eija braced, expecting pain and death.

But the blur of ebony collided with a Draegis who'd appeared behind her, its weapon-arm rippling with a red heat wake. Their movements were surreal, violent. Terrible. A *swoosh* of black exploded. Spat in all directions.

Skin tingling from where a projectile singed her, Eija dropped back against the bulkhead, stricken. Terrified. Amid thundering heartbeats, she took in the Draegis raining into an ash heap on the deck.

"What. The. Scuz?" Reef muttered, shifting to her side.

The movement drew Lavabeast's attention. He pivoted. Crimson eye slits expanded. Homed in on Reef.

Realizing the move for what it was, Eija flung her hand out and slid between them. "No!" It was foolish to confront a beast that could weaponize his own limbs, especially when she only had . . . what? A loud mouth?

"Eija, no!" Reef barked.

The Draegis stopped, staring at her. Through her.

Unbelievable.

His body tremored, his anger and desire to destroy evident in the rhythmic pulsing that warbled around him. As if he *wanted* to attack, *wanted* to kill, but . . . he wasn't. Wasn't attacking. Wasn't moving.

"What . . .?" Eija watched the weaponized arm morph back into the black paw—claw—whatever. Slitted eyes stayed locked on her, and he remained in place.

Glowing faintly with a hint of blue light, a hand-shaped depression in the center of his chest drew her attention.

Had that been there before? Somehow, her mind made a connection between that shape and . . . *Where I touched him.* Mentally, she saw her hand landing there when he'd hauled her up and tried to kill her. *Can't be . . .*

"Why'd the others leave?" Reef asked.

Numb, she shook her head.

"Why'd they attack *each other*?"

"You're doing it again—asking what I can't possibly know."

"Well, that . . . *thing* listened to you."

"No, it didn't."

"Then why's it just standing there?" His breath skated along her neck. "Like he's waiting for orders."

"Don't be stupid." Yet, Eija swallowed, because that's exactly how it seemed.

"It wanted to blow my head off, but you told it no, and it *yielded*! To *you*!" Reef eyed her. "Even turned his comrade into ash."

"He *protected* her," came Marco's weary voice. "From the others."

Eija jerked to him, then back to Lavabeast and what just happened. "That's asinine!"

"Why would it protect *her*?" Reef glanced at the ash pile.

"Good question," Marco breathed.

Eija eyed the Lavabeast, fearful he'd rearm and incinerate her, Marco, or Reef. She wasn't dumb—the speed at which he'd powered that arm warned her to tread carefully.

"At least the others are gone," Reef said. "So we just have to worry about this one."

"They're not . . . gone." Marco shuddered. "Still docked."

Alarm spiraling through her veins, Eija pivoted toward the instrument panel and verified what he'd said. Sure enough … What was happening?

Heat rippled off the Draegis, red eye slits glowing brighter then softer, brighter, softer . . . brighter . . .

Realizing he'd closed a few more of the inches between them, she flinched away. Why had the others left him in here? Was he supposed to kill them? Stop them from doing something? Like destroy the Sentinel?

"He won't hurt you," Marco said.

She flicked her gaze to him, then back to the creature as she sidestepped to the lectulo. "How can you possibly know that?"

"Because you're still alive." Marco gave her a tired smirk. "Ask him."

She sniffed. "I don't speak Lavabeast."

"And don't we have more important things to worry about?" Reef slipped to the other side of the lectulo . . . which put him closer to a phase rifle.

"No!" Eija snapped, reading his intent. "Don't."

The Draegis chortled, his arm shifting as heat rose around the appendage.

His good hand halfway to the weapon, Reef faltered. "Did you miss what they did to Bashari?"

"I didn't miss anything," she bit out. "But armed, you become a threat. One he will address without hesitation or remorse."

"I'm not going to stand here and let him turn you into ash."

"Just . . . wait . . ." Eyes on Lavabeast, Eija wondered if Marco was right. *Could* she talk to it?

"Can't wait too long. We've set course for Destruction, remember?"

Eija motioned for Reef to stand down. "Let me try something." She swallowed, having no idea where to start with talking to this beast. Which sounded as crazy as him yielding to her . . .

"Like what?"

"Like asking him what's going on, why he's here—I don't know!" Eija shoved her hands against her face, frustrated, and growled.

"Kuru is homeworld," Lavabeast said, his eye slits aimed at her . . . maybe. "Dangerous. They will obliterate."

Startled at the way he magically answered a question she'd posed, Eija eyed the beast warily. "You speak our language?"

"What?" Reef looked between them, cradling his bad arm. "What're you talking about?"

Eija frowned. "What d'you mean? Didn't you hear him? He said their homeworld of Kuru was dangerous, that they'd destroy us."

For several long seconds, Marco and Reef stared at her. The humming of the ship unnerved her as they shared glances with each other but said nothing. Yet a whole private conversation happened right there.

"*What?*" she demanded.

Marco tucked his chin. "You . . . *heard* him say that?"

She gave him a confused huff. "I sure didn't make it up."

"That's *not* what he said. Jadon, is that what you heard?"

Reef gave a slow, wary shake of his head. "Negative. He just . . . growled."

Eija scoffed but didn't like the way Marco was frowning at her. "Wait. Are you serious? He *did* say it. I can't—" Frustration and fear squeezed her stomach. "How can you not have heard him? He said it. Plain as day." When they still acted like she was the spawn of Xisya, she was desperate for an explanation. "Maybe . . . maybe I can understand him because of the uni-coms."

"Negative," Reef repeated. "Mine doesn't translate his language."

She wasn't going to let them make this into something it wasn't. "But the uni-coms *did* affect how we heard the Khatriza, so—"

"*Xatrimaza!*" Slits radiating a powerful red hue, Lavabeast pounded his fist into his other hand, swung both low and out, then shoved both hooflike paws toward her. "Daq'Ti protect Xatrimaza and Uchuvchi."

"What did he say?" Reef asked.

"How should I know?" Eija balked, unsettled. Because she *did* know. Sort of. Xatrimaza loosely translated to Khatriza. But who was ChooChi-whatever?

"Maybe our PICC-lines are compromised." Reef didn't sound like he believed that.

"They're not." Marco's gaze went distant—likely comparing notes with the feedback from the ship's tubes rigged into his body. That alone still nauseated her.

"Then how can she understand him?"

"I. Don't. Know!" Eija bit out. "It's not like I studied exolinguistics!"

"No, that was Bashari. Who's dead—thanks to that!" He swung his uninjured arm at the Draegis, who erupted—mountainous glob of Lavabeast that he was—at Reef.

A roar reverberated off the bulkhead.

Eija stumbled back, her veins icing.

"Guess that answers whether or not he'll protect you," Reef muttered.

This whole thing was wrong. Twisted. Somehow, she felt to blame, which made no sense, but neither did her ability to decipher the Draegis language.

"Either way," Reef grunted, "them destroying us or Marco ramming us into the Sentinel—we're pretty much dead."

Eija cast a glance at the beast. If he understood them, would he tell his friends about their plan to destroy the Sentinel? She slid her hand to Marco's shoulder. "Is there any way to stop them from getting to the Quadrants without killing us in the process?"

Marco grunted. "Not that I can figure out. We have an extreme disadvantage, being unfamiliar with their system, technology, language, how to defeat them, etcetera. And they're still docked to the ship, so . . ."

"But it's the *data* on the ship, right? Not—"

"And me." He gave her a weary look. "They could use me just as the Khatriza did—"

"Xatrimaza!" the beast chortled again.

"Why does he keep saying that?" Reef demanded.

"*I. Don't. Djelling. Know!*"

"But you understand him!"

"I don't—" She growled. "I hear words. Pieces"—no idea how or why—"but that doesn't mean I *understand*."

"Clearly you do if you—"

"Enough!" Marco's tired gaze went to the beast, then to Eija. Back to the beast simmering with readiness to wipe them out. "Khatriza."

"Xatrimaza!" The Draegis made the same motion to Eija.

Marco looked at the beast's chest and gaped. "That mark! Where'd it come from?"

"Why do you two keep asking *me*? I have no idea!" But didn't she? Her hand even now seemed to burn.

"It wasn't there . . . till he yanked you out of the pod." Marco's words came fast, wheezing out at the end. "Put your hand on his chest. Now."

"No way." Eija shifted away from the Draegis. "I . . . I need to check Engin—"

"Do it!"

Eija blanched, studying the beast and how he suddenly seemed more a piece of cargo than a vicious, ash-creating heap of lava. "He'll kill me."

"I'm betting he won't," Marco said.

"Yeah, and you can afford to lose that bet because you wouldn't be the one risking life and limb." Eija hesitated. Touched her temples. "This makes no sense."

"Neither did you sensing Marco in the hull," Reef said.

"True . . ." she conceded. "The Khatriza—"

"Xatrimaza!" Beast roared and motioned.

Eija whirled to him. "Why do you keep doing that?"

"He keeps indicating to you when he says it, Ei," Reef said.

The beast let out a mournful lowing.

"Touch the mark," Marco insisted.

With a huff, Eija saw those crimson slits home in on her. "It's okay," she said with a nod, not sure if she was trying to reassure Lavabeast or herself. Though she caught pieces of his words, there was no proof he understood hers. She hoped he could, or she was about to be blackened Tryssinian.

When Eija finally lifted her hand toward him, a wave of fear crashed through her. She curled her fingers, hesitating. What if he killed her? Saw this as threatening?

"Do it," Reef prodded.

"Shut up."

"He's waiting for you to—look at him!"

Eija peeked at the crimson lines that served as eyes in the beast towering over her and startled to find him watching and . . . yes, waiting.

"Confidently," Marco prodded. "No fear."

"Says the one *not* about to touch a creature who can incinerate people." *Get it over with.* She splayed her hand and reached toward him.

With that lightning speed, he gripped her hand. Pulled it to his chest. He slid to his knees—did he even have knees?—and those vertical slits suctioned closed. His lowing now seemed less mournful, more . . . relieved. "*Daq'Ti ahmoq emas. Daq'Ti bo'ysuning Xatrimaza. Himoya Xonim.*" Releasing her, he pressed his face to the ground. "*Yuzma yuz.*"

Eija snatched away her hand and stumbled backward, stricken. Processing what he'd done, what he'd said.

He once more rose to his stumps. His segmented neck rippled as he inclined his head at her with that lowing noise. "*Yuzma yuz.*"

"Hand to face," Eija murmured, understanding it intuitively.

"What?" Marco asked with a sweaty frown.

Eija blinked. "What?"

"Why'd you say that—hand to face?"

A chill raced through her. "*He* said it—but don't ask me what it means." She shook herself. "I don't know how I can understand him either. What if . . . what if Xisya gave me something . . . *extra* in my PICC-line that enables me to translate him? Them?"

"You said she tried to kill you."

"She did!"

"Then why would she help you?"

Something akin to panic drummed against Eija's ribs. "I have no idea." Her insides twisted and coiled at the way Marco and Reef stared at her.

"Did he say anything else?" Marco narrowed an eye.

Hating this, she avoided looking at the beast. "His name is Daq'Ti. And he . . ." She lifted her chin. "He said he'd protect me."

Well, that was most of what he'd said. But no djelling way would she repeat the rest. Besides, it was likely a misinterpretation.

Yeah. Had to be.

Exhaustion was a formidable enemy, clogging his thoughts. "Five mikes to Kuru Sentinel." Marco struggled to keep his head clear and stay conscious. "In your crash couches."

"Seriously?" Jadon's answer was sharp, but he was already moving, cradling his injured arm. "Why does it matter, since we're the bomb?"

"Harness in," Marco said over the comms. "This will hurt."

"Can't hurt much more than extra-crispy dead," Jadon commed as he jogged through the hatch.

"In death, you don't feel anything. But this you'll feel . . . *then* you'll die."

"Aww," Jadon said. "You trying to cheer me up, Kynigos?"

Marco smirked, shuttering his eyelids as he focused on the trajectory. "Eija . . . ready for hard-g flip and burn. Check Eng—"

She touched his arm. "We're sure we should do this—take it out with the *Prevenire*?"

"No choice. We fail, everyone we know and love dies."

"But . . . you have a wife to go back to."

"I'd rather die . . . and my family live . . . than for *everyone* to perish because . . . I feared death." He gave a nod. "Go. Check Engineering."

She pursed her lips as if holding back more arguments, then turned and walked out of the bay, the Draegis thudding behind her like an obedient pup.

"Should we be worried about that thing?" Jadon commed.

"No," Marco grunted. "It's going to burn with us."

"And the leeches on our back?"

"Like you said—extra crispy."

"Think I'm going to like you." Jadon's grin carried through the comms. "At least for the next five minutes."

Humor. A good attempt, but Marco had too many things pulling on his mental and physical resources. "Pilot, be ready."

"Every day in every way," Jadon promised. "What about you? Doing okay?"

Stay on mission. "Verify course. Systems check. Watch Eija. If that thing isn't protecting her . . . or if his self-preservation kicks in . . ."

"I'll vaporize him."

Marco wasn't sure that'd be necessary. Using his receptors with deep breaths, he noted the ship's readiness. Jadon and the girl in position. The former in pain, both of them stressed but focused. Nothing at all from the Draegis.

Eyes closed, he verified the course, felt the thrum of the ship gliding almost effortlessly through the stream. *Almost* because they had a parasite attached to the hull, the Draegis ship. The added mass was devouring fuel reserves.

Oh no. Hard burns ate up fuel like nobody's business. He calculated the distance, worked through the flip-and-burn maneuver. *There's not enough . . .* The fuel would be depleted. He should've reduced acceleration to compensate, come in on the inertia of previous burns.

No. Mayhap it was a mistake. His calculations wrong. Surely.

But it wasn't. Once they cleared the Sentinel and flipped, there wouldn't be enough fuel for a hard burn.

Reek! That's why the Draegis had attached to the hull. That'd been their intent. It hadn't been to follow them or kill them in here. They knew. The Draegis knew he intended to destroy the Sentinel using the *Prev.* And they intended to prevent it.

Marco's gut churned. "Ancient, help us." Mayhap he was wrong. It was a fool's hope, but he wouldn't go down without a fight. Nudging the trajectory before they cleared the rings could pitch them anywhere in the 'verse. They had to go through. And by the Fires of Pyr, he'd try that burn. Use up every cell of fuel and energy on the slim chance they could smash that thing into oblivion.

Either way, they were as good as dead.

Isa . . . Grief clawed at him, his thoughts flinging back to her. Their last night together . . . She was a gift he'd never expected or wanted. Not at first. Loving her, being loved . . . being pulled away even as he spotted the twin lights in her eyes—hers that pure blue, and another, softer. *My daughter . . .*

His throat felt thick, raw.

Isaura . . . my kyria . . . I am always *with you. Love her well. I would have preferred to be there. To see her born, know her, raise her, protect her . . . Forgive me, my love. I would have been there . . .*

"No! Stop!"

Shouts echoed through the *Prevenire*, pulling Marco back to the present. To the timer. Two minutes. "What's wrong?"

More shouts. Eija's panicked efflux reached him in the sanitized air.

Comms! Marco keyed it. "What's going on?" A waft of something cool and minty hit his receptors, forcing him to suck in a breath. "What was that?"

More yelling.

"Jadon! Eija! What—"

"I . . . it's scuzzed," Jadon finally reported in, his voice thick with the alarm that drifted on the ship's recycled air. "We're scuzzed!"

"What?" Marco probed the system for errors or failures. "What happened?" A claxon sounded, grabbing his attention. "Countdown. Brace yourselves."

Awareness speared Eija as she stared at Daq'Ti from the security of her crash couch. He'd done something to the controls. They still had access, but the console wasn't responding as it had before. Things around them were heinously scuzzed, but there stood the beast, those crimson slits unblinking—*does he even* need *to blink?*—as they approached the Kuru Sentinel.

From the Command deck, Reef shouted epithets, cursing the recalcitrant systems.

The ship vibrated in terror, as if the *Prevenire* knew it hurtled toward destruction.

Cheery thought.

For a selfish moment, Eija wished it'd been Gola on this ship, which Marco was using as a self-guided nuclear device to prevent the Draegis from fast-tracking their way to Kedalion. That was . . . *if* they could get it to respond better. Eija was working furiously and getting nowhere. "What did you do . . .?" She skated a glance to Daq'Ti, still freaked she'd figured out his name, his language.

"Calibration adjusted," Daq'Ti chortled.

"Cali . . ." Gaze tracking the glowing array of instruments, Eija chided herself for not fighting Marco more on this mission he'd undertaken. Argued that there had to be another way. That she should've done something, *anything* to stay alive. But what were their lives compared to the billions back in the Quadrants who would die if the Draegis—she eyed the beast again—followed the coordinates from the *Prev* back to the *Chryzanthe*?

Reef appeared in the hatch between Command and Engineering,

something strange in his expression as he strode toward her.

She started. "What're you doing? Get back there!"

Daq'Ti rotated toward Reef and let out a subtle thrum, his hand reaching back ever so slowly. Like an Eidolon with his finger going to the trigger.

"You should pilot us in. Go." He climbed into the other crash couch.

"Seriously?" She wasn't going to leave the *Prev* without a pilot at the helm, so she freed herself from the couch. "Why?"

"The controls . . ." He shrugged beneath the straps, hissing between clenched teeth as he slid the harness over his injured arm. "He did something to them. I can't get a bead on what. The ship isn't responding like normal."

She almost smirked. "It's never been normal to me."

His brown eyes seemed tortured. "I know . . . But it's even worse since BeastieBoy did something to them." He swiped a hand over his olive face. "I was just thinking . . . Maybe all those times when you said it was off . . . maybe you were right."

Her heart thumped a little. "You said I was crazy."

"Yeah, and who thought we'd find a man hardwired into the ship? This whole thing is straight out of the insanity training manual."

"Still, with Lavabeast's changes, I don't know what I can do." Once harnessed and PICC'd up, she marveled at the difference with Marco controlling most of the ship's systems. She hadn't really noticed it before, but it was obvious now. It could also be a combination of Daq'Ti's recalibration and Marco's . . . connection. Engines were running smoother, not trying as hard. Controls weren't as sticky—not that they were bad before, but now, they were like . . . an extension of herself. She could sense Marco and the finesse his abilities brought to the mix. It made no sense, but it worked. And well.

She relaxed, eyed the countdown, and commed, "Sentinel in five . . ." Head back, she studied the HUD where the convergence of their ship and the blue dot of the Sentinel appeared. "Four." Sweaty palms betrayed her fear. "Three."

Right here. This was when that *off* feeling happened. Just like in training when she'd done everything by the book. Obeyed like a good little candidate. But this time . . . it was real. What if she was wrong and killed them right here—too soon to take out the Sentinel? As Chief had repeatedly said she'd done in the sims?

Trust your instincts, Patron had admonished.

Yeah, but Bashari had said, *You'll get us all killed.*

Well, that was a closed book, anyway.

"Do it, Ei," Reef's preternaturally calm voice sailed into her ear.

Here goes . . . everything.

"Two." Eija drew in a breath and with a subtle nudge of her finger made the correction. She held that breath. Exhaled. "One."

Blue light haloed around them. The drop from the slipstream this time felt like a punch in the gut. She coughed a breath as searing white light expanded through Command. Her split-second thought was that there'd been an explosion. She focused on the routine, the familiarity of it as the ship vibrated with fury. Bulkheads popped open. Cables dangled. Sparks hissed.

At the convergence of the dots . . . she tensed for the explosion. Braced for . . . something that never came. Her gaze hit the array. Saw something that didn't make sense. As if they flowed through a wall that should've smashed them to bits.

Alive. We're alive.

Why are we alive?

Djell! That meant—

Snapped back to the reality that they now had to flip and burn to hit the rings, she fired reverse thrusters. Even as they flipped and she keyed the sequence to restart the forward propulsion, Eija spied a new dot on the radar.

Then three. Five. A lot more.

"Oh no."

The *Prevenire* roared against the strain exerted against the hull.

"Hold for hard g's." She spun up the engines and tapped in the target of the . . . "Holy Voids and Ladies," she muttered, eying the massive ring that gave off the glow.

No, not *one* ring. Several. All embedded within each other. Not a long baton like the *Chryzanthe*. This was massive, sophisticated, with many individual stations. If the *Chryzanthe* was a metal flower, this was a whole djelling bouquet tethered around one colossal station.

Daunted by the size of that thing, she started the hard burn.

The *Prev* shifted, hard. She strained against the blackness encroaching on her vision, bit down on the mouthguard, fought to stay conscious. The ship screamed . . . then whined. Her vision cleared as the crushing weight of acceleration lessened.

Vibrations fell silent, along with her hopes. Their hopes.

"No," Eija whispered. Fuel! She gaped at the tank readouts.

"What's wrong?" Reef commed.

"We're out of fuel," Marco breathed. "They planned this."

Daq'Ti thudded toward Nav.

"What's he doing?" Reef asked.

"No idea."

"Stop him."

"How am I supposed to *stop* him?" She tried recalibrating the tanks. Maybe that's what was wrong. No good. She eyed Daq'Ti working the panel with his hand—fingers, claws, whatever. A console at his eye level slid open. The strange thing had a depression, three holes, and readouts.

"Djell," Eija whispered, staring at it.

"Stop him! Don't let—"

Daq'Ti pressed his appendage against the black console. It fit—perfectly. That's why he'd stayed—to do this. It'd all been a trap!

"Get away from that!" Words still on her lips, Eija felt the ship shift—shudder, something strange. Something she hadn't felt before. "No," she breathed, scanning the array of readouts as they went from green to orange to red. "No no no."

"We're powerless." Marco's voice was strained. "That's why they piggybacked us—to drain our cells faster. They knew what we were trying to do. Eyes sharp. They'll reboard us now."

"Think Big Guy here is helping them?"

A series of thumps sounded against the hull. Sparks flew from the open bulkhead.

Pop! Boom!

The *Prev* shuddered. Whirred. Lighting flickered off and emergency beacons along the inner hull activated. A subtle vibration wormed through the ship.

"What's going on?" Eija balked, watching the various ship's systems go offline, then some come back online.

"Auto-firing!" Marco shouted. "The rings are firing on us!"

The *Prev* lurched to port, then stern, back to port.

"What the scuz! Eija, what're you doing?" Reef grunted.

"It's not me! The ship," she said, bracing against the jarring motions. The incoming barrage … missing. She eyed the Draegis, who hovered over a similar readout. "It's Daq'Ti—whatever he did to the *Prev* gave us a chance against their proximity-based firing system. I think."

"That'd makes sense with what I'm seeing," Reef said.

"Won't last forever," Marco muttered. "But maybe long enough."

As if in answer to his words, the ship silenced its defense.

The cold vacuum of space was murder on his receptors. Yet Marco detected the half dozen ships surrounding them, Eija and Jadon's terror. Strangely—terribly—he couldn't smell those beasts, except when they fired their weaponized arms.

The girl hurtled through the hatch with the Eidolon close behind her. "We're dead in the water—no thrusters or nav. They just took out comms."

Marco slumped against the lectulo. If they were going to be boarded again, he couldn't stay in this contraption. These beasts were primal—they'd see him as wounded prey, primed for the kill. "Get me out of the lectulo."

"How?" Eija came forward, eying the contraption. "Shad said if we do, you—"

"If I stay here, I'm guaranteed to die."

"But if I take you out, you die."

"Then I've got nothing to lose." He reached back and caught the cable feeding into his nape. He'd seen Eidolon with these PICC-lines, and every member of the *Prevenire* had them, too. That the device protecting Eidolon on hard drops was the same device that enabled him to tap into a ship with his senses made him wonder where it'd come from. He had a bad feeling he knew the answer.

Eija's hand closed around his. "What about your wife? Your baby—a girl, right?"

A pang struck his chest and he struggled against it. "Staying tethered to this thing doesn't get me back to them."

"But you can barely talk. How do you expect to fight—"

"I'll figure it out." He ripped the IV out of his forearm. Fire flashed through his veins, but he gritted past it.

A chortling roar came from behind the girl, who glanced back. The Draegis thudded closer, focused on Marco.

"He doesn't look happy," Jadon said.

A stream of unintelligible words warbled as the beast drew alongside the lectulo and those slits glowed—*glowered*. Pulsed with meaning.

Eija looked slowly from the Draegis back to Marco with an expression and efflux of confusion. Did she not understand the thing this time?

"What's wrong?"

"He . . . he wants you to stop. I think he's saying extricating yourself will kill you."

"Convenient." But Marco detected nerves in her efflux, too. There was more to the beast's words. "What else?"

She chewed the inside of her lower lip. "I think we should listen."

"I can see why he'd say that," Jadon said. "If we listen, we make their next culling easier."

The guy's anger mirrored Marco's. "I'm not letting them take me alive—the intel is in my head and this ship." What he anak'ed from her redirected his anger. "Already giving up on me?"

"No," she said, startled.

"What aren't you saying?"

"He . . ." She deflated. "He said help is coming."

"Help for *him*." Glancing at the weapons lockers, Jadon balled his good fist—he'd used a strap to anchor his broken arm to his chest. "Remember phase-blaster for arms? Bashari being reduced to ashes?"

A loud clank reverberated through the ship, and with it came a noise that drilled the air, driving their gazes to the hull.

Marco felt the explanation in the lectulo, in his senses. "Another ship docked—starboard."

The Draegis chortled again.

Eija balked. "Why another?"

"There's no good answer to that." No matter what ship had mated with the *Prev*, Marco wasn't going to take the new arrivals sitting down. He ripped off the nodes attached to his temples and from behind his ear. More fire zinged his neck. He grimaced but reached for the ones on his chest.

"No!" Eija's command came in a tone and decibel that drew Blue closer, his arm weaponizing. She lifted a hand to the beast and stilled him before refocusing on Marco. "Stop. Please."

Wondering if he should be concerned that the black monster obeyed her so readily—surely the girl wasn't a traitor—Marco hesitated. The thoughts grew louder, more pervasive. What did he really know about this crew? How had they *not* known he was stitched into the ship, just as these cables were stitched into him?

No, he wouldn't stay down like a dog beneath a master's boot. He pushed up from the steel slab—but wobbled. His arms trembled from disuse.

"Please." Eija pressed a hand against his shoulder.

He glared up through his brows at her. "If I die, you will answer to my family—my wife, my daughter, my kingdom, and the Brethren."

She swallowed. "You won't die. Daq'Ti will protect us."

"He'll protect *you* because you marked him. He bears your mark. We are nothing to him. And if there are dozens of his kind coming through those airlocks, even he can't stand against so many." Making another attempt to stand, he went slower to give his muscles and limbs time to adjust. Reached for the chest cables.

A deafening sound erupted, like the howl of wind through a lonely cave. Marco saw a black blur rush him. Knew he'd been right—that thing didn't care two scents about him. He threw up an arm for defense as a wave of heat struck. He careened into a fathomless void.

"Day five, fifteen twenty-three Kedalion Universal Time . . ."

Sevtar "Rhinn" Crafter had no idea if that mattered on this planet, with its unusual day-night revolution. No matter how hard he tried, he couldn't get a bead on time marking with his chronometer. Maybe it was damaged. Or he was crazy, losing his mind after dropping from the *Prevenire*.

Definitely a possibility.

Voids—he couldn't unsee what happened to Bashari at the hands of those Draegis monsters. Then there was the horror of finding Marco wired into the ship. What kind of sick slag does that to another being?

Visor autodarkening to shield his eyes from the sun high in the sky, he glanced to where he'd last seen the *Prev*. It'd jumped, though he had no idea how Marco managed that with the ship's damaged systems and his wrecked body *and* the Draegis piggybacking like parasites. But they'd been there one minute, gone the next.

"What're you doing?"

At the voice whining through his comms, he lowered his gaze to the horizon of this blank-slate-of-a-planet. Nothing out there. Just cold, white. How there was this much snow with that sun confounded him, but what did he know about this alien galaxy except that it sucked?

"We need to keep moving," Gola Tildarian snipped.

He gritted his teeth. Ignoring her hadn't worked for the last two days, so he wasn't sure why he thought it would now. "You need to remember your rank."

"Rank? You want to fight over rank?"

Rhinn rotated and slammed his visor against hers. "Excuse me, *Shepherd*?"

She wasn't backing down. "There's no Command here. No HyPE. Therefore, *no shepherds*. In fact, there are no other people. No point—"

"Stand down," Rhinn growled. "It's even more important now to maintain chain of command. Obey orders, or I'll leave you behind. Now, grav down." He scanned the empty landscape again and huffed. "We're taking a break."

"Again? But we've only—"

"What'd I say?" he barked.

She drew up but wisely kept her mouth shut.

"Voids, why couldn't it have been Zacdari or Jadon who dropped with me? At least they'd be useful!"

"How dare—"

A strange howl bellowed on the cold wind, making Rhinn draw up short. Yeah, he had snagged a pulse pistol and rifle from the weapons locker on the *Prev* before dropping, but—

"We'll be fine," Tildarian squeaked. "We have weapons."

"Nothing big enough for whatever made that noise." And anything that survived out here had to be hard to kill.

Tildarian glowered. "You're just trying to scare me."

"Only if it worked." Crouched by the pod sleeve and cradling an unconscious Shad, Rhinn ran diagnostics to be sure the kid had what she needed until they could get help.

If help existed out here.

The crash landing had destroyed her pod, leaving her with a goose egg on her head. Although the swelling was going down, her brain activity wasn't coming up.

"C'mon, kid," he grumbled, tapping the panel. Didn't need another death on his conscience.

Small and quiet, the kid had a name bigger than her one-point-five-meters—Ildanis Shadrakrian. She'd earned his respect after the way she'd dealt with the sabotage, crewmate illnesses and death, and then fast-dropping without complaint.

Unlike Tildarian.

He dug into his ruck for a ration bar, and his gloved hand thrust out the bottom. "What the—"

With a soft *thump*, a critter screeched away, its hairy, spiked backside vanishing into the snow.

"No." Those ration packs were all they had left, and with no civilization in sight, he needed every one. Especially if Shad ever came to.

"You idiot! That's our food!"

Rhinn slammed his forearm into Tildarian's chest. "Call me that again!"

She stumbled back, her face thick with shock and fear.

Soft *ploofs* of the escaping creature yanked him around. He sprinted after it. Within a few meters, he leapt headlong into the snow as the thing dived. Must be a vole or something, digging tunnels for safety from the elements and predators. He shoved his hand down into the depression after the creature.

Frozen earth dug beneath his nails and soaked his fingerless gloves. Rhinn felt the brush of coarse fur and lurched to grab the thing, groping blindly for the thief. "C'mon, you scuzzer!" On his knees, he swept away snow to get a better angle on the tunnel.

"He stole all our food! You have to catch him."

"No slag." Rhinn wasn't getting anywhere. He whipped around and snatched his collapsible shovel. He hacked at the hoary ground . . . only to find more tunnels. "When I catch you," he hissed at the thing, "I'll slice and dice you for dinner." He grunted at the mouthwatering thought. Hadn't had real meat in months. He'd willingly waste a whole power cell cooking the thing. It'd be worth it.

An hour and four additional unearthed tunnels later, Rhinn had to accept the blasted thing had escaped—with said rations. Pitching the shovel aside, he bellowed his frustration and fought the futility that wanted a voice, wanted to erupt with fury. He dropped back against the ground.

"Why are you giving up? Find him!"

Rhinn shot the shrieking shrew a look and flipped up his visor. He took more than a little sick pleasure when she shrank back. Swiping a hand across his cracked and blistered lips, he glanced at Shad's pod sleeve. At least in there she didn't have to worry about hunger, frostbite, or hypothermia. She'd die quietly, her O_2 eventually running out.

Of course, he wouldn't let that happen. It's why they were hiking till their legs fell off every day, trying to find people or a village. He huffed as he squinted out into the emptiness. Just had to stay alive until the *Prev* returned. *If it returns.* Which depended on Marco surviving the jump. And avoiding the Draegis ambush on the other side of the Sentinel. And the slim possibility of Marco, Zacdari, or Jadon knowing how to navigate back to this planet.

We're scuzzed.

If things didn't change soon, they'd die on this rock.

Can't give up. Not with two subordinates depending on him. Rhinn lumbered to his feet. After throwing another curse at the furry thief, he slung on his ruck, shouldered into the harness he'd rigged to drag the pod sleeve, and started trudging to Baru knew where . . . At least he wasn't sitting idly by, waiting for Death to come.

"We're *leaving*?" Tildarian whimpered, shuffling after him. "But I'm hungry!"

Rhinn walked for several minutes in silence. "Day fifteen million and five," he subvocalized into his personal comms. "If I kill her, it wasn't my fault."

"Day seven: It's been two days since the vermin stole our rations. I've dug for bugs and can't even find that in this Baru-forsaken place. Tildarian's complaints are endless. Where's a good airlock when you need one?" He didn't want this record of their journey to be all about the whiny shrew. "We . . . uh . . . we took shelter on the plain again—not that we had a choice. Built an ice hut like every other night. That's when I noticed Shad's pod sleeve freezing up, hardening the gel nutrients. Ya know, the ones designed *not* to freeze? Well, they froze." He rubbed his eyes and fought off the exhaustion. "I hope she makes it."

"Day ten: The kid—Doc—came to the same day the pod nutrients froze. So that was good. She's good." The repercussions if she hadn't . . . "It was real nice to see those soft eyes looking back at me. She's something else." *Since when do you care about that?* He kept walking. "Anyway—that's when we got attacked. This enormous elephant-mammoth thing snatched Tildarian right out of our ice shelter. It was . . . I . . . no time to prepare. But even that beast couldn't stand her—found her a half klick out. Ripped up pretty bad. When I was rigging her to the stretcher, the thing returned and finished her off. Nearly killed me and the kid, too. Had to use my pulse rifle to drive it off . . ." Spent way too much ammo. His legs tangled and he dropped to all fours, narrowly avoiding a collision between a rock and his face. "Doubt we'll survive till the *Prev* returns. Just a matter of who dies first and last." He peered through the distance.

What was that? Light was breaking over the horizon, casting strange shadows. *Probably the sun, idiot.*

Man, he was tired. Dead tired.

His eyelids drooped. Felt himself sagging. He growled and pushed up. But his boot slipped, and he went down hard, head bouncing against the hardpacked ground. Light winked out.

Laughter a melody and face a beauty, Isaura threw back her head in the field of wildflowers. The river rushed past them a few feet away, adding to the symphony caressing his ears. Gold hair lit by the morning sunrise splayed around her head like a halo, a perfect addition to the Heavenly that she was. Her delicate touch caressed his face.

"When I first saw you in Moidia, I thought my heart would drum out of my chest." Her smile went wistful. "Your pale eyes, so like the storm clouds, seemed to know my pain, what I'd been through."

Marco smoothed a hand over her forehead and into her hair, savoring its silkiness. "I felt a protectiveness regarding you that I couldn't explain. A compulsion to be near you that had no name." He brushed his lips over hers. "You fulfilled something in me I did not know I needed."

She cupped his face. "Come back to me, Dusan."

He frowned. "I'm right here, my aetos."

Sorrow etched its painful talons along the edges of her eyes. "I wish you were."

Propping himself up to see her better, he traced her cheek . . . Only, his fingers went through *her. Were roughened against grass that was no longer green but more haylike. She wavered. Her existence wavered.*

His heart thumped. "Isa."

Tears spilled down her rosied cheeks. "I need you. Please . . ." Somehow she was standing over him. Moving away. She turned. "I miss you so much it hurts."

"I'm right here!"

"Our baby, Dusan . . . please . . ."

"Isaura! Reeking plagues—I'm right here." *He darted forward. "I beg you— stop!" He couldn't lose what he'd only just found. He snatched for her but caught empty air and stumbled. Fell into the river . . . The dark, churning, roiling river snatched him down into its icy, angry depths.*

"Augh!" Marco jerked upright. Every muscle and ligament spasmed, slamming him back down against a hard table. Agony hammered him, drawing out a howl.

A strange noise blared as he dragged himself from the cacophony of fiery pain. He blinked to get his bearings. His surroundings swam and blurred. He blinked again. A dark, looming shape reached for him.

Marco snapped out a hand. Caught the offender.

Trilling wafted over his receptors.

That wasn't right. *Noises* didn't pervade his receptors, smells did. But with the trilling came a surreal peace that cooled his panic and temper. His mind scrambled for coherence. He squinted, struggling to orient himself. Recall where he was. At the Citadel.

No, Drosero. Kardia . . . Isaura. Her face swam into his thoughts, golden hair splayed across the pillow. Yes! He'd been . . . Where had he—

Bed. He'd been abed with her when a noise had pulled him awake. Men converging on him. Dragging him away. The reek in the air—grief, fear, panic. Then cold, chemically treated air.

Recollections flooded him. The *Prevenire*. Bulkhead. The *beasts*! The crew. One being killed. Others screaming. The pods dropping.

A face shifted into view over Marco—not a memory. Real. And not human. *Draegis!*

Vile beasts with a thirst for violence. As the thing stood over him, he vowed to wipe them out. Every last one.

More calm hit his receptors. Eyeing the beast, he fell quietly into that air bath of comfort. Relaxed.

Wait. No . . . no, he shouldn't be calm. That wasn't right. His brain was getting mixed signals or something. But there were sparks of thoughts, cold cruelty permeating the calm. Warning swimming against the current of placidity. All enough to tell him he wasn't safe. But suddenly, he rushed headlong into darkness.

Again, Marco found his way out of the emptiness. He tried to move his arm, only to find himself restrained. A terrorizing split-second flashback to the *Macedon* and Xisya sent him crashing down onto the metal table. Thrashing against the voltcuffs, he strained to pull upright. Struggled, but the fight was leaching out of him. Strength draining as if each attempt he made deprived him of willpower. As if this apathy fed off his panic. Once more he fell into that black void.

When he next opened his eyes, the room was darker. Colder. The air had a different tinge. He could smell people. How long had he been out? Recalling the Draegis and voltcuffs, Marco jerked. Scanned the room for threats, realizing he was no longer in a lab now. He lay on a flat surface—not really a bed. No restraints. Hesitation guarded him as he again skated a look around. Grays and whites blurred and pulsed, making his corneas ache. But he was alone. Doors unguarded. He lunged upward to seize that freedom. Instead, weakness weighted his limbs and drove him back down with a thud.

"Easy."

The soft voice reached him, sweet, and he nearly sagged with relief as her blurry form came toward him. "Isaura." Where was she? He blinked his vision clear.

"Sorry, no." Eija came into view and gave him a halfhearted, apologetic smile. "Just me."

Right. Of course. Shaking off the disappointment, he waded through the mental fog that jumbled his world and thoughts. Should've known it hadn't been Isaura. They'd stolen him away. Light-years from home. From anything good.

He leaned to the side, angling his legs over the bed, and pushed himself upright—with her assistance. Humbling how much he needed the help. "Where . . .?" Vibrations ran through the hard surface beneath him. Chemical smells. Sanitized air . . . different from the *Prevenire*. But it had oxygen, which meant these creatures had a similar makeup to humans. "A ship?"

With a nod, Eija stood back. "A Draegis dreadnought orbiting Rohilek, their homeworld."

The Draegis had killed a *Prev* crewmember and would've killed others if they hadn't used the drop pods. So . . . *Why aren't* we *dead?*

Again, images flickered through his mental eye. Danger. Pods . . .

He growled. There was something about the pods. Something he should know. Something he . . . "The pods—" Marco stood, the room spinning. His knees buckled. He was careening. Dropped back onto the bed. "Augh!"

"Hey, hey," Eija said, catching his shoulder. "Slow down there. We—"

"The pods . . ."

"The pods malfunctioned for me and Reef, remember? The others got away."

Right. Marco felt his heart rate slowing. Calm descending. "We have to get out of here." He wasn't sure why he said it. There was nothing to fear. He was calm. Which . . . wasn't right.

"We can't," she said quietly. "Look, there's a lot to catch you up on— you've been unconscious for a while. Sadly, there's no way out. At least not that we can find."

Marco locked onto his objective: destroying the— "The *Prevenire*."

"Still there."

Right. They'd failed. Fuel spent too fast because of the docked Draegis, who then reboarded. And the Sentinel had been far more advanced than anything he'd anticipated. It had protected itself.

Marco hung his head. "Then they already have what they need."

With a little sound of disagreement, Eija slid onto the foot of his slab bed. "I don't think so. You deleted the logs before they boarded, so they aren't getting data or coordinates from the *Prev's* systems. Not easily, anyway. I think they're still digging."

If they got those coordinates, the beasts could find their way to Herakles. Wipe out humanity . . . Drosero . . . *Isaura*. "We have to destroy it." He glanced around the room. "No bars."

"Ah, no." Eija pursed her lips. "But the electrostatic barrier will fry you into the next life if you cross the threshold."

Even as she said it, two Draegis morphed from the shadows of the passage, pulsed those eye slits at them, and continued on. A third remained in the corridor, the faint imprint of Eija's hand still visible on his chest.

Eija's reasoning made sense. If the beasts had found the coordinates, they would've killed them and jumped already. If they were keeping Marco and—"Where's the Eidolon?"

"In his room."

"*Cell*," Jadon corrected as he appeared around the corner, the static barrier crackling as he entered. "This isn't the Academy, Ei. They're keeping us in *cells*, not rooms." His gaze skidded to Marco. "D'she tell you the name of this ship?"

Marco slid his attention to the girl, still struggling to get his thoughts together.

"The *Yo'qiluvchi*," Eija supplied.

"There you go again, leaving out the important bits." Jadon sniffed. "It means 'Destroyer.' Three guesses who they destroy and your first two don't count."

The girl bristled. "I told you, you're reading—"

"You're scuzzing right I'm reading into it. They turned Bashari to ash!" He jutted his jaw at her but looked to Marco. "She's been playing cute and cozy with BeastieBoy while you've been fighting your way back from the brink and I've been caged in this hole."

Though the girl didn't argue, her expression and her reddening complexion said she wanted to. What was going on here? They were still alive. He'd been healed . . . Why? Why not just get rid of them? "They need something from us," Marco murmured.

"That's what I've been saying," Jadon said.

"But what?" Eija held her palms out, then tugged at the strange clothes she wore. "It's not like any of us is tech-savvy enough to reinstate deleted data. They haven't even asked us to try."

Wait—why wasn't Eija in her HyPE uniform? She wore a crimson velvet bliaut adorned with silver threads and black crystals. Black pants and boots completed the outfit, oddly reminiscent of Droseran attire. "Your clot—"

"Don't ask. Please." She shifted, folding her arms as if trying to hide the bliaut. "It's not by choice."

Aches wove through Marco's back, demanding he lie down again, and although his limbs felt as heavy as anchors, he refused to give in.

"They've been treating her like royalty," Jadon noted. "Calling her Xonim and allowing her to go wherever she pleases. You and I? Onboard security protocols allow us in and out of the cells in this brig module, but not beyond it. And we're in standard blacks."

"Not wherever I please," Eija shot back.

"Okay, a couple exceptions—the bridge and CIC—which she's accepted without objection."

"Stop making it sound like I had something to do with that."

"Did you?"

"You know I didn't!"

While the two argued over privileges aboard this dreadnought, Marco processed the information boiling away his confusion—the *Prev* was still out there and likely operational; this ship was large enough to have the bridge separate from a Command Information Center, which collected, parsed, and analyzed data, as well as threats . . . meaning it'd be harder to pull off an escape; and though he had been weak and barely conscious on the jumpship, he felt a lot better now. That meant they'd treated him medically.

Temple itching, he scratched it and found ridged flesh. That'd been where a port had connected him to the *Prev*. What about the other junctions? He touched where cables had fed into his body and arms, finding scars. Not scabs. Even Reef's arm looked healed as well. "How long was I out?"

Silenced by his question, they said nothing, but he still had his receptors. Smelled their nerves. "*How long?*"

"Three weeks and change," Jadon answered.

Curse the reek. Marco cradled his head and bent forward. Three weeks.

Add that to the months in the hull . . . away from Isaura . . . He couldn't change the past. But he could—maybe—change this. After all, the Draegis hadn't killed them. The *Prev* was still intact. "Have they launched?"

"Unknown," Jadon said.

"We're pretty sure they haven't," Eija added, "though it's possible they've sent some sort of scouts through as a precursor to the full-fleet invasion."

Marco considered the girl. "Three weeks you've been walking around the ship, and you don't know?"

Regret bled through the small sterile room as she shifted. "I . . . they let me walk around but nothing else. No access to panels or controls. All I've gotten is a feel for this place and how they operate."

Jadon shook his head and leaned against the bulkhead. "She understands them. They're like best friends or something."

The Eidolon's jealousy . . . Curious. Marco considered the girl. "That true—you understand them?"

"Not . . . completely. I-I don't know." Burrowing into herself, she shrugged. "When he speaks, as long as it's not fast, I can sort out the meaning. Sometimes it just feels . . . intuitive. The other Draegis are more difficult, if not impossible, to understand. Have no idea why."

Interesting. Marco eyed the Draegis lurking just outside the cell. The faint blue mark on his cheek was still there, but it seemed . . . different. In fact, the beast itself seemed different from when he'd been on the *Prev*. "Is that the one you touched who then protected you?"

"He didn't . . ." She hunched her shoulders. "Yeah. Maybe. It's like"—she squinted—"I get him, ya know?"

"No," Jadon grunted. "We don't know. That's why he's asking."

Noticing Blue tense and suddenly hyperfocus on Jadon, Marco warned, "Easy." Heat corkscrewed through his brand as a thought struck him. "You touched his chest and marked him."

"What?" Jadon laughed. "The way wild animals imprint on each other?"

"*Nothing* like that." Eija glowered, her chest heaving with emotion that whipped her efflux into a frenzied mess of confusion and panic. "Look. When he yanked me from the pod by the neck, I *shoved* him backward!" There was more despair than disgust behind her words, as if she, too, knew something significant had happened in that moment with Blue. "I just wanted him to stop. That's all."

"That's not all," Marco argued. "They dressed you up and gave you run of the ship."

"I *don't* have run of the ship. I just—"

"It's not a bad thing." Marco eyed the handprint on Blue's chest, convinced that was responsible for the beasts' treatment of her.

While there was something else off, something pinging his brain, mayhap . . . mayhap this thing between the girl and Blue could be a means to an end. At the same time, if she could understand them . . . "Dance the dance." He used a colloquialism in the hopes of keeping some of their convo protected from this beast. "We know he reads body language, but can he—they—understand what we say?"

Eija shrugged. "I don't know. But with the way they let me walk most of the decks, I don't think they see us as a threat or think we can escape, which I'm inclined to believe, because this place is massive."

"Works in our favor to be underestimated." Marco had to look at this with a strategic mind. "Tell me everything you know."

She drew in a long breath and slowly let it out. "From what I can tell, their fleet is some serious business. This ship is one of dozens of dreadnoughts, and there are just as many battlecruisers. Thousands of ships—easily ten times Symmachia's fleet." Weariness tugged at her youthful face. "If they find a way back, the Quadrants will not stand a chance. If I were to guess, I'd say there aren't thousands of Draegis—there are *millions*."

Jadon grunted. "Great, just what Kedalion needs—millions of weaponized grunts coming for our friends and families."

"This ship," Eija continued, "has three counterparts that are the vanguard of the Draegis fleet. There's some other intel on a moon or something that I couldn't decipher, and another thing I can't really make sense of is that this ship, apparently, hasn't moved since they brought us aboard."

"So maybe scrapping the flight logs worked." Marco winced at a pinch of pain from digging into that memory. "But if they somehow figure out how to reverse-plot our course or—"

"*. . . She's threading her DNA into your brain . . . Implanting memories for her to use against your olfactory senses.*"

Implanted memories. Olfactories . . . If Xisya was able to implant her memories, could these beasts *extract* his? A year ago he would've scoffed, but now the idea wasn't a leap . . .

Deep dread thrummed at his core. "How advanced are they?"

"*Very*," Eija warned, her efflux infected with awe. "We watched them extract you from the lectulo. It was . . . incredible. Had we removed you as planned, you would've died just like Shad warned."

"They hooked an entire contraption into the dais," Jadon added. "It was something straight out of a sci-fi docuvid."

"At first, I thought they were killing you, so I tried to stop them."

"Yeah." Jadon's voice took on a shade of disbelief. "And when one of the silvers accosted her for interfering—BeastieBoy there came unglued. Unbelievably, Silvermark, who seemed to have authority, yielded. Nobody would touch Ei after that."

Nerves thick in the air, she shifted.

It came back to the girl and that strange connection. "We use it."

Eija's eyes widened. "Use what?"

"The deference they show you. It's our tool." Yeah, that was a logic leap, but if they dolled her up and let her roam freely . . . "You're their queen." Major logic leap. "At least, for Blue there."

Eija sniffed. "I'm no one, let alone a queen." A half smile wavered as she looked at Jadon. "Recall, I almost didn't even make the HyPE team."

"But you *did*, which no one could understand," Jadon said. "Now, here we are. With that beast responding to you. *Protecting* you." He had a strange edge to his voice and an even more telling efflux. "I say nuke them all, even if we have to go down with them."

"Don't be stupid!"

"There you go, defending them again."

"I'm not defending. I'm—"

"What is it with you and this beast?"

Marco noted Blue's eye slits start glowing. "Easy."

"I didn't hear you complaining when I asked him to heal your arm. And it's not about defending them. There are innocents here."

"Now they're innocent?! Slag, Ei. I never thought you'd—"

"Yes. You never *thought*! That's hard work for you, isn't it?"

"Hey! *Easy*," Marco hissed.

"You've lost your bearing, Corporal! You have that thing following you around—"

"Not by choice!"

A roar thundered as the Draegis erupted into the room. Blue shoved between Eija and Jadon, cuffing the Eidolon's neck as his rage trilled in the air.

As Marco lunged to intercept, he heard Eija shout to stop. The Draegis was lightning fast, weaponized arm aimed at Jadon, heat warbling, ready to incinerate him.

"No!" She reached to the protector-beast but fear snatched her hand back. "Daq'Ti, no!"

Command received, Blue bellowed an objection at Jadon, then pitched him aside before adjusting to Eija's flank.

Groaning, Jadon rubbed his now-raw throat as he sagged against the wall. "Point made." Despite the Eidolon's bravado, his efflux said he'd nearly wet his pants.

Taking it all in, Marco definitely had something to work with here. He'd need to sort and execute a plan. Yet he couldn't very well talk tactics with an enemy combatant in the room. Just how far did the girl's authority go? "Will he leave if you tell him to?"

Shaken over the event—or possibly her control of the Draegis—she looked to the beast. "I . . . Maybe."

"Try it."

Reticently, she shifted to Blue. "Wait outside. Please."

"Slag, Eija," Jadon grumbled. "Give him an apology and offer to clean his feet while you're at it."

Blue swung to Jadon, chortled what seemed a threat, then clomped out and joined another Draegis just beyond the static barrier.

"Good to know." Marco couldn't get away from things nagging the back of his head. Things they needed to force into play for their benefit. He shifted aside to shield himself as much as possible from the beasts, then lowered his voice. "I've been going over a few things that stand out as significant concerns. First, not only did they not kill me, but they healed my injuries. That implies—second—they want something from me, and—third—apparently, I need to be healthier for them to get it since they're healing me." Voicing these thoughts felt a lot like opening a vault to the Fires of Hieropolis. "I think it's my memories. This is too much like that creature on the *Macedon* digging around in my head using tech I didn't know existed."

"Xisya," Eija offered.

He nodded. "As with that Khatriza thing, I can't smell the Draegis, which makes them dangerous and unpredictable."

"Or it puts you on level ground with us mere mortals," Jadon said.

Ignoring the snarky comment, Marco studied his enemy. There he read the deference the Draegis laid so wholly at the girl's feet as he hovered within reach. Blue had stood against his own kind to protect her. How far did his loyalty to her go? "Ask him if they've sent ships to the Quadrants yet."

"He won't answer that," she balked.

"With the way he just yielded to you, I suspect he *must* answer."

Guarded and fearfully reluctant, Eija turned to the beast outside the cell.

"Daq'Ti, have the Draegis gone to my homeworld?"

Trilling the air, Blue stared back. A scent wasn't needed to know the beast didn't want to answer, especially when the other Draegis stomped forward, nudged Blue's shoulder, and bellowed in their garbled native tongue.

"What's going on?" Jadon asked. "Did he not understand?"

The girl looked worried. "I-I don't know."

Marco might not be able to read Draegis scents, but he could read that interaction. "He understood. They both did." The first tinge of hope stirred in his gut. "If Blue answers, he betrays his people." Which in itself *was* the answer.

Excitement flinging through his Signature, Jadon eyed him. "They haven't jumped back."

That seemed to spark courage in the girl. "Daq'Ti—*tell* me." She squared her stance. "Have the Draegis sent scouts or warships to my home system?"

The beast sagged. A chortling sentence broke free, far quieter than anything else that had come from him before. "*Hali ames. Uler yulduzler jedvelini eidirimoqdeler.*"

"Oh, thank the Ladies," she whispered, facing Marco again. "They're still looking for coordinates."

Purpose and determination dug a crevasse through the desperation that had entrenched his receptors. "Before they can dig them out . . ." He rubbed his jaw. "Like I said, Eija, we need to put your freedom to use. The handprint"—talk about logic leaps . . . this one had a jetpack behind it—"see if you can turn any of the other Draegis."

She went ice white. "What?"

"Next opportunity—be strategic, of course—see if you can turn another Draegis."

"Are you out of your djelling mind?" she gritted out. "I don't even know how I did to Daq'Ti what I did. It just . . . happened."

"Try. That's all I'm asking."

She swallowed, still pale.

"Also, learn their weapons capabilities—armaments, number of missiles, and if they're vector controlled or attitude jets, so on."

A strong nod this time. "Why?"

"Because we need to figure out how to send two missiles into the *Prevenire.*"

She widened her eyes, incredulous. "*Nuke* it?"

"And find a way to take down this ship, too."

"*After* we get off it, right?" She blinked. "The *Yo'qiluvchi* is a *dreadnought.*

Massive. How're you going to destroy it—without killing us?"

"At this point, our only concern is stopping them. Our lives are nothing if they make the jump back to the Quadrants."

Jadon grunted. "Nothing like a suicide mission to motivate a Marine."

"I'd always figured this was a one-way trip." Eija just hadn't expected to be actively inducing her own death. When Reef jerked, she saw the scowl that darkened his beautiful eyes. "For me," she clarified. "I didn't care if *I* ever went back."

"Well, I do! But this isn't just about you," Reef said. "Did you forget—"

"I haven't forgotten anything. I just . . ." With the whole handprint-subservience thing with Daq'Ti, she had a desperate need to talk to Patron. That's what she'd done for the last few years anytime there was something strange or stressful. "What if there are innocents here that we harm?"

Reef gave her a dark look. "Any creature whose arm turns into a pulse cannon needs to be converted to slag ASAP."

Did worrying about the Draegis make her a traitor? Maybe. But this churning in her gut brought back memories from Tryssinia of the way flying ore-rats protected their young.

Yeah, totally not helping, Ei.

When they'd first been brought aboard the *Yo'qiluvchi*, then through the initial week of Marco's unconsciousness and their isolation, Reef had been a pillar of strength, kept her going. Quite simply, he'd been there for her. Let her lean on him, figuratively and literally.

But as this thing with Daq'Ti became more apparent, Reef had become a pillar of antagonism. And it was exhausting. His scathing comments made her feel as if he were starting to see *her* as the enemy. Frightening enough having a beast defend her, but being alienated from Reef? Slag.

Confused with herself and weary, she pushed back the loose strands dangling in her face. "I . . . I should get going on my intel hunt."

Marco stood, though he didn't do it with much vigor—he was still regaining his strength. "Remember." He had that brooding thing down to a science. "Be careful—we don't know where those boundaries are for the Draegis with this hand thing. It's possible the only assist we'll get from his buddies is a fast track to death."

"I'll be fine. I-I can sense . . . him. His thoughts." *Again, not helping, Ei.* "Feelings." She flinched at how that sounded. "Daq'Ti *is* trying to help us."

"This thing with you and him, it's . . . disturbing."

"I know."

"But use it."

"Right." As she left with Daq'Ti and the other Draegis, Eija wasn't even sure where to start this reconnaissance mission. Marco had more confidence in her than she did. Eija Zacdari wasn't some hero or genius. She was an accident, an anomaly. Always fighting for the smallest, dingiest corner of the Quadrants to stand on. Fighting for everything had just been a way of life—of surviving.

The first hour of their trek around the ship, Eija felt the slitted eyes of the green with them monitoring her. Perhaps he was reporting back on everything she did. Probably an unfounded fear, but it was strong all the same. With each juncture and lift, she became more determined to be rid of him. But how?

"But use it." Marco's admonishment echoed in her head.

"Daq'Ti," she said quietly, deliberate in her use of the Quadrants tongue, "why is there another guard?"

"Qo'riqchi yo'q. Eskort Xonim."

Escort? She wrinkled her nose. "But *you* are my escort."

"Daq'Ti guard Xonim. Protect Xonim."

So there was a difference. "And if I preferred not to have an escort?" Would it be that simple to shake the extra detail?

Green trilled at them, his words blurring in her thoughts. Should she try the hand thing with him, too? The idea of touching him spiked fear through her. Yet, curiosity plagued her. What if she could easily turn the entire Draegis race to their side simply by touching them?

She eyed him, plotting how to do this without looking like she was hitting him. Maybe feign stumbling? With him beside her, that'd be awkward at best. They rounded a corner, and she deliberately let him pull ahead. When he rotated to see why she'd fallen behind, she stumbled forward. Aimed her hand at his chest and willed with everything in her for the same mark to appear. Willed whatever it was in her that transmitted change to Daq'Ti to be imparted to this green.

Her palm landed on the thick, cracked surface of his torso. Feeling nothing different, she pushed harder.

Green howled.

A wake of superheated air stung her cheeks, and she instantly felt the terror of her mistake. Saw the weaponized arm. No sooner had her mind registered the situation than she was jerked back.

Daq'Ti stood between her and Green, howling and his own arm weaponized.

She stumbled back. "I am sorry."

Towering over her, Daq'Ti guided her into yet another lift. "Dith Nur'Ok asks why dishonor him by asking for absence then trying to attack him."

Dishonored? "No slight was intended. And no attack—I just . . . stumbled," she lied shakily. Now more than ever, she knew she couldn't let this green stay. He now saw her as an adversary. If he remained with them, she'd never get any real intel. "In my world . . . having an escort is dishonorable—means you aren't trusted but rather looked down upon." She turned innocent eyes to them. "Is that how I am viewed by Dith Nur'Ok?"

The green chortled and thumped Daq'Ti, who did it back to him, but when the lift doors opened, Daq'Ti blocked Green, forbidding entrance.

Nur'Ok howled his objection and rammed into Daq'Ti, whose arm weaponized faster than ever before. He shoved the business end into Nur'Ok's face.

"Her ways are higher. Respect Xonim as is our law," Daq'Ti commanded. "Or die."

Startled at both his words and his ferocity, Eija stilled.

With plenty of anger, Nur'Ok bowed his head, the pulsing of his slitted eyes slowing as the door slid shut.

Stunned, Eija released the breath trapped in her throat. It'd worked!

As if shaking off the confrontation, Daq'Ti rippled a grunt, then turned to her. "Where would you like to see?"

Asking to see the missiles would be too obvious. Besides, it could put him in danger, and she couldn't risk losing the only protector she had—at least not until she figured out how she'd turned him in the first place.

But she had an idea . . .

Eija slowed, turning to him, though it was hard to meet his gaze. "Daq'Ti, I want to see schematics for this ship's missiles. Can you show them to me?" Her conscience squirmed at using Daq'Ti like this, deceiving him, when he so readily made her will happen.

Indecision throbbed in those red slits, his lava-black skin seeming not quite as dark beneath the passage lighting.

Somehow, she knew that he wrestled with obeying her and betraying his own kind. While his subservience was weird, something deep in her warned Eija not to abuse the gift. She wasn't ignorant—she saw how his decisions on her behalf, though absolute, were causing him issues with higher ranks and even with lower ones. They resented his obeisance to her.

Well, they had that in common with Reef.

"Just a schematic." She didn't trust herself to explain. The request seemed innocent enough. But even as he considered her more, she saw the end result of using the missiles against the *Prevenire*—the concussion that would impact this dreadnought. But, considering the size of the *Yo'qiluvchi*, it'd be nothing more serious than a tornado on a planet.

With deft movements of his massive paws, Daq'Ti awakened some technology. A digital array floated before them, stealing her breath as she watched him dive into the ship's systems.

"How're you doing this?" She inched closer, amused and surprised.

He rotated his arm to reveal that the weapon-arm was more than a delivery tool of destruction. Technology was laced into one of its subdermal layers that allowed him to access the ship's system.

Hope surged. Was this how they could nuke the *Prev*, using him to pull up the firing array? "Can you control parts of the ship and actually, like, open doors and bays with that?"

"No," he growled. "Only information and diagnostic readouts here." Again moving his arm, he brought up a display of weapons. "And meals."

She blinked. "Meals?" *Here.* Did that mean he could access controls elsewhere?

"I order my meals and supplies. But not navigation or tactics." He motioned, and she followed his thick paw.

Wait. She'd thought it resembled a dog's, with indistinct pads, but now that she followed his movements, she saw clear delineation of thick digits . . . fingers. Was her initial reaction to encountering the Draegis so strong that she'd seen him only as a monster, a beast?

Before her eyes flashed a menu screen with—

Missiles! Eija sucked in a breath at the lineup. So many missiles. Her stomach churned. This dreadnought had more than the entire Symmachian fleet.

The Quadrants have no hope.

Overcome by a sharp need to immediately eliminate the path back home, Eija glanced up at her protector. "Can you get me into Engineering?" Again, she sensed his uncertainty, his hesitation. And while she would protect him, was this not why Patron had sent her to Kuru? To protect the Quadrants?

Marco believed that was his mission. Was it hers, too? "Please."

With a somber trill, he swayed his head and shoulders in what seemed to be a nod and starting thumping his way there. It took nearly an hour to navigate decks and lifts, but he finally guided her through a small hatch. "Help me get into the system."

It was a fool's hope, but Eija had this feeling that what she'd learned, what they'd been trained on at the Academy had been a mirror of or modeled from systems here. At least, she hoped so.

Daq'Ti palmed a wall panel and it sprang to life.

Eija bent closer, the illumination nearly painful in the semidarkened deck. Her confidence vanished when she saw the strange symbols. "I . . . can't read this."

"Rohileri."

"Great," she muttered. While she could understand the spoken language, she had no experience with it in written form. Even as discouragement wiggled into her thoughts, she let her fingers dance over the screen, recalling the way they'd been taught during HyPE training. The system blipped and blinked beneath her ministrations. Giddiness stole over her until . . .

Womp-womp.

She lifted a hand at a symbol dancing before her. What did that mean?

"Denied," Daq'Ti read.

What had she done wrong? She closed her eyes and tried the sequence again.

Womp-womp.

She growled.

A stream of angry Rohileri flew from the other side of the deck.

"Restricted," Daq'Ti trilled.

Eija glanced across the room and spotted a Silvermark watching, nearly defiant. Where was that subservience Marco and Jadon insisted the beasts were required to show her? But this wasn't the time to fight. This was the time to play dumb. Come back later. Again and again. Until she got into the system and fired those nukes, because that image of this ship's arsenal would haunt her until she destroyed their way back to the Quadrants.

KARDIA, LAMPROS CITY, KALONICA, DROSERO

"He would have been proud of you, my kyria."

Words so well-meant had a powerful ability to penetrate walls Isaura had erected around her heart. She took her time lifting her gaze to the newly installed Commander of Armies, Elder Bazyli Sebastiano. With Prince Darius recently relieved of title and office, many changes had been forced upon her shoulders. "As you intended a compliment, I will take it as such. Not with the hidden undercurrent of a medora dead."

Bazyli's cheek twitched, his guilt apparently sparking before his own eyes. "I beg your mercy—"

She lifted a hand, noting the other Council of Elders members moving down the hall toward apartments arranged for their leisure during the weeks-long meetings. "I know your heart, or you would not be wearing those epaulets, General Sebastiano." She drew in a breath and slowly released it. "However, vigilance is required to keep Medora Marco alive in all our hearts and minds. What I do here is done with the explicit expectation that he will soon walk through those doors, so I may return to days of quiet reflection and improvement of my skill with sun discs."

"And protecting the heir until he is safely delivered."

"Or *she*." With a tired smile, Isaura reflexively laid a hand on her belly, which had the slightest curve. Four months she had been without Dusan, alone in Kardia.

"There are means to ascertain the sex, with the Kynigos here."

She recalled how Dusan had named Kersei's babe a son. Soon, they would know if he was right. The hunters around her likely knew the sex of the babe she carried, but she had sworn them to silence regarding the matter. "If I am to learn that before this child makes its way into the world, I would have it from our medora's lips or with him at my side. Never would I rob him of that honor."

"Of course." The general bowed his head. "Good rest, my kyria." He nodded to her father. "Mavridis." He started down the hall.

Her father touched her elbow. "I would have a word with him."

Sensing his anger, Isaura caught his arm. "Do not be overly hard on him. He did not intend ill."

"But he wounded all the same and knows better." Mavridis's stony expression softened—to the extent it could for the Plisiázon leader. "You seem much tired. Go rest."

She laughed. "Another time to extend grace and not take offense."

He grimaced. "I did not—"

"Aye, I know."

Mavridis considered her for a moment. "Bazyli was right—Marco will be proud to see all you have managed in his absence."

"I anxiously await that moment."

He locked gazes with Hushak, one of her four guards, who had long served him as a Stalker. "See the kyria to her apartments."

After accepting his kiss on her temple, Isaura laced arms with Kita, her friend and lady's maid. They started for the stairs, following Kaveh and Hushak, who were trailed by Ramirus and Ulixes, two Kynigos sworn to her detail by Master Hunter Roman deBurco. They were brooding, intense men, and despite their ability to blend into shadow, their presence could never be hidden. She *felt* them as she had Dusan.

Reaching the residence, Ramirus and Hushak entered first and cleared the rooms, verifying no threat.

Once they stepped back out, she went to the sideboard and touched the warm pitcher from which spirals of taunting cordi aroma filled the air.

"Shall we get you into a more comfortable dress?" Kita offered, moving to the dressing closet. "How do you fare after all that politicking with the Council?"

"Exhausted," Isaura groaned, following her. "I daresay the elders do not take lightly to seeking my approval for their actions." She sat and allowed Kita to remove the tiara from her updo.

Done with that, Kita began unbuttoning the heavy brocade bliaut. "But yield they will, or to be sure, Ixion will generously share a piece of his mind."

Ixion. Not Mavridis. Odd that her friend used his given name. "He is even now gone to remonstrate Bazyli for a slip of the tongue." As the heavy garment slid from Isaura's shoulders and arms, she let out a soft moan, relieved to be free of the weight. If only she could be so easily freed of the burden of ruling. Yet she would never disgrace Dusan by abandoning her duties.

"It is entirely unfair that you have been unaffected by your pregnancy," Kita teased as she helped her into a lighter, more delicate dress.

"I have endured enough in the last few months that I do not see the lack of morning sickness or whatever trials other women face as unfair." The cool material cascaded over her.

"Indeed. You are right."

She traced her curving belly, marveling at how that had increased in the last week. "What will you look like, little one?"

"That, too, is unfair. With your beauty and our medora's rogue looks, this child will undoubtedly be blessed by the Ancient."

Tying the belt of the evening coat, Isaura sat and allowed her friend to let down her hair. Tension along her scalp eased with each removed pin. She tilted her head to the side and massaged her shoulder.

A knock came at the outer doors, then the click of the handle. Only Mavridis dared enter without invitation.

Kita glanced at the door. "Let me see what he needs."

Watching her friend in the mirror, Isaura continued digging out hairpins, anxious to let down her hair. Last pin removed, her blonde locks fell over her shoulder, and she was reminded of how much Marco loved touching her hair. She felt the press of his lips at her nape, which sent exhilaration scampering down her spine.

Murmured words intruded on her reflection, and she glanced over her shoulder into the solar. Kita had not yet returned. Was it not Mavridis then? Mayhap something was amiss. Isaura stood and crossed the dressing room. About to step into the solar, she stopped short at what she saw.

Near the door stood her father's familiar, tall form, cupping Kita's elbow as her friend allowed him much closer than propriety allowed. Soft words whispered between them, and Kita was glowing—her cheeks blushed! Intensity always coiled about Mavridis, and though it yet existed, in his countenance there was also something . . . piqued as he looked down at her friend.

Isaura drew back, surprised. *What is this? Intimacy* between her father and friend? A bitter pang struck her. Suddenly aching more than ever for Marco's touch. His husky words. But . . . *this* between two not bound . . .?

She cleared her throat and rounded the corner. Easily noted their startled responses.

Kita touched the back of her neck as she stepped back. "Mavridis is here. To-to . . ."

"To what?" Isaura wondered how they would explain being so intimately set.

"Tomorrow." Her father's voice rang true and clear—yet with a strangeness impossible to hide. His face tightened as he met her gaze. "Your meeting with King Vorn and Queen Aliria is moved up. Seems there have been some uprisings in Jherako as word spread of the ships."

"Disappointing that we could not harbor that secret a while longer." She shifted back into her role as kyria. "Let us hope we can delay those rumors from so heavily influencing or infiltrating Lampros City or Kalonica. We need more time so that the introduction of electricity is not a sharp shock. Duncan has been so fastidious about it."

"We may not have that time." Mavridis handed her a small device. "Delivered moments ago from Jherako."

Recognition hit her—she'd seen Dusan use such technology. "A message." Isaura took the communiqué dot and moved to the wardrober where Dusan's things awaited his return. She inserted it into the vambrace, the same one Bazyli had shrewdly used to contact the master hunter and alert him to Dusan's kidnapping.

Vorn's rugged face wavered before her like some ghoul. "*Queen Isaura, I thought it best to send this via technology to limit what eyes could intercept it. I fear our efforts to segue our peoples into technology may yet defy our careful planning. Word has come out of Hirakys of ships and weapons with technology. It may be that we have no choice but to thrust advancement upon the people. We will speak about this on the morrow, but I thought it imperative to warn you to prepare a contingency plan. I am pleased we will attack this together, our two lands a united front against a terrible enemy. Until the morrow.*"

Daunted and worried over the news that might force her to go public alone with the technology initiative, she lowered herself onto a seat, a yawn cutting off her groan. The Council surely would not appreciate this. She must be stronger and more direct. She, the woman who walked a league around confrontation. Oh, the irony!

"It is late and much have you endured this day. Rest now," Mavridis said from behind her. "If it please you"—it was not the first time he'd said that to her, and still she almost laughed that he, the Stalker, would defer to the daughter he had never named—"I will join you to break your fast so we may review contingencies."

"It would very much please me." With a nod, Isaura removed the dot, returned the vambrace, and stored the dot in a hidden compartment in her dressing room. "We should have General Sebastiano and Baron Tyrannous with us as well."

Mavridis stiffened. "The baron—"

"Regardless of his faults and crimes—which I concede are many and painful—he is a brilliant strategist and tactician. Also consider," she added, again rubbing her neck, "there are few so wholly aware of what threat comes from the skycrawlers. Please recall that Roman said there was deep regret in Darius for what he did."

"Aye, the guilty usually do regret being discovered," Mavridis bit out around a dark gaze. "Give him not your trust, Isau—my kyria."

Though impressed he caught and tempered his anger, Isaura noticed Kita cringe. Her poor friend was not as well acquainted with that aspect of him. "Trust Darius? No. But I would have his advice, and with the hunters at hand, we will know the truth of what he offers."

"That is not foolproof."

"Well I know." Dusan, one of the most adept Kynigos, had not been able to detect the threat that had stolen him from her until it was too late. "Yet . . . I would give Darius a chance." Was she foolish to hope that by the time Dusan returned, his brother could be . . .

What, Isaura? Redeemed? Reformed?

"Why?" Mavridis growled. "Why waste your time—"

"Because Dusan wanted his brother back. He did not want the divide. If it is in my power to make that happen, or at least start the process, then I will do it."

"He could get you killed! Never will I be responsible for that."

"You are not responsible for it! These are my own actions."

"Be sensible, Isaura!"

Indignant, she lifted her chin, feeling every bit the child beneath a father's rebuke. "I am quite sensible, thank you."

"You are not—"

Approaching with a tray of tea cakes, Kita drew in a breath and reached for Mavridis, who jerked away—a move that made Ulixes and Ramirus emerge from shadow.

Jaw muscle bouncing beneath his beard, Mavridis scowled at the hunters and then her. "I will leave you to your rest." He started for the door.

Isaura mustered every ounce of resolve to speak evenly to his retreating back. "I look forward to breaking my fast with you on the morrow."

He tensed in the doorway, gave a nod, then left.

Recovering her courage, she let out a taut breath as she acknowledged the hunters, who bled back into anonymity. Weary, she faced the balcony overlooking the sea. Even at night with moonslight dancing over the raging waters, it offered serenity. Comfort.

Behind her, she heard Kita moving closer.

"If you do not need me, I must . . . take my leave." Why did she seem nervous? "For Mnason."

"Of course," Isaura said, pulling her gaze from the tumultuous waters. "Thank you. I do beg your mercy that you must always witness my arguments with him."

Kita firmed her lips into a practiced smile, then wilted. "He would only protect you."

"Aye, as a father a child, but—"

"No, as his kyria." With what authority did Kita speak of Mavridis like this? "With Medora Marco gone, you are all that holds Kardia and Kalonica from slipping into the hands of the Grand Duke, or worse, Symmachia."

"Already two nobles have challenged my right to rule in his stead."

"And they will continue until our medora returns, but we will not let it go unchallenged—that is what Ixion intends to ensure." Kita dipped her head. "I must go." She curtseyed again and hurried from the solar.

Ignoring the prepared tray, Isaura glided out onto the balcony. She stared out over the small columned garden to the fountain of Eleftheria below and beyond that to the cliffs of Kardia and the raging Kalonican Sea. It seemed as angry as she was about Dusan's absence. "Please, Dusan . . . I cannot do this. I am not trained or equipped for this role." Fresh tears fell, evidence of the long day, the child within, and the hole in her heart. "Come back to me."

That night, she fell into a deep sleep, and into Dusan's arms.

Peering out at the training yard, Kersei held the parchment that might restore control. Protect her unborn child. Her *son*, as Marco suggested on Iereania.

How had it come to this, she powerless and Darius the villain? Scores had he killed with his complicities in the attack on Stratios—her parents, her sisters, their friends, sergii, machitis, regia, his own father and brother. Now possibly his only remaining brother, the man she loved with every beat of her heart, Marco. Arrogance so thick blinded a man she once had been proud to know and call friend.

The cord of their union had been severed in the throne room when Darius confessed his guilt before all. Kersei ran a hand across her overlarge belly, swollen with his heir, and grieved that their child would bear such a tarnished name and legacy. Naught could be done to repair the damage. Her hand tightened around the parchment.

"You are sure of this, my lady?"

Kersei sniffed at Myles's question, the same one posed by another on a very different day, when she had been brash, daring, and reckless in challenging the aerios who now challenged her in this solar. Gone were those days and that woman. In her place stood a woman broken. Bereft. Bitter.

Ma'ma had warned not to give soil to the root of bitterness, but those were the words of someone not betrayed. Now she was dead, and the bitter root—the one that had dug into Kersei's heart on Iereania when Darius removed all hope of life with Marco—had been watered at the trial with the blood of her family and loved ones. Judgment that day stripped him of title and sentenced him to death, the latter stayed by a very unexpected person: Isaura.

The woman who had been delivered to Kardia a few short months past with the hearts of Kalonicans and the regia firmly in her hand. A woman who had also powerfully stolen Marco's affection. The woman who now possessed everything Kersei had dreamed would be hers.

Kersei hated Darius. Ladies grant her mercy, but she did. Hated his foolish, feckless actions. For the toll she and their child—even Marco, now missing four months—must pay for Darius's vain conceit.

Batting aside a tear, she swallowed against a raw throat. Glanced again at the parchment, as if doing so could infuse her with the necessary courage to see it through. It was there, in ink and parchment, her only chance to give her son a future.

"Never has it been done in the Kalonican court." Myles's brusque words were filled with caution.

"Aye, neither has Kalonica before seen the murder of two medoras and the slaughter of hundreds in a cowardly act of arrogance by one of its princes."

Face grave, Myles frowned. "It is not known that our medora is dead. We must yet hope—if not for us, for our kyria and the heir."

The heir. Marco's heir. Carried by . . . Isaura.

Had it not been for her, the one person Kersei had thought to resent for the rest of her life, Darius would be in the cold earth with their parents, and she would be penniless and homeless. Yet Isaura, with her beguiling naïveté and wastelander strength, had shown royals and nobility alike that their haughty lives were shallow, frail, and weak. Empty.

Though grateful for the kyria's well-intentioned transfer of Stratios Hall and its lands—a royal decree ensuring her provision of shelter and sustenance—a curious anger simmered within Kersei that her father's legacy had been laid in the hands of the man who murdered him.

With her family's lands conferred upon Darius, her family gone, Marco and his love attached to another . . . what was left for Kersei but the child she carried? So she must protect him in the only way she knew how. As for her . . . "I no longer remember how to hope," she murmured to herself. "He has stolen everything from me."

"He is much changed, my lady."

She scoffed, pulled from the morose. "Aye, he lost his crown and coin, thereby forfeiting the ability to buy loyalty and favor. It is no wonder he has changed."

"Baron." Myles's tight utterance of Darius's new title came even as the door clicked shut.

Kersei stiffened as steps drew closer. She hastily tucked the parchment beneath her woolen wrap. With vigor, she drew up the walls around her heart and mind, the only way to shield herself. Never again would she believe his lies or smooth talk. Even as she brooded, she sensed her regia's disapproval. But she would not—could not—cry for Darius. Plenty had been shed in the first weeks after the trial.

"Kersei." Gone was Darius's authoritative tone, but no longer would he beguile her. "Please, speak to me. Even if it is to say you hate me." He touched her elbow and angled in. "I cannot endure this."

"Good." She turned aside to the fire, her belly a constant reminder of him. "Then you know what I feel—"

"I cannot know your feelings if you will not speak them."

"You did not care about my feelings the night of Adara's Delta Presentation."

"Not true!" The wound of that accusation pricked in his blue eyes. "I saw your anger and we talked—"

"*You* talked!"

He hesitated, considering her. "Do you so wholly regret me? Our relationship?"

"*Yes!*" She whirled on him. "I regret everything about you. Knowing you. Binding with you. Letting you have your way with me. This child!"

Darius staggered, his scarred face white. Eyes as round as his gaping mouth.

Hot tears raced down her cheeks. At his clear hurt and stunned disbelief, Kersei finally heard her own words through her fog of anger. Shamed by their sting, she turned to flee and tripped on a table leg. Stumbled.

Darius caught her.

"Leave me!" She threw off his grip and stumbled again, steadying herself on the desk. She slapped the wood. Swept everything aside, sending pens, inks, and papers flying. The crash of ink bottles made her still. Palming the desk, she hung her head. Choked back a sob. Bent, she cupped a hand over her mouth. Cried.

Within her their son squirmed, likely responding to the eruption of grief and rage. A momentary flicker of alarm—what if she somehow stressed the babe and lost him?—forced her to calm. Considering the cruelty of life this last cycle, she dared not tempt the Ancient's Hand.

Darius was at her side, arms encircling her. Though she wanted to pull away, she had neither strength nor will to fight. Long had it been since she had been held. Since she felt comfort.

"Somehow, I will make this right," he breathed against her ear. "I swear to you."

"You have done enough, thank you. Is your conceit so wholly intact that you would risk us more injury?" Then, she did nudge him aside, feeling the parchment close to her heart. "Leave it, Darius. It is done."

She who wandered the wastelands now ranked among kings debating the fate of their world. The audacity of it struck Isaura as she sat near the man named the Errant. Vorn had come forcefully into his role as king and owned it. Much like Dusan.

"We will not yield authority over the regia or machitis to Jherako," General Sebastiano growled. "Think you we are fools?"

"I thought," King Vorn said with an edge, "Kalonica wanted to ally with us. It was your king who toured my facility, and his father before him who sought an alliance. Marco said our Interceptors were needed to defend Drosero against the Symmachian skycrawlers."

"Our medora's visit was preliminary," Mavridis stated calmly.

"But his agreement was not!"

"A southlander knows the mind of our medora?" the general demanded.

This Council meeting regarding technology and airships was making Isaura heartsick. How was she to save this realm for Dusan if she could not even keep its leaders and allies from spewing venom at one another?

"Are tours of this . . . facility available for the Council?" Darius's first question of the meeting injected firmly into the division.

"Not to you." The loyalty of Grand Duke Rhayld waxed and waned so violently—even against his own kin—that Isaura took little counsel from him.

Thus, she would not allow him to decide who could and could not have a voice in the tricky efforts to bring technology to their people. "I—"

"There is no legal authority to refuse my participation. As Baron of Stratios, I sit on this Council," Darius argued. "My past failings have been dealt with, and at the instruction and mercy of our kyria, I yet serve this realm."

Rhayld muttered something that sounded a lot like him naming her "a hormonal, sentimental woman."

Isaura pulled straight. "Du—"

"Mister Secretary," barked Mavridis. Seated at her right, he looked to the aged recused iereas, Ypiretis. "Did you catch the duke's mutterings?"

Eyes bright and nearly mischievous, Ypiretis inclined his head toward the parchment where he recorded all that transpired in this meeting. "Every word, Elder Mavridis."

"Good," her father said. "I would have our medora understand the loyalties of his Council and how we all treated his kyria in his absence." He nodded to Darius. "Go on."

Even bolstered by her father's shrewd warning to the duke, Isaura desperately wished Dusan would walk through the door and take command of this situation. He had saved her before . . .

I need you, Dusan. Please return.

The door opened.

Her heart leapt, jarred when she saw a dark duster and black hair. Dusan! He turned—and hope crumbled. Roman deBurco fixed his fierce eyes to her as he entered with Rico Ohlsson. "Forgive us, Your Majesty," he intoned, inclining his head to her. "I think our invitation to this meeting was lost in delivery."

"Nay, naught was lost," Grand Duke Rhayld grumbled.

"How strange," Rico added with a rueful smile. "Surely there is no other explanation for not inviting the only men on this planet who've had flight training and are experienced scout pilots. Especially considering the insistence of your kyria that we attend."

"Scouts are one thing," the blond Jubbah Smirlet said. "Interceptors are a different class of aircraft."

Shoulders square, jaw tight, Roman stood before them. "Kynigos chose scouts for their ability to endure longer hauls, but all hunters are first trained on Vipers, fast-attack craft similar to Interceptors." He focused on her. "Kyria Isaura, are we welcome at this table, despite our tardiness?"

"Always, Master Hunter." Some of the building pressure in Isaura's chest eased as they joined them at the table. "I am grateful for your presence, as Medora Marco would be as well."

"All the same, Kalonica will not release her warriors to space dogs," Rhayld growled this time, spittle at the edges of his beard.

"Grand Duke," Mavridis spoke, his voice sharp. "Is that how you would name your medora?"

"Of course not!"

"Then I suggest you reconsider your words, as our medora numbered among these revered hunters."

"I speak nothing of our medora, though you would twist my words to turn our kyria against us. I only—"

"Seek peace." Isaura stood, once more surprised with herself. "The implementation of the technological advancement and flight-readiness pact is crucial. However, it will not be ours without an effort to protect our right to it. Our world is in danger, but we have at our hands the means to defend our people *and* this planet. The Kynigos deserve our gratitude, not our censure, for they help defend Drosero. There is no room for 'us' or 'them.' Downworlders, skycrawlers. We each fight for the survival of our people, so it is imperative we join forces, learn together, fight together." She indicated to the hunters. "As the Kynigos are not from a rival kingdom, we lose nothing in terms of political capital and gain everything in the training of our men for flight. Only fools would reject their help and counsel."

Mavridis and Hushak smirked, and somehow, their approval always made her feel as if she had Dusan's as well and that she had yet again stepped on someone's pointy shoes. Deliberately.

"My kyria," Rhayld sniveled, "taking protection away from yourself and Kardia—is that wise? Besides, what good is it to train our aerios when we have no airships?"

So she would have to come clean, as she feared last eve upon the arrival of Vorn's message. "As it was Medora Marco's wish to ally with Jherako in bringing ships to Drosero, I have authorized the treasury to disperse the necessary funds to secure at least a dozen Interceptors."

Stunned silence echoed in the council chambers as elders shared wide-eyed glances.

Insides churning, Isaura stood tall, refusing to cower.

"And how much is that?" Rhayld demanded, then flung his hands into the air. "Do you plan to run us into the ground while we are without a medora? Heed my warning—continue on such a careless path and you will not stay kyria long!"

Like lightning, Ramirus and Ulixes rushed at the ruddy-faced grand duke, who sputtered at their reaction. Hushak and Kaveh slid hands to hilts, forming up on Isaura.

"You dare threaten our kyria?" Mavridis roared, slamming a hand on the table.

"'Twas no threat, for plagues' sake!" The ruddy duke was not used to being challenged. He thought too much of himself and too little of her. All the same, he could not toss around careless words without consequence. "But she would do well to listen to men with much more experience and less . . . feminine sensibility."

Mavridis shoved to his feet, but Isaura stayed him. How easy it would be to let the men fight her battles. "We may well be without a medora at the moment, but we are not without a kyria," she reminded him. "I suggest this Council take the advice and direction of the Kynigos in selecting those of all rank to be pilots. At once. Our enemy will not wait till we are ready nor until archaic minds accept change." Her heart pounded. "They are coming. Already they have stolen into Trachys and kidnapped our medora. Let them not steal our very lives, too."

Vorn leaned forward, his brawny arms resting on the table as he glanced at the others, then to her. "I suggest the perfect place to begin these preparations is the Conclave of Sovereigns in two weeks. Jherako is host this time."

"You cannot mean to attend," General Sebastiano balked. "Bringing together all of Drosero's leaders to one place at a time like this—blood and boil. Symmachia could wipe us out in one strike."

"And you sit here, mentioning it right in front of the baron," Elder Elek commented, his expression as stone.

Though Darius hid the wound that comment inflicted, he did not hide it completely. "My loyalties are to Kardia."

"And who else?" Rhayld glowered. "You betrayed and killed your blood, boy. Never will you be—"

"Enough." Isaura tried to steady her frustration and nerves. "The Conclave *must* happen, and I will attend."

"Do not think measures have not been put in place. I have a queen and heir to protect as well." The steel of Vorn's words and gaze silenced more objections. "The event will be held in secret, its exact location concealed until the day of the meeting."

Wits gathered, Isaura swallowed. "The timing cannot be helped. We are in danger, but it is imperative we meet and converse. Symmachia already has us drowning in fear. We cannot let them smother our will to rally. And rather than an empire stubbornly clinging to outdated practices, we must rise to the challenge of the day." Her chest rose unevenly, so she took a moment to calm herself. "Now, can you men attend to this, see to it that our machitis are chosen and deployed for training in the airships, or must I direct that endeavor as well?"

Vorn barked a laugh, which he vainly tried to hide behind the back of his hand.

Mavridis rose. "Our kyria has rightly spoken. Shamed us for forgetting our priorities." He nodded around the huddle of tables, then settled on a still-red-faced Rhayld. "Gentlemen. Shall we consider the closest machitis—the regia and aerios?"

"Though I am no admirer of the duke," Hushak said, "he is right in this: it is not wise to strip Kardia of regia. No one of us wants to answer to Medora Marco should he return to rubble and ruin and a dead kyria because her protectors went south to learn to fly skyships." He faltered. "I beg your mercy, my kyria. I only—"

"I appreciate your counsel, Stalker, and count it as wise," Isaura said, deliberately ignoring the duke's seething. "None will be forced into this endeavor."

Relief seemed to fill the hall, but General Sebastiano shifted. "No one hates war more than a warrior, but it is the warrior who will bring it when necessary. As will the aerios and regia to the skies."

"And the Plisiázon. On to selection then," Mavridis suggested, which earned a chorus of ayes. Plans were made to recruit the right candidates and begin their training under the direction of the Kynigos. A while later, he brought the Council to a close.

Isaura rose, and once the gathered were on their feet, she exited and made for the private passage to the royal residence. Nerves flayed, she felt the tears coming, burning her eyes. A reaction she could only attribute to stress and her pregnancy. Unwilling to be seen crying, she motioned Hushak and Kaveh to stay and turned into the library. She eased the door closed and pressed a palm to her forehead. Squeezed shut her eyes. The first sob was more a breath that bloomed back at her. More demanded freedom. She would savor the solitude, the moment to let down her guard, cry. Not feel the need to perform or be composed. Likely, Kita would search her out soon. And if Mavridis noticed the guards . . .

I just need . . . She slipped away from the door, afraid they would hear her cries, and slid onto a small bench. Burying her face in her palms, she drew in several calming breaths.

Oh, Dusan. I cannot do it any longer. I need you. I'm tired. "Please, Dusan . . ." she whispered against her hands.

"Forgive me, Kyria Isaura," came the even voice of Ramirus. "I came through a side passage. I did not mean . . . Are you well?"

Ashamed to be discovered in this state, Isaura straightened. "Yes," she said, gathering herself, keeping her gaze down. "I thank you." When she finally stood, wobbled—mercies, she was exhausted—he was at her side. Cupped her elbow. She laughed off his concern. "In earnest, I am well."

"Of course. Your strength is obvious."

They were words she did not deserve. "You are too kind." Feeling awkward at being alone with him, she moved to the door. "If you will excuse me." In the hall, she met Kita, who scowled at Ramirus behind her. Yet it was an overly excited Kersei rushing up the passage that alarmed Isaura. She glanced at the baroness's belly. "Is it time?"

Kersei flushed. "Nay, a few more weeks."

"Of course." If she were ready to deliver the prince, she would not need an overcloak but a pharmakeia. "I mistook your urgency . . ."

"Oh. I-I must away. An errand." Kersei's gaze darted down the stairs to the main foyer. Light spilled across the marble from the north courtyard, where the Council made their way to the aerios training yard. "I am told Stratios is being readied, and I would see it before it is too late."

Of course. Before the babe was born. Yet guilt panged Isaura that Kersei would soon have to leave Kardia permanently. "I beg—"

"No." Kersei held up a hand. "You did more than I could have dreamed, considering the situation and certain people's actions." The baroness's venom surprised, though it should not. She had been a victim of her bound's scheming.

Part of why Isaura had orchestrated the transfer of title and lands. A mistake, mayhap . . . "I have heard it much angered you that Stratios lands were conferred upon Darius."

Kersei flinched. "You meant it well, and I hold no grudge."

But did she not?

"I . . . Before I leave—on these errands . . . only"—curls bounced along her olive complexion as she shifted nervously on her feet—"I wanted to tell you . . ." Kersei looked crestfallen. "Sometimes, we do things . . ."

What was this?

"Kyria Isaura," Ramirus interrupted, "your presence is requested at the training yard."

Plagues and boils. Could they not manage on their own? "Thank you." Isaura refocused on Kersei. "Please, continue."

"'Tis nothing," Kersei lied so obviously. "Only . . . If you need me—for anything—Myles can find me."

Find her? Isaura frowned. "Very well." She glanced at the burly aerios behind the baroness. Sergii could easily locate the princessa—she still could not think of Kersei as "baroness," despite that being her official title—and pages could run messages, so why tell her that? Something was off . . .

"Your Majesty, they say it's urgent," Ramirus prompted.

"Go." Kersei squeezed her hand. "When Marco returns, be happy."

A certain sadness lingered in that charge. Isaura almost spoke to it, almost addressed the rhinnock in the room, but before another word could pass, Kersei turned and descended the stairs with Myles, who guided the very pregnant princessa into the sunlit bailey.

"Strange," Isaura muttered as she and her lady's maid were escorted down.

"She seemed in a particular hurry," Kita noted.

"And distraught."

"Sergii say her relationship with the baron is quite strained."

"How could it not be when he is responsible for so much of her loss?" Redirecting her thoughts, Isaura crossed the north lawn to the training yard beneath the great wall of Kardia.

Elders and Kynigos had the aerios and regia arced around them. On a small dais, Darius signaled to her as he explained to the warriors what was happening, how their medora wished them to be able to defend themselves in the coming war with Symmachia. The aerios were respectful, but even these seasoned fighters had grim expressions and postures. They were daunted when it was revealed twenty would be chosen from among their number to learn to fly.

How strange it must be for those who had not yet seen electric lights. Even Isaura, though she had been in a skyship, found it difficult to fathom trusting a flying hunk of metal.

Darius spotted her gaining the dais. "Our kyria!" He yielded the center stage to her.

"Vanko Kalonica! Vanko Marco! Vanko Isaura!" the aerios shouted, fists thumping their chests.

Aware of the trepidation they likely felt, she must direct their attention to courage. "Your medora," she spoke from the dais, "before he came to the throne, was a Kynigos who loved flying. Months past, we visited Jherako together, and King Vorn showed Medora Marco airships. Never had I seen his eyes so vibrant or his heart so alive. He was thrilled, not only at the idea of flying again, but also at what this could mean for our world in the face of such an overreaching enemy. When he returns, you can be sure he will be among the pilots, fighting alongside you. So while it is hard to imagine, I charge you to be strong and of good courage, give no room to fear where flying is concerned. In fact, I think many of you warriors may find it thrilling." She thought of her own roiling stomach. "Once you get over airsickness."

Nervous chuckles carried around the yard.

Stepping onto the dais, Roman nodded his approval, then addressed them. "Marco was one of our best hunters and a top-notch pilot who aced his flight modules. Here in the training yard, we'll go through exercises to determine which of you have the best aptitude for flying and science. Your kyria will keep close watch as you must have her pardon to leave the service of Kardia for training in the south."

"Our kyria has decreed that *no one* will be forced into this program," Mavridis announced. "Only those with an excitement and passion to take to the skies will be considered. And believe me, engaging this technology for the first time is unsettling."

"Those not interested in flying, return to quarters," General Sebastiano said. "The rest, head over to the sparring yard."

To her surprise, not one aerios returned to the barracks. All to a man followed the general and Mavridis to the sparring yard. As she watched, Isaura slowed, wondering what had been so urgent about this talk with the aerios and machitis that she had to be summoned.

"Everything okay?" Roman asked quietly.

"I—" She blinked at him. "Why was I requested to come down here?"

Roman tilted his head, considering her. "You weren't."

She frowned and glanced at Hushak, who wore a similar wrinkle on his brow. "Ramirus said it was urgent."

A cloud moved over Roman's face. He turned to the younger Kynigos, who stood out of earshot but his gaze swiftly swung in their direction. Likely smelling the reaction Isaura could only see.

"What is this lie you perpetrated?" Roman demanded.

Chin tucked, Ramirus joined them. "Forgive me." The lanky hunter nodded to her with an earnest gaze before focusing on his master. "In the house, I detected something amiss with the baroness and her regia, so I used the quickest route to remove the kyria from them without alarming her or warning anyone."

"Something amiss?" Isaura drew back.

"*What* was detected?" Roman's gaze homed in on Darius, walking with General Sebastiano to the sparring yard.

Isaura prayed there was no ulterior motive that involved the man she had all but pardoned in Dusan's name.

"Deceit, fear," Ramirus said.

"Fear? Of me?" she balked.

Ramirus flicked a hand. "I cannot know. Only that I am to protect you in the name of Marco and the Brethren."

Why would Kersei be afraid of her? Insides swarming with concern, Isaura recalled Kersei's urgent, harried manner. "Something *was* odd when she stopped me in the hall . . . but deceit?"

"A guess, but I believe she withheld something." Ramirus remained confident. "If there is a threat—"

"We do not know there was a threat," Roman countered, shooting the younger Kynigos a scowl. "Only fear and deceit. There is no proof either were directed *at* the kyria. However, we use this information to watch and learn what is concealed."

Her gaze sought the former prince, surprised to find him rushing from the field toward the house. Curious.

"Perhaps it is wise," Hushak offered, "that the baroness and baron not be allowed near the kyria for now."

Aggressive tactics would interfere with developing a friendship with Kersei. "Surely such measures are not nee—"

"I agree," Mavridis pronounced as he strode up with Kita. "Our kyria should rest now. Escort her—"

"No." Isaura could not believe she so openly defied him, but even greater was her disbelief that he should order her around as if she were nothing more than his daughter. "I stand in place of our medora, and this is where he would be."

"Mayhap, but our medora—no matter where he is—would not be with child."

Cheeks heating, Isaura bristled. "That has—"

"Kyria Isaura," intruded Roman. "I welcome your opinion regarding two aerios as candidates for the pilot program." He offered his arm, gaze slamming into her father's. "You would do well, Mavridis, to remember to whom you speak and how you do it—especially in front of others."

No one dressed down Mavridis.

Expecting a reprisal as she was escorted away, Isaura felt the heat of his gaze and fury following them. Yet, none came. Near the training yard, she was delivered to a small dais and provided a seat.

"They are nearly done with this one." Pointing to the field, Roman took a knee beside her, his head yet at her own level. "This exercise is to judge their spatial ability." Wood blocks were laid out at strange intervals with net ropes strung between poles. "It's important to understand how the body moves in different environments and, once that is understood, to learn how to control it. Sense of direction is also important, but that is tested in other ways."

Though she watched the men, half her focus remained on the argument with Mavridis. She gulped the adrenaline that had jumped through her veins during that tiff. His presumption—

"He is a father and would protect you."

"Aye, but I am no longer a child."

"You will always be his child." Roman smirked, reminding her so much of Dusan that the ache in her heart blossomed anew. "He is also not used to yielding command."

"Especially to a woman."

"Nor one who is his own daughter." Another smirk, this one bigger.

Handsome, brooding, he had a casual confidence that commanded both attention and respect. "You are much like Dusan."

"No, he is much like *me*." Amused, he narrowed his gaze on the field. "Watch them and tell me what you see."

Why did he want her opinion? She would give it merely because he asked. He had been a stalwart presence since the trials, one she was increasingly grateful for. From her balcony, she had seen Kynigos ships taking off and the hunters going through their rigors in the training yard. They had even done drills along the cliffs, believing it an unprotected route to the castle, a terrifying prospect.

After an ora or so of watching the aerios and machitis test for aptitude and agility, she felt confident enough to offer thoughts. "That one is adept on the blocks . . ."

Roman monitored the aerios she pointed out. "But?"

But his actions were familiarly slow, hesitant. Just as she had been most of her life. "He is afraid."

"And the little one?"

A few moments of watching and gauging delivered her judgment: not as agile but a fast learner. Ready to face a challenge. "My opinion matters little." It should be Dusan giving counsel. He was a hunter—wiser and smarter, since their far superior skills and gifts enabled them to see beyond the visible. "If Marco were here—"

"Focus on being his beacon, to him and these people." Without another word, Roman stood and made his way onto the field. Over the course of the afternoon, he and the other Kynigos would whittle the candidates down to thirty, then to twenty.

Isaura removed herself to the grass and quickly felt the presence of Kita at her side again. "I am an inexperienced girl who was never meant to rule a kingdom, let alone pick out warriors to be pilots."

"But you are kyria by all rites and laws," Kita said, "and you honor these warriors with your presence, and your aerios with your strength and courage while our medora is away."

"Oh that he *would* return."

"My kyria?"

Resisting the groan that crawled up her throat, Isaura plastered on a smile and turned. Before her stood the lanky apprentice of Ypiretis. "Duncan."

He gave a quick bow. "I . . . I want to ask . . . to suggest . . ."

"Go on, boy," Ypiretis said, joining them. "Speak."

Duncan shifted, flashed a smile. "It's just that—being not from here. That is, not being from here, from Kalonica—Drosero even." His nervous laugh was adorable. "Thing is, I have a way with technology and was thinking that maybe I could work with some people I know to implement security."

She did not want to dim his excitement, but the suggestion confused her. "I have regia."

"Yes, but they cannot be everywhere," he said. "Technology can, because I'll wire it around the city. I even thought we could secure some channelers to help information move faster among your regia. Minutes could be crucial in saving—"

"Do it," Isaura instructed, pleased both to have more security and to give this young man a purpose, which she sensed he needed.

His brown-green eyes brightened. "Honestly?"

"I would not lie," she laughed. "Draw up a writ of necessary supplies, what you plan, and I will review and approve it."

"R-right. Of course. Thank you, Majesty."

Isaura inclined her head, watching as he backed up, then spun and darted toward the quarters.

"That was very kind of you, Kyria Isaura." After a nod of thanks, the recused iereas followed his apprentice.

As she made her way to the royal residence, Isaura realized this was yet another of Dusan's dreams—to see technology come to the City of Light—and it made her ache for him more.

That night as she lay in bed, restless from the day's events, wondering how Dusan might have done things differently, worrying that change was not happening fast enough, she was drawn into a deep sleep by Dusan's laughter and warm touch.

"You must return to me, safe and alive. I make decisions in your stead and am terrified they are the wrong ones."

Dusan's calloused hand traced her cheek as he aimed those pale eyes at her. *"The most important decision was saying yes to me."* His lips teased hers.

"Do not think to distract me with kisses."

"Why?" he asked huskily as his mouth captured hers in a long, languorous kiss. *"Is it working?"*

"Mmm . . . Always." She blinked, and he lay next to her, his pillow puffing beneath his stubbled cheek and jaw. *"I love you. Please . . . please come back."*

"My aetos, I never left." His hand came to rest on her womb.

Isaura sat up with a start, the room dark, save the light of touchstones on the far wall. She glanced at the empty spot on the bed beside her, certain if she looked hard enough, she could still see his imprint on the pillow. Her hand went to her belly, expecting to feel the warmth of his hand placed protectively over their child.

As the haze of sleep vanished beneath the cold breath of reality, she choked a sob. Dusan was *not* here—he was gone, and she alone.

08

Wind beat Kersei mercilessly, whipping her dark curls into her face with a thousand tiny stinging reminders of what she'd done.

She slowed the Black and glanced back, peering around her hood to the glow of Lampros City in the distance. Had he yet realized? Had the regia she encountered leaving the city reported her presence to him? She had been sure Isaura would detect her subterfuge, but when Ramirus had drawn the kyria away, Kersei seized the opening for escape.

What anger there would be that Isaura had been the last to see her and not realized what was happening. Would anyone chastise the kyria?

She sniffed. Hardly. All who encountered the Moidian beauty became besotted with her. Admittedly, more than once that jealous twinge had stolen Kersei's good sense, that longing to have the way back into Marco's arms cleared of obstacles. Then she begged the Lady's mercy for thoughts that inherently implied the death of another.

You are wicked, Kersei. Truly.

"Baroness, we must hurry," Myles shouted over the wind. "Storm approaches. We must get you to shelter."

Cloak tugged tighter, she refocused on the well-trod path and urged Bastien onward, skirting the ruins of Stratios. She took in the nearly complete restoration of the gardener's cottage, intended for her and Darius until the main house was finished. Compared to the ancient stone hall that had been in her family for generations, the cottage felt more a hut than a home.

An ache swelled in her breast. Neither would again be home to her. She knew not where Myles was leading her except that it was far from Darius.

Rain splatted her cheek, as if it spat upon her for abandoning her marriage and bound during his darkest hour.

She gritted her teeth. It was one thing to endure his disgrace, but quite another to live with him day in and day out, knowing he had killed everyone she loved, perhaps even Marco. No, she could not endure it. Neither did she want her child living with the stigma of being the son of a disgraced prince.

As they journeyed farther from Kardia, Kersei felt the weighted shackles slipping from her wrists. Now she inhaled the fragrance of freedom as her Black overtook Myles. "What is this?" she asked with a laugh. "Would you have me unseat you again?"

His expression had gone wan, then hardened as he looked at something in the near distance.

"What?" Kersei glanced back and sucked in a breath. "No."

Gathered on the southernmost side, riding toward the house that would have been hers, was an entourage of five or six. None other than Darius rode at the lead, followed by his regia, Caio and Hadrien, and his assigned Kynigos.

"We divert to the east," she said, urging her Black that way.

"There is nothing for it." Myles caught her reins, slowing both destriers. "We are seen."

Kersei snapped her gaze toward the contingent and struggled against the urge to cry out, to sink deeper into despair. More than a little fear attacked her sense of freedom. No doubt Darius would be furious, demand she return with him . . . She bit her tongue, withholding her slew of rancid thoughts, fearing the wind would also betray her and carry her words to him.

"Promise me your protection," she pleaded with her guardian over the howling winds.

Myles aligned their Blacks as they waited for the gap to erase. "I will not leave your side until I have delivered you safely."

She managed a smile. "Thank you." She swallowed as the riders met them.

Darius swung his Black around next to hers. "What do you here?" Despite the casualness of his question, he locked gazes with her. His blue eyes conveyed loudly his concern.

But no anger. Had he not found the parchment, then?

"The house, of course," Kersei lied, nodding to the structure. "Word came that it was near completion. I would see it."

"In your condition, you should be resting, not riding horseback." He glowered at Myles. "Why did you not order a carriage for the baroness?"

"Because I would have air and control of the Black," Kersei shot back. She must distract his temper and questions. His anger was missing, and that meant she still had a chance to pull this off. "Why are you so far from Kardia at this hour? I thought you were helping the kyria."

Darius hesitated overlong before offering, "The house." His eyes were shadowed, but that could be the falling sun. He cocked his head toward the cottage. "Shall we tour it together?"

Kersei held the reins firmer in gloved hands.

"Mayhap before the rain drenches us on our return?"

Not trusting herself to lie convincingly, she spurred her horse toward the cottage, deliberately away from him. A spiteful move, but she had little mercy for him these days. At the house, she guided Bastien to the hitching post.

Before she could dismount, Darius was there, helping her to ground.

"I am not incapacitated." Peeved, she looked at Myles, and though he averted his gaze, she caught his irritation at Darius's manhandling of her.

Scowling, Darius also did not miss the protective reaction of her aerios, yet he focused on her. "I have a surprise for you." His words were ones of reverent excitement. "I had hoped to show you in a more official manner"—he lifted her hand to his lips, depositing a kiss there—"but this will have to do."

Kersei jerked her hand free. "There have been enough surprises for a lifetime." With more than a little annoyance, she entered the house, glad to find it simply yet elegantly appointed with foyer, drawing room, library, kitchen, dining room, sitting rooms, and four bedrooms, all done in fine papers and linens. Far finer than the gardener had kept it, no doubt. Clearly Darius worked to ensure she felt no deprivation other than the size and location.

Until taking up residence in Kardia, Kersei had only known Stratios Hall with its great gray-black stone hewn from a nearby quarry. As an elder of Kalonica and First of the Medora, her father had kept a steward, many sergii, gardeners, kitchen staff, a stable master, a smithy . . .

"What happened to the Mardlines? Or Mr. Kerit? As laborers, surely they were not at the hall that night."

Darius lowered his gaze. "Most found work among your father's grandees."

Grandees. The higher ranks . . . "But were they not at—"

"Our binding?" There was something about the way he said that, the way he bit off the ending . . . "Aye. Some. Which is why some went also to Prokopios to find work and another elder to serve." He guided her toward a door on the right. "I grant, though this cottage is smaller than either of us are used to, it will do fine. Would you not agree?"

Her stomach squirmed—and it was not the babe this time—as she stood with him. Guilt harangued her, but resolve hardened. "None of this would be necessary if—"

"This is the evening parlor." He paused at the door as if it had a special meaning.

It did not. She would not be lulled into distraction over a home now empty because of his actions. Punishment she must endure because of his foolishness. "What are these games? I am tired and my back aches." She charged past him into the room with chairs, a writing desk, sofa, table, lone shelf stocked with leathered spines. Repulsed that he seemed excited to share this with her, this place that had been someone else's home, she whirled on him, irritated. "What is this game you play at—"

The words fled back down her throat as her gaze rose to what towered behind him.

Kersei let out a strangled cry, covered her mouth, and stumbled backward, dropping hard onto a chair. Heart thundering, she could not tear her eyes from her parents and sisters standing over them, forever immortalized in canvas and oils. "By the Lady . . ." she whispered, hot tears coursing down her cheeks.

On a knee at her side, Darius thumbed away her tears. "I worried it might be too much. I had thought to show you sooner, but . . ."

Ma'ma looked so regal in her favorite cream gown. And Adara—frozen forever at ten cycles of age, tugging on the ribbons as she had always been wont. Father . . . Her chest constricted at his firm scowl and silver-threaded beard.

Oh, Papa.

She struggled to her feet and went to the mantle. Reverently, she touched the canvas, half expecting her fingers to graze the leather of Father's boots or the delicate silk of Ma'ma's gown. Instead, the rough texture of the oils once more shoved the truth in her face.

Grief tore over her. They were gone, dead. All of them. Because of the man who had commissioned this painting. She fisted her hand.

"Are you pleased with it?"

She braced against the mantle, gaze lost in the empty firebox . . . empty like Stratios Hall . . .

And my heart.

"I thought it would make you happy to have remembrance of them."

"I would not need a remembrance if you had not betrayed them."

He had commissioned the painting as a gift, a way to show his sorrow and regret. Never could he undo the loss he had caused her. And this . . . this was his way of admitting that.

"Speaking of betrayal . . ." He swallowed, then gathered himself. "While on the north lawn selecting the aerios to go south for flight training, I was pulled aside by Caio. He urged me inside, said 'twas something regarding you. Naturally, I assumed it had to do with the babe and raced off the field. Once inside, I realized you were not there. Odd, I thought, considering your condition." His gaze rose to her and saw that she was still. So very still. Pale. "I know things have been . . . strained between us since . . . the trial. The judgment." He twisted the family ring that had not been taken from him, thanks to Isaura, and watched as Kersei slowly lowered her hand and stood like a statue in the near dark. "But . . . I never expected what I found in my office."

She shuddered, her wide, dark eyes finding his. Watering.

His heart drummed. "According to the laws of Kalonica and Kardia . . ." He sniffed. A deep chasm opened in Darius as he recited that parchment and he studied the floor for several long seconds, his anger wrestling grief and regret. "What I cannot sort is how you managed to have my brother sign it."

Kersei started. "What?" It was but a gasp.

He shifted aside and folded his arms. Swiped a hand over his jaw. "See, Kersei, since permission for all bindings is granted by the medora, so must all annulments also be granted by him. Since Marco is not here to sign it, the parchment is invalid."

"Not true." Her words were strained, angry. "It was signed by—"

"My own uncle." He shook his head. "And still incomplete, unexecuted."

"No!" she gasped. "It is signed. Rhayld and the commissioner told me it is done."

"Without Marco's seal, it remains simply a parchment." His anger was real but the wound much greater. He thought they had been repairing their relationship. "How could you, Kersei?"

"Me? *You* have ruined everything. This annulment is the only power I have left to protect myself and my son—"

"*Your* son?" He saw it in her eyes then, the guilt she carried like a crimson banner. "You mean to take him from me." Shock riddled him. His own guilt mirrored in what she intended. He deserved this.

"It is better. For him."

"You mean *for you!*"

"Blame yourself—"

"Try to take my son from me!"

Kersei drew back.

He pushed himself away, tremors of rage threatening his restraint. "I meant to come here . . ." He lowered his head, hating himself. Hating what had become of their relationship. "I thought . . . I thought we were working things out." Darius searched the face that had always been the sun to him. "Is there nothing I can do or say that would . . .?"

"That would *what*?" Kersei's small frame rattled with anger that flushed her cheeks. "Bring them"—she stabbed a finger at the painting—"back? Make me stop hating you?"

Agape, he took a step back. "Kersei . . ."

"No!" Her shout echoed through the empty house. "Nothing will change that. You are a monster. A cruel, selfish boy who could never see past his title. And I will not allow your foolishness to darken my world any longer!" She hurried from the room, the door flapping behind her hasty departure.

Grieved, Darius hurried after her. "Kersei."

Before the trial, she had shared her warmth—her smile, her laugher, her love, her passion. Now, in their place were cold, icy responses. Brittle shouts. A frozen tundra between them that would likely never thaw.

Yet he must not stop trying. For her. He would do anything for her. To heal this hemorrhaging marriage. He reached her as Myles assisted her onto Bastien. "We should name our son Xylander." It was a concession, a great one.

Myles squared his stance before Darius.

"Stop me not, aerios."

"Will you force your will on yet another?" Kersei drew Bastien around. "My son will be named Xylander not because of your permission but out of my ardent insistence upon keeping my father's name alive in whatever manner possible."

"Ker—" His shoulder struck Myles's as he tried to stop her, and it took everything in Darius not to lay the aerios out. Hooves trampled his heart as the Great Black ferried her away. He glowered at Myles, then shifted back a step. "Protect her."

"With my life." The man's gravelly voice was fierce as he hauled himself up onto his horse and barreled after her.

Stricken, Darius felt his knees shake. Buckle. He knelt, fighting the squall that threatened to overtake him. He peered out across the field as she faded into the stormy distance. Swallowed hard. Knew there was little he could do to gain her mercy. Doubted he could ever convince her that he was not the diabolus himself. His greatest fear realized—she was lost to him.

"Insufferable beast!" Growing angrier, Kersei felt the heavy weight of her sodden wool cloak as they galloped through the downpour. Talking in the storm proved impossible, which served her well, as she wanted no conversation. The punishing ride sated her anger but beat her back and ridiculous stomach hard.

Myles pulled ahead, then dropped back, only to surge ahead again. Repeatedly this happened, and she realized he likely felt the need to hurry, but she could not take the rigorous pace. Yet the chill stealing into her bones from the rain and driving winds forced Kersei to urge Bastien on.

Ahead again, Myles glanced back at her, his expression a mixture of surprise, relief, and concern. But she braced herself on the saddle, burrowed in, and suddenly wished for the speed and smooth ride of Marco's airship.

One day Drosero would have such technology. Sadly, this was not that day.

Bastien pounded the earth, his gait gentle for a destrier, yet jarring to Kersei. She felt strong kicks of the babe and grimaced. *Just hold on,* she willed her body and son.

Shivering felt more like convulsing. An ache spasmed up from her lower back and across her belly. Kersei tensed and grabbed her back, stiffening through the pain. Her teeth clacked, and she squinted through the downpour to Myles, but the sheets of rain were too dense. She saw only emptiness that forced her to slow and search her surroundings. A twinge of fear raced through her. Where was he? In fact, where was *she*? Unable to discern her location, she slowed more. If she were lost in this storm . . . She strained to see through the thick, wet veil.

A Great Black shape erupted from the side.

Kersei yelped. Felt herself sliding sideways. She grabbed the reins to retain her seat. Bastien misread her yank on the leather straps and reared.

"Whoa, whoa!" Myles's deep, resonating voice cut through the elements. He caught Bastien's bridle, encouraging the beast to calm.

Kersei expelled the breath trapped in her throat, body convulsing from being cold and wet as Myles led them a few strides further.

A dark hulk emerged from the sheeting rain, a building.

"We should shelter while the storm rages. To go further risks your health. You are frozen through." Her burly guardian considered her. "I would help on this mission of yours, but not if it puts your life—or the babe's—in jeopardy."

Rubbing her arms to generate some heat, she glowered. "H-how are you n-not c-cold?"

"I have more meat on my bones." He dismounted and went to a door, which he tried, but it would not yield. Not easily deterred, Myles shouldered into it and, with a loud crack that mixed with the thunder, the door surrendered. He vanished inside, then reappeared. Taking the horses' reins, he led them around the side to where a large section of wall had crumbled. Once inside, he released the lead and reached to Kersei.

Hands on his shoulders, she let herself slide from the saddle, trusting the aerios to break her fall and keep her steady on her feet. Only, as her boots struck earth, her legs buckled from the long ride and the chill eating at her strength.

Myles lifted her into his arms, a move that both startled and shocked her—she was not used to being so easily touched by men—and strode across the musty room. His scent was one of earth and air, strength and courage. She had long admired the aerios, the rank he held as one of Zarek's fiercest fighters. Only in this moment did she wonder at this man, who he was. Where was his family? His red beard was neatly trimmed, his chest hard, round and solid as a barrel. His eyes were gray and clouded with concern as he set her on a sofa.

Their gazes met, and Kersei flushed for the way she studied him. "I beg your mercy." She turned to the fireplace that had defied time and elements, standing straight as the day it had been erected. Uneasy at the dirty old cushions she sat upon, Kersei tried to ignore her crawling skin and the thoughts of the insects likely infesting this place. But it felt good to sit, to feel her legs and backside once more.

With a heavy thud, Myles deposited a bag at her feet. "Change into dry clothes before you catch your death of cold."

She bristled at his commanding tone. "There would be no point—this . . . house is only a reprieve from the storm. We—"

"If anything happens to you, it will be my head. We stay." His grim expression warned he would not budge. "Change."

"If he catches us, alone in this shanty . . ."

"'Tis not like that!"

Kersei took a moment's pleasure in his discomfort. "We know the truth of this, but how would it look?" She batted away loose, wet curls. "Nay, we shelter for a while, then must be on our way. It would be insupportable to remain longer."

"My head will roll if we are discovered, but I would risk that to see you safely to the protection of those I trust better."

Trust better? "Who?"

His contrition returned and he huffed, shook his head. "I should not have agreed to this. If you die, all is for naught."

She, too, regretted this course, that it was necessary, that it imperiled her stalwart aerios, who offered something no one else could: sanctuary. "I beg your mercy." A cold tremor wormed through her spine. "I would not have you suffer for aiding me. My impatience is born of a desire to avoid being forced back . . ."

Another spasm riddled her back and abdomen. Not wanting to alarm her champion, Kersei bit down on the inside of her cheek. The babe kicked hard, reminding her that he was clearly as willful as his father.

And me.

"Are you having pains?"

Curse the man. But she would not lie. "Aye," she breathed. "But not the kind of which you speak." At least, she hoped not. "These are just from the ride and rain." Had her desire to escape put her in danger of an early delivery? Had she jeopardized the babe?

The warm sun wrapped Isaura as she stood at the far edge of the inner wall with her moon discs. How strange, even still, the sound of the waves battering the cliffs. Growing up in the desert had deprived her of the sea's mighty voice, one that comforted.

She whirled and flicked the first disc, then the second, at a tree. Each gave a satisfying *thump* as it chomped into the bark. Strolling over to retrieve them, she recalled the way she had fought alongside Dusan against the Irukandji in those woods of the Altas Silvas. An involuntary shudder struck at the thought of those blue-marked raiders.

Much had changed for her in the forest, which was known as the Sanctuary of Secrets for the many secrets it had stolen through the years. Now, it also claimed her confidence that Kalonicans were safe. As a child, she'd believed living in the north would keep her well. Yet, it was in the north—farther north than her home in Moidia—that Marco was taken.

Overcome by the memory, she lowered her head and closed her eyes. That night had been so perfect, so sweet—like his love. She swallowed, remembering his kidnapping. The scuffle. His shout. Desperation in his pale eyes as the intruders dragged him away. The strike against her skull that rendered her useless.

Tears speeding down her cheek, Isaura felt the presence of another. After drying her face, she clicked the discs together and straightened. Turned with a plastered smile to the master hunter. "I love the sound of the sea."

"We should return to the house."

Of course. Stuff her behind walls, alone. Make her miss Dusan more. But she had enjoyed enough time out of doors this rise, so she would not argue.

"Where's Mistress Lasdos?" Roman had an unmistakable tinge of annoyance as they walked.

"There on the patio with a book, as I suggested she enjoy the time to relax." She swept a hand in an arc, indicating the great barrier that nearly blocked the view of the mountains and the city huddled around it. "With so large a wall, I am safe to practice with the discs. And mayhap enjoy a walk to the cliffs. Dusan so enjoyed this view . . ."

"Forgive me, but your grief—"

"Sadness. Not grief." That might come later, but for now, she keenly held to the belief that Dusan was alive and would return.

"I never left . . ." His words from her dreams moved her hand to where his had rested before she jolted awake.

"He does yet live," Roman said quietly, acquiescing to the walk.

They reached the steps to the lower courtyard with its three arches flanking the fountain of Eleftheria. "I know." Isaura squinted a smile as she set her discs on the wrought-iron table nestled among the flowering cordi bushes. "I confess, with each passing day, that belief grows more difficult to hold on to . . . yet I do . . . will."

"Just because you cannot see him or feel his touch does not lessen his existence."

"As can be said of Vaqar and Eleftheria. Alas, they are immortal. Dusan is not." She continued down to the lower terrace that would lead to the green overlooking the sea. "Yet I know he will do everything in his power—even to the detriment of his own well-being—to return." She hugged herself, avoiding thoughts of him doing something rash that would cost his life. "I do not believe the Lady brought us together, gave us this child, for it to end there. And I . . . dream of him."

She shifted around before the steps and gazed up at the massive palace. Admired the cream plaster aglow from the sunset. Green roof tiles. The sparkling city beyond. Only then did she realize she was looking for someone. She eyed her regia a dozen paces behind. Were they the reason she turned, half expecting to see someone? They had mastered staying out of sight, but still . . .

Roman studied her in a way only a master hunter could, one that made her feel . . . well, not a criminal but more a . . . specimen.

Feeling awkward—too aware that he knew how she felt—Isaura descended the last steps, taking to the carpet of grass that softened her steps and relieved the ache in her lower back. In the months since Marco's abduction, she had grown accustomed to Roman's presence and instructive ways. How everything seemed to become a lesson of some kind. "You must think me foolish."

"Not at all." Hands at his sides, Roman was prepared for anything, just as Dusan had always been. "Do you talk to him?"

She plucked a waxy leaf from a shrub along the northernmost wall. "Who?" Veering away calmed her—on that side, the cliff plummeted eighty feet, though scree plunged at least another fifty. A fall from here would mean certain death.

"Marco. In your dreams, do you talk to him?"

With a shrug, Isaura tried not to frown at the strange question. "They are but dreams. Is there a way to control what we do in them?"

He walked to the edge and eyed the foamy surf. When he came around again, he was smiling. "You did not answer my question—do you talk to him?"

Shoving her braid back over her shoulder, she wondered at his question. It irritated that he pressed her regarding something that was treasured, private. Somehow kept her from despair. It was not for him to know or not know. Yet, considering him and this line of inquiry, she expected he would wait until she answered. "I do." Even now she saw Dusan, head on the pillow, smiling at her, his hair . . . That was for her, *their* moments, and she would not share the details.

Yet something seemed off. What? Why did her insides quaver as those memories were conjured?

"What unsettles you?" Roman cupped her arm and directed her from the cliffs.

Isaura blinked at the maneuvering and at being read so openly by one other than Dusan. "Nothing really." Why was he urging her back up the steps? "Do you fear I will fall?" she asked with a laugh. "I have never been careless or clumsy."

But Roman motioned to the regia. "Take her to the house."

Fright overtaking her at his sudden change in tone and manner, she grabbed his forearm. "Wh—"

Something glinted in the air, flying straight at her. She shifted away.

With a bellow, Roman became a blur. Shouts erupted.

Alarmed, Isaura reached for her discs, only to remember she had left them on the table. She turned to run for them, but black dusters flapped as swift movements caught her up in a gust of tension, thrust her up the steps, almost without her feet touching the ground. "What . . .?" The erupting chaos, confusion, and panic were surreal. She tried to avoid stumbling or falling as they shoved her toward the castle. "Please, wh—"

A horn of alarm trumpeted through the yard.

Face washed white, Kita looked at Isaura and rushed ahead. "Get the pharmakeia!"

Peals from the belltower bounced off the fortress walls. Why were the bells ringing?

Isaura hurried, her heart and mind racing wildly, unsure what was happening. What caused the panic. Her head ached as the doors to the keep flung open and regia bled from the halls.

"Protect the kyria!" Hushak shouted.

Isaura glanced past the throng, back toward the cliffs, to Roman there on the edge. Her heart seized at three brown-clad men attacking the master hunter. Regia swooped down from the terraces to join the fray.

"Where is the pharmakeia?" Hushak demanded.

"Here!" a gruff voice replied.

Who needed tending? Isaura glanced around, a bit dizzy—from the excitement, no doubt. Being hurtled by Hushak and Kaveh into the library only heightened her fears, especially when her guards swung around. In the seconds before the doors slammed closed, a dozen or more regia formed on the other side, swords drawn.

Breathless, she gaped. "What is—"

"Let me see to your wound, my kyria."

The pharmakeia startled her. She'd nearly forgotten he was there. "Oh, it is not I who is injured," she reassured. "It is Roman who—"

"Please. Sit." He caught her shoulder.

Even as he forced her onto a settee, Isaura argued. "In earnest, good—"

"You bleed, my kyria." His grave expression stilled her.

She followed his gaze to her bliaut, stained crimson. Blood marred the beautiful brocade. "How . . .? Where . . .?"

"Your neck, Majesty."

Her fingers found the wound and stinging line she had not yet registered. "Oh." The room swam, and she was urged to lie back. Foggy curtains veiled her vision.

"Finally, the queen returns."

Eija stiffened at the acid in Reef's words. "What's that supposed to mean?"

"Ignore him." Marco dropped from the bulkhead, where he'd been doing pull-ups. "He's worried about you."

Not what she'd expected. She eyed Reef, still not sure how to read his antagonism. "Why?"

"I'm *not* worried." His expression betrayed the lie.

"What'd you find out this time?" Marco asked, wiping the sweat from his brow.

She'd spent the last forty-eight hours gathering intel, and every time she stepped back through the cellblock barrier, he asked the same thing. And excepting that first day when she'd learned about Daq'Ti's limited data access through his arm weapon, she had little to report. It was stressful work, stealing moments, looking around, trying not to seem suspicious. Which was impossible with the night-and-day differences between her and these Lavabeasts, not to mention their strange deference to her.

"He got me into Engineering, but when I tried to access controls, just like last time, a huge Silvermark interfered. I was afraid to draw more attention until I had things better figured out, so I chose to leave. Fight another day, and all that. But honestly—no time to waste. The arsenal they're carrying— it is annihilation equipped. Extinction-event capable—our extinction. The Quadrants'."

His silvery eyes seemed to search the cell for something. "And they targeted you once you accessed weapons?"

"Never got that close. They were hypervigilant about me being near controls." Which annoyed her, though it made sense. "If only the others would comply with my wishes as easily as Daq'Ti," she said with a half laugh. "But since they don't, there would have to be some significant distraction in order for me to access weapons, initiate launch sequence, and fire a nuke. Not impossible, but . . . challenging."

Brooding mastered, Marco cocked his head. "Keep trying."

"Will do. Patron didn't send me here to be ineffective, so I'll find a way, someh—"

A warning trilled from Daq'Ti, who stepped forward, making them all tense.

"What's wrong with him?" Marco asked.

"Not sure."

Reef angled forward. "Someone's coming."

"Several someones," she muttered, not liking the way Daq'Ti turned toward the passage that led to their brig. Like he anticipated trouble . . .

Thudding echoed in the passage, then pushed its cadence into their cell. Four Draegis appeared, their eye slits pulsing violently, with intent. Two entered, arms weaponizing as they aimed at Marco.

"No." Eija balked at the idea of them taking him, worrying his comment about them trying to dig the intel out of his brain was a very real, screaming possibility. "No, you can't."

Daq'Ti responded to her alarm. Trilled at the newcomers, who chortled back.

A blue emerged from the rear and motioned to Marco. "Take him."

"No!" Eija moved with Reef toward the Kynigos. "Leave him alone."

The third Draegis faced them, aimed something at Marco, and a light flashed. Something whisked past Eija, and she heard a solid thump.

Marco clamped a hand over his neck, where the projectile had penetrated. The look of shock vanished, his silvery eyes blazing to white-hot anger. Shoulders squared, he raised his arms as if to confront the Draegis. But rather than launch at the Lavabeasts, Marco wavered. Slumped onto his bunk with a growl that morphed into a groan. The two Draegis clomped over and caught him as he canted forward.

"No!" Eija pivoted. "We can't let them take him." All she could think of was them digging in his brain, getting that intel, and leaving Marco a vegetable. Or worse.

Reef swept to her side. "Wait."

"We can't—"

"*Wait*," he hissed.

Surprised at his tone, his vehemence, she eyed him, then the four.

"If we start a fight, they'll lock you down."

"But Marco . . ." Heart thundering, she watched them carry him off and felt every ounce the ineffective Tryssinian she'd vowed not to be. "If they get into his head . . ."

Reef pulled her around to face him, his hand sliding to her waist.

"Hey—"

His nose against her cheek stunned her into silence.

"That was the exact kind of distraction you could've used."

"If I were in Engineering," she countered. "I can't do anything here."

"Just saying . . . you'll figure it out." There was something crazy in his eyes as he looked at her. "You always do. Marco gave you a job. Find a way. Get it done."

Stilled, she nodded. Knew he was right. Yet . . . it just seemed so futile to destroy the *Prev* if the Draegis could just extract the intel from Marco's head, likely killing him in the process.

"Daq'Ti could've stopped them," she said around a pout.

"That's it," Reef said, eyes widening. "Use BeastieBoy. I know I don't have to say this—but with them taking Marco, our timeframe likely got cut short. Much shorter."

She understood. Swallowed. "Yeah, you didn't have to say that." She started for the static shield. "Wish me luck."

Passing countless Draegis required courage she didn't think she had. With those thick-muscled, black-charred, intimidating bodies, they were flat-out monstrous and took up most of the corridor, forcing her to lean toward the bulkheads. Her boots clipped in the corridors, every hesitation a scuff-slide fracture in the irregular rhythm. When a green-marked one swayed into their path and didn't correct his trajectory, she faltered. Fear deepening with each thudding step toward her.

"*Chatge*," Daq'Ti chortled at the green.

Green maintained his course, despite the "to the side" order.

With a violent thrust of his arm, Daq'Ti enforced his command, cracking Green across his head, sending the lower-rank into the bulkhead.

"*Yotub turing*," Daq'Ti growled the warning to stay down as he prodded Eija past.

With the other Draegis behind her, she was soon in stride with her guardian again. Gave him a sidelong glance. "Thank you."

"*Yuzma yuz.*" Hand to face. Maybe it was a motto, similar to the Eidolon saying "Drop, shop, and crop" to each other before a mission? Or the Kynigos saying, "For honor."

After another turn and a couple flights of stairs, Eija struggled to remember the route. There were now a lot of access panels, hatches, and Draegis between her and Marco and Reef. The daunting truth— she was too far from human aid if she got into trouble—made her skip a step to stay closer to Daq'Ti.

At a hatch, he accessed a panel. With a nod to her, he stepped back.

Gliding inside, Eija scanned Engineering. Draegis both sat and stood at various posts. Their beefy size and the threat they posed always made rooms feel cramped, but this bordered on suffocating. She navigated her way through, having to squeeze sideways to avoid bumping one or another Draegis.

Another blue-marked Draegis clomped toward them, eye slits thrumming with indignation. "*Siz bu erda nima qilasiz?*"

At his demand to know what she was doing here, Eija swallowed. Wondered how to ans—

"*Xonim buni ko'redi,*" Daq'Ti replied.

Yes, indeed—the lady *would* see it. Feigning ignorance of their conversation, which fell into fast, terse dialogue she struggled to keep up with, Eija shifted around, eying the consoles, arrays, and controls. As always, the Rohileri lettering proved disorienting—it was one thing to hear and assimilate it, but quite another to *read* it. Yet as she took it in, somehow the differences fell away.

Djell. The *Prevenire* was a retrofitted corvette, but it'd also been laid out in a manner uncannily similar to a Draegis ship. Xisya must've had a lot of influence over the Symmachians, instructing them not only in the technology to make the jump, but in the design of the ship's interior and controls.

Which made Eija's job a bit easier. *Focus on the similarities.* On the way, the Draegis adjusted knobs and switches, swiped arrays, the rhythm of their movements in responding to the dreadnought's outputs. Almost on its own, her gaze skipped left. To an unmanned console. Averting her eyes so she wasn't completely obvious, Eija shifted. Turned. Noted the ongoing rapid-fire conversation between Daq'Ti and the other blue as she came around and deliberately bumped into the one Draegis.

"Oh." She moved backward. "So sorry." When the beast trilled at her, she lifted her hands and acted sheepish, her trajectory toward the unmanned console looking completely coincidental. She hoped.

Lavabeast heads swiveled to her, radiating their irritation, then swung back to work. Except Daq'Ti's gaze. He was locked on her as the other blue said something. Though Daq'Ti's eyes weren't shaped like human eyes and she had little Draegis facial recognition from which to draw the conclusion, she came to it all the same: *He's worried.*

But if he could keep that blue distracted . . . Heat slid down her spine as she stopped before the unmanned console. She swept her hand over the surface and turned, as if doing nothing other than experiencing the area.

"You yet watch over me, do you not?" Green eyes set against the glow of her tawny skin invited Marco closer.

"It is all I could do, since I am not there." He pressed a kiss to her forehead, agonized over the cut at her throat. "Anything to be sure you are there when I return."

"When will that be? How much longer?" Her words fluttered against his cheek.

"The Lady knows . . ."

"Hurry home, Dusan. Please."

He loved that she called him that. A name nobody else used, fragranced by her love. "Nothing will keep me from you or our daughter, Isa."

Gentle fingers traced his face, the simple gesture providing so much comfort. "You are sure?"

He smirked. A sound behind him drew his glance over his shoulder.

"What is it?"

Darkness swelled in the door.

"Marco!"

"What?"

"Marco, wake up."

"I am awake . . ."

A chuckle. "Yeah, not quite. Let's go."

Marco twitched and the room morphed into the brig, transporting him back from Kardia to a grim, gray existence. Swiping a hand over his face to rough away the dregs of sleep, he wrestled with how easily his subconscious planned to live and return, in spite of his conscious mind's intentions to do whatever it took—including a suicide mission—to protect Isaura. Was it a lie?

What did it matter? They were dreams. At least there he could control the outcome to some degree. What could it hurt for her to have more hope?

"You with me yet?" Jadon asked.

Frowning, Marco lay on a hard surface and glanced down the length of his body to where Jadon stood. Why was he so out of it? "Wha . . .?"

"They took you again," Jadon jutted his jaw. "You have a new . . ." He wagged a hand at Marco, then tapped his own temple.

When Marco tried to sit up, he felt as if something sat on his chest. He fought to get upright but the room spun. "Where . . .?" Thoughts tangled before they made it to his tongue. The Eidolon said the Draegis had taken him. Again. He vaguely remembered being carried out of the room. "The girl . . ." She'd been ready to fight for him.

"Eija? Doing recon, I guess. Me? I'm apparently a status update machine. In case you were wondering."

Groaning, Marco squinted at the Eidolon and felt a pinch at his temple. He touched the spot and found it burning.

"Guessing they decided you were healed enough to go digging in your head." Oh no. "How long?"

"An hour. Maybe a little more."

"Gotta get out of here."

"Agreed. But how?" Jadon squatted against the wall. "If we destroy the *Prev*, how do we escape?"

"Thought it was obvious."

"Right—steal a ship. One neither of us is familiar with or trained on."

Marco cringed against flares of pain. It was like his head had been used for target practice. Wait . . . "If they plugged me into the *Prev*, then . . ." His thoughts squirreled away fast.

"Assuming because you flew the *Prev* means you can fly any ship? That's a leap, man."

"We won't know until we try."

"And die trying."

"Or sit here and wait for them to get what they want, and die then. Along with everyone in the Quadrants." Marco sensed the girl's efflux drawing closer—filled with stress and . . . distress. "Zacdari—something's wrong." He pushed to his feet, hating the lethargy that fought for control of his limbs, and noted Jadon rose as well.

The outer door whisked open and in stepped Eija with a beleaguered-looking Blue.

"What's wrong?" Marco asked.

Hesitating, Eija shot the beast a look. "Tempers are . . . flaring. I think the Draegis are mad over Daq'Ti's deference."

"Did they try to hurt you?" Jadon straightened, arms poised at his sides, ready to fight.

"Only if you deem forced removal from Engineering hurtful."

"What happened?" Marco asked.

"I don't know." She shoved her hands through her hair, which now hung past her shoulders. "I tried to get into the system, but they seemed aware before I even got anywhere."

"Why didn't you use the distraction thing?" Jadon folded his arms.

"It wasn't that simple. They were all over me, watching me. Daq'Ti talked to a Blue, and I thought that would help, but . . ." She shook her head, then narrowed her gaze on Marco. "What about you? How're you doing?"

"Still alive." Marco traced his temple ridges that were still raw. "Which probably means they didn't get what they wanted."

Jadon glanced at Eija. "And it ticked them off." He grinned. "Between the two of you, things are being upended. From you, they can't get the maps. From her, they lost an officer."

With a nod, Marco held her gaze again. "Keep trying with the hand thing—"

"But that green literally shook me off."

"We have to try the others. Keep trying until—"

"What if Daq'Ti is the one in a million that I can turn?"

Jadon leaned against the bulkhead and sighed. "Then we need a bigger distraction."

Eija rolled her eyes. "You don't under—"

"Maybe he's right," Marco said. The two of them stopped and looked at him, waiting. "I might have a plan."

"Good." Jadon nodded. "Because if you're right and they didn't get what they wanted, they're going to keep digging, which means you might not come back next time."

KARDIA, LAMPROS CITY, KALONICA, DROSERO

"Open your eyes. Please."

Eyelashes fluttering, Isaura tried to focus. Light exploded and she groaned. Tried again, the light this time less painful. Finally gaining her bearings, she found Mavridis, Kita, and Roman hovering behind the dark-haired man. The pharmakeia.

Her hand went to a stinging at her throat as she tried to sit.

"Ah-ah, not yet." The pharmakeia shook his head. "The cut is stitched but best not agitate it further for a while."

Stitched? "Why . . . are you all here?" Her head positively throbbed!

"Forgive us for intruding on your privacy, Your Majesty, but the matter is urgent," Mavridis said quietly.

Still disoriented, she was grateful for the water Kita offered. After a sip, she asked, "What happened? I recall but chaos and confusion . . ."

"You were cut by a thrown dagger," Roman said. "Had you not the instincts of an aetos, you would have met with a much worse fate."

Brow knotted, Mavridis nodded. "The danger has been routed."

Danger . . . "The—" Isaura drew in a sharp breath. "Irukandji." Recalling the attack, Roman fending them off, she scanned the formidable master hunter. "You are unscathed. How?"

He smirked. So like Dusan. "Worry not. Concern yourself with that babe."

"But raiders—on the cliffs!" Oh, but her head hurt! "How did they—the heights!"

Sobered, Mavridis glanced at the hunter. "We are uncertain. They should not have been able to scale it or the wall. Better safeguards are in place to protect that area." He gave a grave shake of his head. "Centuries this fortress has stood defiantly against every enemy on land and sea . . ."

"It holds little hope against aircraft," Roman advised. "I will make a list of suggested reinforcements, as well as technology we may need to quietly install regardless of Council approval. It would also be my counsel that the royal residence be relocated to a more centralized part of the castle. With the balcony overlooking the sea, it's too easy a target for pulse cannons and our very agile enemy bent on ending you. I'll instruct the Brethren to begin air patrols around the castle."

"Nay," Mavridis countered. "Those would terrorize Kalonicans. You forget, Hunter, that most Droserans are not used to skycrawlers."

"Don't let fear paralyze you into leaving your kyria and heir unprotected." Roman's gaze darkened, and it seemed his stature grew. "It's imperative technology become a part of your lives, for skycrawlers *are* here, whether you would have them or not."

"I fear he is right, Father," Isaura said. "As well, it would do much for morale to see that we have a force ready to defend Kalonica against what now seems an enemy impossible to defeat."

Roman's eyes sparked. "A wise thought." There seemed something else . . .

"Dusan missed flying." It was hard not to think of that gleeful look on his face when he returned from the Ironesse caves with King Vorn. Isaura struggled to stand from the settee, surprised to find she had little strength. Noting their concerned expressions, she smiled and stayed put. "Odd. I am yet so tired."

"You may feel weak due to the shock and the toll the wound took on your body," the pharmakeia said, "not to mention your unborn child."

Isaura stilled, recalling the dream. The words of Dusan in that hazy world. *Daughter.* Did she earnestly carry a girl?

"Rest," Mavridis urged. "A meal has been sent for now that you are awake. You should also know that we have added to your security, both here and on the wall."

Isaura nodded, still rattled that raiders had made it this far north. It was one thing to deal with them in Moidia, but *here*? Where Dusan had said she would be safe . . . "Why would they attack me? I am nobody, no threat."

"Shed your old insecurities, Isaura. On the contrary," Mavridis said, "you are a large threat—mayhap the greatest. Not only are you kyria, but you are also effective, unbending, and carrying the Tyrannous heir. Your very existence implies Kalonica will yet stand."

"There must be more," she mumbled. "There is no sense in attempting to reach me here, behind lines of aerios, regia, and hunters." She noticed something in Roman's expression. "What do you keep from me, Master Hunter?"

He seemed chagrinned. "Threats *will* come—as a monarch you are invariably a target. And Symmachians are notorious for overconfidence. They've always held a position of dominance because of their ever-expanding fleet." He firmed his stance. "We were remiss in being so lax. Will not happen again."

No, it was not only threats or their state of readiness. *There is more . . . What does he fear to speak?*

Shouts echoed through the house, and Isaura glanced at the door.

"Stay here." Mavridis hurried from the room, Roman on his heels. The pharmakeia was quick to leave as well, muttering something about his aid being needed elsewhere.

What commotion had drawn the men away? Isaura stood on shaky legs.

At her side, Kita steadied her. "Here, the tray of bread and fruit is yet fresh."

With the proffered sustenance, Isaura moved toward the door.

Hushak and Kaveh largely blocked her view as a sergius delivered her meal. The broader Kaveh shifted into Isaura's path. "Mavridis asked that you remain within, my kyria. Until they ascertain the situation."

Down the corridor near the stairs, Mavridis and Roman were locked in conversation with Darius, whose brows and shoulders were drawn tight. Clothes disheveled, hair mussed, he flattened his lips.

He's worried.

He glanced at her then and tried to move past the men, but Mavridis shoved him back. "Yield!"

"I must speak with her!" Darius insisted.

His panic—as she had guessed—pulled Isaura forward. "Attend me." She slipped around her regia, sensing their concern and respecting the safety measures in place. As she met Darius at the top of the stairs, she felt an enormous swell of emotion and stopped, hand to her roiling stomach. "Something is amiss."

Darius snapped a nod, but his gaze fell to the bandage on her neck. "You were injured?"

"It seems we both have concerns." Isaura swallowed the momentary alarm. "As you see, I am well. What of your concern?"

"Last eve, I met Kersei at the Stratios cottage. We . . . argued. She left in haste with Aerios Myles. I guessed she returned to Kardia, yet I return to find she never returned."

"The storm—she likely took shel—"

"Nay." Miserably, he handed her a parchment and looked down. "Kersei sought to annul our marriage and has now fled the Lady knows where. She is *gone.*"

"Keep your hand up!" Tigo shouted across the amphitheater, but Jahmai shied from every strike Beriel attempted. It wasn't defensiveness but cowering. "Hand *up*. Hold your stance."

Irritation dug into Tigo's shoulders as he marched over to the sparring men and gripped Jahmai's forearm. "A *fist*. Not tight, thumb outside, or you'll break it." Though, with the way this one fought, he wasn't likely to break anything—not even a sweat! He swept the man's legs apart into a stronger stance, but Jahmai stumbled. Went down onto his backside.

Void's Embrace! What was wrong with these men?

They weren't *men*—they were cowardly servants!

Teeth gritted, Tigo heard the sniggers around the room from those watching, ripping away the last vestiges of reason he had left. But he hauled his anger into line. "We have the honor to train in the hastati training yard, and our time is short to prepare." Or so Jez had said when she cited the "forthcoming war" earlier. "Do you want to look the fool when you stand beside them?"

"They fly," someone groused. "We'll never be *beside* them."

"Believe that and you hand the enemy the victory."

"What enemy?" a younger male whined. "We came to Deversoria for peace, to leave behind bloodlust and shame."

Frustration coated Tigo's muscles. He'd never had to work so hard to get men to *fight*. Then again, these "men" had lived too long in the shadows of fierce female warriors, who trained them to believe they were less than those immortals. "You should be ashamed. Across this 'verse, men are *fighters*, providers," he growled. But swallowed that anger, too. Belittling them wouldn't help. "You have a role in this fight. They have a role. Together we must face what's coming. Will you hide in your rooms while the Faa'Cris war? Will you watch them be slaughtered—"

"That will not happen," a sniveling one named Corton asserted. "They're Faa'Cris, the Blade of Vaqar. We're . . ." He shrugged. "Licitus."

"*Laborare pugnare parati sumus!*" Tigo barked. "'To work, to fight, we are ready!' That's their mantra." Man, he missed the 215 and their hard-won discipline. "*They're* ready! Are you?"

Heads and gazes lowered.

"Will you cowardly sit in this stone shelter while they fight for the people as the Blade of Vaqar? Is that what you're made of—weakness?" Voice echoing in the training arena, he turned a circle as the men slowly gathered up from their individual sparring places. "They say we're here to serve, but serving does not mean silence or ineptitude. We serve in power and strength." He lifted a fist. "*Use* that strength. Now!"

"Back to your stations," Ferox ordered the Licitus. As the men dispersed, his man hung back with Tigo. "They're unused to asserting themselves. Subservience is our bread and water here."

"No wonder you have neither strength nor courage—you need *meat*." Tigo shoved a hand through his sweaty hair. "We must change their thinking of themselves if we are to be what the hastati need."

"And what is that?" Quiet Ferox had an earnest expression, not challenging nor angry but also not shrinking. "Faa'Cris are gifted with abilities we cannot hope to imitate. Even using your space technology, we cannot match their cunning. We are dogs at the heels of mighty warhorses."

"It's time to change that."

Ferox eyed him warily. "How?"

Tigo glanced up at the catwalk that ran the length of the coliseum and spotted Jez with her Sisters. "Only one way—tell *them* we need to make changes."

"Licitus do not *tell* Faa'Cris anything, save our reports from the river-cities." Moza shifted closer. "This is how it has been for centuries."

"Doesn't mean it's right or that it should stay that way," Tigo said.

"Do not think they will listen simply because you are allowed here."

"Brought," Tigo corrected. "They *brought* me here." It'd been months since they'd trapped him belowground. Granted, he was unconscious in a bath for half that, but still. "They want me here. Told me to train you. Maybe they'll listen for that reason alone."

"Unlikely," Ferox countered.

The hour bell sounded through the amphitheater, indicating the time for Licitus to yield the training yard to the Ladies. But even as the men retrieved their gear and started from the sandy training pit, Tigo tightened his hand wraps. He hefted the training pistol, designed to carry only enough charge to make the target aware they'd been hit without truly injuring them. With it resting over his left arm, he stood in the center of the amphitheater as fully armored Faa'Cris alighted to the sandy pit.

Had to admit—they were a sight to behold, armor glittering gold and silver beneath the torchlight. Helms slid over faces so markedly beautiful, it seemed a shame to hide them. It'd taken him a while to get used to this, seeing them in both their normal and enlightened forms, just as it had taken him a while to get used to living in this place. The city was so well lit— thanks to well-placed touchstones and mirrors—and massive, it was next to impossible to remember he was belowground. Except for that itchy, crawling feeling beneath his skin that made him want to get out. And there was the fact that the city was entirely too big to actually be underground, which is where the whole supernatural, other-plane-of-existence thing came in. He didn't understand it the first ten times they'd tried to explain it, so he'd stopped asking.

Tigo's heart thumped hard, and this time, it wasn't because he found the Faa'Cris attractive. Despite the elegance of their movements and beauty of their forms, the Blades of Vaqar were terrifying. Knowing the damage their weapons and training could do, he wondered if he was taking this too far by pushing them, demanding change and the confluence of Licitus and Faa'Cris.

No. He was done pandering and being ordered around.

Rejeztia—he rarely called her Jez when she was fully armored, lest he lose more than his ego—held his gaze with annoyance as she hovered before him, deliberately not putting her boot to ground. Her helm ensconced her mahogany complexion and somehow amplified her violet eyes. Cool indifference radiated from her as a reminding that he was nothing more than a fallen. Male.

Their relationship on the *Macedon* had vanished when he'd stepped out of that bath. At least, for her it did. He wasn't one to so easily let go.

"The bell has rung." Rejeztia glanced at her Sisters floating around them but then whipped her gaze back to his. "Clear the yard, Licitus."

The term stung. That she would address him like that. It was hard, he had to admit, to have their roles reversed. Not long ago, Tigo was her commander. "You chose these men, *me*," Tigo said for all Daughters to hear, "to be compatriots, allies in the battle against whatever is coming."

Her impassive expression faltered slightly. "Clear the yard," she insisted, her tone more heated now.

The other Faa'Cris were growing twitchy, lifting a little higher and angling toward him. Sword hands fastened tightly around hilts.

"Allies are not subservient to one another." Still had all his parts intact, so bravely—*foolishly?*—he went on. "We were brought here to train, to fight *with* and *for* you, but—"

"We do not need you and will not dirty ourselves playing your filthy games!" A lighter-skinned Faa'Cris snapped her wings at him.

The stringent smell of rejection gusted the air and nearly knocked the breath from Tigo. He held Jez's gaze, willing her to speak, to engage. "Then you would have us leave, depart back to our homes—"

"No Licitus can leave Deversoria," Decurion Cybele pronounced as she marched into the training yard with her massive blade and additional decurions, their armor a platinum that glinted almost black in shadow.

"It seems we are worse than servants here." Tigo kept his voice clear and even. "I wouldn't have thought those who consider themselves aligned with Vaqar could so easily rationalize their poor treatment of another being."

Cybele jutted her chin, armor sparking with the indignation so clearly running through her. "Licitus should count it an honor to be in these halls."

"We do," Ferox spoke. "In earnest, we do." He swallowed, glancing at Tigo, who encouraged him to say what he knew to be in the man's heart. "How-however, we would fight *with* you, not beneath you."

"It is the way of things—we fly. You do not."

Ferox went crimson. "I did not . . . that is not—"

"She mocks us," Moza said quietly.

Tigo angled his head, looking from the men—only then noticing how many lingered at the edge of the training yard, anxiety and hope churning in their expressions—to the Faa'Cris. "You say you are the army of the Ancient. Is this how He would have you treat those you're tasked with protecting? By mocking them? Belittling them?" He squared his stance. "That is what you were created for, is that not right? To protect mankind, to protect those Vaqar tasked to guard, yes?"

Quiet settled over the training yard, and Tigo feared he'd crossed a line, teaching them about their own purpose. But he was tired of the divide that had swallowed the Quadrants, tired of the endlessly unproductive politicking and posturing. Tired of constantly hitting the end of his very short leash. He could not tolerate it here any longer.

"Our goal is not to subvert you but to better fulfill our purpose," he said to Decurion Cybele. "To become the needed warriors, we must train together."

Dissent and grumbling rattled through the Faa'Cris, and a giddy hope rose in him. At least they weren't dismissing him out of hand.

"As an Eidolon," he continued, "I was trained to work *with* the mechanized grav-suit rather than apart from it. Apart, it was useless and I was vulnerable. Together, I was protected and stronger." Then he did something he hadn't intended or planned. He knelt. Above him, he felt the whisper of wings thick as clouds shift, fanning him with their surprise. "We are here to serve you, and it *is* an honor, but we ask that you allow us to learn your ways so we can better fulfill *our* purpose. Teach us how you fight, so we can anticipate. Complement."

The Revered Mother, who had first spoken to him when he emerged from the bath three months earlier, appeared in the group, though he was certain she hadn't been there two seconds ago. This standoff had gotten her attention.

Tigo seized the opportunity. "Alanathina, you said I had a purpose, yet I am kept on a leash and in the dark. Would you not agree we are stronger together than apart? That it is imperative we arm ourselves with knowledge and training before we enter the battle?"

In a blink she stood before him.

Panicked by the ferocity in her violet eyes, Tigo felt his heart plummet. His senses were packed with the presence and power of her.

"He is strong as you said, Miatrenette, despite this wretched ignorance of his heritage," the Revered Mother said.

Do what? Tigo flicked his attention to Jez for some hint of what this meant or to whom she spoke. Instead, he found only chilled aloofness, so he refocused on the Revered Mother. "Will you not answer my question?"

She bristled. "It is uncommon for a Licitus to so boldly address our assembly." Her searing gaze held his for a heartbeat, two . . . three. "Or me."

Tigo inclined his head. "I have noticed that failing. Will you not teach us?" When she arched an eyebrow, he experienced a cold crack of air. Only as he went airborne did he register the snap of her wing, the thud that had struck his chest, the air that no longer filled his lungs.

He spine slammed into a wall. Flopped onto the training yard floor. Wits flaring awake, he coughed, struggling against the painful deprivation of air as he palmed the dirt, humiliated. Angry, he stared up at her through a knotted brow.

"Lesson one," she intoned, with a smile that warned not only would she enjoy this, but she intended to make a lesson of *him*.

Warbling voices pulled Kersei from the tight grip of slumber. A violent tremor rattled her body, as if trying to shove her the last few inches to consciousness. Stung by the brightness, she struggled to wake. A groan came nearby . . .

"Easy, Princessa." Myles sounded protective and close.

But why was he in her bedchamber? She felt his hand on her arm and straightened—or did her best to with her unborn son taking up so much room and strength. "What . . .?" Smells and aches rushed over her. The farmhouse!

"Take it slowly." He pressed something warm into her hand.

She squinted at the cup, steam spiraling up from the hot liquid within, but that aroma was unmistakable. "Cordi."

"Nutrients for you and the babe."

Bleary-eyed, she frowned at the drink. "Where did you get this?" Only as she looked up at him did she realize they were no longer in the dilapidated farmhouse. "Where . . .?" Stone walls surrounded them, and a warm fire in a stone hearth chased off an apparent chill. A hide of some kind stretched between the low bed—not a pallet as she'd expected—and walls lit by touchstones. "Where are we? How did we get here?"

"Drink." He crouched at her side. "We will talk after."

Eying him, she thought to be affronted at the way he instructed her—but why? Had it not always been his way? Never had he placated or pandered. As well, he had so wholly protected her. He was a good man.

Myles nudged the cup to her lips with a nod. "There are many things to fight this day, but sustenance is not one of them."

Relenting, she imbibed. Tingling warmth slid across her tongue and down her throat, so comforting and . . . healing. This could not be cordi alone, for she felt suddenly invigorated.

Myles pushed back onto his haunches and stood, his head cocked forward due to the low ceiling.

"Where are we?" Was there a reason he had not told her? In needled the tiniest sliver of doubt over Myles and his survival of the attack that left family and friends dead. What if following him had been a mistake? She had so completely entrusted her welfare into his hands. How had they come to be in this place? Where were the others?

"She fears you have brought her here with nefarious intentions," a woman spoke softly from the shadows.

"No, I—" Yet she did. Heart in her throat, Kersei searched the darkened corner of the room. "It is merely strange. I have no memory of leaving the farmhouse."

"Too much respect have I for you, your family, and our medora to risk your life, Princessa," Myles said, his grumbling voice teasing the walls. "We were too long in the rains, and despite your insistence that you were well, fever set upon you. Then came unconsciousness. I had no choice but to bring you here."

"*Ill*? With fever?" she asked, incredulous. It could not be. Yet, she did even now notice his once neatly trimmed beard was a little haggard and the sagging depletion of her strength. "In earnest, how long was I asleep?"

"Three days."

Her hand went to her womb. What if the fever harmed her babe? Her impetuousness in leaving Darius could have injured her son. Pulse racing, she worked to recall if she had felt him since waking. A kick? Swoosh of movement?

No, she had not.

"Though help was found here, and their medicinal expertise drew down your fever, you did not rouse." Thick brows bunched over his brown eyes. "Gave me a fair fright."

Pressing her palm firmer against the cramped quarters in which her unborn son lay, Kersei attempted to annoy him into reassuring her. "Where is *here*?" Why was the babe not stirring? She hunched over. That usually irritated him into pushing back, yet there was nothing.

"I . . ." Swallowing, she glanced up at Myles and the form still in shadow. "My baby . . ." she squeaked out, wrought with fear. She may hate Darius, but this child was a part of her.

"The child is well," the shadow woman spoke again.

Both her concealment and proclamation grated. "How can you possibly know that?" Kersei tried to compose herself—and failed, panic stealing confidence. "Ever has he been still since I awakened."

"A streak of defiance rests large in that one."

The words were too confident, too laden with conviction. Kersei stared toward the voice and could almost discern a face. "Why do you hide? Why should I listen to anything you say?"

Though his head remained bowed, Myles looked down, then to Kersei.

"Guard your words, my lady. This place is . . . sacred. We should not be here, and"—his gaze skidded toward the shadows—"it is not yet decided if we can remain."

Why would they be pushed out? "Surely, you would not force me out in my condition." A fierce ache tightened her back. She must have been in a peculiar position as she slept off the fever. "I need rest. You cannot send me away yet. The journey—"

"You have violated the Oath of Binding," came the woman's steel-cut words. "That is why your time here is yet undetermined. Aerios Myles was granted temporary haven while you recover, but you . . ."

Oath of Binding. Her marriage. This woman knew she had left Darius—and only one person could have told her. She scowled at Myles. "I swore you to a vow of silence—"

"Aye, and I kept it."

"Then, how—"

"Do you not know, my lady?" He shifted nervously. How strange—never had he done that, even with Medora Zarek. The aerios had always been a stalwart, seasoned warrior, afraid of nothing. So what was this then?

"You are being ridiculous," she snipped. "I have no tolerance for formality or propriety, not when my unborn son could be in peril. Tell me where I am." She struggled to her feet. "You in the shadows—show yourself. Prove you intend me no harm."

Myles stiffened, his expression crowded with shock and outrage. "Do not, Princessa!"

"No. It is well, Aerios Myles. Leave her," the woman instructed.

"You are bound in loyalty *to me*." Kersei resented his obeisance to this shadowy figure. "Why do you ask her—"

"Like her father, she has the iron of the machitis in her." The dark veil of shadow that held the woman parted.

Kersei startled. Shock pierced her bravado. "Ma'ma."

Wind tore at his cloak and hair as he spurred the Black faster. Two rises wasted sitting idly by in Kardia under the kyria's orders. Two rises had he yielded to Isaura's suggestion to allow aerios to search for Kersei. All to no avail. Then he overheard word in the training yard of a sighting of the red-bearded aerios. Hunching into the destrier's spine, Darius willed the Black to devour the distance between him and the encampment where Myles had been spotted. The ache throbbed that Kersei trusted an aerios, a man of war and blood, more than she trusted him. It had been his own doing, but he was desperate to make amends. He rode hard, the warrior in him unwilling to let this end poorly.

Lady, protect her and my son!

After all he had done, he was not sure the Lady still inclined an ear to his prayers, but he begged all the same that she would hurry this plea to the Ancient. He had lost everything—his parents, brothers, inheritance, and titles . . . *Please not the woman I love.*

After a short sleep in the night on the northern edge of the Altas Silvas, he delved straight through the sacred woods that had been his childhood playground. Now he dared the towering trees to steal his secrets. To stop him.

As he neared the western edge of the forest, he noted through the thick canopy of trees the sun reaching its zenith. Movement to the side flittered through the foliage. A rider—mayhap two or more—on a parallel path. He slowed to judge their speed and direction. Straight at him. Alarm drilled. They were coming for *him*. Who? Irukandji? Symmachians?

He would not be stopped. There was too much at stake.

Feeling the threat at his back, Darius spurred his horse into a hard gallop, negotiating the undergrowth and thick trees standing guard. Branches and fronds slapped his arms and face as he trod the hallowed ground. Shielded from the sun, he shuddered against the chill of the musty, earthy forest, trusting his Black to navigate the trees as he stole a glance back.

The riders had closed up.

Impossible!

"Hiya!" He leaned into the Black, the jarring motion necessary as they dodged one tree and then another. Down an incline. He felt more than saw the rider on his left. Heard a shout—his name? No, he would not be deterred. Could not be. Kersei and the babe were his only concern.

Darius focused on the light spearing the trunks and limbs ahead. If he could just—

A blur flew at him. Rammed him. Thrown free of his mount, he groped for his dagger out of second nature, but his back slammed against a tree. Knocked the wind from him. He dropped onto all fours, fingers coiled around his weapon. Growling, he shoved upward, disoriented but ready to fight. Boot back, arms prepared to defend, he sighted the attacker. "Augh!" He pitched himself forward.

"My prince!"

Darius skidded to a stop, stunned. "Caio."

Blood trickled down the onetime-regia's temple.

"Prince no longer." Darius straightened, glancing at the other two riders who trotted over. "Hadrien." He ignored the other man—the Kynigos assigned him by Kyria Isaura. His jailer, for all purposes. The jailer he had drugged. Or so he thought. "You did not drink the tea."

Acheron gave him a dull look. "Next time, hide your scent as well as the drug's."

He huffed and whistled his Black to his side. "Go back to Kardia, all of you. I must do this."

"She does not want you," Caio groused. "Why jeopardize your standing with the crown and Council to pursue a woman who—"

"She is *my wife*!" Darius's heart pounded. "My bound who carries my unborn son."

"The binding is annulled."

"Only drawn up—not finalized. Not until my brother has approved and I have set hand to quill and inked my name." What there was left of it. "I have lost land and title and will *not* lose her or my son."

"You already have," Acheron said flatly.

Darius wanted to run the Kynigos through with a long, jagged sword. Or javrod.

Dismounted, Hadrien squared his shoulders. "It is foolish to come out here—"

"Then why did you give me the news that she was seen here, if not to encourage me to come?"

"—without us."

Darius stilled. Stared at the men. He grinned as a weight lifted from his chest. "Thank you."

"What do we do about him?" Caio jutted his jaw at the Kynigos. They'd been anchored to each other for the last three months, but none had accepted the hunter.

"I will do as is required of me," Acheron said. Though the hunter was no kin to Marco, the man was maddeningly like him. "I must return to Kardia and report to the kyria."

"You mean rat him out," Caio sneered.

Acheron lifted his chin. "I will tell them you are beyond the boundaries established in the kyria's edict."

"You foul—"

"No," Darius said, planting a hand on Caio's thick chest, then patting it as he watched the strangely serene expression of the Kynigos. Yes, aerios would be sent to retrieve him . . . which would mean Kersei would have more help if things went awry, as he expected them to. Had Acheron planned this, then? "Well thought."

Caio glanced between them. "What did I miss?"

The Kynigos drew his Black around.

"That if the raiders are out there," Darius explained, watching the hunter to be sure he had this right, "and the princessa is in those caves . . . and if I am said to be in the caves . . ."

Caio grunted. Then barked a laugh. "I might have to reconsider my opinion of you, Kynigos."

"Do not strain yourself." Acheron nodded to Darius. "Stay alive so I do not face the wrath of the kyria or your brother upon his return."

"I expect neither concern nor anger from either, but I thank you for your shrewdness."

With one last nod, the hunter started back through the Altas Silvas.

"If not for him," Hadrien said, "we would not have located you."

"A regia does not need a dog to help him track," Caio grumbled.

Hadrien extended his arm to Darius, who—humbled by their loyalty—accepted the gesture by grasping his forearm firmly. But the aerios tugged him in close, their noses nearly touching. "Do not again step on my honor, Darius."

Darius. Not *Prince* Darius. The loss of decorum smarted, yet the aerios had come. That was what mattered. He inclined his head. "You are right. I beg your mercy. I just—" No. No more excuses. He gave a nod.

"Now, into the encampment. Together." Hadrien motioned to the small foothills village where Myles had been seen last.

"Ever has she been stubborn," Caio muttered as he caught the reins of his destrier again. "Pursuing Kersei will do naught but anger her more."

Darius flung himself atop his Black. "At least she will be alive to be angry—as long as we are not too late. Myles is shrewd, but what he plays at with this . . ." He shook his head. "We will check the encampment, but mark my words, if he has her anywhere, 'tis the caves. And we know not who he colludes with or how many."

"Symmachians?"

"Irukandji?" Darius shrugged. "All are possible and her life in jeopardy." Hand resting on his thigh, he stared out from the protection of trees and limbs.

Across the distance, where the foothills ended and the Medoran Mountain range began and grew in size all the way up to the northwestern edge of the Kalonican Sea and Arilamet, huddled a small encampment on the verge of becoming a village. Craggy rocks housing the caves were just visible beyond the tents and shanties.

"We leave the forest," Caio said from his left, "and we will be open. Easy targets."

"If he has taken her into the caves as you insist," Hadrien said, "it is possible we never find her."

Darius cut his gaze to the men. "It does not mean we fail to try." He wanted Kersei back, wanted her safe. Again, he scanned the plain that begged them into the anticipated ambush. The only way into the caves was through that encampment.

At least with his disgrace, he was no longer required to bear the Tyrannous sigil nor carry its banner, so they were not openly proclaiming his identity. Yet, the Blacks would be a sure sign of wealth. Though he had considered a workhorse, the very danger of this situation demanded a horse trained for battle. One that did not flinch at confrontation, clashing swords, or shrieks of savages.

"You know Irukandji now dare these woods," Hadrien said.

"Aye, and they trod Kardia's cliffs," Darius spat back, recalling the attack against the kyria. "We cannot let fear drive us to inaction. We will confront this threat. Take it down."

Caio gave him a look but turned away.

"Speak your mind. Ask the question that plagues your expression."

"Kersei had a writ of annulment. Why endanger our lives if she wills not to return?"

Darius tightened a fist. "My . . . mistakes stripped her of the rightful title she should always hold—princessa. Use it when you refer to her." He tempered his anger. "As said, there are Irukandji about and I would be without honor if she were cut down because I—"

A scream seared the afternoon.

Gaze snapped to the village, Darius urged his Black forward, peering across the low plain to the huddle of tents and hastily constructed structures. Saw figures darting in and out of sight. Grabbing people. Crimson splattering tents.

"Raiders," Caio growled.

Drawing his sword, Darius jabbed his heels into his Black's sides and shouted, "Vanko Kalonica!" The war cry carried him the distance to where a blue-marked raider shrieked after a lad of ten or twelve. Without hesitation, he delivered the raider of that scourged face. Warm blood splattered his own.

A flood of raiders rushed into the rutted path on which he stood. His heart raced, seeing so many, their eyes wild with insane rage, hands and torsos stained with the blood of the innocent. "Ladies, have mercy!" He lifted his sword.

As if hornets roused from their nest, the raiders came alive and pitched themselves at him. Even as they swarmed, Darius wished for the weapons of the Symmachians. A clean, swift kill. Anything to preserve what time he had to secure Kersei's safety. He battled hard and fast, relieving more than one raider of an arm. Hand. Head. Whatever it took to stop them. He fought until each howled in agony, slumped into the crimson river forming around him, and fell still. Shaky, weary from the onslaught, he warred on.

There were many. So many. *Too many.*

One tried to pull him down, but Darius yanked the Black around, its hooves thrusting out and knocking aside a raider, stomping another. Still too many. One launched at him and caught his leg. He thrust his sword at the raider, and at the same time, heard the agonizing shriek of his Black. Felt the horse rear. Stumble . . . back . . .

Darius grabbed the mane and held fast, only to see a pike protruding through its ebony chest. *No!* It had somehow dug beneath the rhinnock armor and sunk into flesh and sinew. He vaulted off, rolled, dirt pluming in his face, then sprang up, sword at the ready. Though not a Plisiázon or Kynigos, he was one of the best warriors in Kardia, as were the two with him.

And Acheron . . . would be too late with that help.

If Darius were to die—

Not until I am assured of Kersei's safety.

He sidestepped a raider who rushed him in an uncoordinated frenzy, stumbling, half reaching to a new-glowing mark on his neck and half clawing at Darius. Sighting another raider behind him, Darius snapped his left hand into the first raider's throat and sliced his sword at the second. The two went down, but there was no time for victory as Darius confronted a third.

"Where are they coming from?" Caio shouted, rending a raider in half.

Good question.

Fire seared Darius's chest. He glanced down, stunned to find some type of hook had dug into his leathered rhinnock armor—right between the scales—and ripped a path down his torso. He shoved his gaze along the length of attached cord to the raider trying to tear him asunder. Though agony demanded voice, he focused on freeing himself. Ignored the terrible fire and slashed at the tether. Another sweep loosed him from the hook, pitching backward. He gripped his chest, hot blood pulsing between his fingers. His palm slick.

Shrieking, a raider vaulted from the side.

Darius staggered, nausea swelling and chills tangling his thoughts. He gritted his teeth and drove the sword into the raider. The rank odor of the Irukandji stung his nostrils as the savage crumpled against him, the extra weight forcing him to a knee. Too aware of the danger that came with being down and vulnerable, he fought to stand. To push up. Scanning the encampment . . . the bodies of raiders and Kalonicans . . . and—

It is a loss. A complete loss.

Caio and Hadrien overrun, wounds gaping. Fighting on, but life draining.

No . . . Please . . . I must find Kersei . . .

It was no good. They had failed. *He* had failed.

"No," he whispered. "I beg you! Please!" He wobbled down, strength leaching from the wounds in his chest and stomach. In vain, he tried to stem the flow. "I begged you—have begged you. Hear me now. *Please!*"

Day burst alight in a blanket of pure white that stabbed his corneas and forced him to look away. Darius cried out. Blinked. And there, before him, stood a woman. He froze, stunned. Confused. It seemed obvious now that he had reached his appointed time. "I am embraced . . . Too late . . ."

Stunningly beautiful yet terrifying, she stood in full battle array. A helm protected her fierce visage, though he even now felt her scorching rebuke. Ferocity raged as she strode closer, sword in hand.

A sword to end him, for he had miserably failed.

Screaming, a raider whipped into view.

Dare not! Darius gripped his hilt with both hands and drove it upward. Right through the raider's throat. The savage spasmed, falling aside as Darius shifted back to the woman. Only, she was gone. And blood and boil, that was not merely a woman.

A Lady. He turned a circle to find her. Saw Caio bloodied, hugging his arm to his side. Burly Hadrien stood over a raider and with a primal shout drove a javrod into the savage's chest.

But the woman . . . "Where . . .?" Had he been granted a second chance? Could it—

A dagger spiraled through the air. Straight at his heart. Too swift, too sudden for him to even cry out. He had but to breathe and it would be over. A fitting end. A *deserving* end, considering the hearts he shattered. He would step into the Eternal Embrace of Shadowsedge. Kersei released from his name and guilt. His heir freed to be whomever he could become. His conscience removed of the weight—

The air swirled with a minty fragrance that coiled around his thoughts, held him hostage as the Lady again manifested at his side. Her bronze-clad hand gripped the hilt of the fatal dagger that both was and wasn't lodged in his chest. That was and wasn't restrained by her presence. Behind her, the savage was no longer . . . no longer visible. No longer there.

Bewildered, Darius gaped at the Lady, struck dumb by intense violet eyes that held him fast as she stared back at him. *Into* him. Breath trapped in his throat, threatening to usher him from this life, he felt the tenuous hold of his existence vibrating in her grip, the edges of his vision ghosting. If she released that dagger . . .

"Darius, you will die on this field."

Her words echoed as he swallowed—or tried. It seemed nothing in his body worked. *"Who are you?"*

"I have said you will die, and that is what you ask?" Reproof seared through her words and eyes. *"Should you not beg for your life? Promise you will act with more honor? Right the terrific wrong you have done against those who have loved you?"*

Kersei. *"I do not deserve another chance."*

Her dark yet delicate eyebrow arched. *"You speak true, Prince."*

Grief struck him. *"So. You are here to deliver me to Shadowsedge."* Did he even deserve that? Should not the diabolus take him?

Blinding light radiated off her, the blade between them glowing as if in the forge, the heat of it pulsing through his being. *"Though death is what you have earned, the Ancient yet has a purpose for you, Darius."*

Surprise sprang from the shadows, his mind warring with the frozen state of his body and mouth. What words could he speak? He did not deserve this . . . gift.

"What would you beg for? Your life? Lands and titles? The crown once more upon your head?" Challenge flashed in her piercing violet eyes.

Beg for his life? The choice was his? How could he choose . . .? *What* could he choose?

"Speak quick and true, Son of Tyrannous."

My life is for naught. He thought of bloodied Caio and Hadrien. Sacrificing all to help him save—"Kersei!" The answer shot from his tongue. "My son. Please." Aye, for this he would beg. For this he would die. "Save them, my men."

She angled her head, considering him, her fingers coiling around the knife. More challenge in her gaze.

Had he answered wrong? No. It could not be wrong. If it was, he cared not. Them. *"Please save them. I beg you."* She must.

"Not yourself or the little crown upon your big head? Do you not want that restored? I can make it happen, Prince *Darius."*

Weakness tremored through his body, that deadly dagger held in the power of her presence. "No," he breathed. "N-no. Please—*them*. Save them." The world tilted out of balance.

Searing light devoured the dagger. He squinted to see, to understand. Amid the blinding energy, the steel blade heated in her fingers. Steel blackened. Fell away to ash. To nothing. She held her palm up, empty, and extended to him.

Darius accepted. Touched his hand to hers.

"Since you did not ask for your title or life, for riches or fame," she said, letting the pause hang unnaturally long in the minty air, *"it will be as you asked. Honor will be restored to your name, to those you love. You will see your son born."*

Disbelief surrendered with a choked sob. Relief covered him like a stone-warmed blanket.

"There is but one condition."

Kersei would be safe. His son born. "Anything," he agreed, tears racing down his face. "Ask it of me, Lady."

13

DEVERSORIA

Kersei strangled a cry and pushed herself forward, falling into an embrace she never thought to feel again. "How . . .?"

Arms came around her in a brief, consoling hug. "Seek peace, Kersei."

Hearing Father's words on Ma'ma's lips shoved out the tears, hard and fast, a torrent born of the storm that had engulfed her these many months.

"Gather yourself, child," Ma'ma instructed.

Kersei eased up and searched the memorized face, the one frozen in terror on the walls of that vile room on the *Macedon*. "Truly? You are here?" She blinked away tears but then once more collapsed against the bosom that had offered comfort during her childhood. "How is this possible? You were dead! Father—"

"I am here." Ma'ma cupped the back of her head, and years of anguish seemed to fall from Kersei's shoulders and heart. "Oh, you foolish girl." Firm hands guided her upright.

Heart and mind racing, Kersei allowed herself to be distanced from her ma'ma. She gazed on a face so familiar yet somehow . . . different. "How are you here?" Why had she not recognized her ma'ma's voice?

"Kersei—"

"Is Adara alive as well?" She looked to Myles. "You said their bodies were not recovered. Adara!" She found herself again scanning the shadows of the room. When that did not produce her little sister, she spun back to Ma'ma, hope surging as it had not in a very long while. "Is she alive? I would even be glad for Lexina," she conceded with a laugh, "though we rarely shared a kind word. But what is that when we are sisters—"

"Kersei!" Ma'ma sounded more strident, more familiar this time. "Listen to me, child. We have much to cover, and I beg your mercy for the sudden revelation thrust upon you. I had not meant to do this so."

"Revelation do you call it? Aye, I would say so. But how, Ma'ma? How are you here?"

As always, Ma'ma kept her spine straight, shoulders back, chin up . . .

"Oh, I care not how," Kersei decided. "You are my mother—and you are *alive*!" Laughing again, she embraced her. "Oh, I have missed your imperious ways, Ma'ma. Yell at me if you must, but I will be glad for it. Never have I been more glad for anything!"

Her touch light, Ma'ma held her peace. Her eyes—

"Your eyes!" Kersei exclaimed. "They are much changed! How is this—"

"There is plenty we will discuss, but later, Kersei." Ma'ma's irritation was not foreign. Many a day Nicea Dragoumis had chastised and been annoyed by one or another of Kersei's adventures.

"Later?"

Easing from the embrace, Ma'ma glanced at Myles. "See that she eats. The time draws near, and she will need her strength."

"Time? What time?" Panic edged out elation as her mother moved toward the shadows again. "Ma'ma, no! Do not leave. Please." Kersei lunged toward the dark corner where the air yet stirred. Cold stone stopped her short. "Ma'ma!" She touched it, disbelieving. "Where . . .?" She traced the wall. "A secret passage?" Glancing at Myles startled her, worried her. Was it a dream?

Nay, it could not be. This . . . this must be— "Like Stratios Hall—secret passages. There must be a groove or catch . . ." She shifted back, tracing the cold surface with her fingers.

"There is none," Myles said heavily.

"Of course there is." Must be. She pushed on different sections. Grunting, she tried harder. Kicked. Slapped it. Desperate to be with her mother once more. "Ma'ma!"

Hands caught her shoulders.

"Leave off!" She whirled and smacked Myles's cheek. "What is this? Why do you play the fool when you know where she is?"

"Please, Princessa."

"Where is she?" Kersei snatched a touchstone from an iron brace and returned to the corner.

Slowly, her rational mind caught up with her emotions. It was impossible, of course, for Ma'ma to be alive. The enormous stone walls of the mighty Stratios Hall had crushed her body. Kersei had viewed that segment of the footage on the *Macedon* thousands of times. Survival was impossible.

I have been sick. This . . . this must all be a dream—a nightmare. "Nay, it cannot be . . ." She turned to the aerios. "Did I . . ." Her voice cracked. "Tell me true—did I dream that?" She held her breath as he stared at her without response.

Myles, with his burly build and scraggly red beard, had never looked so aggrieved. "No, Princessa."

Kersei shuddered a breath. "Thank the Ladies." Again, she eyed the now-lit corner. "Then . . . how?" Once more, she traced the stone.

It reminded her too much of the fateful night. The stones that fell. Her family's deaths. Her head ached from trying to sort the pieces and figure out what had transpired. She wanted to rail, but . . . there was no fight left in her. She had lost her father and sisters.

All this time she believed them dead. Ma'ma as well. Then Marco.

There was a great emptying of her adunatos, of her will to continue. To play at this game. Ma'ma had come and then left so coolly. As if . . .

She does not want me.

Nobody wants me. Marco has Isaura now.

This child she carried . . . this existence she lived . . . *she* had wanted neither. The images from the reminding chamber plagued and tormented. "I wish I had died with them. It would have been less painful."

"Do not speak such evil, my lady."

"It would have solved *everything.*"

"The coward's way!" Myles pressed closer, deep furrows digging into his brow. "You have the iron of the machitis. You are Xylander's daughter. Lady Nicea's daughter."

Lady . . . Baric's words on the *Macedon* . . . Kersei frowned at Myles and cocked her head. "You were not surprised by her presence." Her mind wrestled with the truths peppering it. "Have you seen her before—since the attack, I mean?"

He stared back, neither denying nor acknowledging.

She made her way to the cot and lowered herself to the edge. "But . . . before you brought me here." That strange tight band over her belly constricted again. She drew in a quiet breath and rubbed the spot, then realized Myles had yet to answer. In fact, that was the second question he ignored. "You *have* seen her, have you not?"

He once more looked at the stone floor. "Aye," he answered gravely. "It is because of her that you are healed and provided for."

"And you never told me." Betrayal seemed the only reality she would know these days. "All this time you knew what I mourned, what broke my heart, yet did nothing to ease my suffering."

"There is a world hanging in the balance," he said with little of the sorrow that hung in his eyes, "but your grief and concern is—selfishly—for yourself alone."

The chastisement stung but was no less true. "You are cruel, Myles."

"I am direct, honest, Princessa. Always have you known this."

"I trusted you. Brought you to Kardia, made you my personal regia—you had ample opportunity to speak this . . . beautiful truth." Again, she eyed the corner in which Ma'ma had vanished. "But no, you would not apply a salve to the wound my heart suffered."

"It is true I came to Kardia."

Wondering at the way he said that, Kersei snapped her gaze to his, ready to protest. Recalled him at the tavern the day she and Darius visited Stratios and the market. Thought of how he slipped out the side door . . . Though she had given chase and lost him, he returned to save her from the brigands. Then gone from sight again, only to appear while she sobbed just beyond the ruin of the hall.

"All those encounters . . . they were . . . planned." Coming and going just as . . . Ma'ma. "Who are you?"

He held her gaze, unflinching.

"*Who* are you?"

"I do not matter. Who sent me does."

Kersei waited, her breath struggling between the demand to know the truth and what might lie in his answer. Ma'ma . . . a Lady. Was it true, like Baric said? If so, how had the Symmachian known, yet Kersei was ignorant of it? It meant her mother was . . . "Faa'Cris."

His stern expression softened. "It is a miracle you did not know before now."

FORGELIGHT, JHERAKO, DROSERO

"I hold fast to my belief that this is a bad idea. Too dangerous."

"Measures were taken to protect the location and timing of the event—all are arriving at different times in varying manner of delivery. It is the best that could be managed. The sovereigns of Drosero must meet." Bracing as the scout descended into the capital city of their southern neighbor, Isaura willed the meal that had broken her fast not to make a reappearance—and she saw much the same pallor on Mavridis. For certain, Dusan may love flying, but she did not.

"This is too dangerous," he grumbled, his grip on the seat turning his knuckles white.

"As you have already said." She sighed. "Is it that, or that I am not the only Kalonican who prefers dirt beneath her boots to air?" She gave him a weary smile as the five-strap harness held her tight, squeezing her stomach and pushing a groan up her throat. She had no recollection of being so nauseated when she made this trip with Dusan. Then again, neither had she been with child.

"You should have stayed in Kardia." His silvered brows drew into a knot.

"This was not a trip I could avoid. Since Kalonica is without its medora and prince, it is my duty to represent our realm at the Conclave of Sovereigns. Not doing so would be perceived as a slight and strain already troubled diplomatic relations."

"And what of your life?"

"It is guarded by you, as well as the Stalkers, regia, and Kynigos." She laughed. "I will be mightily impressed if anyone can get near enough for simple conversation with so many brooding men clustered around me." Straightening and stretching her neck so the strap did not cut into her flesh, she smiled. "Besides, I look forward to seeing Queen Aliria and the ships."

"But Jherako!"

"Father." The name was yet odd on her tongue. "It is imperative we transform our opinion of the southern nation." Between the two of them, her having lived in Moidia and him having been assigned the protectorship of the same, they had seen plenty of maliciousness along the border between Kalonica and Jherako.

"On approach." Roman's voice carried through the communications of the scout as it dipped hard right, making her stomach roll again.

"At least we can be glad," Mavridis grumbled, "Hirakys was refused admittance to the Conclave this time."

Isaura wilted a bit at the memory of the attacks on the caravan that delivered her out of a burning Moidia and into Dusan's life. "I would not have done well seeing those beasts up close again."

"Aye, though the raiders would not have come, the rex is just as befouled," Mavridis growled. "After the attack against you in Kardia, I would be inclined to take a head or two."

Warmed by the sentiment, she looked away, lest he see her appreciation and stiffen, as he so often did. He had been deeply wounded over the injury to her person, and she fought even now not to touch the still-sensitive scar on her neck. The entire event had awakened them all to the vigilance and ferocity of those determined to do her harm.

The scout landed on the south side of Forgelight in a protective swath of the palace gardens and Furymark. With her entourage of guardians, Isaura descended from the ship. Even as sunlight struck her hem, she searched for Aliria and Vorn.

A deafening roar made her falter.

"It is well, my kyria." Kita indicated a bridge from which rained a shower of flowers, ribbons, and cheers thrown by the hundreds gathered there.

Surprised and awed, she smiled and awkwardly lifted a hand in greeting. The cacophony rose.

"You are clearly loved, but we should keep moving. Not all are friend." Mavridis guided her across the lawn to the castle. "I am still of the mind this is a bad idea—too obvious."

She stepped inside, and when the doors closed, her ears still rang.

"I thought to fear Jherakans," Kita said with a laugh as they moved farther into the lavish room adorned in deep reds and blues. "They cheered as if you were one of their own nobles."

"Rightly so!" King Vorn rounded a corner with a very pregnant Queen Aliria. A broad grin filled the king's handsome bearded face. "You are a treat to our hearts, Queen Isaura. Welcome back to Forgelight."

The Jherakan sovereign had a distinct flair to his attire and wore his long hair slicked back from a neatly trimmed beard. His queen was no less a statement, unhindered by her large belly.

Isaura inclined her head. "I thank you, King Vorn and Queen Aliria," she said, remembering the decorum demanded upon first introductions. "It is an honor, and I do beg your mercy that—"

"No." Vorn shook a meaty finger at her. "No formality between our houses, especially not in private. Here, you are among friends. We are allies, yes—but more importantly, *friends*."

A weight lifted from Isaura's chest. "My heart is in agreement, and Dusan felt the same." She tripped over her casual use of the pet name and hoped she would not be corrected or taunted.

Vorn clasped her arms, a gesture that made the regia tense and Vorn grin. "Our enemy has stolen my friend, your love, and I vow they will regret it." He pulled her into an enthusiastic hug. When he straightened, he lifted his eyebrow at her womb. "Perhaps in a couple of decades, if we have a son—as Aliria insists—and you a daughter, our houses will have a greater celebration by joining our lines. Eh?"

Isaura laughed.

"He teases—mostly." Aliria glided forward and kissed Isaura's cheeks. "I am glad you are returned to us. It is a pleasure."

"For me as well." This time, Isaura was prepared for the hug and welcomed it.

"Ba'moori will see you to your apartments," Vorn said. "Unfortunately, we must quickly attend other guests. The strategic and secretive arrival schedule has greatly complicated our efforts to ensure all feel welcomed, though they are in the lower reaches of the keep. Even now, the Emperor of Avrolis docks after a tumultuous journey. He would be rather put out if I made him wait long to be received."

"As you already have for the last hour," Aliria noted.

"That long?" Vorn gave a mischievous grin. "Hm, well, yes—we had more important friends to attend, did we not?"

Isaura smiled at his implication. "You honor me."

He barked a laugh. "Do not flatter yourself, Marco's beauty. I only do it to annoy the emperor and to give my ears a rest—their manner of speech is painful to decipher. Enough of that—we will see you soon." He gave her a curt nod, then motioned them toward Ba'moori, who waited patiently to the side.

Once the two were gone, Ba'moori led Isaura and her entourage to their apartments. Though Kita went about the rooms, investigating, Isaura could not move. She had . . . this room . . . it was . . . the same room she had shared with Dusan. The same bedchamber in which they had first experienced each other's passion. She swallowed as she approached the bedchamber and stared at the coverlet. In her memory—the near tangibility of it—he was there, whispering sweet words. The scruff of his stubble against her cheek. His ardor. She recalled how, at first, when he'd intended to make her his own but got called away, he had been so furious.

"Bleeding fires of Hieropolis! If someone is not dying, I will change that!"

She covered her mouth to hide the smile. He had not returned that night to resume what had been interrupted, but the next night . . . And the next.

Oh Dusan . . . The ache bloomed stronger in her breast as she touched the settee he'd sat upon while telling her about the ships. Her gaze rose to the windows, and she moved there to look out upon Ironesse, which he had said hid the entrance to the underground facility that gave safe harbor to the scouts. Nigh on two weeks since the first machitis arrived to begin training. She wondered how they fared beneath the instruction of Roman and Rico. How Dusan would have loved to have been a part of that.

Somehow, the ache of his absence felt especially raw here. *Will he ever return?*

"You are well, my lady?"

Isaura started. Turned to a frowning Kita. "I am."

After a skeptical look, Kita motioned to the dressing chamber. "Come. We must ready you for the opening dinner."

Oras later, Isaura was summoned to the antechamber outside a lower ballroom for a private pre-dinner reception with the other dignitaries—largely the rulers of the various countries on Drosero.

"Mercies," she whispered as she stood, feeling the weight of the Kalonican crown on her head and the order pinned to her breast that marked her of House Tyrannous. Dusan's family. Escorted by her guardians, she made her way to the gallery on the second level.

"Just smile and look pretty." Grand Duke Rhayld lifted his nose at her. "It is all they expect from you."

Affronted, Isaura bristled. "Where would I be without you to guide me, Duke Rhayld?" She chided herself for again using the wrong title for him, but could she claim nerves?

His mouth tightened. "Yes, well, that is why I am here. After all, if you cannot get my title right, how will you manage theirs?"

"I have no idea why I cannot seem to remember that." *Catty, Isa.*

He grunted something and moved toward a man in a suit that struggled to restrain his wide girth.

"You take much pleasure in mocking him," came Roman's deep, resonant voice.

A giggle burst free of her restraint. "Too much I fear." The smile she did not want to hide vanished as she surveyed the nobility mingling in this gallery and floundered under a powerful sense of not belonging. These were not her people. They were rich. Soft fingers, perfect coils, refined manners. "Perhaps, I *should* let him lead. These are, after all, his peers. He knows—"

"How to grease pockets and egos. You speak truth and sincerity. That's what is needed in this hour, Isaura. The Ancient did not put you in Marco's path to be a rug beneath their feet but a beacon to guide them."

"Would that I were merely Delirious Deliontress's daughter again," she mumbled just as she saw a young, handsome man striding toward her. His black hair and dark skin were more of those from the far south, mayhap farther than Hirakys.

"Kyria Isaura, I believe?"

She inclined her head, recalling what Ypiretis had taught her of greeting other sovereigns. *Never bow, but show them respect.* "Indeed."

Kaveh was there to do the introductions. "Majesty, this is Prince Rezik."

The young nobleman seemed to wait for her to make the connection, but when she didn't, he angled his head. "Of Waterflame."

"Of course." A principality, if she remembered correctly. "It is an honor, Prince Rezik."

"No, the honor is mine," he said, his youthfulness—he could not yet be twenty cycles—charming and full of promise. "Word of how you won over Medora Marco swept Waterflame." His gaze slid to the side for a moment, then returned. "In fact, my sister, Princess Sheyli, could speak of nothing else for weeks. She was furious when she learned I would get to meet you."

Heat rose into Isaura's cheeks. Truly, why would anyone want to meet her? "How very sweet."

"I would like to express my condolences regarding Medora Marco."

"Your words are kind but unwarranted." She stifled the trill of anger at the assumption. "He will return, and we shall be the better for it."

"Rightly so." His expression was earnest, yet his gaze again strayed, and this time, Isaura caught the object of his distraction.

A lovely young woman stood alone in a corner, a crystal glass cupped genteelly in gloved hands. She looked of the same age as the prince. Was he enamored with her?

"Prince Rezik," she began softly, "do you know who that young woman is?"

His face flushed. "Princess Lirra of Giessen." His voice was a hoarse whisper. "She is here to stand for King Mamoru, who is ill."

"Have you an acquaintance with her? I would be grateful for an introduction."

"I am afraid . . ." He stiffened. "I should not—"

"Oh come. I must meet her." She did not know why he hesitated, since he had clear interest in the princess. "You would not deny me this favor, would you?"

"I . . ." He straightened. "Of course not." Offering his arm, he walked her to the other side of the ballroom, her guards never more than a few steps away.

When she saw them approaching, the princess jolted and went white as milk. In fact, she looked as if she might be sick.

"Princess Lirra, it is my great honor to introduce Kyria Isaura." Prince Rezik's tone was suddenly haughty and cold.

What was this?

The princess cocked her head and gave the slightest of bows but stopped halfway, as if realizing her error. "My qu—I mean . . . I did not—"

"Princess." Wanting to allay the girl's nerves, Isaura shifted around to stand beside Lirra. "I am so glad to make your acquaintance. The prince was very kind to accommodate my request for an introduction."

The young man inclined his head. "If you will excuse me." His stony façade hardened as he left.

Curious. "I had thought him quite nice until this moment. Perhaps I gave offense," Isaura thought aloud.

"The offense is mine," Lirra said, tucking her chin. "Of late, Giessen has fallen out of favor with most empires. Many do not believe my father-king is truly ill but that he shuns them."

"What an insult to suggest you speak falsehoods." Isaura studied her for a moment. "It would seem there is more to that than what is spoken."

Lirra started, wide eyes darting away.

Had she pushed too hard? "I—"

"Isaura!"

At the cold snap of Rhayld's voice, Isaura felt a dart of irritation slash her spine. Deliberately, she focused on Lirra. "Forgive me if I trod where I am not welcome, but I feel we should put rumors to rest. Speak clearly and openly. We will show them, shall we not, that women are made of stronger mettle than—"

"Isaura," Rhayld gruffed, "did you not—"

A large shape manifested beside her just as Rhayld reached her. "The kyria is occupied at present, Grand Duke," Kaveh said evenly, his posture and tone brooking no objection.

Grateful for her regia, Isaura kept her back to the men. "Do you know the sovereigns here, Princess?"

After skating the two men a wary look, Lirra returned her attention to Isaura. "I am afraid not." She shifted, hugging herself nervously. "This . . . my bro—the crown prince typically carried out these duties. But he . . . he died last winter." It seemed to take a great bit of courage to mention that. She drew in a breath and let out an addendum. "A hunting accident. In the wilds. Which made no sense. Rotrick was an excellent sportsman."

"I am sorry for your loss and for your father's poor health," Isaura said. "What of Giessen's queen?"

"It is a wonder *you* are queen when you have so little knowledge of other Droseran realms and rulers," Lirra snipped but then faltered. Looked away.

Though the words pierced Isaura, they fell short of their mark—and revealed what she had seen so often in the wastelands: a person who felt threatened or lesser striking first to avoid being struck. A love lost, the crown prince dead, and the king ill . . . Those events conspired to leave Giessen with an uncertain, unconfident princess. A scared one. It would be easy to take offense at the girl's brackish manners.

She refused to let one more person become an enemy. "You speak truth, Princess Lirra. This night, I could use a friend to aid me in bettering that knowledge. What say you? Shall we show these men the combined strength of two women in power?"

Lirra released her pent-up breath and smile all at once. "I would be most grateful."

Seated at the long, narrow table, not far from King Vorn and even closer to the grand duke, Isaura was grateful for the young Lirra beside her. The ever-stiff Prince Rezik sat across from them and worked quite hard to ignore the beguiling, skittish princess. Conversation tittered, swelled, and fell. Mostly around Isaura but not *to* her, making her again feel as if she didn't belong, no matter how often she argued the lie. It also made the ache for Dusan much keener, the longing for his smooth baritone, his steadiness. His strength.

A laugh resonated from across the room.

Dusan!

She was turning in that direction before she caught herself. No. Of course it wasn't him but the Master Hunter. Their gazes connected, and she could not help but smile. *Her* hunter had not landed far from the Citadel. The parallels between the two were uncanny. Roman deBurco's ancestral line bred strong, powerful men. It had been his influence, his sage words that had grown Dusan into the man she met in Moidia then fell in love with. What was Roman's story? His journey to become the man who taught Dusan to choose honor over selfishness, sacrificing love for a people and realm he did not even know.

"He is a . . . hunter like Medora Marco, is he not?" came Princess Lirra's quiet voice at her left.

Isaura smiled. "Aye. His name is Roman, and he trained Marco. They are very alike."

"Kyria Isaura," punched a commanding tone from her right.

Isaura jerked toward the voice and flinched at the man now seated there, having replaced Rhayld in the chair. Black-haired and olive-complected, the man smiled at her. His dark beard and neatly trimmed hair were a striking complement to his near-black eyes. She straightened, somehow feeling caught in some wrongdoing. Where had he come from? More importantly—who was he?

He inclined his head but little. "Would ask speak true, yes?"

His broken use of the Kalonican language made her work to understand his meaning. "I . . . of course." Or was he saying *he* would speak true? She silently begged him to supply his name and relieve her ignorance.

"Months four past, seen on waters queen and king." His eyes seemed to spark. "Yes?"

She faltered, her mind untangling the strange manner of speech—and the offended inflection in his jumbled words. What waters? When he said king and queen, did he mean her and Dusan, or Vorn and Aliria? She and Dusan had been on a waterborne vessel *once* about four months ago on their way here to speak with Vorn.

"Yes?" Even as she answered, she recalled the king mentioning an emperor whose speech gave him a headache.

His lips flattened. "Yet no come honor to Strune and Selqie."

"I . . . I do beg your mercy," she said, shifting to face him, hoping that might help her decipher his meaning, "but your words confuse me."

"Strune and Selqie are the sigils of Shadar and Saigo," whispered Lirra at her back, a slight touch as she leaned closer. "He's Czar Asrak, twentieth of his name. He implies you and your bound dishonored him by not coming to see him when you were on the ship."

How the plagues did he know they had been on a ship? "It was a very short trip," she reassured him. "In fact, we fled in fear of Medora Marco's life. There were raiders—"

"Nej."

"No," Lirra whispered the translation.

Asrak jutted his jaw, the silver and gold threads of his tunic—finer than any she had seen before—glinted beneath the candles and touchstones. "Nej, did not honor Strune." He spat to the side. "Spit out aetos." He made a *pfft* noise and brushed his hands as if to dry them off. "Shed disgrace by not bring."

Aetos, she assumed, referred to Kalonica. Her heart hammered hard, indignant that he would assault Dusan's honor, especially when he was not here to defend himself. Surely, he would know what to say, how to salvage this. "I see your point," she began, remembering a first rule her father had taught her long ago to help soothe wounded egos. "I do beg your mercy . . ." Yet something in the air or his demeanor warned her not to placate. "You saw our boat?"

"Jes! With eyes two." He pointed at his black eyes. "Rude. Disgrace." He spat again. "Peace make not with aetos."

"And yet," she said, cocking her head as if parsing his meaning, "*you* did not honor *us* with your visit. To see us, you must have been in close enough proximity to make an introduction possible."

"It land not."

"Shadar and Jherako are not on the best terms, so he was unlikely to come," Lirra explained.

"But you were close enough to see us."

His face mottled, reddened. "Jes! And nothing say to Strune honor. Dis aetos king no great."

Fury tightened her chest and made it hard to breathe. His stubbornness and insistence on clinging to a perceived slight when she had apologized . . . Mayhap she would take a turn about the hall. Anything to remove herself from this man, who thought to chastise her and Dusan. "You dishonor me again, Czar—"

"Shame!"

She rose quickly, unwilling to hear him assault Dusan any further.

He clapped his palms together, pressed the fingertips to his nose, and inclined his head. "Jur servant me. With all mercy beg."

Chin lifted, Isaura stared down and to the side, where his black hair shone nearly blue beneath the massive iron candelabra light. She suddenly became aware of the near silence of the hall. Eyes fixed on their encounter. She swallowed the rising anger, her stomach churning with nerves and nausea. What was she to do? She needed fresh air and some breathing room. To leave these nobles to their politicking.

Don't walk away, don't walk away.

Roman watched from the side with King Vorn as the encounter between Kalonica and her uneasy ally, Shadar, played out before the gathered crowd. The young beauty his nephew had taken to wife had no idea the quagmire she stood in and how easily she could upend those tentative relations.

"I thought she didn't do politics," Vorn muttered with more amusement than was proper.

"Doesn't do them and doesn't understand are two different things." Roman anak'd the room, taking in the nervous scents. Shadar was small, but they were fierce, relentless about their perverse sense of honor. Not like the

Kynigos Code, yet not terribly unlike it either. Where hunters would remand a subject to authorities for justice, Shadarans would simply chop off the heads of those who dishonored them.

Unbelievably, the older dark-haired man pressed his palms together and inclined his head to her. Shock rippled through the room, melding with Roman's.

"Well." Vorn huffed a laugh. "I know not the last time a czar of Shadar bowed to anyone."

Yet this young queen in her green silk gown, golden hair, and crown had reduced the ferocious Asrak to cowering. What would Marco think? Likely, he would've laid this man out for speaking to Isaura so rudely.

"He is making things worse. Save her," Vorn prodded. "Before this is undone."

Isaura glowered at the czar, her efflux rank with disgust and censure.

Roman almost chuckled. "I do not think it is the kyria who needs saving."

"You misunderstand." Vorn nudged Roman forward. "He will now want her for his harem. With Marco missing, it would be too easy for the czar to say he was dead and claim the queen for himself." He strode forward. "Go."

Stranger things had happened on this planet. "You take care of the czar."

"I prefer my head where it is, thank you," Vorn said with a wry grin but aimed for the two all the same.

Roman homed in on Isaura and kept his expression dark as he erased the distance.

Her gaze struck his and she started. Others would not see it, but he did—as well as the spurt that rushed through her Signature. She was stressed, tired, overwhelmed, all agitating into an angry concoction that had stolen over her by surprise. He extended an arm to her.

"I think it is time to present our proposal to the masses." Delivering a seething glare to the czar, who indeed reeked of admiration and much more, Roman put the lascivious man in his place as he guided her away.

Relief emanated from her, then scurried into a ball of nerves. "From one fire to another," she muttered. Halfway across the room, she sighed. "When is he coming home, Roman? I tire of politics."

"If you think politics will draw Marco home, you are gravely mistaken. He detested them."

She laughed, then touched her forehead. "Aye, more than I do, which did not seem possible." Her Signature now swirled with grief, ache, and desperation as they settled into a quiet corner. "Was it that obvious I needed a rescue? I could think of nothing but throttling him or sending my moon discs spinning."

"You do Marco justice here, but not all are of the same mettle. Asrak, according to Vorn, will now want you for his harem."

She scoffed but then paled. "Does he not know I am with child?"

"That likely makes you more attractive." He appreciated the way she recoiled.

A bell tinkled through the room.

"I would welcome you all officially to Forgelight and the opening of the Conclave of Sovereigns." King Vorn's voice boomed across the ballroom. Forks came to rest, glasses set down, and chatter died as the formidable ruler stood at the head of the feasting tables. "It is an honor to host this event. While no expense was spared to bring in the finest food from across Drosero, the real treasures sit here at these tables."

"Roman," Isaura said, turning to him slightly, chin tucked. "I would ask—" Her hands were on her stomach—womb. "Dusan knew . . . he knew Kersei carried a son. Are you also able to tell gender?"

An easy deflection. "Marco was gifted with the brand that enabled him to see the adunatos of a person reflected in their eyes. Kersei had two lights— hers and the babe's—a boy. I'm afraid I have no such gift."

"I thought . . ." Confusion rippled across her tawny brow. "So you . . . you cannot tell . . ."

"Ask him, Isaura. Ask Marco when he returns."

"You are right." She fell quiet, her sadness nearly palpable as she gazed up at Vorn on the dais. For several long ticks, she stood in silence, but her efflux swam with a gamut of emotions. "Dusan invades my dreams . . ."

Something in her Signature shifted with those words, with whatever she recalled, and betrayed a fervent hope. She was dreaming of Marco, but did she realize . . . "The dreams . . . how often?"

She blushed prettily. "Often. A lot, yet . . ." She sighed. "Not enough. Never enough. I would have him back."

Mayhap he had guessed right. It ignited hope in him that mirrored hers. That Marco would return and bring the answer, the response to the great war foretold for centuries.

"The thing is," she whispered, as he led her back to the table where he assumed the now-empty seat beside hers, "the dreams are not like most. It is like we are together. Really *together*, not some intangible place in my thoughts. And he speaks of things too impossible for my mind to conjure—things *I* have never before heard, so how I can dream them?" She sighed. "He tells me what is happening with him, and I tell him of all . . . this."

So it *was* more than dreams. "It keeps hope alive."

"Yes," she said urgently, nearly laughing. Tears glossing her eyes. Then she remembered the speech Vorn was giving and whispered, "Yes, exactly."

No, he would not tell her. Not yet. "Keep dreaming, Isaura. *Dream* and lead him home."

Darkness collapsed on the ballroom, stealing her response. Isaura stilled, attuned to her surroundings, wishing she had her discs. "What . . .?"

"It is well," Roman said calmly. "The king's demonstration."

"And now," intoned Vorn, "lights!"

A strange but powerful light surged through the ballroom. Too bright, yet not as bright as the sun, it made the guests squint. Fingers to her brow, Isaura looked up to the candelabra. Wicks still smoking, the candles were not what gave off the light, but instead a different candelabra lowered.

"Electric light," Vorn said with a barked laugh. "Is it not magnificent? The entirety of Forgelight even now undergoes renovations to be fitted with the electrics. Revealing it here seemed appropriate, considering what must be addressed on this floor before you return to your fortresses and palaces."

"You cannot push this on us," Emissary Rudan of Iaizon snapped. "The people are not ready, and Iaizon's infrastructure is complicated by the tundra."

"Regardless of readiness, with the Symmachian infiltration, technology *is* upon us and we must either seize it," Vorn asserted, holding both hands as if he gripped horns, "or be destroyed by it!"

"Destroyed?" balked a short, bearded man.

"President Sotui," Roman muttered to her. "Afraid of his own shadow."

"How can we be destroyed by technology that is not present?"

"Surely, he cannot be this naïve," Isaura whispered.

"It *is* here. Kalonica has been directly affected by technology," Vorn said. "I would have Elder Mavridis speak to what he witnessed."

Her father stood, his gaze striking hers for a moment. "It is not every day one must put his disgrace on display." His grumbled words earned a few chuckles, though she saw the pain it cost him. "Months past, we were in Trachys along the eastern shore of Kalonica. Medora Marco and our kyria"—

he inclined his head respectfully to Isaura—"were there for a short diversion. Marco was stolen from us in the middle of the night. The Plisiázon and I, along with the medora's regia, gave chase to the enemy, losing them when they boarded an aircraft with our medora and stole away into the sky."

His words shoved that terrible night into her mind's eye again.

Dusan's gaze hit hers. "Isaura."

Alarm speared her, aware that something was terribly wrong. Shadows moved, tore at them. "Dusan!" She thought of the garden, of the man who attempted to harm her there. They were here. They had come for her—them.

His expression went wild and frantic as men ripped him away from her.

A painful crack against her temple plunged her into darkness.

Tears burned, but Isaura restrained them, the memory all too fresh. She suddenly wondered—had Dusan seen two lights in her eyes as they touched, as he was taken? Is that why his eyes widened? By all accounts, she *had* already conceived . . .

"Dream and lead him home."

A touch at her elbow pulled her back to the present, to the table. Roman nodded to the crowd, who sat watching her. She had the uncomfortable realization she'd missed words directed at her.

"Kyria Isaura," Vorn said, likely repeating his words, "would you please share what Medora Marco told you, what he saw . . . here?" He nodded, encouraging her.

The ships? Earlier, they had agreed it should be mentioned, but she had not fathomed being the one to do that. "Of course." She wet her lips and managed a smile. "During a tour of the wastelands, Medora Marco, who is also a Kynigos"—she indicated to Roman—"detected a scent in the air that both excited and concerned him. He was certain there were airships here, somewhere on Drosero."

Nervous titters and gasps skittered around the room, but she plunged onward. "Marco was determined to rout the fetor, as he called it, so we traveled south to meet King Vorn and Queen Aliria. One night, he inquired."

"*Inquired?*" Vorn barked a laugh. "No, that is too tame for the medora in the north. Marco was a bloodhound on the hunt. He all but demanded I come out with it."

"With what?" grumbled Emperor Yhachi.

"Forgive me, Queen Isaura," Vorn said. "Please continue."

"As a hunter responsible for the care and maintenance of his own ship, he recognized the fetor easily and asked King Vorn if he had ships, though he knew they were here." She looked to the gregarious Vorn. "When he returned after seeing the ships with you . . . in earnest, I have never seen him so giddy. He loves flying and knew that, faced with a formidable enemy in the skies, Kalonica needed more than blades or discs."

"What ships?" Prince Rezik demanded. "Where?"

"That," Vorn said, his grin vanishing, "is a very well-guarded secret."

"Why?" Princess Lirra asked quietly. "The purpose of this conclave is to encourage openness and unity. If you are to keep your secrets, why taunt us with them?"

"And your treasure storeroom vault, Princess," the king challenged, "will you grant us all access to the jewels and coin locked within?"

Lirra blanched, her gaze skimming the room until it fell on her plate. But then she straightened. "Treasures of Giessen do not hold the hope for our planet. Those ships do—can."

"Aye," Vorn said, a dangerous glint in his dark eyes, "and how am I to know you, a beautiful young princess with her throne at stake, has not been bought by Symmachia the same as our Hirakyn neighbors?"

Lirra startled. "I would never!"

"Perhaps." Vorn remained unyielding. "And neither would I." He scratched his beard, glancing to his queen. "The time will come when their location will no longer be a secret, but that time is not now. The skycrawlers have made no secret of wanting Drosero as their own and have shown their willingness to do whatever they must to make it happen, from controlling the rex next door to stealing the medora in the north."

Isaura's heart sputtered at the way he trampled those words so quick and light, as if he talked of nothing more than a dog in the street. She knew that was not his intent, but it smarted all the same.

"Symmachian traitors are here. They may even be among us," Vorn challenged.

"They may be you," Prince Rezik asserted.

Vorn sharpened his gaze on the young prince at the same time Isaura noticed Roman ease forward, narrowing his focus on Waterflame's ruler.

What was this?

"Aye," grumbled Emperor Yhachi, "the sapling has a point. What if it is you and you are controlling the ships?"

"Then," Vorn said with the charm of a man courting a woman, "you are all in a trap and as good as dead."

A wave of something rushed through the room, and Isaura drew away from it as she would a flame.

"Good friends." Queen Aliria rose, her belly nicely round with the Jherakan heir she carried. "It is true what the king states—the enemy has shown itself shrewd and swift, willing to seize both doubt and fear. Capitalize on them. Twist those fears into irrationality and"—she gave them a sorrowful look—"mistrust and mistakes."

She glided to Vorn's side, and though she was a good head shorter, she seemed completely his equal in stature and presence. No wonder the king was smitten with the lady . . . Or was it *Lady* as Crey of Greyedge and his men had insisted? "The pilots are training, learning—an enormous feat as they must understand the mechanics of an aircraft before they have even used electricity to light their homes. So please—let us guard those heroes with zealous fervor, as they are our best hope."

"But what can a few skyships do against the skycrawlers?" someone shouted.

"It's true," said a man Isaura had not yet met. He leaned forward, sliding his plate out of the way and resting his forearms on the table. "Symmachians have thousands. Their armada is comprised of people from across Kedalion and now Herakles. They are trained, some new to flying, some having served in the fleet for decades. There are even those known as Eidolon, the elite of their elite. The best. They are said to drop from the sky and are equal to your"—he looked to Mavridis—"what did you call yourself?"

"Plisiázon," Mavridis answered with a scowl.

"Then this is impossible!" Rezik proclaimed. "We should just surrender—"

"No!" Czar Asrak banged a fist on the table, porcelain plates and cups rattling. "No, not surrender."

"There will be no surrender." Vorn's ferocity charged through the debate.

"But it's impossible to win," President Sotui balked, his face a mixture of terror and rage. "They outnumber us. One planet against an entire Quadrant is madness!"

"No." Vorn thrust a fist up. "It's a *start*."

"A start? What does that mean?" Yhachi demanded.

"There are others who can help us. Who were long ago sworn to assist mankind." Vorn glanced at his queen, and the look she gave him seemed to silence the room. "Please?" he whispered quietly.

Mouth tight, she appeared stricken. "I told you they will not—"

Vorn considered her for a long moment before turning to the gathered. "I have a hope that my beautiful Lady tells me is foolish and impossible."

Aliria now looked livid, shaking her head as if to beg him.

"I would beseech the help of Deversoria in defending this planet."

Silence gaped, then a swell of laughter rushed in, mocking the king. "No wonder you are called the Errant."

Being hit with a wing wasn't as soft as one might expect. In fact, it pretty much felt like being thrown into a bulkhead. Groaning, holding his shoulder, which had taken the brunt of the impact, Tigo rolled and stared up at the cavernous ceiling of the amphitheater. Then he let his eyes focus on the Lady, whose wings angled to slow her descent as she alighted next to him.

"It's not fair, you know." He grimaced as he sat up, testing his shoulder joint and wincing.

"Few things are."

Tigo squinted at Jez. "For creatures who invented the concept of mercy, you give little."

She might not be one of their Resplendent—the Ladies who basically acted as generals—but she didn't behave much differently. Then again, in his mind, she *was* resplendent. Always had been.

She stretched her neck, the helm shuttering from her face and receding into . . . well, nothing. Just vanished. "It is for the weak or corrupt. Are you either?"

"Ah." He snorted. "More instruction." He whipped to his feet in front of her.

Her wings snapped out, thrusting her backward.

Tigo laughed. "You're too easy." He reached for the weapon she had effortlessly knocked from his grip. "If there was a way to anchor this to my arm or . . . build it into the armor . . ."

"Be careful the things you wish for."

He eyed her, packing up his gear. "Why's that?"

"There is a dangerous race out there who indeed weaponized their arms."

Tigo guffawed. "Unlimited supply of energy for the pistol, ease of deployment and storage—sounds perfect."

She stared at him as if he'd just forgotten a basic rule of warfare. Suddenly he felt like a child to his instructor. Haughty. Cool. Aloof. Worse, she didn't look as if she'd broken a sweat, yet he was drenched. Another thing that wasn't fair.

"What?" He shook off the sense of inferiority. "You can't just declare something is wrong and not explain why. So what? I'm not endless, so no endless supply? But if I'm dead, I wouldn't need any weapon." He shrugged. "You haven't convinced me yet."

"Do not be so cavalier."

"That's not cavalier. That's Survival 101." He slung his ruck over his uninjured shoulder, getting a whiff of himself—and cringing. They left the coliseum and headed in the direction of the square. In the old days on the *Macedon* or *Renette*, they'd meet up over chow or in the rec room with the 215. Here, she went her way, and he went his. In the pause before the separation, he tried to meet her eyes. To connect. "I hate this."

"You are making strides with the Licitus." Jez acted as if he hadn't just said that. "The Revered Mother is pleased."

"You'd never know." Voids, he sounded petulant. "I mean, there's no reward or advancement. Even when we excel, we're treated more like *lichen* than men."

"*Licitus* are fallen." She inclined her head. "Boundaries are in place for a purpose."

"Do you hear yourself?" He couldn't stand this. "*Fallen*? Do any of these men act fallen to you? Do I?" He hesitated, recalling how she'd never liked the way he flirted with women. "Never mind that last question."

Rejeztia pulled up straight, and somehow, though he looked her in the eyes, she towered over him.

"I hate when you do that." He pivoted toward the juncture. He missed his friend, his first officer. The woman he'd grown to trust more than anyone.

"Tigo—"

"Catch you tomorrow." This? *This* was having purpose? They treated him like a rhinnock, a beast of burden. *Their* burden. He'd stood his ground for the men weeks past, and yet here they were still. Him subservient. Her beautiful and so superior.

Fingers closed around his arm as Jez pulled him around. "Tigo, please—"

Reflex had him shrugging off her touch, but he stopped. "This . . . this doesn't work for me, Jez."

At the informal name—one that'd been good enough for the last four years—she again drew up.

"Yeah—*that*!" He pointed at her. "You acting like Mother Superior or something. We're equals, Jez."

"We are not." The decisive cut of her words was sharp. "I know it is hard for you to understand—"

"Real enlightenment there."

"—but here, we are not Eidolon. I am neither your lieutenant nor under your command." She stood straight and tall. "I am Faa'Cris, and you—"

"Yeah, yeah. Got it. Cattle dung. Dirt under your shiny, shapeshifting boots."

"Remember yourself, Licitus!"

The rebuke shoved his gaze down. With a sniff, he fisted his hand. Deep breaths. *Count it off. Ten . . . Nine . . .*

Nah. Forget it. He was done.

With one last look into those violet eyes—so strange after all the years he'd appreciated her golden eyes—Tigo turned the corner and headed to his assigned quarters above the sanctuary in a room with locks and security measures that would defy even Symmachians to break in.

It wasn't much different than his time in the brig after he'd helped Marco and Kersei escape. At least with them, he'd had a purpose and friends. Here? Neither. No friends, no buddies to chat with after chow, because all Licitus left the city each evening. He couldn't even talk to the Faa'Cris because—of course—he was *fallen, depraved.* They were high on their position and power, and the men were defeated and discouraged. Neither side willing to change.

He'd spent the last eighteen months—in Quadrants time, that was . . . well, he had no idea exactly, except it was different—training the men, fighting for basic rights among beings who were the equivalent of demigods. Let's not even go into how painful it was seeing her every scuzzing day. And rather than getting to know her better, the chasm between them widened.

After showering up and grabbing chow from the cantina, he returned to his prison and sat on the edge of the bed. He wanted to fight, wanted to be furious, but what was the point? What good would it do? Should he look for a way to leave?

"For so gregarious a young man—"

Startled by the voice, Tigo leapt off the bunk and pivoted to find the Revered Mother standing there, flanked by Decurions Cybele and Ithriel. Irritation shoved away the shock. Still, he would not be disrespectful, so he lowered his gaze, eighteen months of strain forcing that response into his brain.

"—you are quite depressing."

"Guess that's what happens after being locked in a room night after night in complete isolation."

"Solitude was intended to deepen your relationship with the Ancient."

"Yet even He wanted companionship," Tigo shot back. "That's why He created us, right?"

She smirked, considering him for a long while. "Among those you have been training, are there any whom you trust unequivocally? Those you know without a shadow of doubt would and have obeyed the edicts set forth for life here?"

Unbelievable. So no answer to his question. Again. And now she wanted to discuss the obedience of the men. He tried to stare her down, but it was impossible to hold her penetrating gaze, so he shifted his focus to the stained glass backlit by a touchstone. "Banishment and death are strong motivators to *obey* said edicts."

Irritation flashed through the room.

He was pushing his luck. There must be a point to this line of questioning, and he didn't want to arouse her anger because then nothing would change. So, men . . . faithful to the edicts. "Yes."

"Name them."

"Moza, Xeros, Ferox, Aegeus, Ancile, Picus, Vasilis, Savill—"

She lifted a hand. "Not *all* your officers."

"They are my officers for a reason. I trust them. They're good at what they do. Because they bow to your whims without—" Okay, maybe that was going a little too far. Even if true. Risky when dealing with a Faa'Cris, whose wings could slice open a man's throat.

The Revered Mother arched an eyebrow. "Your anger is well known to me, Tigo."

"Jez," he muttered, then realized his mistake and huffed. "Rejez—*Triarii Rejeztia*." Curse his inability to use her correct title! "She told you." Ratted him out. Their little minion spy.

"It annoys you that she does not treat you as she did celerus."

Celerus. Their word for aboveground, all that took place outside these stone walls. "What annoys me is"—*Easy, easy,* he warned himself—"this whole thing. Bringing me down here to train men you have held captive—"

"No Licitus is captive," she countered, authoritatively but calmly. "Each has chosen to live here."

"It's the only home they have! Even if they wanted to leave, where would they go?" He narrowed his eyes, fed up with this charade. "Some have been here since infancy, brought as rescues from aboveground by a Faa'Cris. Where are they to go? How are they to live?" His heart writhed in his chest. "It's a mockery to suggest *free will* keeps them here. They leave and they have nothing! No job, no one to recommend them on a planet that is as backward as—"

Tigo faltered, seeing his mistake in the glimmering of the air around her—a sure sign of her anger and the oncoming armor—and the blur of Cybele rushing forward.

"No!" the Revered Mother said, stilling the violence nearly unleashed.

In a blink, Cybele was back at her side, face clear of the aggression she'd just been willing to deliver. Uncanny how they were diabolus one second, benevolent daughter the next.

Man. He just wanted to leave. This room. These halls. He detested games like this. "Look . . ." Where did he begin? "I greatly respect you. Revere, even!" He could concede that much.

"That seemed to hurt to confess."

He cocked his head in a shrug. "It's not something I often say. Or ever."

Her violet gaze held him fast. "But . . .?"

Tigo roughed a hand over his face. "I can't reconcile that this is the right way—isolation."

"You could live among the riverfolk."

He'd considered it, but that . . . that would mean leaving the Sacred City, leaving . . . Jez. And though she now only saw him as a lesser, he just . . . Voids, he couldn't give up. Not yet.

"I have been weighing your complaints," the Revered Mother spoke into the gaping silence. "The Resplendent have decided to allow you to choose four Licitus."

"A mission?" He'd finally get out from belowground.

"An experiment," she corrected with a smile. "There is a dwelling recently vacated here in the Sacred City, and I grant dispensation for you and your favored four to assume the residence."

"To live?" Tigo gaped. "Here? In the city."

She walked the tiny flat. "Yes, freely. Come and go as you please."

Tigo stared at her, stunned at the offer, but he saw a notable drawback. "No."

She blinked and frowned. "No?" she faced him, imperious as ever. "But you—"

"No. Things stay as they are."

Arms folded, the Revered Mother scowled. "You confound me, Tigo

Deken." She sighed and paced. "Miatrenette said you would reject the idea."

He had no idea who that was. "Then why offer?"

The Revered Mother moved to the window overlooking the church courtyard and fountain. Uncertain what this was about, he glanced at her decurions, who were as motionless and unaffected as the stone walls around them.

"Was I not supposed to ask that?"

"You have every right to ask." Her voice was strange now, wavering. Sad, surprising enough. She faced him again. "You are right . . . in so many ways." A smile flickered into her features. "When the Resplendent decided to separate ourselves from humanity, it was . . . bliss. No more worrying if the men would become consumed with power and control, trapping us aboveworld by breaking pacts to give us Daughters. No more did their females fear us or feel threatened by our presence. The hatred, not limited by gender, no longer stung our nostrils or endangered our lives. It was a haven, and we took certain pleasure in men understanding how great our influence was—that without our consent, they would have none of what we could bring to their realms and worlds."

Now it was his turn. "But?"

"Do you recall the first time you challenged the Daughters?"

"Cracked ribs didn't let me forget for weeks."

"We could have healed you, if you had let us."

In that bath thing, he guessed. Tigo shook his head. "Too easy. I wasn't willing to forget what cost came from underestimating the Daughters."

"There are not many Licitus—"

"Men."

She held his gaze for a long second. "There are not many *men* like you." She spread her hands. "In fact, there have been none in Deversoria, but already I see the benefit of your presence. The Lici"—she tucked her chin—"*men* have rallied. Even the Daughters are more alive."

Tigo glanced at the decurions, uncertain how to read this.

Now she lifted that chin. "I will trust the four you name. They will live with you in the house mentioned. Eat, come, and go as you please."

"I told you—no."

She frowned and shook her head. "But why? It is—"

"The perfect way to paint a target on the backs of your best five. The other men will quickly resent that we live here and are treated better."

"So you are saying men *are* given to depravity?"

He gritted his teeth. "You twist my words."

With an acknowledging nod and arch of her eyebrows, she said nothing.

"You've reduced men to one aspect, which is unfair. We are the way the Ancient made us, just as you are. We are men—passionate, physical, and fierce. Designed as protectors and providers. If you call that depravity, then what of you, with your armor and violence? Also gifts from the Ancient." His words hit their mark.

Her spine lengthened. "The *Faa'Cris* are His warriors, designed to protect His Creation. We—"

"There is no denying how beautiful or powerful you are. But you categorically confront the Fallen. Give them no measure or grace. Only judgment. So much that you are going to tell me only five men can live in your city because only those men are not given to passions? I have seen already that your decurions here do not like what you offer, but I would say if five are acceptable to live within this sacred city, why not the rest? How do you define the others as depraved? We all seek freedom to choose where we live, where we work." He inched closer. "The Ancient gave us free will to choose—whether to serve Him or not. To decide each day between right and wrong. Deprive us of our ability to choose, and while you may not see violence for a time, you will also not see courage or heroism—which, if you search your hearts, may be what you truly seek once again from men. Give us that chance."

Fiery images darted through his mind's eye of places—Kynig and the Citadel, Cenon . . . the white palace of Iereania, the Temple. Then memories of people—Father with his deep voice and jet-black hair, a much younger Sylvanus in the halls of Kardia, the master—Roman—spiriting him away and becoming a father figure to him, Rico and his near irreverence. As each image leapt into that visual vortex, it seemed . . . blurred but . . . forced.

The priest Ypiretis . . .

Darius.

What is this?

Agony whipped through his head, down his neck and along his shoulders, as if a hundred daggers sliced muscle from bone.

It's not real . . . it is not real . . .

Unable to convince his body, Marco arched his spine and howled. "Augh!"

The echo of his pain bouncing against the hull snapped his eyes open. He blinked hard, trying to focus on where he was. Disoriented by the lack of scents from beings, he startled to see several shapes hovering over him. He thrashed, trying to free himself, as blurs of black and harsh lights swayed above him. The strange warble of Xisya's voice somehow wobbled along his eardrums.

What . . .?

He saw her . . . but she wasn't here. Right? This planet was filled with Draegis, not her. Yet he felt her tendrils, the silvery-sharp slice of her words and intent against his adunatos.

"Xonim!" one of the Draegis trilled, excitement in his tone that easily bled around their garbled tongue.

Though Marco couldn't understand the language, he didn't need to understand it to see the parallel between him thinking about Xisya and them mentioning Xonim. Fire crackled through his head, then along his field of vision, faces taking shape once more, like a docuvid of his life. Ixion. Bazyli. Palinurus.

Again, the Draegis chortled, the sound irritated, authoritative.

What is going on?

His brain fired again—High Lord Kyros. Darius again. Kersei . . .

Somewhere in the torture, the sensation of daggers and fire, Marco realized where his thoughts would lead. Awareness flared a warning.

They're digging in my head. Just as Jadon had said. Accessing his memories. He'd been warned that Xisya had threaded her DNA into him to use his memories against him.

Panic erupted. He thrashed, his hands and legs tethered. He wouldn't let them go there. Couldn't. They'd find—

No! Don't think about it.

The chatter around him made his instinct rage, though he could not tell what they were saying. Just knew it wasn't good. Couldn't be. The warning shoved Marco the rest of the way into consciousness, into full fight. He growled against the bit in his mouth.

A loud crash sounded nearby, followed by chortles and a flurry of words that his own growling muddled. Heat shot through his veins, then ice. And he again fell into darkness.

In a rush Marco came to, finding himself in the barren environment of his cell. He peeled off the slab and sat up with a groan. Heels of his hands to his eyes, he recalled narrowly evading their attempts.

Time was short. With the Draegis' advanced technology and digging into his memories, they were likely forming a map back to the Quadrants. It'd probably go faster next time. And if he was unconscious again, he could unwittingly betray everyone.

He lowered himself to the deck and started doing push-ups, sit-ups, crunches—anything and everything until his body trembled from exhaustion. It was imperative he get in shape and keep himself alert.

Arm trembling from a one-handed push-up, he lowered himself again, noting the blue glow against the deck from his brand, pulsing with life. A constant reminder of what and who depended on him.

"Can I ask you a question?"

Staring through his hair, which had grown unruly in the months since he was taken, Marco eyed Jadon. He'd had a deep appreciation for Eidolon after Commander Deken and his team helped save Kersei. However, this pup didn't have the maturity inherent in Tigo under all his swagger. Out of respect for the commander, though, Marco pushed up, his arm violently objecting, and hiked back onto his haunches. He shoved sweaty hair from his eyes.

Jadon held his gaze for a tick. "This . . . feels pretty hopeless."

Hopelessness crushed the soul, but it was also where defiance, an integral seed of courage, rose on feeble legs.

The Eidolon leaned against the bulkhead with his arms folded, gaze glued to the deck. The guy clearly had something occupying his thoughts, making him hesitate.

"That wasn't a question."

Jadon shoved a hand over his hair as he dropped onto the rack. "Eija—that thing . . ." He was distraught, frustrated. "She doesn't even hesitate to trust that beast. Goes with it without thinking twice. Has no problem with the way it follows her around."

After toweling off, Marco threaded his arms through a provided black shirt. Which he found interesting—the Draegis had weaponized arms and didn't wear shirts. So where were these clothes coming from? "Worried she'll *side* with him?"

"No!" He flinched. "Maybe." He groaned. "I have no idea. How can we know anything at this point? I mean, those creatures have no compunction about reducing us to ash, and she talks to him like they're best friends. You've seen how it's changed since she touched it. What does that mean?"

Marco had no answer for what he could only describe as bizarre. "Eija doesn't see him as a best friend. Her intentions are more altruistic."

"Intentions? Is that some downworlder speak for 'she's attracted to him'?"

"You need to check your feelings for her."

Jadon came to his feet. "Feelings? Yeah, I have feelings. Worry. Fear. I'm worried about her betraying us and our plans to the Draegis."

Marco turned to the static barrier, peering as far down the passage as he could to count the number of Draegis nearby. "She won't. Eija's more mission-focused than you give her credit for." There were three, maybe four lurking around this passage.

"I don't think she is. She wanted this—to leave the Quadrants. She hated her life in Symmachia. All she cared about was getting away."

"Maybe, but I disagree that she'll betray us. But we have bigger problems than that—if they dig into my brain again, they'll find what they're looking for. They got too close last time. So set aside your jealousy—"

"Excuse me?"

"—and let's focus on destroying the *Prev*."

"What happens to *us* after that?"

"Vaqar knows." Marco bent to strap on the provided grav boots, and his hair poked his eyes. Growling, he straightened at the same time a trill of alarm hit his receptors. He eyed the passage. Even as he did, he detected a heated incoming scent. "Move," he snapped, shoving his hair back, wishing for his pistol or even a webbing gun.

"What's wrong?" Light and fast, Jadon shifted to the side of the door for protective cover, his hand reflexively searching for a weapon that wasn't there. "Slag."

"Yeah, same," Marco said, nodding to the corridor. "The girl—" Drawing in her scent, he angled for a narrow line of sight outside his cell. Heard a Draegis thud closer, a bit of dialogue between her, Blue, and another. "Get back. I'm going to test a theory."

More thuds reverberated closer to the static barrier. There came the *worp* of the shield drop, and then a Draegis clomped in.

Marco swung around and grabbed the thing by the throat. He heard the whistle of the arm weaponizing, felt the searing heat beneath his fingers. Met the blaze of livid slits. A wake of heat wafted off the creature, and Marco felt himself lifted from his toes. Air squeezed from his lungs even as the thing punched him backward, but only enough for the weaponized arm to take aim.

"No!" Eija screamed.

Marco gripped the arm now holding his throat, still not quite sure how he'd lost his grip on the Draegis.

"Stop!" Eija shouted, trying to wedge into the fray.

Blue chattered in their weird language.

Fire burned Marco's neck, and only then did he notice that Blue seemed to have a neck, too. He hadn't before, had he?

Yeah, who cares—focus on staying alive.

The beast hesitated, his eyes still pulsing with fury, but his violence . . . stayed.

"*Itlimos! Chiqarish! Uni tinch qo'ying.*"

Did the girl realize she was *speaking* in their tongue?

The acrid scent of burned flesh—his—made him tense. Hiss against the pain. His stunt had given him the needed knowledge. He just hoped he wasn't going to die for it.

"*Chiqarish!*" she shouted, her tone brooking no argument.

The beast pitched Marco aside and turned to Eija, bellowing in her face so hard the wisps of hair around her temples riffled.

Blue charged forward, chortling back.

Holding his throat, Marco eyed the two beasts having a Draegis showdown. Noted the size disparity—Blue was much taller but less bulky as he trilled and chortled at the other, who finally backed out with a braying that alerted Marco to the thudding approach of more Draegis.

Registering the difference between the two—not just in size, but physically—he climbed to his feet, watching the enraged beast as the static shield crackled to life.

Eija whirled, her brow knotted. "*What* was that?"

Though he thought to close his receptors to her anger and fear—a lot of it—he welcomed the scents, which were far too rare here. "A point."

"It was stupid!"

Her scent . . . "What has you alarmed?"

"Besides you nearly getting reduced to ash?"

"There was no threat because you were here." He touched his throat and flinched again. "Though I wasn't entirely sure of that until just now."

She gaped at him. "Are you insane? We already knew that from earlier!"

"No, earlier, we learned he will comply with your wishes, but I needed to know if he'd stand up against one of his own and still obey you. And even though that green was mad as plagues, he did yield. We had to know what would happen."

She stifled a scream. "It was an unacceptable risk."

"Disagree." Marco understood her anger, but they had to know where the boundaries were. "What were you worried about when you came in here?"

"Besides you losing your life?"

"That fear came after—I'm talking about the one before."

She huffed. "You drive me crazy."

"And you both make me crazy," Jadon groused.

Marco waited for her answer.

"I hate that you can know that." Eija folded her arms. "Right now, I'm very angry with you."

"Anger is good—use it—"

"Stop! Just . . . stop." She splayed her hands and stabbed the air, then took a moment to calm down before she sighed. "I think they know what's happening." Her voice was small as she hugged herself.

"What d'you mean?"

"I was with Daq'Ti trying to find another way into Engineering, when everything went sideways," Eija said, her eyes bright. "Suddenly, I'm locked out of access I've had since we first boarded." She nodded to Blue beside her. "He even lost access to certain systems, too. Not as comprehensive as my lockout, but yeah."

"Both of you." Marco considered the implications. The girl losing access to vital ship's systems he could understand, but Blue? Yet, still they obeyed her. These beasts did not like the trouble she created or the subservience she somehow commanded. "Not good."

"That was *my* point."

"We *have* to destroy the *Prev.*"

"You keep saying that, but we're locked out. Like I said last time, I think they know—it's the only explanation. And what I learned makes me believe they may not tolerate Daq'Ti's . . . subservience much longer."

"Why?" Marco asked warily, eying Blue, who scanned him and Jadon, though his every move was centered off the girl. Always close enough to protect, far enough away to deliver death blows without endangering her.

Was it him or was Blue's skin changing? Less lava, more basalt . . .?

Marco was losing his mind.

Eija's face reddened. "*Ovqatlanish.*" She sounded as strange as the beasts. "In our language it roughly translates, *The Taming.* The Draegis believe Daq'Ti has been tamed—by me. The handprint . . . somehow. In their violent, high-alpha structure, a Draegis who has been tamed is . . . outcast. Shunned because the others are afraid it will happen to them. Like it's contagious or something." She dragged both hands along the sides of her face. "I don't understand it—just know that because of that handprint they're locking him out of systems. But not all at once. That's what's weird."

Jadon formed up on Marco. "You see what I mean, right? What I was saying—"

She blinked between the two of them. "What were you saying? About me?"

About her betraying them. If she was partial to the beast, if she'd tamed him . . . No, her Signature held respect for Daq'Ti, along with a plethora of other scents—confusion, fear, uncertainty. But more than all those, she was concerned about them. That's what he'd detected when she came in. He shook his head at Jadon. "Still disagree, but there are too many unknowns, too many variables to navigate and unlock."

"If they're locking him out," Jadon added, "it won't be long before Eija is confined to the brig as well."

"Not necessarily. She's an anomaly to them. While it's true they obey or yield to her, they also hate her and the compulsion—if we can call it that— to obey. Regardless, we're out of time." A scent riffled across his receptors. "Wait." He frowned and slowly approached the beast.

Spice . . . That *was* a scent. Unsettled that he now anak'd something from

Blue, he homed in on it, cocking his head, opening his mouth to pull the note to the back of his throat. Why? Why could he now detect pheromones, emotions, from this emotionless Draegis? Strange . . . It was woodsy . . .

Oh! Curse the reek! Not just one note. Two—there were *two* notes. Strange but powerful. One acrid yet empty, a confusing note. The other one surprising: cypress.

"Concern." Marco stared at the triple slits in the face . . . ones no longer quite so thin. It was as if the third slit might bleed into the other two. Just like the scents—because that's the tick he noticed a third note lurking behind the others.

"What's wrong?" Jadon asked.

Marco hauled in a breath. "Balsam."

"Wait!" Eija balked. "You can *smell* him?"

He anak'd the roiling scent. "What has you panicked, Daq'Ti?"

Eija had been a fool to think she could hide anything from the hunter. "The Taming has them turning against him, shutting him out," she said hurriedly, placing a hand on Daq'Ti's arm and feeling his muscles constrict beneath her fingertips. She stared at the limb, shocked that his lavalike "skin" now was . . . smoother. No, not so much smooth as less . . . bumpy.

Yeah, okay, not really great with adjectives right now.

Different. It felt *different*. Enough that she could feel the contraction of muscles. She looked up at him. At those strange red slits. They also had changed, seemed more orange . . . *ish*.

What the djell? She was going crazy. The light must be different in here. Right. Different from the last umpteen times she'd been here with him?

"There's definitely something happening here that we don't understand—I can anak him now. But only him." Marco's words were somehow calming. "He's changing."

Eija held his silver gaze, then slowly nodded. "He is."

"With him locked out of systems, we have to deal with the *Prev.* ASAP."

"And escape," Reef added. "Let's not forget that part."

"Live or die, we cannot let them find the coordinates to the Quadrants," Marco stated flatly. "We have a chance to save humanity. Our lives are of secondary consequence."

"Yeah, but one way or the other, we have to get you out of their reach," Reef said. "And I'd like to try the *living* route first, if you don't mind."

Expression grim and hair dangling in his eyes, Marco radiated meaning and authority. "Fair enough. But our time's up. If we don't do this now, we might as well hand them our loved ones and friends on a platter. So first—" Intensity radiated through those silvery irises as he studied Daq'Ti. "Can you understand me?"

A trill of heat and noise riffled the air.

Guess that's a yes. Though she didn't like the way Marco seemed ready to challenge him to a death match. What was with him coming on so strong? Daq'Ti might be subservient to her, but he was still fiercely violent.

Marco faced him. "They're blocking you from accessing parts of your ship, restricting your access to vital systems. That, by its nature, puts you at risk." He paused as if to let that sink in. "An important part of our team is Xonim. She's with us and we're with her. We will not go down easily in our efforts to protect her." He pointed to Eija. "You would protect her, too. Yes?"

Another trill made Eija shift. She really, really hated the whole Lavabeast-protector thing. It made no sense. And honestly, she resented how much Reef hated it, because he was getting the translation of this thing with her and Daq'Ti wrong.

"There is a threat against us, against our existence. If you don't help us," Marco said, pointing to her, "they will kill Xonim."

Nausea swirled at the reality of his words. She recalled the confrontation in Engineering. *Remember—heaps of smoking ash, Eij.*

"We need to get to the weapons systems." Marco was preternaturally calm as he stared down the monstrous Draegis. "Can you help?"

"*Daq'Ti Xonim himoya qiling,*" Daq'Ti said.

Words flowed into Eija's mind easily, and she didn't know whether to be annoyed or glad. He'd said before and shown that he would protect her, but that didn't answer Marco's question.

"What'd he say?" Marco asked.

"Daq'Ti just reiterated that he would protect me—oh, that reminds me!" She reached into a pocket. "I asked Daq'Ti for these—it's their version of a universal translator. I thought they'd come in handy." She held a device toward each of them and nodded. "Just a pinch, and you can stop asking me what they say."

Marco tensed at the proffered comms. "Not sure I want any more Draegis tech in my body."

"Yeah, but it'll be a pain to keep asking what he said," Reef muttered as he clicked the piece into his PICC-port. "And it eliminates a tactical advantage they had when we couldn't understand them." He nodded at her. "Gotta give it to you, Ei. Thanks."

With a grunt, Marco relented as Eija stepped toward him.

"So . . ." Reef began as Eija pressed the little device to Marco's nape. "You. BeastieBoy will protect *you,* but not us."

"He'll protect *us* as long as she wants us protected," Marco murmured, scratching one of the plug scabs on his temple. "As for the other Draegis, whatever this Xonim—lady?—thing is, it seems to be running out or losing its effect." He straightened and bobbed his head toward her. "It's on you, Eija. I know that's not fair, but we have to protect the Quadrants. It's vital we get into the weapons. You said they already blocked you and Blue, but not completely. There's no more time for tiptoeing around looking for an easy out. Ask him to figure out a way to send two missiles to the *Prev.* That should be enough." His silver eyes were downright haunting.

Tucking a rogue strand behind her ear, she felt as if tempting the anger of the Draegis was like playing with the nuke itself. Then again, Marco was right. They were out of time. The *Prev* must be destroyed, and Marco must be removed from the Draegis' reach . . . one way or another.

"Since I'd rather not make Eija's job a suicide mission," Reef said, "maybe while she's doing that, we figure a way out of this brig and to a fast-attack craft to make our escape."

"Where are you going to get one of those, and where do you plan to go?" Eija balked. "Kuru is enemy territory—all of it!"

Reef shrugged. "The way I see it, we got nothing to lose. Especially him"— he indicated to Marco—"because his only options are escape or death."

Eija flinched at the stark pronouncement. Frustration coiled in the pit of her stomach as her heart railed against the inescapable truth of Reef's words.

"Priority one is destroying the *Prev,*" Marco repeated, leveling a hard stare at each of them in turn. Then he put a hand on Eija's shoulder, and she glimpsed the war within him. Hope and resignation. Longing and sacrifice. "But Jadon's right. Once you set these events in motion, we have nothing to lose by trying to escape."

"Granted," Eija growled, "but even if you can get out of here, how do either of you expect to commandeer a ship? It's not like they're sitting around, powered up and unmanned."

"If we wait for everything to be ready, we'll never leave."

Desperation clogged her ability to think. He couldn't be serious about this, but he was. She saw it in the firm set of his bearded jaw, the way the hairs twitched. The way his eyes seemed as hard as the hull. She huffed. "Fine." With more anger than courage, she turned to Daq'Ti. "We need to go to Engineering. We—"

He pivoted and clomped ahead, almost as if he'd anticipated her request—command. Whatever.

She felt Reef's gaze, his irritation that she had a connection with Daq'Ti that enabled him to know her thoughts. No, it wasn't that. It was . . .

Djell. She had no idea. But she hated the look Reef gave her, hated the insinuation that she had somehow gone to the dark side.

Maybe she'd *become* the dark side.

What is he *doing here?*

Through the throng of bodies and staff, Isaura searched for the face that had flashed into her awareness on this, the fifth day of committees and meetings that were not accomplishing anything. She longed for Kardia, for the quiet of her balcony and the nights alone in bed, feeling her child move and dreaming of Dusan.

But even amid the exhaustion, she knew it had not been in her imagination. She had seen Crey of Greyedge. But he should not be here. From a sergius, she accepted a goblet of warmed cordi and moved to the side, using the motion to scan the crowds in the ballroom. She liked Crey, rough and calloused as he was, but he didn't belong here. Why it worried her, she wasn't sure. Dusan had also liked the man, though he didn't seem to wholly trust him. He'd said something was off. "Discordant," Dusan had called Crey's scent and actions. How she missed his ability to anak, to rout a scent! Perhaps she should ask Ro—

"What is it?" The master hunter swept up to her, his powerful presence relieving yet overpowering.

Isaura gave a small laugh and caught her amulet in her hand. "I . . . I thought I saw someone."

Roman's hand closed protectively around her elbow. "Something is amiss." His gaze roved the crowd. That look—so fierce, so formidable, so . . . familiar.

"If you mean to frighten, you are excelling," she said quietly, still searching for Crey.

"Who did you see?" Roman's gaze narrowed on her. "Speak!"

Surprised at his sharp tone, she glanced at him. There truly was something wrong. "Crey of Greyedge." Shadows of movement blurred and coalesced in the shapes of several hunters, who bled from anonymity to converge on the master. On her. It had taken her a while to get used to their ability to do things like that, to sense her concern. To read her like an open book.

"Trouble," Rico growled, his chin tucked, gaze probing the teeming ballroom.

"Aye." Roman guided Isaura out of the thickest part of the crowd. "We should leave. Forgive my touch, but do not fight me." As he directed her to the side, he never looked at her but kept his focus on the people milling about, oblivious to the threat the Kynigos had detected.

"Should we not tell Vorn?"

"He knows," Roman said, his voice ominous.

Isaura then noticed the way he stared across the room and saw he had the king's attention. Beside Vorn, Queen Aliria . . . Isaura drew in a breath. "What . . .?" With every pulse of her heart, she saw a different form of the woman. One minute, calm and collected in brocade and gems. The next, arrayed in bronze armor with ferocity in her expression. Then again in brocade and gems. "*What?*"

"Move!" Roman whirled her toward double doors.

Amid an eruption of light, the floor wobbled beneath her feet. Isaura stumbled, her slippers sliding across the marble. She cried out. Blinding light swallowed the people, the gilt columns, the castle . . . her hearing.

"On your kyria!" came a distant shout.

Fear flared through Isaura, but another, cooler, calmer wave buffeted it. Pushed it back. Curled it away, leaving only a crisp, minty fragrance that brushed her face repeatedly. Like . . . feathers.

If the disorientation weren't so great, Isaura would vow she saw the soft gray edges of feathers fluttering around her—not gently or peacefully. But with force. Violent thrusts that whooshed against her, knocking her off-balance again. In the explosion of light came gold sparks. Here. There. Glints of armor. The song of steel. Blood spilled.

A terrifying sense of flying—backward—rushed at her. Then a distant roar that snatched her into its white embrace. Silence drowned her. How long she lay in its unmerciful grasp, she knew not. But slowly, hollowly, she heard something. Her name.

"Isa."

She turned, the voice warm and tender—like the visage before her. "Dusan." Giddy, she threw herself into his arms, safe, relieved. Though she vaguely sensed danger around him, she cared not. He was here. She was in his arms. All was well. "How I have missed you!"

"Never have I left." His voice was deep and soft, a tickle against her ear. "I've been right here." He lifted her amulet and, with that ever-present smirk, drew her mouth to his and sealed the moment.

Letting the worries and the trials fade away, she savored the tenderness of his kisses. "Come back, Dusan. We need you."

"With every breath, I work to make it happen."

Isaura stared at him, surprised. Every time she had said that before, he promised he had never left. Yet this time . . . "You are safe? Well?"

His eyes—so very silver now—searched her face, his dark brow rippling. "I don't know. It's . . . strange here. Strange things are happening."

Her courage tripped. "I . . . I do not understand. What is this? What's happening?" Heart racing, she reached for the quiet solace of their dream times. She did not want the waking world to intrude. This was her time with Dusan. Only her and Dusan. Only them.

He cupped her face. "How is our daughter?" His hand slid to her womb. "What name should we give her?"

Tears pricked at the edges of her eyes. "When you are returned to Kardia, we will name her together." This confounded. How could they talk as if they were in the same place, yet be separated? Confusion thickened the air. "Please, Dusan. Come back."

"I'm trying. Petition the Ladies and Ancient for me, Isaura. If I do not return—"

"No!" The word echoed in the dreamspace. Tears burned as they wrestled free of her restraint. "No, Dusan. You must come back."

His arms encircled her, pulling her into his embrace, and he pressed a kiss to her crown as she held him. Inhaled that fresh, crisp air that always clung to his black cloak. Yet there was another smell, a different one . . .

"Do not let her forget me, Isaura."

"Stop it! Please." She fisted her hand into the folds of his clothes. "Do not speak like this. You will come back. See our child born. She will know you, not from memories or words but flesh and bone."

"There's an enemy here, powerful and numerous. The odds are . . ."

What he left unsaid hung like an anchor in the air. Isaura pushed her face farther into his shoulder, tugged his cloak tight, drawing him into a crushing embrace.

"Promise she will know I did not leave—"

"No!" She pressed her mouth to his, silencing his words. Refusing to let him speak. Her tears mingled with the rough kiss, his stubble scratching her mouth. A sob broke free.

The edges of their dreamspace wavered like a plume of heat on the horizon.

Isaura drew in a breath, afraid he was leaving her now. "No," she gasped, feeling the tether between them melting away. "No, Dusan!"

He and the world washed gray. "I love you. Promise me—"
"Please."
Slowly he bled into a white agony.
"Yes! Anything." Isaura screamed as he dissolved. "Dusan!"

YO'QILUVCHI, ROHILEK HIGH ORBIT, KURU SYSTEM

Marco jerked upright, leaning to the side, nauseated. In his mind's eye, he still saw her. Felt her terror. Swallowed hard at how the gray washed away in that last instant, and her face had become clear, bruised, bloodied. Her neck scarred.

She's hurt. Hurt and in danger.

His gut heaved.

"You okay? You blacked out or something for a while there."

Marco hesitated at Jadon's words, trying to get his bearings. He'd been ready to die to save Isaura, but her palpable terror . . . "We must get home."

"Yeah, working on that, remember? We need a plan to escape. Worried—Eija's been gone a while."

Marco couldn't miss the jealous efflux from the young Eidolon. "Not surprised." About the guy's jealousy or about the girl taking long. He was, however, surprised by that dream . . . A waking dream?

"How can you not be bothered?"

Harnessing his wits, Marco focused on the anaktesios, needing some sense of normalcy, familiarity. Reached out . . . anak'd humans somewhere but not on this ship. And that made him wonder about his own sanity. Granted, Xisya had said he'd been taken because of his ability to anak farther than others. But he realized that gave him no satisfaction. Because that wasn't what he needed.

Reassurance. That's what he ached for. Desperation made him search for Isaura's scent, to know she was okay. That'd just been a dream, right?

"What if she's injured or in danger?"

"What?" How did Jadon know about Isaura? Wait. No, he meant *Eija.* Was the girl in danger?

Snap out of it! Widening his receptors, Marco scoured the bulkheads of the dreadnought to Eija and pored over her efflux. At least he could anak her.

That kept him slightly less irritated. But the block against the Draegis worried him. What he knew as a Kynigos, the training, the processing of scents, the guiding during the hunt were nearly moot here. Mayhap he'd put too much stock in anak'ing.

"D'you fall asleep again?"

"She's alive—fine," Marco bit out. "She's just distracted, confused. Scared but not in a panicked way. Likely afraid of being discovered or—"

"Killed?" Jadon's voice pitched. "Is that what you were going to say?"

"Stopped," Marco growled, his strength sapped for some reason. "I need to rest."

"You were just asleep! What? Is this because you don't know Ei, so she doesn't matter?"

Angling to the side, Marco glowered at the pup. "You either trust the girl to do what needs to be done, or you don't. I do."

"So you're not worried?"

Marco swung his feet onto the deck and narrowed his gaze on the Eidolon. "Let's cut to the chase here. This is about your jealousy—of her and Blue—"

"What? No!"

"Were I not able to smell your rancid jealousy, your pitched objections would be enough to tell me I am correct." They should work on that plan, but this had to be dealt with, neutralized. "You fear she's leaving you for that beast, which is illogical since, as you believe, it's inhuman—"

"It is!"

"But it's also committed to her. One hundred percent. And not romantically."

Jadon gave him a long, measuring look. "So you trust BeastieBoy?"

"Not one note."

"Note?"

"It's a Kynigos thing." Marco rubbed the back of his neck. "When Blue was full-on Draegis, I couldn't detect him. But now I catch these subtle tinges. It's odd. There's . . . something." He shook his head, unable to understand what his straining, aching receptors were relaying. "He's changing."

"She said that. So, what? You think, like, his character is changing?"

"No," Marco said thoughtfully. "It's deeper somehow."

"Does . . . that put Eija in danger? Us?"

"Her—no. Blue will protect her to his own detriment. She's better off with him than with us. He's weaponized and the only defensive measure to stay alive and get home."

"I reject that," Jadon snapped. "She doesn't belong with him."

"And you say you're not jealous?"

Jadon huffed, then met Marco's gaze. "She's tough, ya know? Smarter than most Eidolon I've met. She holds her own, and that . . . that's something to respect. But with her out there, among those beasts who have no problem reducing humans to ash with those powered arms . . . I'm ready to make this escape happen."

"Agreed. Tell me everything you saw when they brought you aboard."

A presence manifested beside her.

Eija twitched, her heart racing as she peered up at the slits, and sagged when she recognized Daq'Ti. "I need to get in," she whispered, her gaze skating around the Engineering deck. There'd been a dead silence since she had appeared with her protector, yet nobody interfered.

Daq'Ti brushed the screen, and with a *whoosh*, he bypassed the obnoxious symbols that kept her out.

She nodded her thanks and shifted closer. "I need to access the weapons. Help me." Keeping her voice neutral was tough—and she had no idea if he even understood tone, but she hated putting him at risk when he had so fastidiously protected her.

Again, he complied.

Swallowing, she studied what he'd just given her access to. The symbols were unfamiliar, but as she had with the layout of the instrumentation and arrays here, she tried to see familiar patterns. Something that looked similar to the layout on the *Prev*.

She flicked the screen a few times. Grunted, noting the way Daq'Ti hovered very close.

"Stand down." His warning was hot against her neck.

With a gasp, Eija glanced up at him—only to find those slits aimed behind her. She glanced over her shoulder and saw a green moving toward them. Her pulse sped. *Hurry!*

Wait. Hold up . . .

Login—the interpretation leapt into her mind. She copied the gesture from her console on the *Prev*, and it brought her to a ground-floor categorization of options: Thermals, Shields, Engines . . . *Weapons*. She stared at the triple script icon that glared back. *Could it be that simple . . . ?*

She tapped the icon.

Another screen.

Right. Just like on the *Prev*—verification. She tapped it.

The screen winked black, then the blue screen populated with a table of weapons. "Yes!" Thrilled, she scrolled down.

Without warning, Eija was flying through the air. She tensed seconds before she struck a bulkhead. Heard a cacophony of roars and thuds. Blinking her vision clear and coughing for a pain-free breath, she flipped around. Saw Daq'Ti and another blue thrashing each other. The flurry of movements.

Blood splattered.

Daq'Ti powered up his arm—as did the other.

"No!" Eija leapt to her feet and vaulted at the Green. "Stop!"

The Lavabeast howled and stumbled back, shielding his chest from her. He glanced down, looking at something.

Recognition flooded her, seeing the same faint blue imprint that Daq'Ti bore. Startled, she looked at the green, then at the mark. Astonished—she hadn't expected that to happen—she wondered why it hadn't worked on the other green. If she could control them, turn them to—

He bellowed at her. His slits pulsed hotter.

Awareness flooded—the other Draegis in Engineering had risen, noise crackling through the now-silent deck. Arms were powering.

But she had two protectors now. Daq'Ti and Gree—

Shock riddled her she glanced at Green and saw the imprint fade away. He lunged at her. Daq'Ti was a blur of violence, intercepting the blows and onslaught. Something struck her temple. She staggered, confused as the world canted. But in the split second of time as her protector hauled Green off, Eija let her fingers fly over the screen.

Deafening claxons rang through the ship.

Eying the groaning pipes overhead, Marco went still, dragging in what few scents hung in the sanitized air. His head ached from the strain of pulling in empty draughts—empty save Eija's. Her panic shot out to him. "She's in trouble." On his feet, he moved to the static barrier.

Jadon jumped to his side, punched the barrier, earning a powerful rebuke from the ship.

Between the shrieks of the claxon came bellows. Sparks flew in the brig corridors.

Weaponless, he and Jadon were trapped and useless, yet they needed to capitalize on the chaos. "We have to do something," Marco yelled over the din.

"Like what?"

There had to be a way to get free. Even if they did, whatever was happening out there would not be good for them. They'd have no way to defend themselves. But staying here . . .

He anak'd a stirring in the sanitized air. "Back! One's coming."

"How do we take them down?" Jadon hissed, backing into a corner. "They have every advantage."

"Except size."

"Did you miss the part where they're nearly twice as big, twice as strong, and have cannons for arms?"

"Did *you* miss that dreadnoughts are enormous? They can't turn on a data disc?"

Jadon's expression smoothed in understanding, slowly prying a smile from the guy.

"Make him angry." Marco crammed his shoulders against the hull.

"You sure this isn't your way of getting me out of the way?"

"Trust."

"Says the guy who's going to hide in the corner and *not* have a pulse cannon aimed at his chest," Jadon muttered. And just as quick, he started shouting, raising his arms, and challenging the beasts who must be in view now.

The static barrier popped off and a Draegis swarmed in, trilling something neither of them understood. But they *did* understand the retracting arm and heat wake pluming around it.

"Any time now," Jadon hissed at Marco.

Slamming forward, Marco drove his entire weight into the arm and shoved it upward just as it fired. Heat seared the side of his face as the blast caught the beast's head.

Flesh, blood, and goo erupted with a definitive *splat*.

Cringing, Marco hiked backward. To keep the barrier from zapping on again, he forced the beast's now-limp bulk across the threshold. It hit with a thud that rattled the deck. Dark ooze spilled out into the corridor.

"Ready?" Marco glanced back at Jadon—and flinched. The guy stood motionless, coated in the biomatter of the now-dead Draegis. It took everything in him not to laugh. "You good?"

Jadon glowered, raking a hand down his face to clear the slimier chunks. "Next time, *I* hide in the corner."

Marco sniggered as he started into the passage. "Let's go."

A swirling of air pushed him back, right into Jadon. Two Lavabeasts barreled past the brig juncture, arms weaponized, completely missing them. Once safe, Marco skirted the bulkhead, making his way along the curving juncture. He caught the girl's scent to the right. Almost as he thought it, one of the walls became a door—at the same time his brand lit with a thrumming fire. Startled, he glanced down, then to the panel—a narrow door—that slid aside. *What . . .?*

Unnerving. Didn't like that. But he wouldn't complain now that this black mark on his life was finally serving *him*. Sparks glittered into the passage, searing his nostrils. He stumbled through the opening, Jadon at his back.

"Want to explain how you opened that panel?"

"Nope." Had his brand done it? He didn't know.

"Figures."

A frenzied Eija slid around a corner. Wide brown eyes struck them as she sputtered to gain traction. Behind her, Blue was moving backward, his weaponized arm firing. She shouted, but claxons swallowed her words.

Marco anak'd her scent—trouble. A lot of it.

She caught his arm and pulled him toward Blue and an open passage. The same one receiving live fire.

He resisted.

She rose on tiptoe and put her mouth to his ear. "This way!" Her shout came dimly amid the grating noise. "Stay behind me."

Right. He was a hunter, a warrior, and she wanted *him* behind *her*? But he had no chance to argue—she sprinted away with Blue. They made a dozen turns and maneuvers, Marco just as lost as the Draegis apparently were.

Blue rotated to a bulkhead, palmed it, and an upper panel swung open. He withdrew small phase pistols and passed them out.

Though Marco felt better with a weapon in hand, it was a false sense of security. They were in a Draegis dreadnought with a complement of well over thirty thousand beasts. All with weaponized arms. And he had—he glanced at the small phase pistol—what amounted to a water gun.

Curse the reek!

Eija yanked Marco forward as Blue shoved Jadon. His chortle could be heard over the pistols and the tinny whine of weapon-arms and claxons. In a queue, they advanced down the passage. Unhindered for what felt like an eternity, they scrambled down a ladder to a lower deck, moving quickly through the shadows, avoiding clusters of Draegis running in the opposite direction.

Spotting two Lavabeasts at the other end of the passage that looked less steel military ship and more posh luxury hotel, Marco jerked her back. "No!" When she tried to wrest free, he swept around to protect her. She was clearly important to the beasts, and it'd be handy to have a Draegis on their side if they got off this ship.

She grabbed his face, her eyes uncannily ablaze. Not brown. Not even caramel, but this fierce, pale color he couldn't even name. "Trust me!"

Shamed—hadn't he told Jadon to do that very thing?—he swallowed. "You'll get killed!"

"Maybe," she said. "But I doubt it."

As if to prove her words, shots pierced the sterility of the ship yet completely avoided her. Jadon yelped, clapping a hand over his shoulder, where an angry red welt manifested.

Blue bellowed and gave another shove, through a narrow service corridor and out into the next luxury passageway—officers' quarters?

They wound through the maze, Eija in the lead, occasionally encountering minor resistance, though never a full-on force. Even as Marco fired at the beasts—the weapon's pulse no more than a slap to those impenetrable hides—he wondered if she had succeeded in nuking the *Prevenire*. If she hadn't, this was all for naught.

"Did you destroy it?" he shouted as he sighted another Draegis and aimed at the eye slits, a target that seemed to have the most slowing power against their lava-armored bodies. It was a sweet spot, soft, blinding.

"What do you think set off the alarm?" she called over her shoulder.

The *Prevenire* was gone. Marco took a calming breath. Now he just had to make sure the beasts didn't get in his head again. These demons couldn't reverse his data wipe, which meant they'd undoubtedly take every measure to ensure he did not escape.

They can try . . .

A black blur erupted from the side. He pivoted and fired, but the thing kept coming. He fired again. And again. Again. Only then did the thing start to slow—but not before it drew back its arm, a wake rippling off the front.

Reek! Marco dove into Eija, knocking her forward. Heat seared his back and he growled through it. This wasn't going to work. At this rate, they'd die on the ship.

Something grabbed him from behind and lifted him off Eija, into the air.

Suspended, Marco tried to find what held him when a sharp pinch needled his spine. *No!* Panic lit through him. That felt like the medbay injection. He struggled to free himself. Or rather . . . he thought he did, but a terrible realization hit—his limbs weren't cooperating. His mouth wouldn't open. His fist wouldn't punch.

Paralyzed!

The beast that held him turned him so they were face-to-face.

Silvermark had come to exact his vengeance.

Eija and Jadon were firing at the high-ranking beast, who seemed oblivious and unharmed.

Fear gripped Marco. He knew what they'd do—dig out the memories, find the route back to Herakles and Kedalion. To Isaura. Venom spiked in his veins. He cried out—silently—to the Lady who had spoken prophecy over him. *Please! Please help.*

Feeling infused his arm—fire. The fire of the brand. Unable to move, he couldn't see it, but the pure white glow of the brand seared the passage with its light. Marco saw it rippling over Silver's slits. The beast froze. Stumbled back, extending Marco out as if he were a rotten, repulsive dead rat.

Something flew from a panel and clamped onto Marco's forearm. Coated it. Talons dug into his flesh, and amid his growl, feeling returned to his limbs, like a million pricking needles.

Howling reverberated through the ship, Lavabeasts shrieking as they all fell still.

With a low mewling, Silvermark set Marco down, inclined his head, and backed away . . . away . . . away, until the corridor was empty.

What was going on? Why'd they stop? This had to be a trick. A ruse to trap Marco, kill the others. Though his body was no longer paralyzed, he didn't dare move, other than to glance at the thing wrapped around his arm. He shook it. Nothing happened. He tried to pry it free. No good.

"Go!" Jadon shouted and darted away. "Go go go."

Rattled, Marco took longer than usual to gather his wits. With no answers and a fire the size of Pir in his arm, he pushed himself into a sprint. He raced around the corner behind Eija and Jadon, Blue bringing up the rear. His ears rang with trepidation. This ship made no sense. It was like being immersed in a dream with all its distorted twists and turns and his limbs feeling like they were anchors. Surreal things happening that made sense one second then became even more convoluted the next.

They banked right and headed toward a bay door. In seconds, they were through it, and Marco felt a spark of hope when he spotted a small craft inside. Unbelievably, heat plumes warbled off it. The fast-attack craft was already powered up.

Blue trilled and kept moving, intent. They boarded the craft, and Marco glanced back, his heart crashing against his ribs as he saw five Draegis at the open bay door, arms powered up.

Marco aimed back, but his gaze twitched from the pulse pistol to the thing ensconcing his forearm, the brand. Had it somehow attracted the armor? Unsettled, he rotated his arm and watched the armor flex and crackle against the shield. Black formed the foundation for an intricate network of joints and flexible material. Had he not seen the thing leap from the hull and attach to his arm, and were it not for the distinctly poly-alloy joints and veins that added to its lightweight sturdiness, he wouldn't believe it himself. Despite the solid feel, it was crafted of some type of hide. On top of his wrist, two nubs sprouted silvery-blue veins that crisscrossed and ran to the underside of his arm, vanishing into a transparent material that melded . . .

Right into my brand. When his brand pulsed, so did the veins of the vambrace-like device. *What . . .?* Somehow, he felt the thing . . . vibrating deep down. Gut clenching, he flicked his wrist to dislodge it. Didn't work.

"They're not firing." Jadon backed up, past Marco. "Why aren't they firing?"

Good question. One Marco couldn't answer. Yet he felt the answer churning through the fire in his adunatos. Through the brand. Through this armored thing that now had a wake rumbling around it. *What the Reek?*

Jadon's gaze hit Marco's arm and he scowled.

"Don't ask."

"Watch out!" He shoved Marco aside as a blast seared between them and struck the elevated cockpit, where the girl and Blue were strapping in, talking hurriedly to each other in that strange language.

Jadon arched an eyebrow toward the girl and beast. "Believe me now?" They stumbled back as the bay door started closing.

Yeah, Marco saw, but whatever the connection there, it couldn't be changed right now. "Gotta let it go. Get secured."

Jadon harrumphed as he dropped into a seat behind Blue.

Forearm strangely heavy from the Draegis plating suctioned to his limb, Marco struggled with the harness of the auto-adjusting seat that molded to his body because the torso kept shortening. Apparently, Draegis were massive beings, more so than he'd realized.

Had to admit—the girl's calm, focused efflux was strange. Considering what they were facing, what was at risk, why wasn't she worried? Then again, piloting an aircraft required a lot of concentration . . . Still, there should've been some thread of concern in her Signature.

Let her worry about ensuring their escape. He was glad she was in the cockpit, because the last thing he wanted was to be plugged into a Draegis system or anything else ever again.

Light flickered through the bay door.

A hulking Draegis spirited preternaturally fast into the opening, his weaponized arm spitting off several bursts, the acrid odor scorching Marco's nostrils.

Heart in his throat and harnessed in, he couldn't escape. Couldn't hide. They could recapture him. Get the coordinates. They'd need him alive, right? Or could they somehow extract the data from his corpse? It was a very real risk he hadn't before considered. If that were true—this could be it. They'd kill him. He'd never see Isaura or their daughter.

He would not go down without a fight, though.

Instinct aimed his armored arm. Light erupted from the thing, sending a bolt of pure energy through the forcefield, across the deck, and straight into the beast. The creature evaporated even as its volley bounced off the very shield Marco's shot had penetrated, causing it to ripple with a strange blue-silver shimmer.

The hatch groaned shut as the ship lifted from the flight deck.

"What the scuz was that?" Jadon shouted, his voice carrying through comms that operated across their seats. He stared wide-eyed at Marco, apparently still as shocked as he was at the blast from the armor clinging to his forearm like some self-aware vambrace.

Marco felt another pinch at the back of his neck, his PICC-line receiving a cold jolt as the craft shot forward. Pinned in the crash couch, he felt his tangled thoughts coalesce into one drive: survival.

They dove hard. He gripped the armrests as they went into what he could only describe as a death dive. Breath in the back of his throat, he struggled to shift his gaze, angle his head to see the cockpit where Blue sat with Eija on his right.

Our lives are in the hands of a Draegis.

The thought terrified him.

Pain-wracked tremors clawed his spine as Roman struggled to move. A great weight pressed against his back, pinning him to the ground, face down. Eyes burning, he coughed. Disorientation collapsed and in rushed a thousand thoughts. The light. Dust and rancid panic. Searing odor of accelerant that threw him toward—

Isaura!

Blinking the grit and smoke from his eyes, Roman shifted to see what held him down. A large plaster column stretched across his back. He growled as he struggled onto all fours. Pushed to no avail. "Isaura." Where was she? Was she injured?

The weight against his back suddenly vanished.

Startled, Roman looked back as Ramirus and Ulixes hoisted aside the heavy column. Shoulder screaming, he scuttled free and hopped to his feet. "Where is the queen?" Gritting against the pain, he turned a circle, searching the debris. "Isaura! Find her!" His heart punched against his ribs as he bent, shoving aside fallen chunks of the roof. "She was right here!" He'd been hurrying her to safety.

"We must take shelter," Ramirus urged. "The remaining columns are unsteady."

Roman glanced to where the Brethren indicated, saw plaster dribbling from a trembling column. "Not until she is found." He pivoted, cradling his shoulder as he studied the disarray, knowing she was here somewhere. "Find her!"

Worried, he scanned the forms, covered in dust and some in blood, moving through the hazy hall that lay half in ruins. Sunlight shoved itself through the gaping hole that had once been the southern wall, the sea glittering spitefully in the distance. Stained glass from the eastern and western walls clung to the frames but were at risk of destruction. Bloodied and haggard, a guard crawled from the crater of what had been the dais. Across the way, Vorn helped Aliria, who was holding her bloodied skirts, her face streaked with dark rivulets from her tears.

Ancient, help us!

"Skyships!" someone shouted. "I saw skyships dropping something."

Symmachia. Anger churned as Roman wheeled back to the area around him. "Isaura! The kyria is missing!"

Focus yourself, Kynigos!

He drew in a long, shaky breath as he probed the mounds, bodies. Shrieks of grief matched the sharp scent of death stinging his receptors. Stark red blood gaped against the gray of ash and dust. He scoured the wafting effluxes for her Signature. *Show me . . .* He saw the battered form of Sasada's ruler. The sobbing princess, cradling the bloodied head of a wounded prince. Sergii unlucky enough to have been along the wall were obliterated. Rage sparked through his veins. It was preventable. Unnecessary. On so many levels.

"We must go," Ramirus urged.

"Find her!" Roman ordered. "Do it, or I will end you myself!"

You are much moved by emotions, he chastised himself as his hunters resumed the search.

Roman had seen worse. Knew the prophecies. Knew what was coming. But the losses this time were so . . . personal.

Out of the blue, he recalled what he'd detected in the seconds before that fetor of fuel hit his receptors. Definitely preventable.

They were still here—those who liked to remain hidden, conceal their presence yet intrude into the lives of others. "Show me!" he demanded. The fragrance of their realm was unmistakable. "I sense you! I know you are here. Where is she? Do not let *her* die on your watch, too!"

Ramirus and Ulixes gave him a furtive glance before turning their gazes on what they obviously anak'd as well.

Gritty air could not hide the flare of illumination. He yanked around to face it. A primal shout scraped his throat even as he took in the glow of armor over a fiery form.

In that tick, beneath those powerful rays of light, he saw —a gown! "Isaura!" He surged toward the hem of that illuminated being and found the kyria. The light guardian crouched over her, protecting her. A fragrance of reassurance washed over his receptors.

Though she bore a large knot and had blood on her temple, Isaura was largely unharmed.

"You protected her." Roman nodded his thanks.

Familiar violet eyes met his in the thin veil that separated their worlds. *"She will need rest."*

"You could have protected all in this hall."

Grief emanated from her. *"She is necessary for what must come."*

"Marco," he guessed.

She shifted back and stood, her armor and wings bleeding into the air. *"Alana—"*

Wings snapped him into silence. Forced him to look away—down into the face of the woman who held the future in her hands . . . and womb. Duly diverted, Roman scooped her off the debris-littered floor and straightened.

"Is she . . .?" Doublet torn and dusty, the grand duke was worse for the wear, but his efflux betrayed ill hope that the kyria had not survived, that power would be restored to his own hands.

Disgusted with the man, Roman turned and shouldered past him. "You will not have the throne." His priority was to ensure Isaura's safety and that she received prompt medical attention.

"That is not—I did not mean—"

"Get my queen to the ship!" Vorn motioned two Furymark, who carried an injured Aliria, toward a scout waiting on the shoreline. He saw Roman navigating the rubble with Isaura in his arms. "Here! Bring her."

Gratefully, Ramirus and Ulixes assisted him in getting down to the lower level, past the wounded crying out in pain.

Vorn scanned the crumbling hall. "Furymark—tend the wounded. Set up triage. We'll bring Vipers and use whatever medpods are necessary. Understood?"

"Yes, Your Majesty."

He eyed Roman, then the precious cargo he carried. "My ship—there is a medbay with two medpods. Come!"

Following the king, Roman negotiated the crowded passage into a cavern that held the ship. As he hurried across the deck, he heard Aliria's staccato breaths from where she labored in the medpod that had shifted into a birthing chair. With the aid of Ulixes, Roman laid Isaura in the tube, tapped the panel, and the pod activated. Closed over her. He initiated the treatment sequence. Tubes snaked into her arms, feeding her both saline and any nutrients the pod detected she needed.

Hands on the clear shield, he stared at her still form and swallowed. Marco would never forgive him if she died. He sniffed—he'd never forgive himself.

"They can track us here," Ulixes said quietly. "Symmachian tech is far beyond this scout's."

"No." Vorn spoke from where he held Aliria's hand as she breathed through a contraction. "Jubbah secured stealth tech for our ships and installed it for this very reason." Worry tightened his expression as he monitored his queen. "For now, we shelter with the ships."

"Stealth tech is useless!" Ramirus spat. "Besides, Droseran pilots are far from ready for flight, let alone aerial combat."

A concussion slammed the ship, the hull vibrating as if Symmachia agreed. Or sent a warning.

Vorn shoved to his feet. Punched the bulkhead of the ship. "Cowards!" He lasered Roman with a glower. "Infuriating—to have the means to fight back but be too late. The ships are beneath our feet, and I can do nothing but watch those skycrawlers slaughter my people!"

Ulixes sneered. "Long have I despised Tascan Command, but this . . ." He gave a grave shake of his head. "Authorizing an assault against a people at such a significant tactical disadvantage . . . Repulsive."

"Evil does not play by the rules of civility," Roman said quietly, silently beseeching Isaura to rally, to heal.

Aliria cried out, then strangled it as she struggled to bring her child into the world.

There was much to do, and Roman felt it inappropriate to remain as Aliria labored. He removed himself to another corner of the medbay to give the couple privacy but would not leave until Isaura stabilized. He leaned against the bulkhead, then slid down into a crouch, his legs and shoulder aching.

"Symmachia violated the Accord," Ramirus said, stating the obvious.

"They did that when they took Marco," countered Ulixes.

"Aye, but we must yet prove that. This . . ." Reviewing satellite images via his vambrace, Roman nodded wearily to the wreckage of Forgelight. "Symmachia has started a war." A war they'd known was coming. A war tied to the *Trópos tis Fotiás* prophecy brand.

The attack here was no accident. It'd been strategic. Intended to eliminate as many rulers as possible from Drosero. To weaken the defenses. The will to fight.

In the shelter of the caves, the lusty cry of Vorn and Aliria's son defied the savagery perpetrated against their people.

ORBITING ROHILEK, KURU SYSTEM

Boom! Crack!

Sparks glittered on the bulkhead of the craft they'd absconded with, rattling as if an enormous jolt had hit the ship.

"What was that?" Jadon shouted over the din.

"Shields," Eija hollered from the upper deck of the cockpit, where she sat beside Blue. "They took out our shields."

Which meant it'd be easy for the Draegis to do serious damage to this craft, if not blow it out of the sky.

Marco gritted his teeth, the harness biting into his right clavicle as Daq'Ti put them in a hard burn. Escape would mean outmaneuvering. This would be interesting—Blue fleeing his own kind. The same beasts who had the same training on the same ships.

"Where's he taking us?" Jadon called to the girl.

Eija didn't answer, her head bent to the brightly lit array over which her fingers danced as if she'd operated one all her life.

"Where we going, Eija? We safe with him?"

Again, no answer.

Jadon slid Marco a concerned look with an efflux that toed the line of outright fear, then he again eyed the Draegis armor attached to Marco's arm.

The thing didn't resemble a Kynigos vambrace, but the way it cocooned his forearm felt like one. Save the prickling pain this thing generated along his nerves. Marco wanted it off, but couldn't figure out how to remove it. Besides, maybe it'd prove helpful. The way it'd shot off that volley could come in handy. Yet he saw the questions Jadon wasn't asking and wondered the same—would this thing somehow turn Marco into a Draegis?

And why wasn't Eija responding? Initially, he'd thought her distracted with piloting, but now . . . now he wondered if it was more. Had Jadon been right? Was her loyalty compromised? Did something happen to *her* when she made that handprint connection with Blue?

Marco clenched his jaw but said nothing. He was no Draegis. And even if Eija was somehow aligned with Blue now, there wasn't a thing they could do about it. At least between Eija's and Blue's piloting skills, they had a reasonable chance of survival. For now.

Thunk-groaaaan-pop!

The ship shuddered. Jerked Marco forward as if someone had gripped the back of his head and slammed it.

Jadon cursed, touched his mouth. Blood dripped down his chin.

"Lost navigation!" Eija announced as her chair swiveled toward different instrumentation panels. "Daq'Ti said it's not a problem."

Right. Not being able to control where you were going wasn't a problem.

Marco eyed the beast. Dug through that confusing efflux that somehow seemed ever easier to rifle through. He caught a whiff of confidence buoying him, but there was also faint concern. Blue no doubt knew exactly how to cripple their ships—it was the way of a pilot and his craft, knowing every in and out, electrical system, engines, weapons . . .

"Djelling—" Eija ducked some unseen enemy.

Sparks danced along the bulkhead. Had weapons' fire shorted out another system? Smoke filled the cabin. Alarms screamed through the ship.

Daq'Ti bellowed something over the din that sounded a lot like, "Hold."

The roar and violent vibrations of shoving through atmosphere rattled Marco's teeth for several terrifying seconds, making it abundantly clear that wherever they were headed was on planet—what had Eija called it? Rohilek. Friction warred to dig its destructive fingers into the hull and pry the ship apart, but the thermal shielding held.

The roar vanished. A strange silence hung throughout the ship, and there was a release of tension—a burgeoning sense of hope that they'd just improved their chances of making land without dying by clearing the atmosphere. Not a huge improvement, but one all the same. Getting into the atmo was one thing. Making it to the surface safely was another. If Draegis ships were still on them, this could be for naught.

Daq'Ti bellowed.

"Hold on!" Eija shouted. "We've lost main propulsion!"

Deafening, terrifying silence once more crackled into existence.

The ship nosedived. Marco's gut clenched. Pain chomped into his clavicle. He grimaced and held on tight as the craft canted left, then right. Jerked around. His head sunk into the back of the seat as Blue fought to steer the ship into some semblance of an emergency landing.

Peering up and around the various consoles and seats to the upper deck, he eyed the beast piloting the craft. Never in his life had Marco expected to be so wholly at the mercy of a being that looked more death and darkness than human. And yet, it struck him, even amid the grating alarms, flashing lights, and punishing g's, that Blue's shoulders seemed more pronounced now, less . . . glob-like. He thought of the Draegis he and Jadon had killed in the brig. Larger. Much larger.

Marco had been so mortified when they'd first encountered the Draegis, he'd seen them more as diabolus-reborn than living, breathing beings. And this one was fighting for all he was worth to control an out-of-control craft. If they had a prayer—it was Blue.

The shield in the cockpit popped. Webbed cracks threw the light of a powerful sun in a thousand directions.

If they were going to die, there was nothing Marco could do. At least they'd destroyed the *Prevenire*. Protected the Quadrants. The bone-crushing power of gravity against his body pummeled him. He gripped the seat tight and again closed his eyes. No way they could come out of this one.

Isaura . . .

He saw her in his arms again, that current of flaxen hair a halo arrayed around her and glittering in the light of the firepit. This was where she belonged, where he belonged. Together, in the comfort of each other. He pushed into the dreamscape, away from the near-death experience engulfing him.

"There is nowhere I'd rather be."

She levered upright and peered down into his eyes, her tawny complexion glowing . . . yet . . . hazy. Though she did not speak it, he knew she begged for his return. Reminded him that she needed him.

"I am here, Isa. Where I want to be—with you." When he reached for her, the haze proved thicker. Dulled the sense of togetherness. Though he cupped and lifted her face to meet his in a long-awaited kiss, though he sensed it to be tender, there was something different. Something . . . separating. He willed himself into the dream deeper, forced back the awareness of the chaos consuming the plummeting ship.

Do not lose yourself.

Swiping a thumb along her cheek, he frowned. Lose myself? Was that not the point of marriage, of these dreams?

As the veil thickened, gathering more distance in its arms, Isaura brushed her hand against his bearded jaw. She said something . . . about someone coming, but the haze struggled with her words.

"Who?"

Panic retched into the dream.

Tears pooled in Isaura's eyes, then slipped free and splatted his cheek as she bent and kissed him gently, firmly. Her arms encircled his neck as she lay with him, her face resting near his throat.

"Who?" *Desperation choked him. Alarm grew that he could not feel the swell of their child between them.* "Isaura! What is this?" *Who did she warn him about?*

She lifted her gaze. Blood sped down the side of her face from a gash at her temple. Her lip was cut and bleeding, her eye nearly swollen shut.

"Isaura! What—" *Anger tightened his chest. He swatted the haze, trying to clear it—like fog on glass—but it did no good. No!*

"Do not worry about her or the babe. They are in Her hands."

The voice was not Isaura's. Who? What—what was going on? Marco lunged, but the dream fell away. The haze victorious, Isaura was gone. Lost in the abysmal void that devoured him, held him hostage. "Isaura!" Her name echoed through a cavern of darkness.

Groaning, Eija struggled to free herself of the oppressive weight restraining her. She moaned and pushed at the thing against her shoulder. Jagged pain tortured her body. Arching her spine, she cried out, adrenaline snapping her awake. Slumping back, she realized her fingers were sticky. Mentally, she knew there was blood—but from what? Her blurred vision and mind wouldn't make sense of the distorted scene around her.

"Careful," a voice trilled. "You're injured."

"Reef . . ." she murmured, the fog of unconsciousness lifting. Relief whispered through her body, not only that she had survived, but that he had, too.

"I'm here, Ei, but this beast won't let me near you."

The sound of a scuffle ensued—a huff, a thud, a few more thuds, then a shout. A chortle-growl.

"Back down, BeastieBoy," Reef ground out. "I was here first."

Wait. Eija blinked furiously, her thoughts a jumbled knot.

The shape returned and zoomed into focus.

She went cold at the red slits staring back. Undulating ashen black surrounded those eyes. "What . . .?" The few beats her heart skipped seemed trapped in her throat as she realized it hadn't been Reef extricating her from the harness. "Daq'Ti." Something about his nearness proved disconcerting, strange—her brain finally processed it: *he* was changed. Different.

You've djelling lost it. The crash—it'd addled her brain.

"With care, Xonim," Daq'Ti trilled, the noise gentler, less . . . beastly.

Eija frowned, trying to discern if it was her imagination or—

No. No, his eyes were definitely changing. Still red, but less . . . slitted. More full, though not quite oval. "I don't . . . How are you . . .?"

He pried her harness apart with little trouble, and she stole a greedy breath of sanitized air. Clearly his strength hadn't changed, but his lavalike skin had resolved to an ashen gray that mirrored plague-infected Tryssinians.

Right—not creepy at all.

The ship suddenly canted. Dropped. With a yelp, Eija dug her fingers into the armrests, her rear still sliding left.

Reef, his balance upended by the jolt, stumbled into her couch. As the hull groaned in complaint, he fell forward but steadied himself, narrowly avoiding a full-on collision with her by planting his hands on either side of her couch. "Slag."

"Keep still," she hissed, doing her best not to stare into his brown eyes. Or to let her thundering heart betray her. *It's just fear, that's all.*

"Trying."

They hesitated, waiting for more shifting, for a heavier, bigger fall. For death.

Reef's gaze held hers. A smirk hit his dark eyes, mischievous. "If you wanted me in your lap, all you had to do was ask, Ei. Didn't have to knock the ship off its support."

There went those beats again. Eija shifted. Swallowed, hating the effect he had on her, yet . . . glad for it, too.

Daq'Ti chortled.

Reef flinched, apparently expecting the same blow from the Draegis as she did. "Easy, BeastieBoy," he muttered.

But Daq'Ti's eye slits glowed brighter.

"Maybe you should step off." Eija focused on their dilemma. She nudged him aside and pulled herself upright, which was tough with the ship listing portside, threatening to drag them down. Her foot slid on the deck.

Reef hooked an arm around her waist, angled his leg against hers, forcing her to draw in a breath.

What was he doing?

Daq'Ti's chortling warned he didn't like the close proximity. Though Eija certainly wouldn't complain, this wasn't really the time for . . . whatever this was. But then she felt the clunk of his boot against hers and the subtle magnetic pull of the deck against the back of her legs.

"Oh." Amused at how effortlessly he'd used his own boots to magnetize hers, she felt foolish for having thought it was something . . . else. "What happened—did the dreadnought hit us?" She did, however, notice that he took his time removing himself from her personal zone.

Reef grinned, unfazed by the intimacy of their position. "Could be, but it'd be weird."

"Why?"

"They were all over us when we broke atmo, but it's been quiet since. If they were targeting us, they could have easily destroyed us since we crashed."

Daq'Ti trilled his objection and pushed Reef away from Eija.

Reef thrust the hand aside. "Get off me, BeastieBoy."

Her Draegis protector seemed to grow by several feet as he bellowed, the encounter reminding her of docuvids of otherworld animals guarding their territory.

Reef went livid. Pitched himself at Daq'Ti.

Eija scrambled around and wedged between them. "Whoa-whoa-whoa!" Holding them both at arm's length, she struggled with the way the odd angle exerted gravity against her—which, nice to know Rohilek had gravity at least close to 1g. Both palms rose and fell on their chests that heaved from the anger roiling through these two. She homed in on Reef. "What's wrong with you?"

"*Me*? He wouldn't let me near you. I've been trying for the last six hours."

"Six—*what*?" Eija jerked to Daq'Ti, then back. "Are you kidding me?"

"It was dark when I came to." Reef shrugged and motioned to Daq'Ti. "He was moving around but wouldn't let me check your head wound."

Reflexively, Eija touched her temple, which she finally registered was throbbing. Ah, so that's where the blood came from. The blood was drying, so she guessed the injury wasn't too bad. "I'm fine." Her gaze hit her protector's. "How'd we land? They were firing . . . we were *crashing*."

Daq'Ti bobbed his head. "We come in fast, but they stay with us. The only way to evade was to cut engines, go out of control."

"Hold up." Reef twitched and frowned. "The spin—that was you?" His eyes went wide. "You put us into a spin to make them think we were crashing."

"Unfortunate but necessary."

So that's why they'd blacked out.

"You could've killed us."

"No," Daq'Ti said. "I am skill at flying this ship. We hit hard, then drop."

Was it her imagination again or was he talking more clearly? "You mean, we dropped, then hit hard."

He stared back but said nothing.

"We *crashed*," came Reef's gruff intrusion. "Does it matter if Lavabeast gets his human grammar mixed up?"

She supposed not. Disoriented and shocked, she sidestepped. Her grav boot collided with a tool case that must've come loose in the *fake* crash landing. Strips of metal dangled from the bulkhead, and she eyed the hole in the side of the hull. Fake crash landing but not-so-fake ship damage. Only . . . there was something weird about that hole. Then again, wasn't everything weird right now?

Once more she looked at Daq'Ti. "How long have we been here?"

"One journey of Coliex and Ju'Mar," he said.

"One journey—is that their version of a day?"

"I don't know." She gave Daq'Ti a sidelong glance. "Is it just me, or is he easier to understand?"

Consternation crawled through the smooth planes of Reef's face as the realization hit him, too. "Yeah, and I don't like it."

Daq'Ti's voice *was* different. Less trilling-rumbling. More . . . human. She shuddered at the realization as she studied him, trying to comprehend what was going on. Aboard the dreadnought, she'd attributed her perception of change to merely getting used to the startling appearance of the Draegis. Now, however, there was no doubt—he *was* changing. As in *transforming*. But how? How was that possible? "Daq'Ti . . ."

Something in his gaze seemed sad, ashamed, and pushed hers away. That's when she spotted an unmoving Marco and, next to his leg, a hole in the hull that exposed them to the hot, dry planet. "Marco!"

"He's okay," Reef said, joining her. "I checked him earlier. No visible injuries and his heart rate is normal. He's unconscious, but okay."

Eija touched the hunter's shoulder. "Marco." Internal injuries were possible . . . but unlikely, since his vitals were stable. "Hey, you with us?"

Eyelids fluttered. His icily pale eyes rolled to her. "Yeah." Barely a breath, the word seemed to hurt him.

"Are you injured? Hurting anywhere?"

"No." Groggily, he struggled to lift his head.

"If Shad was here, she could run a full scan . . ." But she wasn't. They weren't sure any of their friends were alive, and it'd been impossible to find out what happened to the others who'd jettisoned before making the hyperjump to Kuru. "You sure you're okay?"

"Yeah." Marco sighed.

Why did he seem bereft all of a sudden?

Reef braced himself in the shorn hull, then glanced at the hole near Marco. "Guess the air's not toxic."

"Could be we just haven't felt the effects," Eija noted. Or maybe they were—oxygen deprivation could account for the perceived changes in Daq'Ti. Right? Could've made them a little loopy. Though she'd be disappointed if this was as loopy as she got—hearing some alien creature better.

"We'd know if it was toxic," Reef said.

"We can't be sure of that or anything at this point," Eija growled.

"Your BeastieBoy would be clamoring to save you, so"—Reef bounced his shoulders, one of which sported a nasty scorch mark—"no threat."

She ignored his nickname reference as Marco sat up and faltered. What was with the armor clinging to his forearm? It'd become a weapon powerful enough to kill a Draegis, and it looked similar to Daq'Ti's arm when it powered up. Should she be worried that the hunter might change, too?

Marco noted her studying his arm and shifted away. Squinted at the hole, his left cheek twitching beneath those pale irises that were now a creepy silver. If not for the thin black line separating the iris from the white of his eye . . . yeah, she got jeebies thinking about it.

A loud, metallic groan startled Eija—and she felt herself flying backward. Felt a searing fire across her arm even as her back slammed against one of the crash couches. She coughed the air from her lungs and blinked to get her bearings. *What the . . .?*

Her gaze swept the interior. Daq'Ti had pitched her out of the way of a support that had swung loose and now pinned—

"Marco!" With a yelp, she threw herself toward him.

Reef shoved against the beam. "It's crushing him!"

"Can't . . . breathe . . ." Marco groaned.

Daq'Ti pushed himself between Marco and the beam, which he gripped. The digits of his hand seemed more distinct and jointed, rather than the moving molten form that easily shifted to form his weapon. With a chortling growl, he pushed.

The beam lifted.

Marco's eyes widened, and he rasped a breath as he rolled out of his crash couch. He landed on his knees, a hand to his side. Slowly, he unfolded himself, again looking at the large steel beam that had attacked him, but then his gaze settled on the hole in the ship. And stayed there, a frown deepening beneath his long black hair.

What was he looking at?

Eija searched for an explanation and . . . decided there *was* something wrong about that hole. Some oddness that wouldn't let her ignore it. Wanted attention because it meant . . . something. "What is it?" whispering, she joined him, almost afraid to ask, to know. Because this? It felt like a game changer.

Djell. Hadn't they already had enough of that?

"The metal isn't flexing *inward.*" Marco moved his gaze very slowly to Daq'Ti, a stiff tension roiling between the two. His finger danced below that strange Draegis armor on his arm—as if powering it up. "It bows *outward.*"

Why hadn't she pieced it together? "The dreadnought blew a hole in it," she said, knowing it was wrong, yet her brain wouldn't let her voice anything different.

"No." Reef's brown eyes were strange, dark. "That would cause *inward* bowing. And it'd be uniform."

Which also meant the hole wasn't from the crash or from hitting some structure.

Only one possibility: someone or something had forced its way out. And the only one among them who could do that . . .

Her stomach squirmed. "Daq'Ti."

Marco's jaw muscle twitched as his gaze took in something else. Something Eija wasn't sure she wanted to see or know about. "How long were you out?" he asked Reef.

"No idea. It was dark when I came to."

Marco nodded. "It was daylight when we broke atmo."

"Yeah."

She understood their thoughts, what they didn't say. That Daq'Ti had been the only one conscious long enough to have slipped away and . . . "What? You think he's betraying us?"

Marco's sober gaze met hers.

"That makes no djelling sense. He saved us—nearly got killed helping us escape."

"Did he?" Marco asked. "He seemed to always know how to avoid them. Gets away unscathed every time."

"Because they're his people—he knows their tactics, their weapons."

"Yeah."

She was losing this argument. "Why would he come back and play dumb if they were coming for us?"

"To be sure we didn't escape," Reef said.

"We already escaped!"

"Easy." Marco locked onto Daq'Ti, who hadn't moved, responded, or intervened, though she was clearly distressed.

What did that mean? Eija shifted, desperation curling through her midsection. "Tell them!" Her heart thrashed. "Tell them you didn't betray us."

Daq'Ti lifted a pack to her. "We should go. Sun's too hot. Draegis coming."

"Go where?" Marco challenged.

Slits pulsing, Daq'Ti stood facing Marco as if waiting for him to do or say something. Then, he glanced out the hole he'd made. "The ridge. I scouted— there are caves."

They all looked in that direction but saw nothing. Then Eija realized the very thin wavering heat wakes on the horizon, which she'd thought were striations of rock, were actually elevations. The horizon slowly morphed into the skyline of a city with strange red hexagonal structures jutting up from the surface. "Djell." That had to be a day's walk. Newfound fears over Daq'Ti digging out of the craft and scouting that distance dug into her shallow arguments, making her question . . . everything.

Reef cocked his head. "Drop, shop, and crop."

That Eidolon mantra had always sounded dumb to her, but its meaning carried—drop into a location, shop around for the objective, and return with the crop of whatever they'd gone after.

In other words—get it done.

She hated the uncertainty that followed her off the craft and into the Rohilek desert. More than the uncertainty, she hated the nagging thought that by crossing the terrain, Daq'Ti was marching them to their deaths. But no sooner had they covered the first klick than they heard the screaming shrieks of Draegis ships.

Maybe she shouldn't have been so quick to side with the Lavabeast.

"Why me? Why did you give me the brand?"

"Trust, Child."

"But of what use am I? Why did you mark me?" Kersei demanded of the veiled figure she knew to be the Ancient, though His face remained hidden. "To what end? Tell me! Marco is gone—likely dead. My bound has betrayed not only me but the realm. The woman on the throne is a village girl, who—I grant—is beautiful and sweet but knows nothing of ruling."

She braced her belly, which churned like the rest of her. Groaning, she knew she stood on treacherous ground, railing at the Ancient like this, but she must know. "And me? Me . . . I am the size of a rhinnock! Fat with the child of a traitor!"

"Seek peace, Kersei."

"Do You not see? There is war. Marco is missing. It is hopeless! Useless! I thought You had a purpose, a way for us to survive what was coming . . ." She looked at her brand, pulsing and burning with a renewed fire in recent days. "What use is it? I do nothing but get sick and wait to be free of this child!" She gasped, stumbling back, disbelieving the words that had escaped her lips. Holding her belly, she sought to hug the child she had just cast aside with careless words. "I beg Your mercy . . . My words were ill-spoken."

His hand, glowing hot, reached toward her. "The child is a gift. Treasure him. Remember!" Even as His fingertips touched her swollen womb, a deluge of rain overtook her. Blotted out the light that was the Ancient. Forced her to blink and shrink back. She felt the water around her . . . soaking her omnirs, the cream brocade darkening in an ever-growing arc down her legs.

Kersei cried out, jolting awake. Darkness crowded her, the stone ceiling far too close. She couldn't breathe. Sweaty, curls sticking to her face and neck, she levered herself up. Warm liquid pulsed between her legs, and she choked a sob.

"No," she gasped. Her waters had broken. "No no no." Hot tears shoved down her cheeks. "It is too soon. Please, please . . ."

Ma'ma emerged from the shadows.

Kersei strangled a cry. "M-my water—"

"I told you the child was restless." Quietly Ma'ma moved around the room, opening one cupboard then another.

"It is not time," Kersei choked out, terrified her child would die for the words she had hastily spoken. "I should have another fortnight!"

"Your son has decided now is the time." Ma'ma and two other women quickly stripped Kersei down. They put her in a clean shift before transferring her to a room with soft-glowing touchstones and a well in the middle. "In you go. Carefully."

Kersei startled. "*In* the water?"

"It is the way we give birth."

"But in Stratios—"

"This is the way among Faa'Cris."

"But—"

Something in Ma'ma's gaze silenced her—that and the strong band tightening across her middle. Kersei grimaced, the sensation again snatching her breath.

"A contraction." Ma'ma nodded to the other women, who inclined their heads, then she wrapped an arm around Kersei's waist. "Up into the sanitatem."

Kersei took a step as another wave hit her. Trembling, she drew in a breath and let it out shakily, her vision blurring with tears. "Nay, I do not want to do this—"

"In that you have no choice now," Ma'ma said with a laugh.

"I am frightened."

"Not surprising. Bringing a child into the world is a terrific task. Now, into the well." Ahead of her, Ma'ma led her up the last step.

Kersei saw a strange series of supports in the basin, along with a ledge and what might be a seat. "Strange . . ." She eyed the arcs and bars in the water and realized they were for her to lean forward against and rest her arms. Hold on to, she imagined, during the worst of the labor.

"It will support your body while you labor and aid the birth." Ma'ma's entrance into the well stirred the waters as she turned and guided Kersei in.

Warm, silky liquid cocooned her. Once seated and over the initial shock of being in what amounted to a bath, Kersei shivered a smile. "It's not water."

"Not wholly." Ma'ma adjusted Kersei's garments for modest coverage that did not hinder delivery.

Nestled into the hold of the sanitatem, Kersei relaxed. "I cannot believe this."

"Most women feel that way."

"No, I mean you." Kersei eyed her as that band again constricted. She drew in a breath, slowly released it, wincing through the pain.

"Those aren't very far apart. Your son is impatient."

"Like his father," Kersei mumbled, blowing a curl out of her eyes, then batting it back.

Ma'ma glanced at her. "It is the first you have mentioned of Darius."

An odd ache wiggled through her over the mention of him. Over what she had done. Kersei stroked the bath, finding it calming.

"You left him."

"He is a traitor and coward." As Ma'ma rubbed her back, Kersei monitored the other women entering with supplies, leaving, then returning with more. A bed, linens, clothes, blankets . . . However, she could not shake his face from her mind. "Do you know what he did?"

"We do."

"Then you see Darius *is* a traitor. He betrayed Marco, Kalonica, even me!"

"Indeed he committed treason against the crown—"

"He killed you and Father! Adara!" Kersei exclaimed.

"That he did not."

Kersei screwed up her face through another contraction, breathing in . . . out . . . "I mean . . ." Another breath . . . "It is true you are alive, but—"

"No, Kersei." Ma'ma drew her hair back and secured it, unwittingly massaging Kersei's scalp, which proved relaxing. "Darius is not responsible for Stratios. That was Theon, an iereas given to depravity, aligning himself with evil."

Kersei scowled. "No—he admitted it. On trial. They stripped him of his title."

"I am aware of the punishment meted out, but I assure you, the violence perpetrated against Stratios was done at the hands of Theon—"

Kersei gasped as a band seized her, then breathed through it. She would not argue with her ma'ma. "I thought it would be painful, but this mostly steals my breath."

"The sanitatem is helping, healing, but you are yet at the beginning, Kersei."

Only the beginning? "You said he was impatient . . ."

Ma'ma laughed. "As is his mother, apparently." She smoothed a warm cloth over Kersei's brow and neck. "My daughter giving birth . . ."

Kersei sighed through a smile, suddenly grateful. Very grateful to have

Ma'ma here. To be seen and known and loved again. They sat in quiet for a good while as her body readied itself to release the child within. Then a thought surprised—she had not imagined doing this *without* Darius. Strange, surreal to have Ma'ma here for the birth when she had believed her dead. "Parts of me fathom this a hallucination."

"I assure you, I am not."

"But how . . . how are you here—alive?" Kersei saw three women enter the large, open room. This time they didn't have supplies. They simply strode toward the well, folded their hands, and . . . waited. In earnest, she did not want an audience. "Must they be here?"

"All our offspring enter the world attended by the Resplendent. Be glad for the Ladies."

Kersei's gaze snapped to her mother's. "What say you?" Her heart thundered in her chest. She recalled what foul Captain Baric said on the *Macedon*. Nicea. "Lady of Basilikas." She straightened, looking at the women then back to Ma'ma. "You're a Lady." Myles had vowed as much but it was still too much to believe. "How . . .? It cannot be."

"Being Faa'Cris is how I survived and part of why you bore the brand—the blood in your veins."

"But"—Kersei shook her head—"you had three daughters. You stayed with Father, did not—" A powerful contraction hit, suffocating her words. She bent into it, wrapping an arm around her hard belly.

"Breathe, Kersei," Ma'ma whispered. "Your body will deliver the child. Do not fight it."

"What if something is wrong?"

"It is not." Her mother's words were so definitive. So decisive. "Just breathe."

"But you stayed," she grunted, unable to let go of that small fact. The contraction abated. "It is said that once a Daughter is born, Ladies return to Deversoria with the child. But you had three, and we remained at Stratios—with you. It is impossible you are a Lady." Yet the proof knelt beside her.

"Have you chosen a name?" Ma'ma clearly sought to divert the conversation.

Tired, Kersei rested on the well supports, thinking of the many arguments with Darius over the name their son would bear. "We could not agree. He wanted Zarek."

"You wanted Xylander," Ma'ma supplied.

"We considered both but could not even agree which should come first. I told him X was before Z in the alphabet, but he scoffed, said Zarek was a medora, Xylander an elder, so Zarek should be first." She lifted her head. "However, Darius is not here"—strange how that made her throat raw—"so the naming is left to me. My son will be Xylander."

"A decision made in haste may later be full of regret."

Surprised at the words, she considered her mother. "I thought that would please you, naming him after Father."

Countenance no longer serene, Ma'ma looked down. The ache and loss palpable between them. A shared grief.

"Myles said they buried him, but he also said . . ." Kersei would push for an answer. "He said they could not find you—or Adara. Is she here? Lexina? You would not answer earlier." Her heart spasmed.

"Please, do not think on these things. Relax. Focus on your son, who is fighting his way into the world."

"They are gone." She believed Ma'ma would have said if they were alive. "Why did my sisters not survive when you did?"

Her mother held her gaze, as if in a moment of silence, then yielded. "I survived because I was first a Lady who studied here for a long while before being commissioned. Only once I was fully trained did I seek out Xylander."

"Trained in what?"

"We will talk of this later—"

"Wait . . ." A curious thought pushed into her selfish, tired musings. "Does this—you said . . ." She straightened a little, the water lapping gently against her shoulders. Why had it not registered before? "Am I a Lady?"

Ma'ma traced her face with those large eyes that were once gray and now radiated violet but always—*always*—held mystery and elegance in one effortless glint. And more than a little disappointment that seemed yet to search for something in Kersei that did not exist. "Technically, yes."

The words struck like a bolt of lightning. Kersei could scarce breathe. Slowly, wonder spilled through her. Locked in the moment with Ma'ma, she did not know how to respond, what to think, what—

Pain writhed through her body. She yelped and curled in on herself. Worked through the contraction, her mind somehow settling back on her father. As the pain receded—mostly, an ache lingered that stirred nausea— Kersei thought of her father. Missed him. Imagined how, had he lived, he would have taken this child under his wing to train him in the way of the machitis. "I think Father would have been proud for my son to bear his name."

"Indeed."

"He was the best of men, was he not?" *Well, besides Marco . . .* "It is a good, strong name—like him." She eyed her ma'ma again. "Did you love him too much to leave Stratios? Is that why you did not come back here?"

Ma'ma darted a look to the Ladies before lowering her gaze. "It is true I chose him over my Sisters."

"I would not choose that." Kersei regretted how quickly she spoke it. What that said of her, of her anger toward Darius . . . A curious thing pinched in her heart that the anger was there. Still. It seemed a fool thing to choose a man over the Faa'Cris. She could not imagine!

Now, were that man Marco . . .

Aye, she could well imagine.

"Guard your thoughts, Daughter," Ma'ma's voice whispered against her conscience.

Cringing beneath the remonstration, Kersei felt ashamed. But then she jerked, stunned to realize Ma'ma had not spoken with her mouth.

"You may have thrown away the paper that bound your life to Darius, but by the sacred oaths you spoke—"

"He betrayed us and Marco. Killed Father, Adara!"

"No," Ma'ma spoke aloud this time. "That was the hand of the adversary. Well may he have used Darius, but do not mistake the messenger for the one responsible."

"Messenger? Darius stole *everything* from me! By *his* own will, no one else's."

"You never were able to see anyone else's pain past your own."

Bewildered, Kersei gaped. "And you never allowed me the pain I felt."

"You are wrong—I allowed, but you wallowed." Ma'ma angled her head, a strange glow around her just then. "How long will you wallow, Kersei? Your child struggles for birth, and you are yet fixed on a man not your own, nurturing fetid seeds of discord. Why? In the hopes that *you* can have Marco one day?"

"I will!" she cried out, her vision blurring as she thrust her arm up, water sluicing over the well. "The brand ties us together! This says *I* was supposed to be with him. He loved me—*I* loved him. We were supposed to be together!" Her wail echoed through the cavernous room and bounced back at her with a smack. She buried her face in her hands, letting herself cry, grieve . . .

Wallow. She groaned, then felt the nausea build and groaned again. She leaned against the well wall, sniffling. Heard the subtle swish of fabric from the Ladies' clothes. In the corner of her eye, they shifted, and there came the cold chill of disapproval.

She cared not! Had they experienced the grief and torment she endured these last months, they would not stand so superior. Wiping tears that seemed endless, Kersei defied their stiffness, cried . . . Yes, blood and boil—wallowed! It had been unfair. Bound to Darius, she was also tethered to the man responsible for killing everything she loved. She hated him. Hated this child. Hated life.

"Kersei!" Ma'ma caught her shoulder. "Hear me! The babe needs your focus. He is in distress."

Startled out of her self-pity, Kersei blinked. Glanced at her overly large womb and . . . "What? No . . ." But she thought . . . recounted the last ora . . . "I haven't felt him." A whisper of dread snaked into her. Batting aside the tears did no good—her hands were wet and smeared the thick, watery liquid across her face. "What is wrong?" She gripped the edge of the well, straightening. "Why can I not feel him move? There has been no contraction."

Grief struck and brought with it a pound of panic. "What do I do? Is he okay?" New tears rushed down her cheeks. What had she done? So foolishly focused on the past, she had not noticed her own child had gone silent. Had the Ancient, too?

Please, Kersei silently pleaded with Him, *please help me.*

"You must calm yourself." Ma'ma peered over her shoulder to another Lady, who quickly glided forward. "This is Iisil. She is our prima opstitrix. Listen to her. *Obey* her."

Rapidly blinking away the tears, Kersei looked at the dark-skinned Lady as another wave of nausea grabbed a fistful of agony and shoved her backward. "Save my son," she cried. "Please."

"That is up to the Ancient," Iisil said softly. "Your job is to be the vessel for His will." Kind eyes smiled at her. "Lie back against the sanitatem."

Noting the way the other Ladies, with instruments in hand, now moved around the room with purpose, Kersei felt cold, scared, yet she obeyed the order to recline, surprised to find a slight incline in the stone behind her. Eying her mother, she settled, observing her womb had risen above the water. "Darius . . ." His name slipped from her lips, but she swallowed the rest, reminding herself she hated him. Focused on the desperation to feel her son, once so active and wrestling within, move again.

Great emptiness rushed over her at the stillness inside her—no movement, no contraction. "What if the Ancient is angry with me? Will He take my son?"

Ma'ma placed a warm palm over Kersei's forehead. "Shh. Seek peace."

"You were right," Kersei said, feeling the tremors of fear that forced more tears free. "I was selfish." This entire time. Only thinking of herself. What she had lost. "Please do not let my baby pay for my—"

Searing pain ripped through her.

"Agh!" Bending to the side, Kersei splashed her face in the water. She jerked back and gasped, tensing through the wave of agony. Pain roared unabated.

"Keep her still or this child won't make it!"

"Dusan!" Isaura sat up with a start, her limbs shaking, heart racing. A terrific throb of her head dropped her back down with a groan.

"Easy, Your Majesty."

Holding her head, Isaura squinted against the blinding light pouring through the room to find the body that had voiced those words. "Cetus." But he had not been on the trip to Jher—

She snapped awake, the fog of pain and sleep clearing. Remembered the blurring of the room. The sensation of falling. "What happened?"

"My lady!" Breathlessly, Kita rushed forward and fell to her knees. "My heart is so relieved you have awakened."

Isaura's surroundings swam into focus—stone walls. No windows. A damp, musty odor. "Where are we?"

"The caves," Kita said. "Beneath Jherako—apparently they have a full residence down here for the safety of the king and queen, who are even now with Ixion."

Isaura eyed Cetus slipping from the room, and she pushed to sit upright, which clubbed her head with dizziness. "The room spins, yet I am uninjured . . ."

"King Vorn had a device—a box of some kind that healed you," Kita explained. "Ixion brought you here afterward, but mayhap you are in need of sustenance."

Vaguely, Isaura recalled being in such a thing. It struck her again that Kita had not referred to him as Mavridis or as Elder Mavridis as would be proper but used a more *familiar* form of address. She shifted to look at her friend, but the line of thought spun away as the room wobbled. The chair in which Kita had been sitting with a basket of embroidery floated this way and that. Tapestries of warriors and ladies wavered on the walls. A chill of cold and nausea scampered through Isaura.

She closed her eyes and felt Kita lay a thick pelt across her shoulders. "I would not have imagined it cold down here, where the rocks hold the warmth of the sun," Isaura murmured.

"Aye, but the ocean lends its own power to the air," Kita replied.

The door opened and Mavridis stormed in, face awash in concern.

"What is wrong?" She recalled too clearly the dream that had stolen Dusan away from her and the attack that had injured her somehow. "Is he dead?"

Behind him hustled Ypiretis and her regia. All distraught.

As was she. "Please—what is the matter?"

"You," Mavridis said with a near laugh. "You have been unconscious these many days. We feared—"

"Days?"

"Aye. After being stabilized by the medpod, you remained unconscious. The pharmakeia explained that the injury to your head could keep you from us for many days or weeks, maybe even . . ." He did not finish the thought, but she felt the unspoken implication: forever.

Still cowering beneath the thumping headache, she put a hand to her womb. And understood now the dizziness that remained. "The babe—"

"We are assured by the pharmakeia that the heart yet beats steady and strong."

With a shuddering breath, she slumped against the wall, feeling the cold stone through the pelt and her bliaut. "What happened? I recall . . ." What *did* she recall? Being in the ballroom— "The nobles. What of the talks?"

"The talks are over. Symmachia saw to that."

Her gaze snapped to Mavridis, and she saw there anger and intent—to make the skycrawlers pay.

"For now, it is best you stay abed and rest."

She bristled at his instruction. "Forget you whom you address?"

He smirked. "A father to his daughter."

At that, Isaura deflated and felt a thousand aches across her body. "Symmachia, you say." She focused on what she could. "Then the talks are more imperative than ever. Is there no way to—"

"Sadly, no," came Roman's resonant voice as he entered the stone room, his broad shoulders filling what space remained. So like Dusan that. "There are few nobles left with whom to talk. Much is in disarray or destroyed. There is barely a castle in which to even shelter at the moment."

Isaura stilled, gripping the coverlet. "The destruction is so vast . . ."

"We are here and will answer your questions," Roman said, "but Marco needs you and that babe to draw him home, so please heed Mavridis. Rest while you can."

Dusan . . . Her thoughts spun into a frenzy, remembering the dream.

What did it mean? What if he was truly gone? Stolen from her a second time?

In what felt like a blur to her aching head, Roman squatted at her bedside, his gaze sharp, assessing. "What distresses you, Isaura?"

She swallowed. That visage of Marco going gray repeated in her mind, tormenting her. "I . . ." What good would it do to speak of it? "Nothing," she lied, her heart raw over what it could mean. "Tell me of this attack on Jherako." Even as she spoke, the ground rumbled and shook. Rocks dribbled. She glanced at the others. "It yet persists?" But they stood mute, watching her, giving each other glances. "Speak plainly!"

Mavridis tightened his jaw. "For two days Jherako has endured an ongoing attack, initiated with the strike during the Conclave, which was no doubt intended to wipe out the ruling houses and leave the nations of Drosero headless."

"They largely succeeded," Roman added. "Forgelight is in ruins. Most of the Conclave of Sovereign nobles here were killed that first night."

"Vorn!" Isaura gasped, unable to keep the pitch from her voice. "What of him? And Aliria?"

"Alive by the grace of the Ladies," Roman put in calmly. "Aliria was delivered of a healthy son shortly after the attack."

"Good." Isaura did not have time to rejoice more. "How many are dead among the houses?"

"Most. There is but a small remnant."

Isaura turned toward the wall, her own grief materializing with a relentless shiver. "And yet I live." Ignoring their objections this time, she slipped from the bed. Felt the thin carpet beneath her bare feet as she hugged the pelt tighter around her shoulders. "And the city?"

"Thousands dead or injured."

"But the Droseran-Tertian Accord . . ."

"Means nothing," Mavridis bit out. "Symmachia is determined to take Drosero at all costs, which—this day—are high. Catastrophic."

Bitterness glanced across her tongue. She felt sick. "Who is dead among the Conclave nobles? I would have names."

The men again exchanged looks.

Oh, Ladies . . . Panic and fear and grief wrestled within her. Writhed. Turned her restraint to anger. "Speak! I must know what I face and who is left to face it with me!"

"You should rest," Mavridis said quietly.

"I should be the kyria Dusan made me," she snapped, once more hating how little he trusted her. "He is not here, and I must face—*confront*—the terror that has invaded."

"He would not want you—"

"Speak not for him!" Her shout echoed off the walls, startling even her. Surprising her, forcing her to see the tentative grip she held on to her grief and anger.

The world tilting, upending her illusion of control on her body, on feigning strength, Isaura slumped onto the mattress and tucked her head. Fought the overwhelming urge to cry.

Air swirled, and a large hand came to rest on her knee. "You need not do all things at once. It is too much. First you must rest—for your child."

Isaura drew in a trembling breath. "I fear there will be no rest for quite some time." Mercies, why did she have to fall in love with a medora? Why did he have to get snatched away and leave her here to rule? *I am breaking . . .* Through tears, she whispered, "I fear I cannot do this much longer."

What if he did not return? Five months . . . Dusan had been gone five months. Again, that dream invaded . . . the way he faded . . . *What if he is dead already?*

No. She could not afford to think such things. They betrayed Dusan. Weary, she smoothed her fingers over her rounding belly, where his daughter grew, and felt a solid little thump against her fingertips. Eyes slipping closed at the assurance of life within her, Isaura sniffled.

"You do realize it is okay to be human," Roman said at her side, "to miss him, to be afraid he won't return."

"No." Isaura jerked up, wiping the tears away. "I cannot yield to those fears. Thinking on them only allows them to breed." She stared blandly around the room. But how long *could* she continue this? It was hard . . . so very hard . . . "Too many depend on me, and I must never allow hope to be stolen from me as well."

She had survived that attack when so many had died. How? How was she alive with but a few scratches and aches and a knot on her head?

"Why am I alive?" It was a normal question. At least, she thought it was. Until a new quiet smothered the room. A quiet that said something . . . something hid beneath their downturned gazes. The sudden fascination with the stone floor.

The question had been rhetorical, but their reactions lent it credence. Spurred her to pursue it. "Why am I alive when so many others are dead?" Silence yet gaped. "Blood and boil, if I must demand one more answer . . ." She finally noticed a bruise peeking from Mavridis's collar. The cut across the master hunter's brow—and was he protecting his shoulder? Their silence, their injuries injected more fear into this dark rise. "*Speak!*"

Roman lifted his jaw. "The Ladies."

"The Ladies," she repeated, uncertain of his point. Something warm blossomed in her breast. Her babe kicked. She believed in the Ladies . . . or that they once existed. "They are gone." Yet her mind argued, thought of Aliria. Of what Dusan said of the Lady at the Temple.

"They are not," Roman said.

"He speaks true." Mavridis's cheek twitched beneath restraint, as if he struggled to speak something. "When the first explosion happened, I saw . . . a Lady. A, uh . . . bubble erupted around you as she flew at you."

Flew at me?

Roman jerked to him. "You *saw* that?"

Her father nodded.

"Bubble?" Isaura murmured, trying to comprehend the meaning.

Mavridis lifted a shoulder. "I was looking at you when the explosion happened. In the split-second before the roof collapsed, when Roman raced you toward the doors, she appeared above. Flew at you. Ceilings, walls—they were all falling. A rock struck your temple. Then she reached you, and both of you were . . . gone."

"Gone." Oh great, there she went again, repeating his words.

"He's right." Roman eased forward. "You would've been crushed like the others but for the protective embrace of a Resplendent." He lowered his gaze for a moment, then drew in a breath and let it out. "Aliria is a Lady, and I know that is hard to accept—"

"Wait." It was all too much. Too, too much. Suddenly queasy, Isaura cradled her head in her hands. She stood, the room canting, so she waited for it to stabilize. Oh, that she could be anywhere but here with this absurd tale. "I . . ." She paced away from them, finding only an unfeeling stone wall for refuge. "How can this . . .? Why would . . .?" It was hard to even name them now. "The Ladies . . . Why protect me?" She had heard rumors. "Crey mentioned in—" She whirled to the others, feeling that cold dizzy spell again and was grateful when Kita steadied her. "I saw Crey of Greyedge."

Mavridis went very still, his expression hard. "Where?"

"In the palace. Just before the explosion." She squeezed her own fingers, wondering . . . "Think you he was responsible?"

After sharing a frown with Mavridis, Roman shook his head. "I anak'd nothing there that would imply treacherous intent, save the fetor of fuel. Since you had mentioned his presence before the attack, I inquired of Vorn. He and Crey are working on some contingences to protect the southern realms. Crey is not responsible for the attack."

"I am glad to hear it." She turned back to the bed, wishing for a window, feeling confined. Wondering how long she must stay in the caves— "The caves!" She pivoted to face the men. "Our pilots—the ships!" She strangled a cry. "Tell me our hope is not lost."

"It is never lost, as it rests not in man," Roman said firmly. "But the shipyard and men are unharmed. Despite being Symmachia's intended target, they could but guess the location."

"And thankfully, they guessed poorly," Mavridis said. "We must keep them hidden as the siege continues—one launch of a Viper and they will strike. As is, we will need to find other means of training the pilots. Our efforts may have come too late."

"Indeed." Soberly, she thought of those at the talks, of the people she had conversed with, those who would be allies and those who would be foes. "Who among the rulers are known to be alive?"

"Shadar, Saigo, and Avrolis yet live," Mavridis said. "Sasada's shah is clinging to life by a—"

"So few?" Stunned, Isaura considered him. Her heart skipped a beat at a name not mentioned. "The princess." She begged it to be a mistake, a slip of memory. "Is Princess Lirra . . .?"

Her father's features darkened grimly. "Alive, but not Waterflame's prince."

"Sweet Ladies . . ." Isaura eased against the cot, hugging herself.

"It is a miracle any survived," Mavridis said. "Our contingent suffered loss—two of your guards"—he glanced to Roman—"a hunter as well. Little remains now of Forgelight or the Furymark."

Her mind churned against the truth, the implications. "What will happen to Jherako—"

"We will rebuild."

Amid shuffling of feet, Isaura turned. "Vorn."

"Isaura." He gave an acknowledging nod.

"I am much relieved to see you alive."

"Vorn's purpose was not yet accomplished, nor his promise fulfilled." Aliria trailed the king with their babe in her arms, her voice strangely ethereal, full of confidence and authority.

"My son." Vorn gave a proud nod. "And I will make good on that promise to give her a Daughter."

"I meant," Aliria said with a measure of irritation, "Vorn is integral to the great battle that is coming. When he stands with Marco and—"

"Marco." Isaura moved around the broad-chested king to reach his wife, reading into the words she spoke. Trusting, hoping—believing that she was a Lady. "Then he is alive?"

Aliria held her with those violet eyes. "Has he not told you so?"

"Who? Mav—"

"Marco."

Isaura blinked, the joke cruel and unfeeling. "He is . . . gone. You know this."

"He told you of the enemy he faces." Aliria remained unrelenting in her confidence.

A confidence that rattled Isaura's. Dusan *had* told her about the enemy . . . in her dreams. Surely Aliria could not mean . . .

"What did he tell you?" Aliria persisted.

Heat wormed through Isaura as she stared at the queen, stupefied that she knew. "The enemy is powerful and numerous." Her heart stuttered. "But how could you—"

"They will come." Aliria glanced around the room as she gently bounced the babe in her arms. "And they will war with us."

"Wait—what do you mean Marco told you this?" Mavridis edged in.

"It was just a dream," Isaura said with a nervous laugh. She stared in disbelief at the queen, waiting for—*needing*—her to explain, but then looked to Roman. "Did you speak of this to her?"

He frowned, affronted. "I told no one."

Isaura shifted, her heart refusing to believe it, yet recalling her own hope that Aliria was a Lady. "How . . .? How do you know of this? It was a *dream*."

"No, not a dream. Lifespeech," Aliria corrected, lifting her babe to her shoulder. "Because of Marco's mother and his brand, and because you carry his daughter, he can use the *vox saeculorum* to communicate with you."

Hands on her belly, Isaura could not process—*believe*—what Aliria spoke. "Then . . . it's real?" she whispered around the tears stinging and blurring her eyes. "He's real—in my dreams, he's real?"

"As if he stood with you in the same room."

A bubble of laughter trickled up her throat. "It is too incredible to believe that he . . . *communicates* . . ."

"He does, so listen well to what he tells you."

"I said before you were his beacon, and I meant it," Roman said. "This connection between you and Marco—your child—will guide him back. We need his return."

Aliria shifted and seemed more powerful, more authoritative. "The Progenitor *must* return for what is to come, and as Roman has spoken, you and Aeliana are instrumental in making it possible for Marco to return."

"Aeliana?"

Aliria gave a warm smile. "Your daughter—the name you have given her."

"I did?" Stunned, Isaura at once felt as if she'd always known it. "He said I carried a girl—in my dreams. He declared it so." She took a step forward and frowned, her mind finally assembling this strange, miraculous puzzle. "But . . . if you are Faa'Cris, why . . . why can *you* not guide him back?"

"As a Kynigos with broken family ties, Marco sees little meaning in us other than as symbols of values and beliefs he holds dear. You and Aeliana, however, are as life. He will do whatever it takes to return to you both."

Isaura drew in a breath, savoring the glimmer of hope that she could draw him home. She *would* draw him back. Hold him again. Hear his voice. See that smirk. "Why tell me this now? You could have explained it to me before, helped me . . ." She was so very tired.

"The toll you have endured is great and has weighed heavily against your courage, Isaura," Aliria said in that otherworldly voice. "As Marco is vital, so are you, for without you, he would be lost, and that cannot happen." She inclined her head. "The Progenitor stirs the Fallen to a war that will decide the Fates of *Toukousmos*."

"*Toukousmos?*"

"It means, 'the worlds,'" Roman said over his shoulder. "The name given long ago to our Quadrants."

"The Fallen will defy the will of the Ancient and press into lands from which they have been forbidden for millennia. The toll"—Aliria's serene visage faltered for a moment—"will be catastrophic. The victory undecided until that final day. Yet the Faa'Cris see hope in the tellings of the Progenitor, who will lead the battle to completion."

"In more common words," Roman said quietly, holding the Lady's forbidding gaze, "he is the *instigator*. Wherever Marco is, he is instigating the greatest battle of humanity's existence."

"The baby is in distress—dying."

Kersei choked back a sob. "No! No, please . . ." The pain was a cruel one that infected tissue and marrow but did nothing to further her labor. "Please, Ancient . . ." She looked at the women before her, Ma'ma at her side. "You are Ladies! Can you not—"

"We are His servants," Ma'ma stated flatly, "effecting His will, nothing more."

"My son," Kersei whimpered, holding her womb, moaning against the terrible ache in her back that would not go away nor be appeased no matter her position, the herbs, or massages. "Darius!" she cried out and threw her head back as another futile contraction hit.

"Do not push," Iisil instructed. "Each contraction pops him out of the birth canal, and he turned—breech. His heart has nearly failed. If you push, you'll kill him."

"My body is not listening," Kersei said around another whimper. "It hurts. He's dying. I can feel it. Pleeeasse!"

"Give her more herbs—"

"It's too risky for the babe."

"She will lose him! It is too risky *not* to give them."

"Kersei."

She had wanted freedom. Wanted . . . her way. But not this. Not at the cost of her son. Through the last several months, she had fought every act not perfectly in line with her own will—and this is what had come of it. Weak, drained of courage, she collapsed against the sanitatem. Selfishness had cost the life of her unborn babe. If he died, then so should she. Never could she face the world knowing her foolishness caused his death.

"Kersei!"

She started, suddenly recognizing the voice that reached through her despair. Saw blue eyes that now hovered over her as she labored. "Darius," she breathed. Then sobbed. Grabbed for him. A great splash sounded, along with shouts and objections as he climbed in next to her. She hooked her arm around his neck, buried her face in his shoulder, and cried more. "I beg your mercy, mercy . . . mercy . . ."

His embrace was warm and strong. "Peace, Kersei, peace," he whispered, stroking her head and cheek. "I am here. All will be well."

"No! He's dying," Kersei cried. "'Tis my fault. I left . . . He dies, Darius! I beg your mercy!"

"Kersei—"

"Because of me, our baby is dying. There can be no forgiveness."

"Kersei." He framed her face with wet hands and stared hard into her watery vision. "He is not yet dead. We will do this together. Relax."

"He refuses to come, and who can blame him when I said I did not want him?"

Darius twitched at her words.

She saw his grief, the hurt she yet again caused, and hung her head. "I am not worthy to be his mother. That is why the Ancient takes him from me. I abandoned my oaths. Left you. He is dying. Do you hear me, Darius? Dying!"

His touch was firm. His body strong as he pulled her against his chest. "You are in distress and so is our son, but you take too much on yourself. Give yourself far too much credit."

"Relax, Kersei," Ma'ma instructed. "Listen to your body."

Kersei clung to Darius, savoring his strength, his touch. Oh, she did not deserve this, deserve him. "You came . . ." Even though she had run away. "How?"

"Shh." He peered down into her face, his blue eyes piercing, his stubble nearly—

"A beard."

He gave her a sheepish look. "There has been no time to shave while trying to find you."

Find me? He had searched? The idea fluttered through her as she fingered the stubble, leaving behind gently glistening droplets, surprised to find it a bit soft. "I like it."

His eyebrows arched. "You do?"

"Mm," she said. "You look . . . distinguished." She was tired. So very tired. Leaning against him, she let herself drift . . . "I am so glad you came." She lifted her head. Looked into his eyes. "How are you here?" She glanced at Ladies busily working. Even Ma'ma. "How can you be here? It is not . . ."

He simply drew her tight again and cradled her head. "Shh, beloved. Focus on our son."

"Xylander."

Darius grunted a laugh. "If you insist."

"I do." Then she hesitated, realized her insistence had gotten her into this. She looked at him. "Only if you will it."

Surprise wormed through his handsome, bearded face. "Xylander will be in your arms shortly."

A waft of something minty caressed her thoughts, and she clung to him. "I was wrong to leave." Even now, with her body in agony, she felt Darius go still. "The writ . . . a mistake."

His chest sank, as if he'd held and expelled a breath.

"I have begged the Ladies, the Ancient, even Marco's Vaqar that our son would live."

He kissed the top of her head. "I have bargained the same—for you both."

A convulsion of feelings—grief, relief, anger, love—ran through her. With yet another whimper, she collapsed against him in the water, curling her fingers into his jerkin as the last vestiges of strength seeped from her limbs. "Thank you . . . thank you for coming." And she wondered again about that. "How . . . how are you here? It is not as simple as riding down to Stratios on your Black—"

"I told you—I made a bargain."

She eased back again to look into his eyes. Had to admit something about those blue irises and that light brown hair made her stomach swirl. "What bargain?"

Darius cupped her face, as he often liked to do. "I told her I would do anything to be with you."

The words cocooned her broken heart and tethered her tighter to him. "Thank you," she whispered. "I was wrong—about everything."

"Not everything." With a grin he added, "But mayhap many."

"Living up to the petulant prince title again," she teased weakly.

"I take it very seriously."

Kersei pressed into him, glad for his presence, his strength. "I love you, Darius." If only their son would live . . .

He held her fast. "I love you, too."

A contraction hit. Kersei flinched away, tried to strangle her cry against the pain. Then she felt her son moving—violently. Whimpering again, she leaned back, arching her spine to give him room, instinct alone driving the action. Down the length of her body, she saw her belly roiling where it rose above the water, a bulge moving. Felt punches against her ribs. Pressure that made her arch her spine farther.

"What's wrong?" Darius asked, glancing to the Lady who waded in at her legs.

"Nothing," Iisil said, palming Kersei's womb. "The babe is likely turning."

"But there's no room to turn," Kersei complained, as yet another foot shoved her rib out of the way. But then she felt a strange swirl of warmth around her legs. "What was that? What's wrong?" She cocked her head to see around her large belly.

"Nothing—your waters are clearing out."

"I thought that happened hours ago."

"He was blocking some, it seems." Iisil gently probed Kersei's belly, then laughed. "He is no longer breech!"

Kersei's breath caught as another pain struck. She focused on breathing, on this son who suddenly decided he wanted to live, too.

"When you're ready, push, because this baby is ready!"

Darius laughed, then following the instruction of Ma'ma, he slid in behind her to support and hold her. He kissed the soft spot beneath her ear, reminding her of their more intimate moments.

And then it came. The pang that choked thought. Demanded attention. Applied forbidding pressure.

Wanting to cry, to wail, Kersei knew what her body—her son—needed. She angled and bore down, focused on the center of her being. Imagined her baby's feet propped against her ribs, prepared to propel himself into the world with her assistance.

Pressure.

"Another. I see the head."

With all her focus trained on her body—though she clearly noted Darius at her back, his strength and presence a tremendous comfort she could never have imagined, Kersei bore down to give the best push she could. Even as her lungs screamed for air, she felt the shift. The rightness of what her body knew it needed to do to bring this new life into the world. Focused on that, on her son's placement and readiness.

With a *whoosh*, he rushed into the world.

Kersei felt an enormous release. Glanced down and saw in Iisil's skilled hands, a ruddy ball of flailing arms and a silent scream. She gasped.

Iisil lifted his head above water.

Their newborn shot his protesting fists into the air as he took his first breath, then screamed for all the world to hear that there was yet another Tyrannous heir.

ROHILEK, KURU SYSTEM

"Incoming!"

In the split-second it took Reef to pivot and push her, Eija saw the Draegis fighters in the sky overhead, coming right at them. Behind Reef, she sprinted across the rocky planet, dodging broken stones and sparse vegetation, sliding on loose gravel. Her boots slipped as she fought for purchase, tried to run faster. They delved down, skidding, sliding into a gorge and relative safety from the aircraft. She glanced over her shoulder at the ships coming in hard and fast with a whine that made her skin crawl.

White flashed from the fast-attack crafts, ordnance spitting at them.

Dirt erupted around them, showering them with dust and debris.

She stumbled in a depression, then cursed herself for not watching in front of her. Even then, she heard the shrieks of another bombardment. Unable to resist, she glanced back again—just in time to see Reef dive at her. In that instant she registered two things: Marco lunging to safety and crimson rage glowering from Daq'Ti's eyes as he faced the hunter.

Then the impact from Reef drove them both to the ground. Eija hit hard, Reef's head cracking against her chin. Clacking her teeth. Air punched from her lungs. But she scrambled around, afraid she'd see Marco and Daq'Ti killing each other.

Daq'Ti went to a knee and his arm powered up, though it seemed painful, harder to produce—and his aim swung skyward. The wake-field sputtered before flaring to life as he aimed at the crafts screaming overhead.

Taking shelter behind a rock, Marco whipped around and aimed his armored arm at the attackers. Dispelled pulse blasts that hissed through the arid day.

Debris rained down, forcing Eija to squeeze shut her eyes. Heated air gusted against her face, leaving her coated in dust. Were she in another place, another galaxy, she might think the fast pitter-patter of falling dirt was rain. The ground vibrated from the concussion of the weapons' impact and the roar of the engines as the Draegis strafed the gorge.

Amid fire, rock, and dust, Eija coughed. Tried to gain her bearings, clear the dirt from her mouth.

"Go!" Daq'Ti bellowed from nearby, targeting with a secondary weapon this time.

Reef scrabbled aside. "Run!"

"Caves. Almost there," Daq'Ti bellowed.

Caves might not be the best idea but being out in the open was worse. Even as she sprinted toward shelter, Eija marveled at the way Marco moved. He wasn't fast, his injuries from months in the *Prevenire*'s inner hull still evident in his slow, limping gait. Yet he had clear experience that guided him skillfully along the terrain, which in turn guided her and Reef. She appreciated his implacable spirit, the unwavering tenacity to warrior on despite months spent crammed in the walls of a djelling ship.

Blasts pelted the barren lands, spitting rocks at them as they pushed harder for the caves. She hunched, keeping her head down as she peered ahead toward safety, her heart racing. A strange wave of . . . something washed over her. Slowed her. Pulled her around.

What was that? She glanced over her shoulder. Away from Marco and his intensity and agility. Beyond Reef and his laserlike focus to— "No!"

Daq'Ti was laid out. On the ground.

Skidding to a stop and forcing Reef to divert around her to avoid a collision, Eija shoved back toward her protector.

"No!" Reef shouted at her. "No time!" He pointed to the sky, where fast-attack crafts streaked toward them.

Her gaze shot to Daq'Ti, still unmoving. "I have to—"

"We can't!"

Amid the shriek of ships, the shouts of Reef and Marco to keep moving, the pounding of ordnance devastating the desert, and the howl of wind she'd only just noticed, came Daq'Ti's chortle of pain. With a hop, she started for him.

"No!" Reef caught her by the waist, whirling her around and forcing her toward the cave. "He wouldn't want you to."

"No—what?" She jerked back to her Draegis protector. "I can't . . ."

Reef hauled her up off her feet. Hooked her over his shoulder and ran—but no sooner did the darkness of the cave engulf them than he cried out, went to a knee. Cringing, she realized he'd thrown her over his burned shoulder.

Torn, Eija hesitated, reaching to haul Reef to his feet, but her gaze bounced back to Daq'Ti—and she gasped.

Peeling himself off the ground, he was still fighting. Still firing at the Draegis who were preternaturally focused on ending the enemy—her. Marco. Reef. Sacrificing himself . . .

She started forward, but Reef jerked her back. She stumbled, hit the cave wall, and thumped her head. Hopping up, she gritted her teeth. Rushed to the cave opening, but Reef was there again. Holding her. She focused on her guardian. "*Daq'Ti!*"

He swung around, coming to a knee as his red slits homed in on her. He trilled, and in a flash, he was up.

"Move!" She shoved away from Reef, glad to finally be free of him, and focused on a now-running Daq'Ti. If one could call it running. "He . . ." *What . . .?*

"He's missing a leg," Marco noted.

A sickening knot formed in her stomach. "He won't make it. He'll bleed out . . ." Grief assailed her—he had protected her. Sacrificed so she . . .

What she saw did not make sense. As Daq'Ti ran, his leg . . . lengthened. She blinked, trying to process as more and more of the leg appeared. Wait, what? Had she—

No. She hadn't imagined it. It was *regenerating*! With the others, she watched, unable to speak. Unable to understand the creature who had pledged his life to hers. "That's . . . not possible."

"That's *scuzzed*, is what it is." Reef grabbed her arm and looked her over. "You okay?"

"Get off!"

"You have a knot on your head."

Eija wrested free of his grip. "Because your hard head slammed into it and then you threw me into that wall."

"I saved your life!"

"Keep telling yourself that." But she saw something in his expression she hadn't expected—hurt. And it thumped against her conscience as she checked Daq'Ti closing the distance.

He bolted in—on two whole legs again—and spun, facing out, aiming his—

She sucked in a hard breath. "Your arm!"

His skin was rough and ashen, and the weaponized forelimb remained in place thanks only to a strap he'd rigged around the melted skin.

Eija swallowed bile, knowing it hurt. And ashamed over how she recoiled from the sickening sight and smell of charred flesh. "You're . . . injured." Concern washed through her.

Glancing down, as if noticing the injury for the first time, he let out a chortle-whimper that was little more than a whisper. "O'zgerish."

"The change," Eija muttered, looking up into eyes that were more oval by the minute and filled with pain and . . . fear.

"So it wasn't just my imagination," Marco mumbled, eying Daq'Ti. "He *is* changing."

"What will he look like when he's . . . done?" Reef asked.

Eija shook her head. That was the question, wasn't it? And why was this change even happening?

"Change or not, he's on the verge of losing that weaponized arm." Marco turned his attention to the bombardment, to the ceiling as pebbles rained under the fighters' continued strafing of the land over the cave.

"He's of no use to us without that weapon," Reef said.

"And if you lose your weapon, should we leave you behind as well?" Eija snapped. "At least he has codes, knowledge of the Draegis military operations, familiarity with the city on the horizon, this planet, and the surrounding ones. What do you have?"

"Tactical knowledge that says he's a threat!" Reef scowled, his gaze sharp. "And with this change, he probably won't retain the codes."

"You don't know that."

"What I do know is I'm sick of you worrying about him. You're more concerned about him than you are about the rest of us."

"That's not true! I just—"

"Lovers quarrel later," Marco growled. "Safety first." He cocked his head toward the cave entrance, directing their attention to something in the distance. "We're about to have company."

"Slag," Reef hissed. "They're fast-dropping."

Sure enough, what first looked like black shooting stars turned out to be an entire squadron belched into the atmo from a dreadnought.

"We need to move," Marco said.

Daq'Ti, weary and unusually quiet, bobbed his head. "Go—in!" He motioned farther into the darkened cave, then held something out to Eija.

Wary, she accepted it, the weight hitting her palm similar to the one in her stomach. She refused to look at Reef or Marco, who were no doubt studying this encounter, too. They didn't like her deference or protective instincts toward Daq'Ti. To be honest, neither did she. It was impossible to understand and even worse to find herself not only yielding but . . . *embracing* whatever this—he—was. She shuddered involuntarily.

"Safer." Daq'Ti pointed to the rear of the cave and squeezed her hand. "Go."

Light flared from between her fingers, the device he'd passed her suddenly warm. Guarded, she moved a few steps back and shot her protector a furtive look. Another nod, this time with a message in his morphing eyes. One she couldn't understand, except that he was again protecting her, putting his life in defense of hers. As the light flared and danced, the black walls glittered, amplifying the beam. Then she saw what Daq'Ti was urging her toward. "There's an opening! Maybe a tunnel."

Reef's shoulder nudged hers as he edged closer, weapon trained on the blackness that was always a few steps ahead, escaping the light's reach. "This is either a really bad idea or a really scuzzed one."

"Would you rather take your chances with the Draegis?"

"No!" Marco's shout pulled them around in time to see Daq'Ti aiming at the mouth of the cave.

Boom!

Stunned, Eija jerked away, narrowly avoiding the blinding flash and fallout debris from a detonation. Sucking in a breath, she got a mouthful of dust. She jerked around, confounded. Light no longer struggled into the cave.

Unbelievably, Daq'Ti had sealed them in.

She felt more than saw Reef launch at the beast.

A roar erupted. Daq'Ti and Reef were going at it. Arms and fists. Reef losing badly and not caring as he threw another punch—right at Daq'Ti's injured arm.

Coughing and blinking against the dust, Eija lurched toward the fray as Marco tried to pull them apart.

"Stop," she shouted, eyes and throat burning. Whatever was in the rocks here . . . she might as well drink acid. "Stop, please!"

Boom!

The ground rattled. Dust rained again. They all stilled, staring at the ceiling. In the deafening silence that followed, Eija coughed again, eyes watering.

Boom!

More rock trickled loose, freeing larger chunks.

"They're trying to breach it," Marco growled.

"He just buried us alive!" Reef shouted over the ordnance rattling the planet. "If she dies"—he pressed closer to Daq'Ti, strangely on equal footing and height somehow—"I will personally kill you. And keep killing you until you can't regenerate!"

"Reef!"

"No. He led us here, moved you to safety before he caused that cave-in.

Now we're trapped and losing air by the second. His buddies are bombing the slag out of this place—"

"Tunnels," Daq'Ti said with a very human glower.

Marco jutted his jaw. "Show us."

"You trust him?" Reef lifted his arms in frustration.

"We're dead if the ceiling comes down, so we have little choice. Besides, like she said—he's got the know-how of this planet." Marco faced her Draegis protector. "Get us out of here, safely." A warning hung in his tone.

When Daq'Ti glanced at her, Eija felt their strange connection. And hated it. But what could she do except use it to their advantage? Somehow, she even knew that he waited for her approval, so she supplied the encouraging nod.

With a chortle-trill, he took the light amplifier and led them into what seemed a sea of black. The illumination barely advanced, as if it, too, feared what lay ahead. A dozen steps more in forbidding blackness proved suffocating. Though she'd been a pilot, familiar with flying through space, this somehow felt more oppressive, more . . . threatening.

Seemingly awakened to their presence, the ground rumbled.

No. That was an explosion. The murmuring rocks beneath her feet warned of danger seconds before a concussion slammed her into Reef. She knew in that instant the Draegis had breached the tunnel. Giant boulders leapt from the sides. Light punched holes in the darkness. Something hit her shoulder. Her cheek. She threw up her arms to protect herself.

"Cave-in!" Reef's shout was barely audible over the horrendous *whoosh* that enveloped them. Walls crumbling, ceiling collapsing, air unbreathable.

Eyes clenched against the debris, Eija braced for the inevitable crush of earth. They'd survived the *Prevenire*, survived the Khatriza's initial efforts, escaped the dreadnought . . . only to die on the Draegis homeworld.

No!

Pitch black swallowed her. Panic thrust its way into some strange, distorted timing, things slowing around her. Even her scream amid the cave-in warbled across time's wavelength. Boulders dropped.

Cold air swirled. Rustled across her face. Stung her cheeks. Light pushed against her eyelids, begging her to open them.

When she did, Eija drew in a sharp breath at what lay before her. Not the cave. Not Reef or Marco, or even Daq'Ti. Instead, there stretched to endless impossibility: an expanse of white. A world held hostage in the violent grip of a deep winter. Snow. Ice-covered mountains.

She turned, unable to comprehend. Unable to believe—

"What the scuz?"

She spun, startled to find Reef behind her. "Where are we?"

"How am I supposed to know? You shoved me into this place!"

Standing once more in the halls of Kardia should have provided a measure of warmth and encouragement, familiarity. At least, that was what she had believed when conviction told her to return to the heart of Kalonica and be visible to the people. Roman and Mavridis argued vehemently against the idea, but she insisted they return to the capital immediately, despite legitimate fears of being shot from the sky by Symmachia. However, once she entered the grand halls, the chill that had begun in the caves of Jherako clung with renewed vigor, seeping into her bones and infusing her with foreboding.

War. Dusan was instigating a war.

This morning, Isaura stood on the balcony, hands knitted over her belly, allowing the tumultuous wind off the stormy sea to buffet her body, toss her hair, and remind her once more that there would be no peace in the days ahead. Learning their child created a tether between her and Dusan had given her hope. Joy. But this ominous cloud that hung over her after the haunting dream of Dusan fading to gray . . . Was it possible her baby somehow knew something about Dusan's well-being that she did not? Was he . . . dead?

Isaura recoiled at the thought. Hated that it had pushed into her consciousness again. Yet . . . it had been a week since waking in the cave after that dream—Lifespeech, they called it—and there had been no more dreams. Or hope.

"Where are you, Dusan? I ache to hear your voice. Speak!"

Loneliness curled around the edges of her failing courage, planting worry into the very marrow of her bones. For two reasons she had insisted upon returning to Kardia: one, to show strength to the people by not abandoning them, and two, her irrational belief that Dusan would not know where to look for her if she did not return. As well, she wanted the familiar rhythm of life she had found since coming here months past. Strangely enough, she even missed Kersei's company. But upon her return, she found the staff here at Kardia had no word on Darius or Kersei. Which stirred more worry and stress into the rancid concoction Isaura tasted in the air. Grief beat against her attempts to lift her thoughts and spirits. Everything she knew and loved was gone. Like Dusan.

Oh, Ladies, let it not be! I beg of you.

"It has been four days since our return, yet your countenance is unchanged." Roman had hovered since their scout delivered her to Kalonica.

"As is our circumstance." She was unable to hold his gaze and was doing her best to avoid Mavridis's, too. "Worry not for me. I am well."

Boils, if he did not give her the same look she had seen many a time on Dusan's face. "Do you forget that I can anak your feelings?" Roman asked kindly. "You are connected to my nephew through his child, and I grow concerned that you have seen something you're unwilling to share."

Isaura returned to the solar and poured herself some warmed cordi. Growing up, she had never preferred the drink, but consuming it made her feel closer to Dusan. And mayhap even allowed their daughter to grow an affinity for the sweet, fruity concoction.

"What have you seen?" he prompted, chin tucked as he homed his discerning eyes on her.

Lifting the cordi to sip, she met Roman's gaze. She would hold her peace, her fears. Not share them. *Because it scares you.* Speaking those words to him, confessing her doubts, felt a weakness. That mayhap their notions of her being a beacon were wrong. "I have had no dreams in days, which is not usual." What did it mean? Why did it feel . . . permanent? "And what dreams I did have most recently . . ." She shook her head. In truth, she hoped they were not real. Begged the Ancient for them not to be.

"You are a formidable woman, Isaura, and I can see why the Ladies chose you for Marco. These times are difficult—and that is mildly put."

Roman appreciated the weak smile she offered with that mute nod, but there was yet a coldness that hung about her, like mist shrouding a mountain. Her vague reassurances and deflections did little to dissuade him that her dreams were dark and frightening of late.

He was convinced of it. "Be glad for the dreams, though they alarm and make you fear for his safety."

"Glad?" Her green eyes glittered with the challenge so ready in her

Signature. "He speaks of strange creatures. Dark, numerous—terrifying. Powerful. He seemed . . ." Distress ran a tight cord through her efflux. "He was *scared*, Roman. Nothing scares Dusan. He is a fortress!"

"He has always wanted to think so," he said gently. "But the creature Xisya tortured him, awakened him to new realities, new cruelties. Marco has a right to be scared, and I am certain he is aware of that."

"These creatures . . ." She nodded, then shrugged, squinting. "I am not certain . . . They were massive, black—terrifying. Moving like nothing I've seen. There was some strangeness to them, starting one place, flitting to another, and ending . . ." Her mind seemed to drift to a place that shocked her scent with an icy, bitter stench.

He marveled that she had seen the creatures. "He is the Progenitor and has much to fight. Much to see to conclusion, including returning to you and seeing the birth of his daughter."

Chin pebbling beneath an attempt to restrain her tears, she sat elegantly poised, so young and beautiful. So intelligent, strong. "I saw . . ." Emotion thickened her words. "He looked injured—there were cuts on his face that had not been there before. Then as we talked, he simply started . . . fading." She flickered her fingers like the wings of a bird. "The dreamscape went white, and I have had no dreams since. If you are right, if what you speak is true about this being Lifespeech, why can I not reach him now?" Her gaze rose to his again, radiating an undercurrent of terror. "What if he is gone, Roman? What if those . . . creatures killed him and he does not return to us?"

Drawn by her grief, he went to her side and knelt. "Marco *will* return. He is the Progenitor."

With a huff, she stomped to her feet and whirled away from him. "I would not speak of his brand or that prophecy. They . . . they only ensure more violence, more darkness, and I—" She put a hand on her unborn child and shuddered around a breath.

He stood to face her. "Fear does not become you, Isaura."

"Then you have my most ardent apologies because that is all I seem to have left." She inclined her head, then glided to the side. "I . . . I am overtired, so . . . I bid you good rest." With a curt nod, she left and closed the door.

He drew in a long, heavy breath and smoothed a hand over his face. The times were certainly dangerous. It was uncertain who would stand and who would enter the Eternal Embrace before the end.

The air stirred minty and he sniffed. "You are late, maybe too late."

"I am not."

He angled to the Resplendent who appeared there, her face framed by black hair and shocking violet eyes. "She is gone."

"No," she said with no small amount of condescension, "she is in the other room. Choosing a green night dress. Green, for the father of her child."

Frustration tightened his muscles. "Why do you not speak to her, show yourself? With the enormity of what she carries, Isaura could use an ally, yet as your kind do in every other situation, you stay behind your stone walls and icy façades."

Oozing more condescension, she lifted her chin. "She has powerful advisors around her, and she is strong, or she would not have been chosen to bind with Marco or to bear his Daughter."

"If she does not need your help, why are you here?" Annoyance rifled the air, and Roman could hardly hide his smirk. So she *was* here for the girl. Good. "She is surrounded by men and—"

"Mm, I will give you that one—a most grievous thing."

He ignored her taunt. "She needs a woman's voice and touch in her life—your touch. That is why you have come, is it not?"

"And how do you know the inner workings of the Faa'Cris, Roman?"

"Enough games! Do what you have come to do—be an ally for Isaura. She's crumbling and needs help to bear this burden, someone—" He gritted his teeth.

"Someone with their hand in the River of Eternity?"

"Someone *not* swayed by circumstances or politics."

She considered him, quiet and contemplative, then her gaze drifted to the door, beyond which Isaura was preparing for bed.

"Vaqar would be ashamed of what has become of his legacy here."

"*Eleftheria's* legacy is thriving and—"

"Thriving?" He scoffed. "You are collapsing from within and know well it is time to come out of the caves."

"You know not of what you speak, Roman."

"What do you fear, Alanathina? That she will learn you are Marco's mother?"

25

D E V E R S O R I A

In his arms he held the world, and all was right and beautiful.

Beneath a mop of curly, sandy hair, Xylander slept soundly, peaceful in a nest of blankets and hide to keep the chill of Deversoria at bay. It was the first time his son had been quiet after making his triumphant entrance in the world.

As he bent forward, his arms forming a wedge in which the babe lay, Darius absorbed every detail of his son's round face. He balanced him with a leg and drew out a hand, then nudged his pinky into the small fist. Tiny fingers flexed open, then coiled tightly around his in a fist-hold. One day that grip would take hold of his broadsword.

"You are so perfect," he whispered, then glanced across the small chamber to where Kersei slept, recovering from the enormous miracle of giving birth. Warrior and beauty, she had it all. She was his all. Never had he loved another as he did her. Never would.

And he had failed her so miserably. Cruelly.

Xylander grunted, then squirmed, his jaw jutting as he grunted some more.

"So like your mother." The thought warmed Darius, realizing this tiny babe had parts of him, parts of Kersei. Together, they had created this beautiful little human.

So untainted, unfettered by ill choices, desperation . . . jealousies . . .

"Take care of her, Xylander," Darius whispered to his son, wondering what he would look like as a boy, a youth. A man. "I know you cannot yet swear it, but I ask this great thing of you, my son." His throat was raw with strangled emotion. "You are a Tyrannous, so I know you will succeed. Always protect her . . ."

With a staccato series of grunts, his son broke into a yawn. Stretched, his arms jutting up into the air. Reminding Darius of the birthing well. Seeing him drop into the world with vigor and objection.

"Fight for her, for what is right, for Kalonica."

Do what I did not.

Grief cut through him, aching to be there as Xylander picked up his first sword. Brought down his first deer. Earned his aetos wings as an aerios. Then the days he would be told of what his father had done, the title he should have held—prince, not duke.

Shame would follow.

"I beg your mercy," he whispered as his vision blurred, "for the burden I have laid on your very small shoulders and at your feet, my son. I plead for mercy with all my heart. Be as Marco, as Isaura, as your mother . . . Be better than me."

His eyes stung as Xylander once more gripped his finger and yanked it to his face, searching to suckle. *You are the only right thing I have done . . .* "So amazing and perfect."

"Beautiful, is he not?" Kersei's voice drifted into his awareness.

"Like his mother." Darius dashed away the tears and looked to the bed, glad to see she had not noticed his weakness as she climbed from the mattress. "What do you?" He was on his feet, curling Xylander against his chest as he moved to her side.

"I would use the privy, if you must know," she said with a lazy yawn.

A Lady appeared from behind a wall and assisted Kersei. Had she been there the whole time, listening to his chat with his son?

Xylander whimpered in his arms, then screwed up his face. A moment later, his healthy peal danced over the walls. "I think he knows you are no longer asleep," Darius called, bouncing his son to quiet him.

When Kersei re-emerged, her hair secured with a ribbon and wearing clean bed-clothes, she looked radiant. In the time it took the Lady to help Kersei get situated once more in the bed, with pillows and blankets around her, their son had vaulted into full-on screaming his demand for sustenance.

Darius delivered him to her and watched as Kersei set him to her breast as if she had nursed a dozen babes. So natural, so comfortable with motherhood. "I am relieved he is more your son than mine." His heart was a millstone as he smoothed Xylander's curly, sandy hair.

"Forget you his entrance? That was all Tyrannous." Laughing, she peered up at him.

"I seem to remember a certain fiery Dragoumis heir sparring with aerios and regia in Kardia's training yard and unseating one of the medora's fiercest."

"I had permission," she reminded, and there flickered something in her brown eyes that whispered of the betrayal he and Rufio had visited upon her and their realm.

The reminder pushed between them, trying to erase what little healing had arisen between him and this woman he loved more than life itself. It was also a reminder of the bargain he had struck and its price. This time with her, with their son . . .

He eased onto the edge of the mattress, studying her. Memorizing her features and dark eyes, shadowed with exhaustion from childbirth, yet she had never looked more beautiful.

"Why were you asking him to take care of me?"

That she had heard his moments with their son, his candid requests of the babe, made Darius's heart thump in his chest. He wanted to tell her. Wanted to explain—

"Darius." The authoritative voice came from behind, strong, compelling.

Standing, he did not need to turn to know which Lady addressed him. He touched his son's head again, the ache sharp, painful. Forbidding him from drawing an easy breath. "I have done wrong by you . . ."

"That is forgot." Kersei smiled.

He started, searching that fair face. Startled by the compassion there, the beauty, the richness of her adunatos . . . Though he had longed for her to grant him mercy—forgive him, as Marco said—he never expected her to do so. Now, she handed it to him. "I do not deserve it, or you."

"We are bound," Kersei said, something matter-of-fact in her words. "We have a son. There is no room now for the past. He is our future."

"Aye." How raw his throat! He bent closer, taking in those rosy cheeks, her black, unruly curls bunching around her shoulders. "Always know that I love you."

"Darius," she whispered, her eyes wide. "What do you?"

"Could I go back and repair what I have done, make it right . . . For you, I would. For our son." He leaned in and pressed his lips to her forehead. "I thought I was doing the right thing. I thought . . ." He shook his head. "I was wrong. So wrong."

She caught his sleeve with her free hand. "What do you?" she asked more urgently, as if she somehow knew . . . But then, had not she always known him best? Seen into his adunatos unlike any other.

"What I do, I do for you, for our son."

Panic scratched into her fair features. "What is wrong? Why do you speak like this?"

"Darius," the Lady called. "It is time."

Kersei looked between them, her eyes wide and panicked. "What? Speak to me!" She gripped the back of his neck. "Darius! What—"

"My beloved . . ." He caught her hand and pried it free. "If this works, perhaps the stain will be washed from my name, the burden from your shoulders."

"No! What is this? No! Darius, where—"

He cupped her face and kissed her, silencing her words, but knew he could never silence her cries, which followed him into the dark passages of Deversoria and into an act he could only hope would redeem him.

What was that?

Bathed in dust and debris from the collapse, Marco coughed and strained to see as he regained his feet. Eyes burning in the gritty air, he blinked, searching around for the two. "Eija! Jadon!" The mounds he checked were too small. The larger boulder had no limb sticking out from under it. They weren't here. How could they not be here?

Instinctively, he flung out his receptors, monitoring for threats, forgetting for a tick that he couldn't smell these infernal beasts. Except that light spicy note of Blue and something else . . . something familiar he struggled to place. But where were the others?

He couldn't pick up any hint of Eija . . . anywhere nearby. Her Signature still existed, but . . . not on this planet.

Should I be worried that I can tell that?

No, he needed to worry that Eija was missing. So was the Eidolon. And while the guy was useful and effective—though addlebrained over the girl—Eija's absence created a big problem. A *really* big problem. One that stood a little over two meters with a weaponized arm that outshot anything Symmachian.

Marco felt more than heard or anak'd the attack. Dropping into a crouch, he narrowly avoided the powerful arm of Blue barreling in with lightning speed and laser accuracy for his head. This beast had never really liked Marco— then again, did Draegis like any human? The only reason Blue protected the girl was because of the handprint. But with his objective missing, Blue had come unhinged.

Fingers on the ground, Marco swung his boot around. Swept the beast's leg out from under him. But not enough to knock him down. And it only enraged him more. This was going nowhere fast.

Marco leapt away, stumbling and struggling over the rocky piles. "Stand down!" He planted his feet, aiming the weapon that had attached itself to his arm over the brand. It was part vambrace, part killing machine, though neither made sense to him. Didn't have to in order to be effective, though. "Stand. Down!"

Blue came on, unyielding, trilling.

"Do it. Now!"

This man—creature, Draegis, whatever—might be transforming into something more humanlike, but he still had Draegis training and instincts. And undoubtedly, he would have no compunctions about killing Marco, should it fit his need.

Daq'Ti plowed on, his arm glowing and his maw chortling the volatile fury that made people—and Marco would be people—fear his destructive abilities. An energy pulse sputtered from Daq'Ti's arm. He chortled in rage and retracted his arm, powering it back up.

They didn't have time for this. "Enough!"

A squall of fury erupted again even as Marco pulled off a shot that went high. Daq'Ti's blow pitched him into the obsidian wall. Clacked his teeth. Warmth slid down his temple. Unwilling to be a punching bag, he toed the cavern wall and sprang up and over the beast, grateful there was at least that much room. But not enough for more than that. He firmed his stance, avoiding breaking a leg on the rubble, and faced Blue, who bellowed that warbling noise.

Teeth gritted against the agony of sound, Marco tensed, forcing himself not to show weakness. These creatures were primal. They understood basics—fight, rage, kill. Something in the air felt too much like that creature Xisya. Marco leapt up and drove a roundhouse kick at Daq'Ti's chest.

As he flew backward, Blue's eyes flared with anger and something else. Shock. Probably not used to anyone attacking *him.*

Making sure the beast was down, Marco vaulted forward. Landed hard on him. Dug his knee into Blue's throat. "Stop!" he roared. "She's gone. If you don't shut up, they'll locate and kill us. Then she'll be in danger, *unprotected.*" Was it his imagination or did the thing seem to look distraught? "Which means you failed her."

The beast's crimson eyes pulsed a few times, each one a little later than the last. Slowing. A mournful lowing issued from Blue as his eyes softened to a dull orange. Grieving.

I can work with that. He eased back and let him up. "Listen." Marco heard the thumping of the earth, the groaning of rocks around them. "We have to move. Get out of here before your buddies show up or the entire place collapses."

"I must find her," Blue trilled.

Unnerved, Marco couldn't hesitate. "She's not here—they're off-planet. I don't know how. Only way to find her now is to borrow a ship. Know where we can get one?"

Blue stared for several long pulses of his eye slits. "The city."

Marco motioned to the only remaining part of the tunnel that was open. "Let's go." Surprised when Blue scrambled up and trudged into the darkness, Marco followed him. And for the first time in a very long while, he was glad for his brand, which had drawn this device with its weapon and still gave off the subtlest of glows. They walked until it seemed his legs would fall off. The dark cocooned his mind, thrust him back to being in the lectulo. Which was much like being buried alive. Only he had air, though his mind wanted him to think he didn't. The sounds of the ship. The aching, relentless cold . . .

Marco stumbled. He grunted, hair falling into his eyes. Shaking off the memories, he was pulled to his feet by the Draegis, who urged him ahead. He remembered being trapped in the lectulo as the Draegis boarding party docked, then searched the ship. Killed the dark-haired pup.

Pup? That guy had to be in his midtwenties.

Marco wasn't even thirty yet and already felt like an old man. The crew of the *Prev*, by and large, were young and inexperienced, save the other Eidolon, Rhinn. Tigo's man. Regardless, too young to have been ripped from families.

Families . . .

He reached out beyond Void's Embrace. *Isaura.*

"Oh, Dusan! I am here. How good it is to hear your voice."

At the soft, sweet timbre of her voice, a tired smile tugged at his mood. *"I'm glad you're there and not here, my aetos, but I would be there."*

"And I would have you here. I have missed you. It has been so long."

So long? He laughed. *"We talked but a few hours ago."*

"Hours? It has been weeks, *Dusan."*

He slowed. *No . . .* He recalled the girl saying time moved differently here. *"The cycles are different. I will be home soon."*

"We need you. It is . . . bad here. Symmachia has attacked Drosero."

Heart in his throat, Marco stopped short. *"When? Are you well?"*

"Safe—at the hand of the Ladies, I am told. Symmachia seeks to destroy Vorn's fledgling fleet."

It made sense from a tactical standpoint—cripple Drosero, restrict their ability to fight so they have but one option: surrender. Which meant subjugation.

The beast behind him chortled, "Keep move."

Not realizing he'd stopped, Marco glanced over his shoulder and glowered before resuming the seemingly endless march. He had wanted to tell Isaura to stay strong but shied away from placing yet more weight on her shoulders. Also, he wanted to encourage her to keep counsel with her father, but what did he know of the political climate there? The only thing he knew unequivocally—he loved and trusted her completely. Strange how absolute that trust was, born of love and a common brand. He flicked his wrist involuntarily. The brand united them—not as it had him and Kersei, burned into their arms. But Isaura had been inspired with the symbol as a child and her ma'ma crafted it into an amulet. That necklace had been assurance to him that she was to be a part of his life. Told him she was important.

"Your uncle is relentless about my protection—and that of our daughter. I am not sure who is more ardent—him or my own father."

Marco frowned as he came to a juncture and hesitated, his mind warring with the options before him. Wait. Rhayld? He had not imagined the grand duke would show any concern for her, what with his desire to take the throne.

Daq'Ti's hand slid into view over his shoulder—Marco flinched, expecting a blow, but the beast pointed to the right. Thick in the heaviness of exhaustion, he trudged in that direction. He couldn't feel his legs and was growing clumsy. Weary, he wondered how much longer.

"Indeed—how much longer in this accursed system?"

"I ask myself the same each day you are gone," she said.

He knew not how they could communicate like this, but he savored it, believed it was true. Perhaps the Lady had given him a way to keep his hope alive despite the galaxies between them. Or mayhap a more plausible truth: the loss of scent by which to guide him was slowly eroding his sanity.

"Somehow, I will find my way back." They were the only words that would not unnecessarily burden her with worries that none could control. And they were his lifeline, his desperate prayer to Vaqar that he would not die in the belly of a planet that bred creatures from nightmares.

"Soon, I hope."

"Aye—"

Thump-creech . . . thump-creech . . . thump . . .

Slowing, Marco glanced back at Daq'Ti, who did that howl-chortle, then blew past him in a dead run.

What makes a terrifying beast run?

Not wanting to find out, Marco broke into a sprint.

DEVERSORIA

A week ago, Tigo relocated to a two-story dwelling near the training yard with his chosen: Moza, Xeros, Ferox, and Aegeus. Against his better judgment. But he'd give the Ladies a chance to prove their sincerity regarding change.

Nah. He was just determined to invade their lives as much as he could and with as much help from the Licitus as possible. He would not go quietly into the dark.

When he'd been aboard his corvette with the 215, he'd endured tight quarters and meals with the team. Privacy didn't exist. He was used to it, but somehow, rooming here with these four . . . was getting under his skin. Tigo rolled out of bed and grabbed his ruck. It'd become his routine, his escape, to hit the training yard before classes started and steal time to himself while working out. Win-win. Hustling down the steps, he heard a door open down the hall and he picked up speed.

"Tigo?"

Slag. Should've been quieter. He kept moving. "I'll be back—"

"We need to talk."

Hand on the doorknob, he glanced over his shoulder. All four stood in the small kitchen, sporting looks of expectancy. "'Bout what?" He hiked the ruck onto his shoulder, itching to get going.

"We think you . . ." Aegeus hesitated and then looked to the other three.

"Since we share a space," Ferox said, his voice clear, though a bit shaky, "we must all do our part."

Tigo flicked the doorknob and stepped back, frowning. "Part in what?"

"You do well with cleanliness, but the meals . . ." Xeros said.

"Meals." Tigo had to bite back a retort.

"It is the best way to foster community. Since we are locked away from our friends, meals are a good way—"

"Yeah." Great. He'd stood up to the most powerful supernatural creatures and ended up living with mother hens. "Understood." He pivoted and stepped out of the house.

He hated this. Hated being here. Raking a hand over his head, he stalked down the cobbled road to the training yard. Unbelievable. Cook meals. He'd freed those men from the outer-river colonies, chosen them to live among the Faa'Cris with him . . . and they complained that he wasn't cooking. Why couldn't they be more concerned about their sparring skills or their weapon accuracy?

Tigo made his way along the sloping hill lined with vendor carts from the river villages. Though there was little trade here in the city, there were armorers, blacksmiths, tanners, and such. Honestly, with the cream plaster walls that reflected light from touchstones, it never failed to impress Tigo how normal it felt here. Well, as normal as a suffocating underground city could feel.

In the training yard, he wrapped his wrists and took out his frustration on the punching bag. He transitioned to the track and sprinted, marveling at how much easier he moved, how much faster he could go, how much farther without tiring. There had to be something in the water down here. Next, he migrated to the firing range, but it was too easy. Even the pull of the weapon and the recoil did little to relieve him of the stress. So he picked up a collapsible javrod and stilled.

This was what Jez had given Kersei on the *Macedon*. A Faa'Cris weapon . . . All that time, his first officer had been a supernatural warrior and never said a word. She'd brought him down here . . . Why? Sure wasn't to be an ally, not considering the way she treated him as a lesser. Something to be crushed beneath her boot. Hide her identity, yank him from the only life he'd known . . . for what? To end up among the lightweights, bored out of his skull with men who wanted neither combat nor the skills to effect it?

With a jerk, he flung the javrod away. It whipped across the training yard and struck a wooden barrier with a resounding *thunk*, landing perfectly in the center target.

Are you kidding me? He stared at the reverberating rod. That . . . how . . . *Not possible.*

Then he sensed her—Jez. Invisible in the air around him, she'd guided the rod, snatched it from the air, and driven it into the wall.

Not interested. Tigo returned to the punching bag. Then again, maybe *he* was the punching bag these days.

"*Why are you angry?*"

"Out of my head," he growled, bouncing on his toes as he threw a right, left, uppercut . . . then a roundhouse. Felt good to be moving, exerting. Sweating.

She appeared at his side, aglow but not armored.

Breathing hard from the rapid-fire punches, he paused and adjusted the strap on his left glove.

"What is wrong?"

"What isn't?"

"She let you live here in the city."

"No!" Tigo forced himself to calm. "She just changed the locks on my prison."

Her violet eyes flared, eyebrow arching. "Is that really how you feel?"

"Have I *ever* lied to you?"

Her touch on his arm was light yet powerful. "Tigo."

Stepping back, he tightened his spine in a mock salute. "Yes, *Triarii Rejeztia?*"

Lifting her chin, Jez studied him, and he had the sense that she could see straight into his soul. And he hated it. Because they'd been friends, allies, Eidolon. Same team, same level playing field. "What you have been given is a great honor."

He locked onto her gaze. "What I've been given is a life I didn't ask for."

"But it's what you were designed for."

"No. *Fighting, protecting* the innocent is what I was designed for. Being the roach under your boot and bunkmate to men who can't remember where their manhood—"

"Tigo."

At her chastisement, he snapped his gaze down. "I hate it. I hate what your kind has done to the men here. They've been worn down, turned into weaklings! Is that how you like men? Subservient?"

Her gaze narrowed on him. "Understand, Tigo, the Faa'Cris have neither asked for nor needed any help. *We* are the warriors. *We* are the supernatural beings called upon to protect those of this planet." She was closer somehow, though he could swear she hadn't moved her feet or body. "Until now. What the Ancient has in store for this galaxy—"

"No."

She drew up, lips parted in surprised.

"I'm not doing this with you." He backed up.

"Doing what?"

"You justifying why things are different, yet your kind—"

"*Stop* calling us that!"

At the command in her words, Tigo gritted his teeth and snapped a nod. "Exactly." She'd been right before—he wasn't used to being the underling.

"I've never treated you as a lesser, Jez. Ever. Not you, Rhinn, AO, Diggs, or Esq. We were a team, worked *together*. Cohesively and ruthlessly because we knew our jobs and did them. That made us formidable and great. But you and the Faa'Cris do not understand the concept of teamwork or commitment—"

"How dare you!"

Void's Embrace. The fury roiling off her could practically be tasted. It scared him. Then enlivened him. *This* was the Jez he knew and loved.

"Love?" she snarled. "What do you know of love?"

In his thoughts again . . .

"You slept with every willing girl on the *Macedon*. Even Teeli!"

"*Teeli?*" Where had that come from? Frustration nearly strangled him. First his father accused him, now Jez . . . He turned into her space, his heart tripping over her words and the possible source of the anger. "I *didn't* sleep with her."

"She was in your bed—dead!"

Hands tense, he made a motion as if he'd strangle her and tightened his lips. "She was grieving—terrified of the mine plague riddling her body!"

"So you made love to her?" she yelled. "Do you realize how that must have hurt her, when she was already—"

"I. Didn't. Make. Love. To. Her!" Stunned by her rage, by her . . . "You really believe that of me? That I'd do something like that?" When she said nothing, Tigo shook his head. Backstepped. "Slag, Jez. I never realized you thought so little of me."

"You are a ladies' man."

"I'm an *advocate*. I believe in people." He sniffed and backed up. "Give it a try sometime. Or are you too arrogant and coldhearted to actually have feelings?"

Wings flared, Jez flew at him.

In the split-second before they collided, he braced too late—she lifted him from his feet. He knew she was going to slam him into the wall. Knew it'd hurt. Bad. The impact proved brutal. Like a sledgehammer pounded the air from his lungs. He hooked his arms around her so she couldn't drop him—but she jerked back and again slammed him into the wall. Released him at the last second with a ferocious twist.

He crumpled amid pops and groans, a howl in his ears. Jagged pain ripped through his body, but he didn't care. As trained, he gained his feet. Sighted her circling above for another attack.

Aflame, she glowered, white-hot daggers shooting from her eyes. Her armor and skin glittered with light reflected from an invisible source.

When she dived at him, Tigo scuttled backward, luring her in closer. Too soon, and she could recover and nail him. Too late, he could get killed. He waited . . . waited . . . adrenaline spiking as she barreled in. At the last moment, he dropped and rolled to the side. Felt the repetitive *thwump* of her span as she snapped them hard to reverse course.

Jez veered upward again, gaining altitude, then whirled around, tucked her feet, and flew at him.

What's going on? How had they gotten here?

She was coming hard and fast.

Tigo stood. Watched her come. Made a decision: No more fighting.

Enough, Jez, he threw his thoughts out there, not sure it would work. He had no idea how the Faa'Cris got in his head, but maybe . . .

She came unyielding.

When she closed the gap to five meters, he launched himself at her—but not at her body. At that dangerous span. Stabbed his fingers into the feathers that were both soft and hard. Dug in. Hung on, hampering her ability to lift. She fought him, her fury plain. When that didn't work, she coiled her wings around her body—and him with them—and whirled like a cyclone, trying to cast him off.

Tigo had been in zero-g spins before. He could handle it. But as her spin continued and his food from last night rose through his gut, he wondered if he'd made a mistake.

Yet . . . he wouldn't fight her.

Blood and fury coursed through her body. He felt it. Tasted it.

No more.

He let go. Let himself fall. It was over. It was truly over—their friendship. His life. He hit the ground hard. Bounced. Heard a distinctive pop and rolled, groping for a breath. Arching his spine, he rolled onto all fours, fire exploding through his side. Growled through the agony. He clenched his eyes. Hands in the dirt, he blinked around the blinding pain and realized there was something hard beneath his right palm. Metal. The collapsible javrod. Shaking from pain, he coiled his fingers around it. Lifted only his gaze to the flickering movement above. Watched as she tucked her wings back and dive-bombed for him—only to suddenly fan out her wings and arms, one wielding a sword.

Seriously?

Should he? What he intended could injure her. He didn't want this. He'd only ever wanted her friendship. Okay, maybe a *little* more. But Jez had always been unreachable. Unattainable. Better than him.

Tigo waited . . . waited . . .

She swept at him without mercy.

Instinct whipped him around, bringing the javrod up with the move. Somehow, unbelievably, he caught her off guard. Knocked her feet out from under her. Not waiting, he leapt forward and pinned her, javrod to her throat, boot on her wing. "Yield!"

Violet eyes blazed as she bucked beneath him.

A screech erupted in his head—a keening that nearly made him lose his focus and grip. "I am *not* . . . your enemy!" he gritted out. Warmth slid down his nose—blood. Felt it slipping down his neck—from his ears. "Stop," he wheezed.

Jez's eyes widened. She stilled.

The keening stopped, but he felt like he'd been vented into space. His head an anvil. Coldness chased the warmth from his veins. His lips grew uncooperative. Shifting to the side, he collapsed, groaning as his vision ghosted gray.

"Tigo!" She was at his side, cool fingers framing his face. "Tigo, talk to me."

What just happened? Why couldn't he think? He didn't want to look. Wanted to sleep . . . forever. Leave this place. This life. He hated it. Hated . . . He let himself fall into it. A better, warmer, quieter, safer place than—

"Tigo, *please!*"

Darkness and solace. Quiet and serenity. He would embrace them. So much easier . . . less painful.

"Tigo, *live!*" Her words echoed through his skull.

He groaned around hollowed hearing. Blackness receded, tugging a grainy gray blanket across his vision until it cleared, leaving the tangled brow of Jez hovering over him. Now she seemed concerned, worried. Not furious. The difference was startling. So was the memory of her nearly trying to kill him.

"Voids, Jez," he breathed, but even that sapped his strength. He moaned.

Something wet hit his forehead and he blinked. Looked at her.

Tears streamed from her eyes onto his cheek. "Please—I'm sorry. I'm so sorry." Cool, strong hands framed his face. "I didn't mean to hurt you." She tucked her chin, and a glorious, silky warmth speared his body.

He arched his back and drew in a shocked breath, unable to release it. Unable to breathe. *What . . . ?*

"Breathe, breathe. Just breathe it in, Tigo. Let it heal you. And please—come back to me. I'm sorry." Her forehead touched his. "It's my fault. I hated you for coming here, for not . . . seeing me." She choked off a sob. "I resented that you went for Teeli, that you were with her. You have no idea how much that hurt."

Tigo coughed, feeling the strain easing as he looked at her, really not sure his ears were working right. She couldn't have just said what he thought she did. That was the oxygen deprivation, right? "You . . . you didn't want me." He dragged his sorry carcass onto his side, propped himself up. "Made that clear." His head spun.

"I couldn't," she whispered, head hung low. "It is forbidden. I was sent to protect you. I wasn't allowed . . ."

Wasn't allowed what?

Scratch that—Jez said she hated him for going after Teeli. She was jealous? Wait . . . wait.

Wait wait wait. He came up into a crouch and tried to look into the eyes he'd loved for so long, eyes that she now hid from him. He tipped up her chin. "Jez . . ."

She resisted, but he insisted. Her beautiful caramel skin, those violet eyes . . .

"I cared for Teeli, yes," he conceded. "There was attraction there, sure, but as you so adequately pointed out to me—she needed a friend, a defender."

"You flirted with her. All. The. Time."

Disbelieving the jealousy rolling off her, Tigo stared. Was this real? He must've hit his head harder than he'd realized. "I know. But . . . I flirted with everyone. I liked letting women know they were amazing, beautiful. It was rarely anything more." How could she not know that "rarely" was her? "Jez." Should he spell it out? She just said it was forbidden.

"If you don't ask, the answer is always no," his father had often said.

"Jez, you said it—loving women is what I do. Granted, I made stupid mistakes. I had a gift for making women feel good about themselves. Now that you've put me in that holy bathtub—"

"Sanitatem."

"—I see now that I corrupted a gift. I was made a protector. And as scuzzed as it sounds, that's what I wanted for them. It's why I flirted with everyone." He swallowed. "Except you."

Her eyes snapped to his.

"What I feel for you—what I've *always* felt for you . . . Ancient forgive me, but it's lightyears more."

They both straightened. Her eyes returned to their normal caramel color, large and molten with expectation and . . . hope. During the time Jez and Tigo were attached to the 215, those eyes had made dreg of his thoughts.

Tigo couldn't get a bead on which way this was going. In their Eidolon days, he'd wanted to voice those words, his heart, but . . . here, every time he suggested anything close to interest, she threw him into a wall. "You always made it very clear you'd *never*—"

Her lips were on his, hungry, urgent. Her armor softened, vanished, leaving her thundering heart against his own.

It took Tigo a second to register the kiss. He'd never been slow with these kinds of things, but this—it was a shock. Yet before she changed her mind, he claimed what he'd sought for the last four years. Drew her into his arms and crushed her against his chest. Returned her kiss. Deepened it. Felt a tightening of the connection between them that reminded him of the viscous waters of the sanitatem—warm, comforting. Drowning.

She eased off, a crimson hue flushing her beautiful complexion even as tortured eyes met his.

Oh no. "Jez—"

"We can't."

"We just did." Noticing she had fist-holds of his shirt, he kissed the edge of her mouth again, wanting more. Wanting another—

She shoved back, nearly pushing him off his feet. He'd never get used to that. Or that *something* in her expression, the hardness that returned.

"Are you serious?" he balked. "You kiss me like that and then—"

"I am disappointed," intoned Decurion Cybele, her voice echoing through the yard.

Voids. Tigo jutted his jaw. "I'm not." Grinning, he retrieved a weighted rope and his gear. "That was an impressive kiss." No way was he going to let them minimize this. "One I didn't ask for"—he glanced at Jez, then Cybele—"or steal."

"The Revered Mother extends grace and mercy to you, allowing you to live in the city," Cybele said, words punctuated with each step she took, "and *this* is what you do—accost a triarii!"

Tigo barked a laugh. "You've got that backward. What happened between Jez and me—"

"*Triarii Rejeztia* is how you address her. Your arrogance will bring you down, Tigo Deken." Decurion Cybele flapped out her wings, lifting off the ground.

They'd become so predictable in their reactions and their maneuvers that he anticipated it. Waited for the opening . . .

She arched her spine to snap that span at him, like a mother trying to whip a rebellious child.

That opening, right there.

He flicked the bolas.

Cybele saw his move and twisted—too late. Her attempt did the work for the bolas, the rope catching across her torso. Weights flinging around her once . . . twice . . . Thumping hard against her chest, closing the wingspan. She shuddered, instantly losing altitude. Stumbling, she couldn't avoid being grounded. She staggered, only going to a knee.

Right before Tigo.

"Whose arrogance brought them down, Decurion?" Shock rippled through the room, and Tigo saw her blanch, then go red. "Humiliation is a bitter crumb, isn't it?"

At once, Faa'Cris descended on him.

Void's Embrace!

As a shout boomed through the training yard, Tigo ducked the blows raining down on him. They forced him to the ground. Shoved him forward. Planted his face in the dirt even as his arms were jerked out to either side.

The attack abated, and he felt the remonstration that hung in the air. Slowly, he lifted his head. Spat the dirt from his mouth. His ribs were aching. His back likely bruised.

Never again. He was done. They could do their own scuzzing training. Even as he resolved to leave Deversoria, he noticed his left eye swelling shut. Before it closed off, he caught sight of the Revered Mother striding across the yard, rage in her left hand and judgment in her right. Behind her stormed the Resplendent.

Yeah, he was as good as dead now.

"Release her," the Revered Mother calmly instructed two Faa'Cris, who rushed forward to free Decurion Cybele. "And him!"

Once on her feet and roiling with fury, Cybele cradled her left shoulder. Blood trickled down once-pristine feathers, the crimson shade matching the one in her face from being bested by a Licitus.

Tigo had the good sense to feel chagrined. He hadn't meant to injure her, but he'd had enough. They wanted slaves, not allies to fight with. They'd brought him to train the Licitus. He'd done that. Now, his job was finished. *He* was finished. No more would he—

Sucking in a hard breath, Tigo locked onto eyes he'd never expected to see again. Eyes that reminded him he'd never been good enough. *"Mom?"*

Whatever was coming at them was big and fast.

Marco sprinted—as much as his still-healing body would allow. He missed the days of flinging himself across rooftops and finding more thrill than exhaustion. Unbelievable. After months in the hull of the *Prevenire*, he still lacked the stamina to run down an underground passage.

He banked right, the dust of Blue's trodden path guiding him. The thunder of whatever pursued them vibrated the ground, and he knew if they didn't find shelter or some pulse cannons, they were going to end up roadkill. But at the next juncture, he skidded to a stop, realizing the path ahead wasn't dusty.

Where did Blue go? It was quiet, still. Too st—

Something latched onto his collar from behind. Jerked.

Marco twisted his spine and popped his legs at the wall. Toed it. Gained traction to do a backflip. Even as he landed, he registered the beast. His heart pounded as Blue again grabbed his shirt and yanked him forward into his chest.

He'd no sooner rolled around Daq'Ti and into a tiny alcove than pebbles were raining down on them, the concussive thuds of the pursuing creature too close. A second later, it rounded the corner and barreled past.

Marco's gut churned at the sight of the massive rodent with hairy hide and wings. Its teeth—

Reek!

Razor-sharp. Two tusklike canines protruded like twin swords.

Blue pointed to something on the ceiling across from them. "There!"

A wooden door secured with an iron latch and lock.

Marco stilled. Where did it lead? What if it was a trap?

A claxon rang out, as shrill as one on a ship, but this one was animalistic. Clear it had come from the oversized rodent, who must've realized he'd lost his quarry.

Blue moved with incredible speed—at least he hadn't lost that in his metamorphosis—and leapt at the door. Caught the handle and shoved, all in one movement. The door flopped open with a crack.

Down the darkened passage spiraled a howl of objection.

With a frantic gesture, Blue waved Marco up into the opening. "Go, go."

"You first." Marco still wasn't convinced Blue had anyone's interest in mind except his own.

Blue didn't hesitate. He hopped up and caught the ledge, sliding through with ease and confidence. As his legs vanished through the hole and into the upper darkness, Marco slipped from the alcove. Even as he did, he saw a blur of black hide barreling at him, thunder rattling the walls as the horn sounded again.

Marco leapt. Gripped the edge. His muscles strained with the effort. Again, he cursed the months in the hull that depleted his strength. Half his body through the opening, he gripped a rock, struggled the rest of—

Fire tore through his calf.

"Augh!" He felt himself sliding, being pulled back under.

Hands grabbed him, hauled him up and away from the vermin.

After landing hard, Marco rolled onto his back, panting, growling around the fire in his calf. Hot pain and blood coursed from the wound.

Blue slammed the trapdoor shut and secured it with an iron crossbar and series of locks.

Good. Marco scrambled backward from the opening, knowing those sword-tusks could easily pierce the boards. He wasn't ready to be impaled again. His leg throbbed violently. He reached over his shoulder and grabbed his shirt, yanking off, then wrapped it around his calf. Hair dangling in his face, dripping with sweat, he felt dizzy.

"I get help," Blue rumbled, those crimson slits changing. What started as slits were now oval. Somehow, the outer two sat wider and higher while the middle shortened and slid down. Eyes and a nose. The change was . . . haunting. Again, he pointed to Marco. "I get help . . . you . . . not rest."

Not rest? What . . .? Marco eased back, leaning against the wall. His head felt like a boulder, his eyelids drooping. Wet hair curled into his eyes, and he shoved it back, fed up with the sweat stinging his corneas.

Weight settled on his shoulder and brought him up sharp.

A somber chortle went through Blue. "Eyes shut. Safe here. Wait."

"Right. Sure," Marco murmured, the exhaustion and weakness overtaking his common sense. He gave himself to the sleep, anxious to find Isaura. Hear her voice. See her beautiful green eyes.

"Isa . . ."

Emptiness held him hostage.

He shifted, turning, his hair once more jabbing into his eyes.

"Isaura? Please . . ."

He needed her. Needed her voice, her touch.

Nothing met him save the cold, hard walls of a dungeon type of room. Shoulder to shoulder. Trapped. In the hull again.

No . . .

Can't move. Can't breathe.

All at once, he relived the day Xisya and Baric anchored him into the hull. First, they'd paralyzed his body so he couldn't fight. But his mind was aware and angry. Livid they were doing this to him. They laid him in the lectulo. The gel cocooned his body. He felt the invasive poking and insertion of tubes and nodes. The tube down his throat, suffocating, choking. Agony. Terror. Excruciating.

"No!" he growled, wrestling to free himself. But the cuffs tightened, yanked his arms up over his head. He couldn't breathe. Couldn't think. Couldn't see. Dark . . . so dark . . .

"Isaura! Where are you?" Tears streaked his face. *"I beg you. Please. Show me your face, your love."* A strange menthol intruded into his receptors.

"Quiet, be still."

Baric. Though his voice was strange, lilting.

"Get off me!" Marco shoved the hand aside.

"Hold him down—it's for his own good."

Weight fell on him. Crushed him.

Not the lectulo again.

Marco cursed. Thrashed. *Please, Vaqar!* Lady! *I beg you!*

Something coiled around his thoughts, his mind, weighted but warm. Reassuring. Blacks shifted and changed to grays, then blues, then . . .

A hand moved from his face, bathing his receptors in menthol. Woodsy. Earthy. Marco relaxed into it. The darkness fell away, taking panic and fear with it.

UNKNOWN PLANET

Eija hunched closer to Reef, her nose practically to his back, following each shin-high print he made in the snow. Not only would it hide their numbers, but it also made each step easier for her, since he was shielding her from the driving winds and bitter elements. Hours ago, they'd spotted a small village on the rim of a gorge and set out for it.

Snow. So much snow.

"I thought I liked snow," she muttered. Feet and hands numb—oh, who was she kidding? *Everything* was numb. She couldn't feel anything, and walking . . . well, yeah, Reef's steps paved the way, but the blank whiteness made it hard to judge depth. More than once she'd stomped, tripped, stumbled. This time, she crashed forward, jarring her knee as she landed on all fours. That's when she realized her hands weren't hurting anymore.

Djell.

Reef circled back and hooked his arm through hers. "C'mon. Up."

"I can't. I can't do this anymore."

"Exactly. I'll give you a piggyback."

"Don't," she said, her jaw stiff. Everything was hard to move! As she struggled to her feet, she felt the air swirl. Heard something. She hesitated and glanced around.

"What?" Reef asked. "Pretending I don't exist again?"

"Do you?"

"Well, you can zap me right out of here the same way you zapped me here."

She growled at him. "Stop saying that. I have no idea how—" Wait. There it was again. Thumping . . . "That noise—tell me you hear it."

Reef jerked. Pivoted, hand going to her side as he nudged her behind him in a protective stance.

A half league out, the snow belched a herd of white-and-gray beasts that reminded her of hairy rhinnocks. And they were charging straight for her and Reef.

"Oh no."

Reef spun her. "Go! Run!"

"Where?" she balked. "There's nowhere to go! We can't outrun—"

"So we die trying!" He shoved her onward. "C'mon. Move!"

Eija stumble-ran, tripping and staggering in a sloppy lope that had to look like someone drunk. But there was a newer, louder noise joining the thunder. A bellowing. Shouts. She glanced to the side, which promptly tangled her legs and slammed her into the crusty snow.

Reef hauled her up again, then he tripped.

As she helped him back to his feet, she felt a gust of air from the opposite direction. Was suddenly lifted from her feet. She screamed, arms flung out as she was hoisted up and laid over some beast. Heart pounding, she glanced up at the helmeted face of the rider who had secured her.

People! They hadn't seen anyone since they appeared here two days ago, the only signs being that village in the distance. But these people had rescued them from the hairy rhinnocks and elements. Their mounts were so like horses but with different, less elongated heads, and the gait! It surged and . . . swam. Almost like surfing an air current, which nearly toppled Eija at every change in direction. The drilling beat of the beast's gait punched her stomach, over and over, despite the way the rider pinned her.

They veered right, as if chasing the sun from the horizon. The relentless pace continued unabated, long after darkness fell over the land, pounding new aches into a body she was sure would never feel anything else again. Her head and neck ached, her stomach muscles exhausted from trying to spare her gut the trauma of repeated impact.

Suddenly, an enormous wall appeared out of nowhere less than a league out. And they barreled straight for it. Anticipating an impact—did they not see it?—Eija strangled a scream as the distance erased and the wall rushed at them.

Without warning, the rider pulled up hard, mounts skidding and sliding sideways to a stop—and had a gap not suddenly yawned in the wall, they would have careened into it. Instead, they straightened and bolted through the opening into a short tunnel. A move they performed with such casual ease, she knew they'd done it a lot.

Eija sucked in a sharp breath and the sudden, drastic difference of scenery. Outside the wall, whiteout. Inside, snowy-draped earth, brown and protected. The abrupt absence of cutting wind felt like a hearth to her frozen body. She wanted to enjoy it, but she hurt too much.

"Hoy!" a man shouted.

Eija's rider veered to him, then lifted her as effortlessly as he had before and handed her off to the man. She couldn't move. Couldn't even protest when he caught her in a basket hold and hurried across a muddy town square and entered a plastered building. He set her on a chair near a blazing fire. The place was as big and open as the gym at the Academy, and its large hearth victoriously threw light through the structure. Women hurried around, two layering blankets on Eija. The warmth should have been glorious, but it proved horrifically painful. She grimaced and bit through the torment. How was—

"Reef!" Eija jerked around—and stilled, seeing men ferrying him inside. They hurried Reef to the fire and placed him before it as several women knelt, cocooning him in pelts and blankets.

Why wasn't he moving? Was he even breathing? Her heart spasmed, anxious to reach him. She eased forward as a woman pushed something onto her hands, but she couldn't take her eyes off Reef.

His face . . . his expressionless face. Eyes staring up, but not blinking.

"He's dead!"

Rising from the sanitatem, Tigo was immediately aware of two things: one, he was naked—again—and two, he was not alone. He re-immersed himself and glanced over the lip of the bath, more than a little embarrassed to find Resplendent there, waiting. Staring. The last time he'd come out of this thing, the attendant told him clothes would manifest. And they had. But not immediately. He'd distinctly remembered a draft. Felt it again as he emerged this time, covering himself.

"The body is natural and—"

"*Naked*," Tigo interjected. "You might be cool with this, but I'm not." It was all kinds of twisted and wrong. Bending to shield himself as he felt the clothing manifest, or whatever it was called. He clenched his jaw at the fierce warriors arrayed before him. "Couldn't summon me once I was, you know— repaired *and* dressed."

"We were concerned," the Revered Mother said, "you would make good on your promise."

Tigo straightened, smoothing a hand over the material molding to his thigh—mostly to make sure it was really there—and glanced at the woman called Revered Mother, who didn't look old enough to be a mother, let alone a revered one. "What promise?"

"To leave."

He frowned, knowing he had not spoken that out loud. Curse their mind reading.

"What is in the heart finds its way into the world, whether spoken through the mouth or Lifespeech."

"Except I don't do"—he waved his hand around—"Lifespeech. Anyway." He tugged the tunic, then jutted his jaw. "My mother, where is she?"

The Revered Mother inclined her head. "Come."

Down a long hall of arched columns, Tigo followed her into a marble amphitheater. The Revered Mother directed him to the dais. As he stepped to the lectern, he eyed the arc of chairs at the front, suddenly filled with the

Ladies who had attended his bath. Except one. The woman in the second seat to the right. "Mom."

Her eyes were as hard as ever. She'd never been cruel, only strict and direct. "Tigo."

My mom. Here. Unbelievable. He'd known she wasn't dead. Told his father he'd find her. And he had. "So. Abandon your husband and son and come here to reign as a queen."

"I am no queen nor ruler."

He gave a cockeyed nod. "Guess we didn't fawn over you enough, the way the Licitus here do." Yeah, he knew it was the wrong thing to say as soon as it escaped his lips. But really, how did they find it okay to leave behind their children and husbands and hide belowground?

The Revered Mother took a seat beside his mom. "Our ways confound."

"Definitely." He squared his stance and folded his arms. "You know, we're all out there, doing our best to live and not let evil win. We hear tales of benevolent immortal Ladies who alter the lives of people, protect women and children. But if they really knew what you were like, that you cowered beneath stone pillars and treated men like worms—"

"We are not immortal," his mother countered.

Tigo snorted. Of all the things for her to respond to . . . "Yeah, that makes everything okay, I guess."

Her violet eyes—which were brown in their other life—sparked beneath a fringe of brunette hair. "We do not expect you to understand our ways or rules—"

"Good!" His voice bounced off the marble walls. "Because it's impossible." He shook his head. "You know, at first, I thought—just *maybe* I haven't given them the benefit of the doubt. Maybe I should learn, give it time, so I can understand." He lifted his hands in surrender. "But I give up. No way can I figure out how you've gone from benevolent Ladies who protect women and children to . . . this—women who lord their power over men. Punish them and beat them into weak, subservient, cowering fools worried about meal prep and tidiness." He shuddered. "Where are the warriors Vaqar sought—"

A stream of heat rushed against him, angry and violent. Tigo staggered back a step. Sniffed and pursed his lips. "Thank you for proving my point. Again."

"We would beg your mercy." The Revered Mother sent a quelling glance at the other Ladies in the arc. "We are not used to anyone speaking to us in such a manner. Yet, you are right, and that is why I have brought you before the Resplendent. Why I have allowed you to see your mother again."

Allowed. They wielded power like a pulse cannon.

He again looked at his mom and could almost swear there was a softening around her eyes. Maybe even her mouth. *Dream on.* "Great. Thanks. Nice to know she's not dead. I'll be sure to let my father know."

His mom stood. "Domitas knows I am alive and where I am."

Sucker punched, Tigo blinked. "Come again?"

She was in front of him, her voice soft, ethereal. *She* was ethereal. Though petite in stature, she seemed all tall elegance before him. "With the impending war and complications related to Tascan Command that endangered far too many lives, I had to leave Symmachia. Too, there were matters more important than myself or my own desires. Domitas knew and accepted that." She caught his hand. "I would explain it. Will you hear, Tigo? Can you set aside your anger and bitterness?"

No, but considering the Ladies' ability to reach into his hidden ramblings, he did his best to guard that thought. "Explaining will not change the past, what you did."

"True, but it could change—perhaps save—the future." Renette Ukat-Deken, apparently also known as Miatrenette, inclined her head. "May I show you?"

He tightened his jaw. Before he even finished his nod, the air swirled, and he suddenly stood not in that marble hall but in the cold, sterile structure he'd called home for most of his life. A shape moved from the shadows, and he flinched, automatically reaching for a phase pistol he didn't have. But then the person registered. "Dad."

Relief rushed through the ruddy, bearded face of Admiral Domitas Deken as he crossed the room, surprise shocking his expression. "Ren, Tigo." There was emotion never heard before in his father's voice as he pulled them both into a hug.

Stunned, Tigo could not respond. This . . . this was not his existence with his parents, the niceties they played at, the façade of caring and concern. He jerked away. Frowning at the two who had brought him into the world. The two who had left him to wade through grief on his own. "I don't . . . This doesn't . . ."

"Make sense?" his father asked grimly. "You were a hellion after she left, and I wasn't sure there was any coming back from the damage our decision did to you."

Tigo eyed them. His broad-shouldered, barrel-chested father. His mother, who now only reached her husband's shoulder, yet in Deversoria . . . Well, to say she was much changed would be the understatement of the century.

Our decision.

They'd made a decision. Together. For his mom to leave. To conceal that and their reasons from him. Never thought to include him in a life-altering change. "Why?" His question felt small and empty compared to what he wanted to say. Voids, he wanted to deride them both. But *why* was the single most important thing he had to know.

"You know that answer," his mother said quietly. "You saw her."

Her? On the *Macedon*? Did she mean Kersei?

"No," Mom said.

Another "her" bled into his thoughts, souring his stomach and erasing the image of the Droseran. "Xisya."

"Her arrival marked the beginning of the war foretold for centuries, the Reckoning," his mom said. "When that happened, most Ladies were summoned back."

"Most."

"Some were too strategically placed to remove. But it was imperative we begin preparations."

"But you spar and train—every day, all the time," Tigo argued. "I've seen nothing but sparring since I entered that underground fortress."

"For centuries, the Faa'Cris have sparred and trained—among each other." She sighed. "Over and over so that it is memorized and rote. But we were not and are not in a place to fight for the people, as we should, as we were designed to. Even you have seen that we have grown . . ."

"Stiff-necked." Had to admit—he enjoyed seeing her cringe. "The Faa'Cris work hard at your version of preparedness, which is limited to being strict and unyielding with those under your charge."

Though she winced again, his mother offered no defense or argument. "In many respects, you are right. It was easy to think of the war as something *coming*, not something *here*. Not a threat that would endanger our very existence." She glanced at his father with a small smile that had both familiarity and affection. "He has ever been your son."

His father stroked his beard and sniffed. "That stubbornness is all you, Ren."

They both laughed, but then his mom sobered, touching her temple. "When Rejeztia brought you to Deversoria, I realized the hour of sparring and recitation of laws was over. Yet . . ." She shook her head. "We did not know what changes to make, so we are forced to accept that we have grown complacent, self-focused—protecting our own, isolating and justifying that isolation. Then brands of Marco and Kersei awakened, starting the clock in a concrete way. That event was like a tripwire. Repercussions rippled through all Faa'Cris, and we realized how unready we were—are. So much had to change for us to not only face this threat but successfully defeat it. So much change. Especially . . . us."

Okay. Great. What did she expect him to do with this? Was it supposed to excuse what they'd done? How she'd left and they'd lied to him? He locked onto his dad. "You were . . ."

"Cruel?"

"Absent," Tigo hissed. "MIA. After Mom left, you vanished. Left me with the fragments of our life. And now, I'm just supposed to shrug and say 'cool'?"

"If you want a pity party, that's out the airlock. You're welco—"

"Domitas," Mom chided, placing a hand on his thick, hairy arm as she turned a pleading gaze to Tigo. "There is no apology large enough to repair the negative impact our decisions had on you. I realize that. But . . . war, Tigo. We face an impossible war. You—"

"Yeah. What about me?"

Her expression cleared. "You were chosen."

Tigo screwed his brows up and struck his arm out, angling to show the bare forearm. "No brand, no prophecy."

"*I* chose you," she said. "Even from a boy, you had a peculiar skill with tactics and soldiering and charm. You could win over the hardest of coldhearted tutors. You have been in Deversoria but a few months—in Quadrant Standard Time—and already, you have trained the Licitus in basic personal combat skills, taught them to respond to a threat instead of cower. And though, I grant, the Faa'Cris have not embraced your insistence upon change, you have challenged us—"

"To what end?" He ran a hand over his face. "You Ladies see yourselves as infallible. As superior. The Licitus still want to worry more about meals than weapons or tactics."

Her lips quirked up.

"Don't do that." He hated when she did that. It meant she saw something he didn't, and it invariably came with another lesson. She'd always been ready with those. Now he knew where she'd gotten that particular gift.

"I can answer part of that," his father said. "The Ladies *are* superior, Tigo. Far superior—they can move across time and distance without issue."

"We are limited, however," she clarified.

"She can also do fancy tricks in the air with her wings," Tigo added facetiously. "But abilities don't necessarily translate to moral superiority. The Ladies reject my every attempt to integrate the Licitus. You treat them—*us*, men—like second-class citizens. You say you want us there, that I was chosen, yet you refuse—"

"Indeed, you are right. We have resisted the very change we brought you here to effect." She glided to his side and touched his arm. "It is not easy to accept that we have been wrong in measures designed to protect our kind." She glanced at her hands, rubbing them nervously. "Rejeztia shared with the Resplendent what happened in the training yard."

Heat washed through Tigo as he fell still. What exactly had she told them?

"Not just about the kiss—"

Well . . . slag.

"—but about how she gave in to passions of anger, jealousy—and yes, even carnal desire toward you."

"Huh." His brain wouldn't work beyond that, and he felt the heat of a blush creeping into his face at hearing this from his mom. Skip the fact that she was a supernatural being and pause right there on him being embarrassed in front of the entire Resplendent council. "Wait." He had no idea why that hit him so late and so . . . weird. "You? You're a . . . Resplendent."

Dad grinned. "That's pretty much how I took it when she told me."

"You're like . . . the queens. The . . . rulers."

"We are the oldest of our kind and tasked with ensuring the Ladies function as Vaqar intended so that, together, we serve the Ancient." She gave him a sad, knowing smile. "But over the years we have lost our way and become the very kind of people we fled—cruel, insensitive, self-absorbed."

Tigo stared at her for a long second. "Wow." Never thought he'd hear that from any of them, let alone his mom.

"After a long, lively conversation, the other Resplendent and I have come to an agreement: in order to survive what yet comes, we must change— ourselves and our methods."

It had a feel-good fuzzy warmth to it, but he'd been in the thick of their stubborn resistance when they'd beaten him to the ground in the training yard. "I don't think you're ready to change."

She took his chastisement with but a little hesitation. "Regardless, we *must*. Or all is lost. The purpose for our existence is lost."

"And what is your purpose?"

"To win a war and reckoning that is yet being initiated by a man you met—and unwittingly saved."

"A man, I might add," Dad said, "who cost you your career."

"Marco." Tigo shifted. "He didn't cost me my career. I sacrificed it, believing what was happening to him and Kersei to be way out of line."

"You have a way of seeing those wrongs in old, well-established cultures and traditions," his dad said as they both nodded. "And rightly so."

"While change is hard—and no, I do not like some of the alterations that must occur—this is not about me or the Faa'Cris," his mom said. "This is about what the Ancient has decreed, what He would accomplish. Humanity needs us to set aside our selfish protective measures. What we are fighting for will far outlast any of us." She smiled at him in that mom way of hers. The one that told him he wasn't likely to come out of this with his own way intact. "I believe your passion for seeing women come into their own identity is a gift of the Ancient. You care about what happens to us, Tigo. And I believe there's a reason for that."

He looked at his father. "You . . . as fleet admiral—"

"I'm positioned and it's strategic. Those around me do not know about your mom, about you, or about me. And they will not. Since they killed Galt—"

"Alestra?" Tigo jerked at the news, feeling a hum of anger. "Alestra's dead?"

"In a manner of speaking," his mother said.

He again stared at her, his brain whiplashing through her tone and words, until it finally caught up. "She . . . she was a Lady?" He'd tried to date a Lady? And now wanted to date another . . . "Ladies don't die."

"That's not wholly true," Mom said, dismayed. "Contrary to many rumors, we are not immortal. If we die outside Deversoria, we *are* dead. It is why Daughters choose to return before the natural world claims their adunatos. However"—she flashed a tight smile—"we are off-track. The reason I brought you here was to lend understanding to the scope of what we face. Why things—our marriage, my departure from Symmachia—were crucial to the overall scheme. Dom had to remain in Command, but I could not stay. If the creature had discovered me . . ."

Xisya. "I . . . I don't understand." But didn't he? "You say she's connected to this?" His mind recoiled, realizing it had all started around the same time he'd become aware of her.

Mom again nodded. "Her kind and the Faa'Cris have a common origin."

Tigo stared at her, disbelief blocking his ability to process those words. "Origin." He was a glitching feed. "What does that even mean?"

"The creature you encountered is from a race that once numbered among the Faa'Cris. But there was a revolt, and a great number were banished for the insurrection. They initially sought shelter on a nearby planet. What the Khatriza did, not only to the people they should have protected, but to the men of the worlds around us, was not just a violation of the purpose behind our existence, but an abhorrent, reprehensible thing. The mine plague arose from their machinations, their efforts to repress and force men into submission."

Mine plague . . . "Tryssinia." Teeli. He rubbed his jaw as her last four words echoed between them. "That sounds very familiar."

"You know not what you say, Tigo. This went way beyond behavioral submission. Because of their violation of the sacred oath to Vaqar, they were thrust away, their abilities dimmed, and they were ordered never to return to the Quadrants or they would face eternal destruction."

"But Xisya is here."

"Yes, and I'm convinced more are coming. That's what the rings and *Chryzanthe* were designed for—to bring more of her kind for war."

"But she's here and she's not destroyed."

"They all will be."

"I don't understand—"

"I know," she said quietly but with a measure of finality. "If we had more time, I would give you the entire history and legacy of all that has brought us to this hour. But our purpose here is more direct."

Tigo felt the old bitterness creeping in and tried to shoulder it aside. "And what is that?" He motioned between them. "Are we supposed to hug and forget everything?"

Irritation carved through her pretty features. "Dom, until next time."

"Which I hope is not as long as the gap between this visit and the last."

That hardness rippled and smoothed for a fraction of a second. "I would will it, too, but you well know there are far greater concerns than our affection for each other."

"Yeah, not helping," Tigo grumbled, uncertain what to do with this tenderness between two people he'd long believed hated each other.

His mother looked at him, and the air swirled. In the space between blinks, he was aware of a grayness, a blurring of realities. By the time his vision cleared from that lone blink, he was standing . . . elsewhere. His heart stammered, as did his brain. Both trying to catch up. "Where . . .?" The air in his lungs struggled, too.

"Cenon," she said.

Tigo nodded, slowly recognizing the market he'd stalked down with the 215, searching for Kersei—having clearly seen her in that terminal with her Droseran kin, yet reporting they hadn't.

To avoid colliding with a hurrying woman and child, he shifted aside. Bumped into a lanky youth, who tucked his chin and scurried away. "Why are we here?" He hated this planet. Hot, humid, and crowded. He just didn't remember it being *this* crowded.

A ship screamed overhead, making him duck. *Void's Embrace*, that was a low-flier. He peered up at the craft, clearly marked a Symmachian. Above it, two more were making for space, likely to join an orbiting battlecruiser.

"Look at them. Look hard." His mother climbed a set of stairs until they were standing on the upper deck of a building that overlooked the bustling port. "With your Eidolon eyes."

Eidolon. What did that mean?

Tactical.

Maybe . . . but he somehow felt it was more about the purpose of being an Eidolon, to protect the people. To do violence on behalf of the innocent. To see things most people miss and use them for a tactical advantage.

So . . . what did she want him to see here?

People. A lot of people. Too many. To the right, a high-end restaurant on stilts rose far above them and accommodated the rich, sometimes known in Herakles as the evengis class, who dined on gold-dusted food, while immediately below was a square filled with the working-class and hovering in the shadows, darting into the open, then bolting back after snagging a scrap of bread or a dropped coin . . . the poor.

His gaze struck a young girl being guided down an alley, the vise grip of a well-dressed man all but cracking her bone. Yet the girl said nothing. Did nothing. Just walked. Right into the south end of the main terminal. And while Tigo didn't have heightened senses like Kynigos or even his mother, apparently, he smelled the truth of this place in the air.

His mom leaned against the rail and took in the scout-littered sky, the low-orbit fliers, cars darting in and out. "The Tertian Space Coalition has added almost a half dozen planets to its roster in the last two months alone. Admiral Lorcan, President Gadar, and Emissary Teumpi are courting the remaining planets, convincing them to join the Hyperjump Interplanetary Trade Channel by regaling them with reports of booming trade routes and economies."

Tigo bent forward, his nerves buzzing with what he saw. "Yet leaving out how HITCh creates crowded port cities, higher crime rates, encourages trafficking . . . and an ever-widening gap between rich and poor."

"But listen to them." Sorrow threaded her brow. "Hear their thoughts."

He nodded, glancing around, trying to pick up pieces of chatter. "I think—"

All at once came a skull-piercing din of conversations. He jerked his gaze to his mom, whose eyes remained focused on the crowds, so he turned back to them. Tried to match the voices in his head with the people nearby.

Prices are jumping, a woman thought as she handed over coins to a merchant nearby . . . the same merchant who was wondering if he should've charged her double because once his dwindling supply ran out, he wouldn't be able to feed his family.

Putrid grief swung out from the alley, followed by a violent growl as a man wagered with another for how much a girl would fetch in the brothels.

Tigo straightened and started for the stairs.

"No," intoned his mother. "We must—"

"I can't let them just take her!"

Even as the objection stabbed his thoughts, he found himself back in the stone amphitheater. He faltered, his balance off as if he'd just been in zero-g. He scowled. "Why'd you do that?"

Her chin raised. "What you have seen, what you heard . . . do you now understand why we need you? Why we must learn to fight—together?"

Tigo balled his fists. "I'm ready to fight, but that whole 'together' thing is something you Ladies need to look up. I'm not the one who struggles to understand teamwork."

"You are right," the Revered Mother said, joining the conversation as if Tigo and his mom had not vanished and just reappeared. "We must change our ways, and we will. From this day forward. As long as you will stay. Work with us."

"Why me?" he growled. "I'm nobody!"

"The time you have spent here—though it felt as a full cycle to you—has only been months. In that short time, you have . . . challenged us, daringly confronted those who have outlived you, some by centuries. Beings who could slay you. Who know your thoughts. Anticipate your desires. Why do you think we have kept Rejeztia from you?"

Not fair.

The Revered Mother smiled. *"Agreed,"* she responded in Lifespeech. "Yet true all the same. Your existence, your timing and arrival here, were no accident, Tigo. Rejeztia was sent out to guard and protect you, ensure you came at the appropriate time. You bear no brand visible to man, but your adunatos has been marked since before your birth."

Tigo tightened his jaw. He'd never been real good with the whole supernatural being, divine destiny thing.

For some reason the cries of that girl being taken on Cenon rattled in his thoughts. He should talk to Diggs or AO, get one of them to do something. Maybe Dad. Huh—yeah. Admiral of the Fleet . . . so perfectly positioned . . .

Xisya . . . the Kynigos . . . Marco . . . Kersei . . .

Talk about being perfectly positioned. Of all he'd seen, all he'd encountered, given witness to, been a part of . . . *They're right. I'm here for a reason.* For a people. For *people*—humanity. He couldn't walk away from that. No matter how much he wanted to. "Divisions end. *Derision* ends. Now." He noticed nobody was objecting. Then again, they'd just heard his entire thoughts, hadn't they?

As one, they all gave a slight nod of acknowledgment.

He couldn't help a grim smile. "And how do I keep you out of my head? What I think about Jez—" *Yeah, not helping your case here, Slick.* "What I feel about another person? Those are *my* thoughts. They belong to me. No invasion of privacy." He deliberately avoided looking at her, lest that kiss leap to the fore again. "Agreed?"

"What you feel for our sister is no secret," Alanathina said with more than a little amusement. "One need not use the *vox saeculorum* to know your feelings." She glanced at Jez. "For each other."

At that, Jez tipped up her chin a little more, her cheeks coloring.

"After that kiss she stole from me in the arena, it wasn't a secret to me either," Tigo said, unwilling to let her hide any longer. He reveled in the scathing look she skewered him with.

Renette—Miatrenette—his mom—stepped forward. The sorrow and determination in her eyes pulled him inexorably away from Jez. Back to the burden. "We are all agreed. The time has come for the Faa'Cris to rejoin the world."

With one voice, the Resplendent proclaimed, "*Para bellum.*"

Prepare for war.

"Marco, it is time . . ."

He groaned, the weight of . . . *Of what?* He moaned and blinked, his skull feeling as if it sat beneath a magged grav boot.

"That's it," an aged, kind voice said. "Keep following that scent."

Scent?

Right. He anak'd and found it, latched on. Drew in a deep breath and snapped open his eyes, his sinuses clearing, his thoughts sharpening as he made sense of the shapes . . . people, upside down. No . . . hovering over him. People he didn't know. An older man and two men near enough his age.

Marco jerked up—but the room spun. He canted forward and felt himself falling.

"Slow down," the older man said, bracing his shoulder and nudging him back. "You're on a table. We didn't have anything else to lay you on, and the ground was too cold."

He tried to make sense of the room—dusty, dank, dirty. Like a stable without the animals, or so the reek suggested. There was an acrid scent he could not attribute to any one person or thing. "Where am I?" He frowned at the older man, anak'ing the three men. The farthest had a dull scent, almost as if confused. The other protective, annoyed, flexing powerful muscles. But the old man . . . that was a strange one. Minty but floral, too. Touches of woodsy dolors. Like a combination of all scents rolled into one.

Marco scowled at him. "Who are you?"

The old man smirked, his bent frame heaped with a tan shirt, brown vest, and a thick shawl the color of cordi, as if all the garments could add to his posture the way a cat's fur sticks on end when threatened. But this man wasn't threatened. He was . . . *What?* Marco could not sort it. But he was glad for scent work at last, as it righted his world. Made him feel like himself again.

Still, the man's clothes were too much on this sweltering mudball. Why was it so hot here anyway? None of this made sense—the man's scent, the fact that there *was* a man and scent here at all, the heat, the thickness in Marco's head . . .

"How do you feel?" the old man asked.

"As if someone switched my cordi for lager." Hair dangled in his eyes, tickling his nose and mouth. Marco shoved it back and felt the world tilt again. "What's wrong with me?"

The old man nudged one of the others with the back of his hand. "The ozuqa moddalari should be ready. Give him a cup, Tutar."

Without a word, the thicker, larger man straightened. He had to duck to avoid cracking his skull on the low ceiling as he started toward a fire that blazed in the corner.

Ah, that explained the heat.

Curse the reek, his leg hurt. And what was that foul smell? This place stunk! "I need answers." And fresh air.

"Of course you do." The old man shuffled toward Marco and motioned a gnarled finger to his leg. "May I check it?"

Feeling odd sitting on a table, Marco leaned back but didn't dare try to stand on his own with the way agony pulsed through his calf. He monitored the man bending to check the bandage that now covered the gored wound from the hairy rhinnock-rodent. "Will you tell me now who you are?"

Wiry, curly gray hair stuck out in sprigs from beneath a knitted gray-and-blue cap over aged gray eyes. His hands were suddenly deft and practiced as he removed a bandage. "You may call me Qadimiy."

That didn't answer anything. "Why are you here?" It was hard to think, to ask the right questions.

"I was asked to come." Qadimiy used the table for support as he shuffled to the end and indicated to the form at the door. "You are very fortunate Daq'Ti sought me out."

Marco startled. That was Daq'Ti at the door? "I thought him one of your men." Why hadn't he registered Blue? He seemed different . . . As pain spiked, Marco grabbed his leg.

"The venom of the kamiruvchi is fast and lethal." Qadimiy let the bindings fall away, revealing a distinct, splotchy mark in the calf. "The poison has been drawn out, but it will never let you forget that you stood against a kamiruvchi."

"Stood? I was more a dangling slab of meat for that thing." Marco eyed the giant, who delivered the wood cup with a steaming liquid. The scent . . . "It smells like cordi."

"And that is a good thing?" Qadimiy tilted his head as if to gauge the response. "Tutar makes this blend for the Uchuvchi."

"That word—uchu . . ."

"Uchuvchi."

Marco looked at Blue. "He keeps calling me that."

The two men shifted, glancing at each other, then avoiding his gaze.

"What does it mean?"

"Pilot," Tutar growled and tugged aside his shirt, revealing on his chest and abdomen distinctive marks. Familiar marks.

Marco had scars in those same places. The sight of them tossed him back to the *Prevenire*, to the walls perpetually closing in, the hollow din, the torture of light on his corneas after weeks trapped in the hull. He knew how he'd gotten his. "What . . . What are they from?"

"Ports," Tutar muttered, folding his arms. "It's where they plug us into their ships."

Gut roiling, Marco was going to be sick. He looked to the old man, then to Blue. "They . . . they've done this before*?" Not just to me?* "This . . . it's . . ."

Curse the reek! Why wouldn't his thoughts form? "This is what they do? To *people*?"

"They care not who or what they use, as long as their ships fly," Qadimiy said.

Anger knocked aside the shock, the revulsion, and charged forward into a white-hot focus. "Unbe—"

"Sentries!" Blue warned. Moved lightning fast toward them. "Hide!"

UNKNOWN SETTLEMENT, UNKNOWN PLANET

Wrapped in a thick pelt, Eija was guided back into the main hall. Hands and feet aching from the warming bath that had stung like nobody's business as the frostbite battled for her digits, she felt the eyes of the village on her as they once more placed her in a seat before the fire.

"M-my friend," she whispered to the lady who'd tended her. "You promised you'd tell me about him."

The woman's smile faltered. "Sit quietly and answer honestly." She rested a hand on her shoulder. "I'll get you some stew."

"I'm not hungry." Eija's stomach loudly betrayed her lie, even as she saw the men closing up around her. The scowls, knives, and hatchets they wore said they were serious and skilled.

The burlier of the men folded his arms over his chest. "You're a guest here. Dependent on our mercy. We can put you outside the gate and see how long you last. Now tell us true—how did you get out this far?"

Irritated, she accepted the bowl of stew from the lady. This was perhaps the fiftieth time this man had asked that question since she'd arrived in this cavernous barn-like structure. And it'd be the fiftieth time she told him the same lie. "I understand you doubt my story. I would, too, but as I keep telling you and everyone else—we got lost in the storm." Which was true, technically. She couldn't exactly tell them *how* she got here because she didn't know. "Thought we were headed back to Kaata Shahar." She had picked up the name from the whispers of the women as they tended her this morning.

The burly fifty-something man cut her a glare. His clothes pulled taut across shoulders that had seen a lot of heavy work. He wasn't one to be messed with. "You're a strafer, then?"

That sounded like a bad thing. But was it a bad thing that would help her cause, or hurt it? Eija bought time sipping the broth of the stew, relieved to see meat on the spoon.

"'At one's not a Marshal," a grizzled man with a beard snarled. "She's too soft, and they weren't in uniform when we found them. I say put them back out there."

Eija didn't miss the pronoun. *"Put them back out there . . ."* So maybe Reef was still alive. He'd seemed so dead . . . It was tactically sound to separate and interrogate prisoners, but what on earth could make these people so suspicious that they'd do that? "What happened to my friend? Is he alive?"

"My problem," Burly said, "is that there *wasn't* a storm."

Eija blinked, hoping her desperation looked more like disbelief. "There was. I was lost in it. I told you." Holding up her hand, she showed the excruciatingly painful frostbite.

"An hour outside the gates does that if you don't have the right gear. And anyone in Kaata Shahar would know better than to even tempt Muzlatilgan."

The round woman knuckled the table, more to support herself, it seemed, than to be threatening. "Leave her, Belcmeg. Let her get her feet under her first."

He glowered at her. "She's not one of us, Delsi. It's village law—no strangers inside the gates during the waxing. And if she escapes and reports our location to—"

"But she's *marked*."

Gasps sparked around the room, slowing movement and drawing stares.

The younger women ceased their knitting, their cooking, cutting roots, mending . . . Men straightened. Hands shifting to swords, axes.

Okay, that did not sound good. "M-marked? What does that mean?" Eija asked but hastily added, "I'm not marked!" She had no idea what it meant—did they mean something like the tattoo Marco had on his nose, or his arm brand? Regardless, they weren't throwing her out—not without Reef.

"She's one of *them*," Delsi insisted, her expression stern yet matronly. "I saw it when I bathed her. We have a responsibility to her. *He* would insist."

"Put her outside the gate."

"We have to," another added. "If they learn our location, we're all done for!"

"No! You can't. I'm *not* marked!" It made sense now—the way the woman had shooed everyone out of the bath earlier. At the time, Eija had thought it was to protect her privacy and give her time to work through the brutally painful process of the water warming and chasing off the bite of winter on her fingers and toes. "She couldn't have seen anything, because I don't have . . . whatever she thought she saw!"

"Silence!" Belcmeg bellowed, seemingly ready to tear her apart.

"I saw it with my own eyes," the woman said, nodding. "You know what it means, Belcmeg."

Face ashen, he stood, arms now resting far too comfortably at his sides. Not relaxed. But ready. It reminded her of an Eidolon about to reach for a pulse rifle. He ignored Eija, looking to the woman. "You are sure?"

"She has a ridge," Delsi murmured with a nod.

What in the Void was this woman talking about?

"Harm her and you'll bring the wrath of the Ajratilgan on this village and all in it."

Ajra-what? Eija's mouth went dry. "I have no idea what you're talking about."

"I would not speak it, especially not against a stranger, but do you want the Ajratilgan razing our village? Yo'qolgan is no more because of lesser crimes. Carefully think about what you do here," Delsi warned.

"*Do* not chastise me, woman! This girl could be a spy."

"Then you should have left them to the wild tishlar!"

Fisted hands seemed as anvils as Belcmeg debated her fate.

"Listen," Eija said quietly, shakily. "I am not an Ajra—whatever. I don't even know what that is."

Belcmeg's brow knotted.

"We don't have tech but we're not stupid," the grizzled one said, advancing on her. "It's obvious you aren't—"

"Wait!" Delsi hurried forward. "She doesn't know . . ." Meaning carried in her tone and expression as she held Belcmeg's arm.

Something twitched in his left eye. "Your friend," he said calmly, "is clearly Azizlar."

Again, no idea what that was either, but they'd now twice referred to Reef in the present tense. "So he's still alive? Where is he?"

Delsi took a step back. Swallowing, she looked to Belcmeg. "It doesn't . . . make sense . . ." She seemed terrified.

"We need to kill her," the grizzled one spat. "It's the only way. Bury them both. Be done with it. Before it's too late."

"What? No!" Eija felt panicked, desperate. Wished she could transport them again or whatever she'd done. "I vow to you, I am no threat. We just got lost. Please—"

"Qochoq," Delsi whispered, then her eyes widened, and she tightened her grip on Belcmeg. "If the Azizlar learn we have harmed one of theirs, we pay with our lives!"

"We can't let her go," Grizzled said. "She's a spy—she'll tell them of our location, and we'll be ash before first break. We must return her to the snow, leave her for the tishlar."

"They'll come," Belcmeg said, resigned as he shook his head. "Either way, whether for her or for him, they will come." He stood considering Eija.

She'd been under a lot of scrutiny for most of her life, but this man terrified her.

He nodded to her. "Show me."

The men in the barn converged on her.

"*No!*" Eija tried to move away, but they caught her. She wrestled, kicking, screaming. As they lifted her off her feet, she saw another man enter with a large shape thrown over his shoulder. But she had *bigger things* to worry about—four of them. She pitched backward, but it did no good against their vise hold.

Screaming as they stretched her out prostrate before Belcmeg, she felt cold, powerless. Terrified. "I am not marked! Unhand me! Stop!"

"Then you have nothing to fear," Belcmeg said, even as cold, small hands moved along her collar. "But if we find that mark, you will not long enjoy the warmth of our fires."

"Leave me! Stop!"

Grunts and words spewed through the room. At the same instant, she saw past the boots and tanned hides, past the wall that ended at her fingertips. And there, deposited on the floor, was the large shape the other man had brought in.

Reef! He lay on his back, eyes closed.

Was he dead or . . . asleep? He was pale. Relief and alarm trilled. Very, very pale. Unmoving.

Oh no. No no no. She felt her clothes being torn away, but she focused on her friend. "Reef." Even as they stripped her—anger and panic warring—Eija strained to touch him. Felt a rush of something heated through her spine. Though she pushed with her toes to reach him, touch him, be sure he wasn't dead, the combined weight of the men held her fast.

"Rahmdil ayollar!" someone shouted.

Then another. Strangled shouts.

As Eija's finger caught the edge of Reef's shoulder, she felt the heaviness fall away. Nausea swirled.

"Kill her!"

Anger and fear shocked her system.

Jagged pain tore down her spine. They're killing me! Somehow closer—which was impossible, but she didn't care—Eija gripped Reef's shoulder. Inexplicably, they weren't lying on the floor anymore. She sucked in a breath to find herself facing Reef, holding his shoulders.

Shocked eyes blinked at her. Widened. Sparked with admiration.

"You're alive!" Eija hugged him, cheek colliding with his shoulder. The air stirred as she felt his arms tighten around her. But even as that registered, she also noted the scalding whiteness. Warmth like a hot spring bath . . . yet, *gelled* like the stasis pods. And some indistinct thing below her.

Reef latched onto her arms. "Eija! What's going on?"

She looked at him, confused. "I don't know—they're saying I'm marked. I don't even know what that means. I just—"

"No, why are we floating in the air?"

She frowned. "What—"

"Wait!" a woman shouted. "Eija!"

She startled, a haze around her vision—no, not her vision. Around *her*—them. Her and Reef. Suspended, just as he'd said, in the air!

What the djell?!

"Eija, wait! Please!"

Through that barrier came a shout of her name. But . . . nobody here knew her name. The realization forced her to focus. Through the haze, she saw two villagers standing in the door. The smaller one rushed forward, looking up at her, arm extended. "Eija, wait! Please!"

Disbelief shocked through her. "Shad!"

ROHILEK, KURU

"*Where* are we going?" Marco hissed as they fled the sentries, hurrying across the darkened city. Skirted walls and slipped through courtyards toward a vast complex and the strange hexagonal buildings he'd noticed from the plains. Crouch-running, he had to force himself to ignore the sting from that beast. Qadimiy had been right—it wasn't something he'd forget, mostly because there was a lingering acid burn every time the muscle contracted.

Ahead, Qadimiy and Tutar banked right around a corner.

Marco hustled forward, but a strange stirring in the air made him hug the wall and slow. When Blue was about to pass him, he flung out his arm to stay the morphing Draegis.

Blue's eye slits pulsed—not with anger but surprise.

"Wai—"

Voices shot through the dark.

Marco nudged Blue into the shadows and edged closer to the corner to peer around. Fifteen yards down the street two Draegis stood before Qadimiy and Tutar. Three things struck Marco as he watched: the Draegis were addressing Qadimiy; Tutar—capable of ripping people limb from limb—stood with his head down, hands clasped; and a thickening scent that did not make sense wafted in the air.

Draegis didn't have scents. What was he anak'ing?

Qadimiy chuckled as he talked to the Lavabeasts. Who was this man that even the Draegis seemed to defer to him? One of the beasts shifted, and his head suddenly swiveled toward Marco, the slitted eyes—four!—pulsing.

Marco jerked back, heart thumping. He waited a few seconds, listening hard, then braved another glance.

Lavabeast2 had broken away from the others and was heading toward him.

"Hide." After warning Daq'Ti, Marco threw himself at the wall to tic-tack, but the burn seared. His foot dragged down the plaster. He stumbled into it. Then pitched himself at the other side, using a window ledge for a boost. Gritting through the burn, he tic-tacked up the corner. Shoved upward and caught the ledge. His arms trembled, hating him, telling him he should've been doing more push-ups on the dreadnought. He growled and pulled himself over. Rolled onto his back, looking up at the sky littered with strange stars, panting. Trying to quiet his breath, he peered over the ledge just in time to see Lavabeast2 confronting Blue, chortling then shoving him back.

Blue staggered.

The shadows were too long, the light too wan, to see if Lavabeast2 outranked Blue, but that might explain the rough treatment.

Lavabeast2 shoved him again—revealing his yellow rank.

This time, Blue held his ground. Pushed back and raged at the other.

Yellow/Lavabeast2 raised his arm, powering the weapon. Blue bellowed and somehow managed to flip the other Draegis onto his back. Stood over him, chortling like a long, deep horn. Yellow cowered, head down, as he pulled himself to kneel. The whole scene reminded Marco of a docuvid showing how among wild animals a younger male might attack and kill a wounded leader. Only, Blue wasn't quite so wounded.

"On your feet." Daq'Ti waited, annoyance trilling in his heaving breaths. "Why aren't you at your post?"

Yellow shifted, trying to free himself. "We heard something. Found the Caretaker out past curfew."

"You sent him back?"

"Yes, Ra'gatira!"

Blue thrust him backward. "Return to your position before someone else goes where they aren't supposed to."

Yellow glanced down at Blue's arm and then to the mark on his cheek. "Yes, sir."

"Got a problem, askar?"

"No, Ra'gatira." Yellow pivoted and scurried back into the darkness.

"Askar!" Blue snapped, waiting for a response or some action. "Search the streets. Make sure he wasn't helping someone escape."

"Yes, Ra'gatira."

Blue watched the underling for several long seconds, then angled his head to the side. "It's safe."

With more than a little reticence, Marco dropped. Stumbled at that fire like a dagger in his calf and came up jogging. "What was that?"

"I've diverted the askars—soldiers." Blue stalked down the street. "They'll go south, away from us. It'll make it easier to get in." He cuffed Marco's arm. "Act subservient."

Jaw tight at the sudden command and redirection, Marco stiffened. Debated arguing. This . . . didn't feel right. Then again, nothing had felt right since coming through the Sentinel.

"I can leave you out here to die," Blue suggested.

"No, you can't. Not if you want Xonim to speak to you again."

Blue's growing eyes pulsed, and it was just then, in the shadows, that Marco realized how very different Blue was now from his compatriots. He was still tall and brawny, but he seemed more . . . human. Slits were shifting even more toward two eyes and a nose. His skin more gray now than black. "The changes . . . I wasn't sure if it was real or my imagination."

"Much pain . . ." Blue grunted a nod to him. "Subservient."

This time Marco complied with the request, wondering if being so compliant made him stupid. These creatures annihilated species without compunction. Did the bidding of the Khatriza . . . Xisya. And Eija. Which was interesting.

Blue led him up the steps, chambered his arm toward an obsidian panel set in the door.

A bolt of pain shocked the air, startling Marco. A wake of heat-infused pain poured from Blue—chambering his arm hurt. It didn't even fully chamber, but was it enough to access the facility? Heavy and mechanical, a *thunk* rattled the ground beneath his boots as the door opened.

Grip tighter, Blue chortled at Marco and roughed him through the door, walking way too fast and powerfully for Marco to get his feet under him. Humiliation heaped upon anger as he was dragged through halls etched with unusual symbols reminiscent of carved machi wood. Only these displays somehow seemed organic. Not like they were *carved*, but like they . . . grew. Patterns covered the walls and crowded the tight space.

Marco stumbled, still trying to find his feet.

With a howl, Blue hauled him off the floor and caught him by the throat with a hot-to-the-touch hand. But not searing.

Dangling, Marco gripped the meaty paw. Resented that Blue could pick him up so effortlessly. He'd be in trouble if he really wanted to escape, but a notable truth ceased his struggling: he wasn't being strangled. He could breathe. The powerful Blue was exerting terrific control over his grip as he stalked the passages with Marco hanging like a dead dog, other Draegis either hurrying aside or nodding approval.

Onward Blue clomped, giving Marco an occasional shake as if fighting with him, through a passage that was more umbilical than corridor to another controlled-access portal. There, Blue chambered his arm again and aimed at the unique lettering. The patterns swirled and shifted, then snaked around and cinched his arm.

Fire surged through Marco's brand. For a second, he forgot to fight against the grip and instead shook out his own arm. When he did, the wall patterns spiraled through the air and wrapped around the armored thing on his forearm as well. Still dangling in the air, he sucked in a breath and stilled, watching as it dug into the plating.

What the reek?

In battle, knowing when to accept defeat was crucial to winning the mental war. It'd been a week since Tigo talked with his dad and mom on Qrimont and had that portentous conversation with the Revered Mother. Since then, he saw the proof of change glittering in the sacred halls of Deversoria. From the side of the arena, he monitored the mock battle. It had been days of planning, preparing, including pairing the Faa'Cris with the Licitus. The blended army was on the sand, swords clacking. Men learning to assist beings they had once worshipped, and the Faa'Cris learning men could be powerful allies, not just servants or means of perpetuating a race.

Tigo watched Moza, who'd fallen into a comfortable rhythm working with the fierce and demanding Decurion Cybele. Surprising. Amusing. One might as well ally an infant with a rhinnock.

A similarly paired set of Faa'Cris and Licitus came in from behind, but Cybele detected them, and even as her wings shifted to change her direction of flight, Moza saw it and pivoted. Spinning around, he crouched and vaulted at the attacking Licitus. Slammed his sword into the man's chest with a loud clack.

Air punched from his opponent's lungs so loud that it was heard through the din. He dropped to his knees with a cough. Thankfully, they'd donned armor and used practice swords, so there was no real injury.

"Brilliant!" Tigo shouted to Moza but saw the opposing Faa'Cris angrily target and dive at him. Cringing, he could only watch the retaliation, his anger rising at her rage.

Decurion Cybele moved to intercept. Slowly.

Too slowly.

Despite the attempted protection, Moza took the brunt of the impact. Pitched forward. His head literally bounced off the ground. Cybele attacked the opposing Faa'Cris in defense of her partner.

Despite his anger—Cybele could have, should have, protected her ally—Tigo folded his arms.

"They are learning." Jez alighted at his side, her span feathering along his shoulder blades.

The flutter felt teasing, taunting. Was that the way Faa'Cris flirted? Like a man who yawned and stretched, his arm *accidentally* arcing around the woman's shoulders? "Your Sisters have surprised me."

She glowered. "I meant the men."

"Of course you did."

"You're angry."

"Disappointed, there's a difference. Cybele should've protected Moza."

"Perhaps," Jez said quietly, "but in true war—"

"*Every* ally counts—if we are to survive." He strode forward to intercept his man as the training hour came to an end. "Well done, my friend."

Wiping blood from his chin, Moza grunted. "They do not give an inch."

"And we must return that favor—as I saw you do. Your ability to anticipate Cybele is incredible. Speak to the others, teach them what you've learned."

Surprised, Moza considered him. Then his eyes strayed to the Faa'Cris as they shed their armor and left the arena. He straightened, his expression strange.

Tigo glanced again and startled to see the ever-severe Cybele tighten her lips, ebony skin rippling as she gave Moza a slow nod and moved onto the cobbled road beyond the gate.

"Never thought I'd see that," Moza whispered as he watched the departing decurion. He twitched at Tigo. "I hated you when you first came."

"Thanks . . .?"

"Yes. Thanks is what I owe you—what we all owe you."

"Don't thank me—there's a lot of hard work ahead." Tigo noticed Jez had left with the others. "Hey. Why don't you start training the others in an official capacity?"

"Ferox is your first."

Tigo nodded. "Aye, and I need him to continue in that role, but I've also taught you what I know. The way you've taken your experiential knowledge of having lived so long among the Ladies, and made it work for you, has turned you into one of the most effective teams out there."

Moza grunted. "I barely have her respect, and you want me to elevate to trainer?"

"Necessity is the name of this game." Tigo clapped the man's shoulder. "Think about it."

He hiked his ruck over his shoulder and plodded to the house he shared with the men. He stored his gear, checked the pantry for something to eat, but nothing appealed, so he struck out toward the market. Down the stone roads of white-stucco buildings under cavernous ceilings that glinted with reflective stones. It was well after lunch, but he hoped for a vendor to still be around. There was one particular guy who had a knack for peppered meat wraps that . . .

Tigo slowed as movement caught his eye. Down the brightly lit avenues, ducking into a narrow street that led to the grand sanctuary, moved an entourage that included all half dozen Resplendent and just as many triarri, including Jez.

But the strangest member of that group? *Dad.* Weird. What was he doing down here? This was significant.

Abandoning his search for a late lunch, Tigo trailed them down a thin, darkening passage. The longer he followed, the further Jez fell behind her Sisters, as if waiting for him.

Keeping his steps light and fast, Tigo caught up. "What's going on?"

She looked straight ahead, her jaw muscle popping as if the answer was one she had to force herself to surrender. "A sending out."

Strange. The level of attention didn't seem right for sending one of their own into the world for reconnaissance or marriage—which they rarely did these days, apparently. He would've expected more. More celebration, more Faa'Cris. His dad sure wasn't getting married again, and they definitely weren't sending him out, so what in the Voids was going on?

They swept through another passage, then a gust of warm, earthy air hit him as the Resplendent moved into an arc. Light—natural light—reached from the other side. Forty or fifty paces down was the opening of a cave. Standing there, silhouetted by the natural light that reached into the cave, were not one, but two men.

"Who's the other man?"

Jez tucked her chin and whispered, "Tyrannous Darius, brother to Marco, husband to Kersei."

"*Voids,*" Tigo muttered. "Why's he here—wait! Is *he* being sent out?" How did that make sense? Could non-Faa'Cris be sent out?

Without answering, Jez moved to join the arc of her Sisters, leaving him alone. *Message received.*

But something . . . Why would they do something so reverent and honoring for a Licitus? Even this one with noble blood? Tigo sure hadn't been treated with such reverence. He slipped around the perimeter until he reached his father, who side-eyed him with a grim smile.

Why grim? It seemed disparate for this audacious event.

The Revered Mother approached Darius. As if on cue, Dad eased back. Surprise leapt through the prince's features the moment he set saw the Revered Mother. With a strangled cry, he rushed into her arms, hugging her and sobbing.

What the Voids?

Dad bumped his shoulder against Tigo's. "She is his mother."

Ah, that explained the grimness. Or did it? "I'm beginning to think everyone I know is either a Lady or spawned from a Faa'Cris."

Dad chuckled. "It would seem that way down here, I'm sure."

But this . . . this couldn't just be a sending out. "I feel out of touch, having been cooped up down here, but wasn't he a prince or betrayer or something?"

"Both," Dad said quietly. "He's done a great wrong but has been forgiven. Now he seizes a chance to redeem himself."

"They act like he's not coming back."

"It's unlikely."

Heavy. Tigo studied the indomitable Domitas Deken. "What're you doing here? I didn't expect to see you again so soon."

Dad's gray eyes took in the array of Faa'Cris, then the sandy-haired prince. "I fear my fate is entwined with his." He stalked forward and grasped Darius by the forearm, gripping the tender, meaty part that stung worse than a PICC-line getting juiced.

Both men turned and walked out of the cave.

An inexplicable draw nudged Tigo toward that opening, toward freedom. He could walk out and be freed of the maddening existence he'd found here. Training Licitus was one thing, but the warrior craved action, honest confrontation. They said a battle was coming, but what good were they belowground? True, they had advanced to sparring as partners with the Licitus, but he'd wager some agreed to do it just to punish the men. Sparring with ultrapowerful women wasn't enough. Not when humanity was on the brink.

Instinct told him to walk into the light—and not metaphorically. Literally. Right out of the cave. Purpose called him forward. He took a step and it felt good, right.

"Tigo, please." Jez was at his side in a blink. "Please, don't."

He met her gaze, felt that surge of love and protectiveness he'd always had toward her. "I don't belong here, Jez. I'm a man of action, a warrior. I can't explain it, but I need to get out of here. Do . . . something."

"I know. But please . . ." Her hand slid behind his elbow, then along his inner forearm, her touch warm and electrifying.

You're trying to distract me.

Her violet eyes glowed as she smiled.

Terrific. Couldn't lie—he liked that her arm was wrapped around his, her hand slipping into his. He held it, but his gaze veered toward the mouth of the cave as it darkened beneath the shapes of his father and Darius. Longed to be with them, to be free, breathing open air. Facing the war rather than hiding from it. Staying was killing him. *I have to go . . .*

"You're right, Tigo. It's time to leave Deversoria." Jez squeezed his hand, drawing his glance. "I'll go with you."

VYSIEN, HIRAKYS

Darius put one foot in front of the other, each move one step farther from Kersei and Xylander. Every one closer to paying for his mistakes. More than once, he stumbled beside the admiral and his forbidding manners. Strange to find this man an ally of the Faa'Cris, when he had sat beside Baric and the other Symmachian masterminds.

"You take pleasure in abusing me, do you?"

Deken said nothing as Darius tripped yet again, nearly eating some dirt. The brawny admiral hauled him up and set him aright as if he were no more than a small child. Darius marveled. Clearly, he should give care not to mistake the silver in this man's beard for old-age weakness. The silver simply marked experience and, likely, the number of times he had dealt with the likes of Darius.

"Let me do the talking." Admiral Deken turned onto the street leading to the royal residence.

"I have been a part of this since—"

"Maybe you missed what I said," he growled. "I talk. You obey."

How odd to be treated like a sergius, but he let the admiral lead him unceremoniously into the courtyard of the Vysien palace. It was an adjustment, allowing himself to be handled so poorly. His men would have put this skycrawler on his back for such an intolerable offense.

Two Hirakyn uniforms stepped into their path. "Hold there! Who goes— oh! Adm—"

"Get out of my way!" Admiral Deken charged onward, yanking Darius with him through the palace gates and into the bailey, which looked more like a city square.

"Admiral," a voice called across the open courtyard.

Darius glanced to the right. His gut tightened at the sight of the treacherous Theon and his minions lurking in the shade of a balcony that ran the long length of the building. *Always in the shadows . . .*

"What is this?" Theon glided toward them, his white-and-red robes pristine despite the hot, dusty day.

"Thought I'd bring this ruffian—"

"*Ruffian?*" Darius wrested out of the admiral's grip. "How dare you! What is this?" Had to admit—this wasn't what they'd discussed, so he hoped the admiral had a plan to right this.

Deken's eyes blazed. "Do not test me, boy!"

"*Boy?*" Darius balked. "I am a prince of Kalonica and your equal, mayhap even superior." They were supposed to go into the central hub of the castle and talk to the new rex. There, Darius would convince them he was not a traitor to the Symmachian cause on Drosero.

Admiral Deken barked a laugh. "Try again, Betrayer."

Darius gaped. *What* was going on here?

"Why are you here?" Theon sounded imperious and a little bored. "And why bring such petulance to me? What am I to do with him, besides rid us of the nuisance?"

At the threat of death, Darius floundered. "I am a part of this endeavor," he asserted, knowing he had to play a long game. "You would not have come this far had I not—"

"Not what? Betrayed your father, wife, brother—your entire people?" Theon taunted, his thin nostrils flaring. "Your own country ripped the crown from your head and put it on your brother, an obstacle we removed. Now you have that harpy ruling Kalonica, and believe me, we *will* deal with it. Plans are in play even now." Nostrils flared, he flicked his fingers at Darius. "You mean nothing anymore. In essence, you are dead weight. Is that not right, Admiral?"

"My thoughts exactly."

No, this . . . What is going on? It isn't— "I am involved in this endeavor—"

"I should cut out your tongue and kill you where you stand," Theon hissed. His long, narrow face seemed unusually pale. "But . . . I must be sure we cannot bleed you of any more benefits first."

"Don't they have a dungeon here?" Deken offered, a grin amid that thick beard.

"Take him to your ship." Theon's gaze snapped to Deken's and narrowed. "Speaking of, how did you get here? We were not alerted to your corvette on approach."

The admiral shrugged, not looking ruffled. "Testing that stealth armor we got off Thyrolia."

Were they really testing stealth armor? What would that do to Drosero's chances of survival? The fighters in Jherako would need to know. What could they do to defend themselves?

For the first time, Theon's sneer vanished. "Then it's ready?"

"Soon. Working out some bugs." Deken thrust his jaw at Darius. "I can't have him on the *Cronus*. There's already too much attention on me after my son's fiasco. Considering this one is Marco's brother and your little mess with *that*, it's better to keep him somewhere he can't be found."

"Do you seek to anger me, throwing that failure in my face?"

Deken said nothing, merely held the high lord's gaze.

Rife with irritation, Theon glanced Darius up and down. "The dungeons here are horrific. They would teach him a lesson. A permanent one, perhaps. If our luck holds."

"What of your oath to the Ancient?" Darius challenged, feeling more desperate than he should. "You wear the robes of office that represent Him— and this is how you do that? Through bloodshed and violence? Through killing men—"

"Even the Ancient has swords wielded for Him."

"So you deem yourself equivalent to the Ancient?" Darius felt as if he should take a step back lest the bolt of lightning from on high strike him instead of Theon.

"I deem myself qualified for the task of the office to which I am appointed." Theon's lips twisted, then he shifted his gaze to the guards. "Put him in the dungeon."

Darius shot a frantic look at Deken, who smirked at him. "You have no right! You do not rule here." Had he been betrayed? By more than Deken? Why had he even thought the Faa'Cris allies? Had they not bartered with him, buying his sacrifice with one last chance to see Kersei and his son. They'd extorted his allegiance.

I am a fool.

Theon sniffed. "For a Kalonican prince, you are woefully uninformed." He nodded to the guards and then whirled away, walking with the admiral up the cobbled steps toward the castle at the end of the courtyard. "Maybe put him in with that raider who killed several of the kingsguard and tried to rape the queen."

"Deken! Do not do this. You are a better man!" Hands bound, Darius was led down into the dank, rancid dungeon that reeked of earth and feces. As they shoved him past dozens of wrought iron and wood doors, he reviewed what he knew of the Irukandji raiders, what Ixion had mentioned to Father more than once. They counted on their savagery, not their wits. Aerios and regia were trained to do violence but only when necessary, relying instead on wit and tactics.

Nerves buzzing when they pressed him against the wall, a key rattling in the lock of a cell, Darius drew a slow, measured breath. Readied himself to meet whatever was on the other side of that door.

A shriek sounded from within. *Thud!* The door visibly bounced from some impact. The guard stepped back, glancing at the other one.

"Just do it," the smellier of the two said. "Open it and we'll throw him in, slam it shut, and be on our way."

The first hesitated. Shook his head.

At last—mayhap an ally.

Then sneered. "I want to see that thing shred this putrid prince of Kardia."

Blood and boil! Darius stiffened as they angled him toward the door. Smelly nodded and unfastened the lock. The door bucked again, making the guards falter once more.

Smelly yanked it open. "Go!"

Darius was shoved forward. He dove into a roll and came up on the left, feeling the wall at his back and crouched, ready. It took a second for his eyes to adjust, but he heard the thud of the cell door.

Yet a sliver of light remained. How . . .? Something was wrong. He glanced there and saw that the guards had failed to close the door. Why?

Only as darkness surrendered could Darius make out the glowing lines of the marks on the raider—who had wedged himself between the door and jamb. Scratching and clawing with his left hand to free himself and gripping a dagger in his right.

Where did he get that?

When the Irukandji shifted and managed to get the door ajar more, Darius saw the hilt. Emblazoned with the Hirakyn emblem. Truly, had he stolen that from one of the guards? He would slaughter the guards and anyone in his path if he escaped.

With a primal scream, the raider leapt from the opening. The two guards stumbled back, shouting as they tried to avoid the dagger. Blood sluiced. Men injured.

Darius darted forward, catching the frenzied raider by the throat and wrist. The man—no, *thing*—bucked wildly. It was like trying to hold a slimy, panicked, newborn rhinnock calf. Howling pierced Darius's ears as he applied pressure to the wrist, forcing the hand back.

The raider thrashed, his feet finding traction. He whipped himself up and vaulted over Darius, breaking his hold.

How the savage managed to maintain grip on the dagger, Darius had no idea, but he felt the fire of that blade against his face. Had no time to consider the injury as the snarling raider rushed him with the blade and wild vengeance for interrupting his attack.

Darius glided forward, catching the raider—who'd likely expected him to back away—with a knife-hand strike to the throat.

He wheeled around with a howl, and this time did drop the dagger as he gripped his throat, gasping for air.

Moving fast, Darius snatched the weapon from the dirt and raced in, driving the blade up into the raider's neck, up into his brain, gliding around the raider. Faced him, ready for the thing to somehow still fight despite the gurgling rasp that had pulsed warm blood over Darius's hand. Chest heaving, he watched the raider drop to his knees, then crumble into the dirt.

The guards stood in stunned disbelief at the seconds-long fight. Their dumbfounded gazes rose to him. They blinked.

They jarred back into action. "Drop it!" Smelly drew his longblade.

"Easy. I am not your enemy." Darius let the dagger thump into the dirt, landing in the pool of blood it'd freed. "I—"

Nervous, Smelly shuffled forward. Cracked the hilt of his weapon into Darius's skull, knocking him from consciousness.

Eija alighted, her spine ripping with pain and . . . light. The weight of it sent her to a knee, but Reef cupped her elbow.

What is happening? Struggling to her feet, she could not miss the shocked and mortified glances of the locals. The whole floating-in-air thing probably hadn't gone over well with them. Then again, she wasn't exactly thrilled with it either.

Still. Locked onto the diminutive girl, Eija started forward. "Shad!"

A large shape appeared in front of her.

Hugging herself, as if that would alleviate the fire, she squinted up. At first, she didn't recognize the bearded man, but then she saw the eyes. Firm set of his jaw. She started. "Gunny."

"Guess you forgot"—his gaze probed the menfolk—"I got promoted."

She grimaced, feeling as if she stood in deep water. "Where . . .? How'd you—"

"You okay?" Shad hurried to her. "How'd you get here?"

Eija couldn't help but hug her. "It's so good to see you. I was worried—"

"Reunion later." Chief took a step forward and tugged Reef toward him as they faced the gathering crowd. "These are my people, Belcmeg."

"People?" Grizzled balked. "She was *flying!*"

"She's marked," Belcmeg said definitively. "No one can argue that after what all here just witnessed."

"Don't know, don't care." Chief shrugged. "She's mine."

Despite the standoff with the chief and locals, Eija reached for Reef, the relief acute that he hadn't died. She hadn't killed him. The stress, the exhaustion overwhelmed and burst from her in a choked sob. His arms encircled her, and she let herself work through it, face pressed to his chest.

"You're new here," Belcmeg growled. "So maybe you don't understand—"

"Understand just fine." The chief was not one to yield.

"You think saving Marilla's life gives you rights. It doesn't."

"Not rights . . . but maybe a mercy. I ain't asked for nothing since I came.

But I'm asking now. Life for a life." Chief backed up toward her. "You have Marilla. I've got Zacdari."

"You were here at the last culling."

Chief flinched. "I was."

"She's Ajratilgan, so that means they'll come. Cull. We can't afford that. Not after the last time and the coming winter. We need every able-bodied person."

"If they come," Chief said, "we'll return the favor and cull them." He gave a nod. "Clear?"

Eija watched, surprised at how the chief had established himself as a leader here in so short a time. Even more surprising was that nobody argued or opposed him further.

"A'right." Chief reached for her and Reef. "We'll talk to her, find out what she knows. Agreed? But no matter what, she's mine."

Mine? Eija thought to object at the possessive terminology, but then again, he was the one saving her from these people, so she'd let it slide.

"Then you take on the risk—"

"I do." The chief never had been one for hesitation. Angling toward Shad, he touched her upper arm, though he continued to address Belcmeg. "We'll be back for Solemnity." Silence crouched in the dark corners of this building, itching to pounce on them as he directed Shad out the door, Eija and Reef ahead of them. She stumbled along, skating glances back, expecting to be charged or attacked. Instead, the people simply watched, expressions mixed—wary, angry.

"What was that?" Reef used Eija for support, as she did with him. "Chief, what's going on? Where are we? You can't tell me we're on the forsaken planet over which your pods jettisoned from the *Prev*." He glanced at Eija. "Right? That was a hyperjump away . . ."

The chief paused, his brow dipping, but he shook his head and stalked on. "Not now," he said in a low tone as they climbed a sloping path cut into a hill.

A series of waist-high stone walls struck off from the path every twenty or thirty paces. Each space between the walls had a door set into the rise of the hill. Homes, Eija guessed as her crewmates led her to one.

Chief pulled it open, and Shad entered first, hustling down a half dozen steps.

Eija followed her down into the underground dwelling and took in the place. A pot simmered over a small fire, whose heat permeated the room. Near the hearth, a little sink had a pipe tapped into an exterior dirt wall.

Nothing that could be described as "modern" filled the space. There was a table with three chairs, a rug surrounded by cushions and pillows. Against the opposite wall sat a cabinet that looked relatively new, if the clean wood was any indication. In the far corner, pelts, blankets, and two pillows lined an inset alcove. Another pelt served as a curtain to shield the tiny space.

Shad went to the cabinet and pulled out a pot and two tin cups. She started preparing what smelled like tea.

"It ain't much," the chief muttered as he eased the door closed and descended the steps, "but it's warm and private." He roughed a hand over the full beard he now sported. "How'd you find us? D'you drop near Kaata Shahar?"

Eija faltered, heat crawling into her cheeks again. "I . . ."

"We didn't drop." Reef met her eyes ever so briefly. He seemed to have recovered his self-possession on the walk. "Our pods malfunctioned when Marco tried to jettison us. Ended up jumping with the *Prev.*"

"Then how—"

"Long story we couldn't explain if we wanted." Reef huffed. "Just know we ended up on Rohilek with Marco and . . . now we're here."

Shad was staring at them, her mouth open while water overflowed the kettle in the sink. She came to herself with a little start when the chief swore.

"Scuz me." He considered them. "And Marco—so he's alive, too?"

"Last we knew. One minute we were with him on Rohilek and the next we were cracking teeth from freezing in the tundra." Reef jutted his jaw. "What about you? How'd you end up here?"

"They found me out there." The chief moved around Shad as he pulled down a lidded tin and opened it. "There's a pretty sophisticated watch system they use to protect the city."

"What city?" Hunched, Reef folded his arms to keep himself warm.

"*This* is the city. Looks small, but it's vast. I've been mapping it since we arrived, trying to get a bead on the lay of it and how we might slip away, but still haven't gotten past the second gate."

"Second gate," Eija repeated, recalling that massive gate they'd come through. "How many are there?"

"Heard tell of a fifth one, but nobody can tell me where it is." Chief gestured for them to sit. "Take a load off."

"But it's nothing compared to Kaata Shahar." Shad came over with steaming mugs and set them down. "It's bigger than Qrimont."

"The big guy—Belcmeg—mentioned it." Eija cradled the cup, grateful for the warmth. "The women thought I was from there."

Shad returned to the cabinet and drew out some roots and began cutting them. She set down the knife with a huff and looked at Eija. "You have no idea how glad I am you're here." Tears glossed her eyes. She looked to the chief. "Rhinn and I were so sure you were dead or you'd dropped somewhere we couldn't reach. It's been terrible being here, stuck among people we couldn't understand, cut off from our people."

Rhinn?

"Unless they came in a ship, we *are* stuck here," Chief said. "I still haven't heard the truth of that." He eyed them, his brown eyes intense as they settled on Eija. "They said you're marked. And that floating thing you did . . . Wanna share with the rest of us?"

Eija sipped the hot brew, wishing she could disappear into it. "I . . . I can't. I don't . . . The woman—"

"Delsi, one of the city's matrons." Shad smiled with a nod. "You're lucky it was her and not one of the others. She's the nicest."

"She ain't nice," the chief countered.

"You're just saying that because she doesn't like you."

"Nobody likes me."

"That's not true." Shad averted her gaze. Was she blushing? "Belcmeg respects you."

"He *fears* me." The chief assumed the third chair, forearm resting across his thigh. "There's a difference."

Reef roughed a hand over his head and yawned, glanced at his digits, which were still sporting a gray shadow.

"Your color should return." Shad tossed the cut roots into a pot and added water. She set it over the fire, then wiped her hands. "Though the medicine they use here is quite effective, let me get my medical kit. I want to be sure."

"Back to the mark," Chief insisted.

Eija lifted a shoulder. "I don't have anything that could be described as a mark. Ask Shad. She did my physicals and wellness checks during the mission."

"And nothing happened after the *Prev* jumped away?"

"A *lot* happened," Reef corrected, eying Eija. "Some pretty scuzzed stuff."

She frowned at him, feeling very self-conscious. "None of that has anything to do with being marked. Which I'm not."

"What stuff?" Just like the chief to not leave it alone.

"Eija imprinted one of the Draegis with her touch, and the beast suddenly became her protector. Wouldn't let any other Draegis near her."

Heat splashed across her shoulders and chest as he went on with the full story. She seized a chance when he took a breath to add some clarification. "Daq'Ti—the Draegis—protected *all* of us, got us off the dreadnought and to the planet."

"Yeah, pretty sure he wouldn't have done that if *I'd* asked," Reef said. "Not blaming you, Ei. It just got pretty scuzzed up there. You have to admit that."

She wanted to argue, but she wanted even more to deflect this uncomfortable attention and the shadow he'd just cast over her. "Again, none of that is relevant. Nobody did anything to me. I'm not marked. So what—"

"Don't dismiss this as irrelevant. You were *flying*. Hovering in the air like some celestial." Chief lifted his eyebrows, and when Eija didn't respond—what was she supposed to say to that?—he studied her for a long moment that quickly became awkward. "Any idea what that was about—the Draegis protecting you?"

"None," Eija said quietly. "It was djelling weird."

"And how'd you imprint him?"

Just couldn't get away from it, could she? "I don't know. I was trying to stop him from killing me, so I shoved him away. Next thing I know, there's the shape of my hand on his chest—like when you put your hand in snow—and suddenly, he's getting between me and the other Lavabeasts. Fighting off the other Draegis. Even crazier, they locked us up instead of killing us on the spot."

"Locked up me and Marco, you mean," Reef muttered.

Head bobbing, the chief squinted. He smoothed a hand over his beard and glanced at Shad, then back to them. "And how'd y'all get here again?"

Was it her imagination or did he sound skeptical?

"After we escaped the dreadnought, we were in a tunnel on Rohilek, fleeing a Draegis bombardment. They were pounding the planet with ordnance when there was a cave-in," Eija explained, her voice going quiet, small as she remembered the fear she'd felt. The explosion of light. Reaching for Reef . . . "Then we were on the tundra."

"There was a light," Reef added. "Same time Eija touched me. Next thing I know, we're here."

Chief stared at them, his jaw offset in speculation.

Behind him, Shad had slowed in her meal preparations. Her gaze darted toward Eija, then diverted. "I . . ." Her voice sounded just as small as Eija's. "Rhinn." That wasn't small. In fact, it sounded cheery. "Can you help me bring in some more wood for the fire?"

He looked at her for a second, then stood. "Yeah. Sure thing."

Something was off. The two were acting strange, likely wanting to talk without Eija or Reef hearing. Why? She slid her attention to Reef, who frowned as the two headed out.

Eija leaned across the table. "Was that weird to you?"

"Yeah."

"Why?"

"Got me."

"And what's with her calling him Rhinn?"

"He's not exactly her commanding officer here—there's nothing to command."

"Clearly." She sniffed. "Not if they're sharing a bed." Eija indicated toward the alcove. "One bed, two pillows."

"Scuz me," Reef muttered, his expression one of disbelief. "Isn't he like twenty years older?"

She laughed. "Shad's not as young as she looks. I want to know what they're saying." She used the table for leverage to stand and hobbled across the small room. Leaning close to the steps leading up to the door, she heard their voices.

"—but that's exactly like the Khatriza," Shad was nearly whimpering.

"She's *not* Khatriza."

"The light, the appearing, wings and flying, the control over the Draegis—*Khatriza*."

Eija peered through the slit in the open door and saw them by the trees off to the side of the hillside dwelling.

Holding her shoulders, the chief bent toward Shad. "Relax, Ildanis."

Ildanis? Eija had forgotten that was Shad's real name. Ildanis Shadrakian.

Chief cupped Shad's pixie face. "No matter what happened or what is going on, she's one of us and we protect our own." That's one thing to appreciate about the chief—loyal to the core and corps. "Especially now, out here. Right?"

Shad searched his face as if she wasn't quite willing to agree, and that hurt Eija. They'd been friends on the *Prev*, stuck together when—

Gola! What happened to Gola? Where was she?

Finally, Shad nodded. "You're right. Of course. I just . . . I never thought I'd see them again. And now . . . knowing what we know . . . seeing all those people die and knowing she has their mark—"

"It'll be okay. I swear. I won't let anything happen to you."

Shad caught his arm and smiled. "You never have."

Oh djell. That sappy look meant one thing—kiss incoming.

Chief dove in for the kill.

Eija sucked in a breath and jerked back, her mind reeling.

"What?" Reef whispered, coming toward her.

"Back!" she hissed, hopping toward him and landing wrong. She nearly yelped at the daggers of pain shooting up her leg. Widening her eyes, she limp-scurried to the table and was planting her backside when the door creaked. Light shoved in, delivering Shad and the chief back into the house. Eija stared into her mug.

As Shad went to the cabinet, head down, the chief closed the door then thudded over to them. Planted his hands on his hips, pulling Eija's gaze up. "I need you to show us your spine."

Reef was on his feet. "Now hold up—"

Chief glowered. "Sit down, Jadon."

"Name's Reef here. No ship, no command structure."

"There is *always* command structure—now more than ever it's vital we maintain it."

"Right. You agree, *Ildanis?*" Reef tossed over his shoulder. "Or wait—is only he allowed to call you that?"

"Thin ice," Chief growled.

"Okay," Eija said, standing and palming the air. "Fine. I'll show you."

"Eija—"

"No, it's okay. Doesn't matter because there's nothing to hide. Besides, we have enough enemies. I want to keep my friends, and if that means showing them something that's not there, easy." She turned her back to them and tugged up her shirt. "See? Not marked."

"Slag," Reef hissed.

Eija frowned over her shoulder, then started when she saw his pallor. "What?"

"A ridge," Shad whispered. "You *do* have a ridge!" She jerked to the chief. "She's Khatriza!"

Darkness cocooned and kept him from the light. From his family.

I have a family. A wife, a son. How much had changed in less than a cycle!

Face stinging and aching, Darius did his best to elevate his throbbing injury to keep the swelling down and the pain manageable. He had torn off a length of fabric from his tunic to cover the deep cut, but the heat of the gash warned of infection. As if the scarring from the burns was not enough. And with no water to spare, he could still feel and smell the raider's blood on his hands.

The moldy bread and dirty water that were provided on occasion did little for sustenance, but they served as a means for counting days. Three, so far. Even still, this dark, rancid place could not prevent him from recalling his son. Xylander in his arms, sleeping soundly. That mop of hair dusting his olive features. So small and fragile, yet larger than life. His tiny tremors of exhaustion that plied yawns. The way he screwed his face into a grimace, before deflating back into a peaceful sleep.

Kersei, so beautiful as she nursed him. She said she felt awkward with Xylander, nervous, yet she cared for him as if she'd been born to it. Did she yet resent it? She had, after all, preferred the javrod and Bastien to gowns and balls. How he loved the fiery daughter of Stratios.

Were they both lost to him now? Would he die here, amid the putrescence and vermin of Hirakys? The irony! He thought to protect Kalonica from the very enemy with which he had unwittingly colluded.

A scritching and murmur at the door drew his attention. Quietly, he unfolded himself and climbed onto his feet, using stealth skills he'd learned among the aerios and regia. Father had long said he was worthy of commanding the armies. Silent on the dirty cobbled stone, Darius readied himself for whatever came into his cell.

The door finally groaned open and was filled by a large shape. Darius could not see the man's face for the light behind him, but he did not miss the arcs and lines over his flesh.

Raider.

This one would not be allowed to finish what the first had started. Darius lunged. Collided with the raider, slamming him backward. They hit the wall hard, the impact felt through the raider's chest into his own. He thrust his forearm into the man's throat.

"Well," came a meaty growl from the side, closer to the door. "I think we are ashamed."

Darius dared not look away, but . . . *That voice* . . . He braved a glance. Saw the way light swung across the face of a man who grinned unabashedly. "*Crey?*"

The smile broadened. "Mind releasing Kakuzo? I think yer embarrassing him."

Surprise coiled through Darius as he stepped back, freeing the man. "I beg your mercy." He glanced at the marks, confused.

Rubbing his neck, Kakuzo glowered and returned to the passage.

"We should go," Crey said in amusement. "We have little time and our luck is even less."

Though confused, he wouldn't waste the opportunity. Darius skirted the door and slipped out, relieved to no longer smell his own excrement. They slunk silently through passages and corridors, clinging to shadows, until they descended slimy, slick stone steps that led to water. He tensed, anticipating the foul reek of wastewater, but the air was clean and crisp. "What source does this water come from?"

"The Dagger, an underground river that feeds out into Rebel's Bay." Crey motioned to the side, where a long, shallow boat no wider than a man's shoulders waited. The move tugged up his sleeve, revealing a dull glow along his inner forearm. "Might first take a dip. Wash some of that stink off yeh."

They both were marked. What did that mean? Darius plunged into the fast-moving water and instantly regretted it—the wound stung as badly as the burns from the Stratios attack. *I deserve it. I deserve this and more.*

Gritting through frigid temps, he came up and rubbed his arms and body as he trudged the shallows of the canal to the boat. Crey and Kakuzo aided him into the craft and instructed him to lie down. They covered him with a blanket, and soon he felt the steady gliding of the boat through the water. Curled at their feet, he let himself fall asleep.

Slowing and a bump yanked him from his slumber. He knew not how long he'd dozed, but moonslight now speared the night.

"We're here," Crey gruffed.

Darius came up and helped them bring the slip ashore, scanning the shoreline. They were south of Vysien, beyond the sight of palace guards or long glasses. They climbed along the sandy bank and secured the boat in a sheltered spot. Crouching against the shoal, Crey pointed to a series of mounds in the distance.

Darius squinted at the lumps, oddly shadowed, though the moonslight shone brightly. "What—"

"Camouflaged airships," Crey whispered.

They crouch-ran along the stone wall that kept sheep and smaller farm animals in check but provided little barrier against horses or rhinnocks. For the next couple of hours, they made their way around the leagues-long shipyard to where hundreds of raiders had bedded down beneath the starry sky, their marks glowing and casting an ominous haze in the dewy night.

Darius wiped his right hand along his pantlegs, somehow still feeling the warm blood of the raider he'd slain in Vysien. With the higher vantage of a nearby cleft, he marveled at the Irukandji, most of whom were laid out in rows, sleeping. The ones not slumbering had set off in a westward direction. In nearly a straight line. The oddity of that rankled and made Darius wonder at the organization and discipline not known to be found among raiders.

After the oras scouting the enemy encampment, they trekked north a couple of leagues, well away from the Symmachians and Irukandji, and set camp for the night.

"Truly, it boggles that the raiders seem so . . ."

"Organized?" Crey passed over a pouch containing dried meat. "It is what we have seen, even with Marco months past. The Symmachians have managed to bring an order to the blue raiders that no one can explain."

"The raider I encountered in my cell was not . . . organized. He was wild, frenzied, panicked . . ."

"And now dead?"

Darius lifted his eyebrows. How did he know?

"Once word came that yeh were in the dungeon, we made our way through the city, picking up what intel we could. Inside the royal residence, there was much talk of the Kalonican prince who cut the throat of a raider."

Darius glanced down.

"It was a good kill, yeh?" Crey's words were barely a question.

"Decades ago, after Achilus left and I became second son, I was trained for war, instructed in combat and weapons by the best. But putting into practice my training, taking a life . . ." Did it make him weak, killing those who preyed on his people? Ravaged cities? "They are responsible for the kyria's losses, for so much death."

"Does it help"—thick brows winged up—"to justify the kill, to say he deserved it?"

Darius considered the gruff man, knew that his own blood deserved to be spilled for what he had done. Yet he was given a second chance, mercy. He pulled his gaze and bit into the dried meat. "No."

"Living here, fighting them is a way of life, a daily battle." Crey gave a cockeyed nod. "Yeh cannot seek justification for every raider we liberate from our lands. Yeh'd go mad."

Darius tore the meat and tucked another piece into his mouth, chewing on it as much as the words. "Marco told of the new rex—that he's your brother."

"Qicien are all brothers." Crey eyed Kakuzo, who spat on the ground, his feelings on the matter quite clear. "And sadly, brothers betray brothers." The man's dark eyes held Darius's with implication.

So he knew about Marco's kidnapping. "You trust me?"

"Haven't killed yeh yet, have I?" The burly man grinned, then chugged water from a skin. "We are enemies of the same enemy. That makes us friends, yeh?"

On that, Darius could agree. "Indeed."

Kakuzo muttered something and started away from the small fireless camp.

Darius stared after him, noticing the hue of marks across the man's back and shoulders. Marks. Like the raiders. And Crey had a glowing mark on his inner forearm—sort of like Marco's brand, yet . . . not. Something was off. Still, this man had extracted him from prison, ferried him to safety. "Why did you free me?"

"Thought it was clear." Crey had no smile beneath that wiry beard. "To take yer crown."

At the jest, Darius sniffed. How many times after the attack had he thought of what Theon and Baric truly intended? That with his father and Sylvanus dead by their hand—*his* unwitting hand—he would have returned and become medora. "I am afraid you are too late. Someone else has it."

Crey edged forward, his expression sharp and fierce. With a nod, he said, "Same."

And therein lay the why. Crey understood what Darius had lost because his brother had stolen *his* crown and bride. Though there were similarities, there were also painful differences. "Kersei gave birth to our son." Darius looked up to the moons. "Four days past."

Crey barked a laugh and slapped him on the shoulder. "Yer a father then?" He slapped his back again. "Well done, princeling."

"They are a reward I did not earn," Darius said softly. "I am come south to pay penance, redeem my name that my son may live in honor, that Kersei . . ."

"Please, Darius, do not leave us. Not after we have just made amends. Xylander needs you. I need you."

The amusement fell away from Crey's gray eyes. A storm took its place. "Yeh killed a raider, yeh?"

Darius flicked his gaze to the Hirakyn, realizing only then that, had things been different, this could have been a meeting between two powerful houses. Instead, they were both fighting for the survival of realms they did not rule.

"It haunts, yeh?"

More than Darius would care to admit.

"There is a great number we must rout from these lands, put to blade, let their blood sate the desert. Ildiron is now lost, but I will take it back. Put to blade many more. So remember, princeling—remember one thing."

"What's that?"

"We have been spared, set on this path to rid this world of the savages, even the ones who do not bear the punishing marks of the Ladies."

Darius hesitated. Not marked? Did he mean . . . "Of what do you speak, Hirakyn?"

"Any who are not with us are against us and must be dispatched to Shadowsedge." The wild fervor in the man's expression hinted at the rex he would have been, but also of something more . . . More dangerous. More . . . wrong. Was he an ally . . . or foe?

A new kind of terror corkscrewed through Marco as the wall dissolved into a discolored mist and coiled around his arm. Over the vambrace. Solidified into a new pattern—one he knew all too well. One that mirrored the arcs and lines of his brand.

Doors whispered open. Beyond the threshold, lights clanked on in succession from closest to most distant, illuminating farther than he could see.

Considering him, Blue shifted.

Marco tugged and flicked his wrist to free himself. The tether that connected him into the building's systems unwound and receded to the wall. Man, that messed with his head. Made him feel . . . violated. He swallowed, itching to look at the brand, see if it was glowing. But no need—he felt the heat charging through his veins.

Blue tossed him forward and stepped inside, the door whisking shut behind them. "Uchuvchi."

Stumbling from the unexpected push, Marco shot the beast a look, understanding that word—name—and not liking it any more than he did the first time Blue trilled it. Less, actually. He shrugged as if he could shake off the invasive feeling and turned toward the large facility. That's when it struck him—

Scents! He could anak *people*. Not landscape or chemically treated air or Draegis-void, but people. The Signatures weren't typical human ones, but they *were* Signatures. People. *Men*, if he read the notes correctly.

Strange . . . all men.

He slowed, turning and scanning the space. Straight ahead, there were bays of rows upon rows of what looked like drop pods, some lit, others dark. Interspersed between them were doors . . . which were opening. "What is this?"

"Uchuvchi," Blue said.

"Not me." He nodded around them. "This place, what is it?"

On the lower level, about a dozen meters ahead, stood a gathering of men.

Most wore black jumpsuits. The crowd shifted, faces swiveling toward them as the group parted and allowed a familiar shape to emerge. Smiling, Qadimiy walked through the gap and approached, the jumpsuits following like a dark contrail.

Marco firmed his stance, calf and brand burning, not liking the way these people were stalking toward them. "What's going on, Qadimiy?"

The man was maddeningly calm as he closed the distance. "Do you not know?"

"I wouldn't have asked if I did." Marco moved in, avoiding the wall and its strange patterns, not wanting to get tangled in its power again. Even as the gap between them shrank, he anak'd deeply—not only for Signatures but for an awareness of his surroundings. How close the upper level was—reachable if he leapt up. The thrum from some kind of system.

"Why do you think to flee?"

Reek, he detested the way he read his thoughts. Hands loose at his sides, Marco knew there was no way to evade so many. At least not on this level. And with his leg still healing and painful . . . "What's going on here?" He took in the men that arced around Qadimiy. Nausea churned when Marco realized the jumpsuits had holes for the plugs—ports, as Tutar had called them. Temples, chest, arms, stomach.

They were pilots. Uchuvchi.

"Why'd you bring me here?" He darted a glance to Blue, then to the old man, and finally noticed Tutar working his way through the men.

"These are your Brethren."

Marco recoiled, his mind tic-tacking those words. "Like the Fires they are." He tucked his chin, glancing at men watching him with curiosity—way more than Marco felt. "The Brethren are back in Herakles."

"The Brethren," Qadimiy said, "is simply a solemn or formal form of address in reference to members of a sect, denomination, or"—he motioned around them—"profession."

"I'm not one of them." He had no idea why those words tasted so bitter, or why he so desperately wanted them to be true.

"You are, in fact," Qadimiy said. "Do you know why you were put in that ship?"

Marco stared hard at the man, wondering how he knew about that. *The port scars, idiot.* Still, he didn't want to answer. Just wanted to get out of here. Find a way back to Isaura and their babe.

"Come, it's not a difficult question, and you're a smart man. Daq'Ti has assured me of this."

This man wouldn't let it go, so Marco might as well tell him. "My gift."

"Gift." Qadimiy smirked, a gesture so familiar and unnerving. "Yes," he said quietly, not so much in agreement, but more as if he liked the word. "Your ability to . . .?"

Teeth gritted, Marco felt his will falling and annoyance rising. The questions were notably leading, as if the man already knew the answers. By the notes in the air, he did. "What do you play at, Qadimiy?"

"Play at? Nothing. Only walking you toward the truth, Marco."

Cold encircled his chest. He hadn't told this man his name. "And what is that?"

"That you are the same as these men—they are called the Uchuvchi here in Kuru."

"No." Hating the burst of adrenaline that hit his tongue and system, Marco swallowed and noted that Qadimiy qualified the location in terms of a system, not a city. It made his nerves thrum. "We're not the same."

Qadimiy lifted his hands and cocked his head. "Ah!" He smiled. "You are right, of course. You are not alike."

Somehow that didn't settle Marco. He waited for the man to finish his burst of enlightenment.

"You were raised among your Brethren, free to learn how to harness your *gift*, master it, excel with it. You became renowned, so much that you spilled that brilliant scent across systems, drawing the Khatriza to you."

Heat simmered in Marco's gut. "How do you know that?" He fisted a hand. "Never mind. We're done."

"You are *not* done. Won't be until you come to terms with the truth that control is but an illusion and that this—your purpose for being here—is not about you."

"Never said it was." He shifted, glancing at Blue. "I served the purpose— got us here. That was the creature's doing. Now I just want to go home."

"Your help is needed here."

"What help? I can't do anything." *Except climb in a ship and jump through that Sentinel.*

"Escape is not the answer you think it to be."

Marco resented that this man could read his mind. "Okay, enough." He was fed up with the pointless chatter. "I need to locate my people and get out of here. Blue will help me find the girl, Xonim."

A trilling rang through the facility, like a long, sonorous hum. Only as it faded did he hear the subtle word he'd just spoken whispered back, unnerving him. He looked at the Uchuvchi and saw the adoration in their expressions. They knew Eija? How . . .?

"How do you plan to locate your people? And *why*"—severity slashed Qadimiy's calm demeanor—"do you persist in calling Daq'Ti by that insipid name? Can't you see he's transforming?"

Of course, at that moment, Blue had to turn those mournful slits-turning-into-eyes on him.

Marco shrugged. "How can I not? It's alarming and unnatural but not my business."

"I quite disagree," Qadimiy pronounced. "You are right that the change is not natural. It is *preter*natural. Extraordinary!"

This meant nothing. Marco just had to get out of here. Before someone caught and imprisoned him again. This man was wasting his time. He started walking, aware that the entire contingent moved with him.

Qadimiy's amusement and merriment fell away. Heaviness, meaning overtook the aged face and eyes. "You forget yourself, Marco."

Something thudded hard against his chest, like the bells of the Citadel reverberating through his being. The glow of his brand had been incessant and increasing in intensity since he and Blue entered the tunnels. But now it fell cold. Lifeless. He twisted his arm, feeling as he'd had the life sucked from him.

What the reek? Even as he wondered, he met Qadimiy's eyes.

There was in the old man's meaning and visage a hint of familiarity, something suddenly reminiscent of the master hunter when Marco had failed to grasp a concept. Like understanding that the will mattered not in accepting a Decree. Only justice, righteousness, honor—the Code mattered. Nothing else.

I've missed something . . .

"Indeed you have," Qadimiy said gravely.

Heat sparked through Marco, and he pivoted to the man. His thoughts had been heard. As they had with the Lady. As they had with Isaura in the dreams. "Who are you?" he asked, careful to keep his tone from confrontation.

"We have much to talk about and little time, but first"—he lifted a hand in the air and rotated his wrist, as if making a circle—"this will help avoid repetition."

Daq'Ti chortled and looked at the corner.

Light exploded through the facility. Marco cringed, afraid they'd been discovered. Or that there'd been an explosion. He shifted around, falling into a fighting stance as he scanned. Spun toward stirring air. And froze. Thoughts backed up into one another, tripping over themselves as he stared in disbelief. "Eija."

Where had she come from?

Arrayed in glittering armor and radiance, she stood with Jadon, who was slack-jawed and stiff, gaping at what now had ensconced Marco's attention—wings. Three spans. Two wrapped protectively around her and the Eidolon, one casually dusting the ground. All sprouting from the girl's spine.

"I . . . *What?*" Marco balked.

"Marco!" She laughed, turning excitedly. "How—we were just—" Her mind and tongue vied for dominance as her gaze swept the surroundings. "I don't—" She screwed up her face. "*What?* We were *just* with Rhinn and Shad. I saw the light and—" She ducked as if trying to get away from something. "What's going on?" She cried out, her mortification evident. "I don't understand. Stop it."

The wings. *She doesn't realize she has wings.*

Jadon stumbled back a step, shaking his head. "Slag, Ei. *What* are you?"

Head bowed, Daq'Ti was on his knees before her.

"Stop," Eija ordered them. "Stop acting—" She tried to reach around to the wings. "I don't . . . *what*—" She shrieked her frustration, pivoting, the span thumping against the walls. Thwacking Uchuvchi, who hummed in nervousness, most going to knees. "No, stop that! Please." She choked back tears and covered her face. "I don't know what's happening."

Qadimiy moved forward and touched Eija, placing a calming hand above her heart.

Same place the girl touched Blue.

The older man said something, his words lost to the rush of Eija's thwapping wings.

In an instant, she was still. Quiet. Peaceful. Shuddering through a breath, Eija lowered her hands. And as if she now controlled them, the wings folded—unbelievably and completely—into her spine. Armor closed seamlessly over her back.

With her head bowed, she pressed a fist over her heart and knelt. "I am your warrior."

Do *what?*

ROHILEK, KURU SYSTEM

Wings. I have djelling wings.

"Can we start with the rhinnock in the room?" Reef looked at her as if . . . well . . .

"Of course. I am Qadimiy." Almost mockingly, the aged man stuck out a hand to Jadon. "It is good to meet—"

"Not you, old man! I meant *her*!"

Eija cringed at the disrespect. "Reef, don't—"

Qadimiy lifted a hand. "All is well."

"Yeah, not exactly," Reef bit out. "Eija—*wings*? How—"

"I don't know." She hated how many times she'd said that since coming to Kuru. They should just rename her Eija "Don't Know" Zacdari.

Qadimiy inclined his head. "Your origin was hidden from you—"

"*Origin*?"

"—because it was absolutely necessary." Qadimiy held his peace and smile as they stood around, dumbstruck. "It will all return to you, if it has not already. Your bigger challenge will be setting aside the identity you assumed for this mission."

"What identity? Mission?" Eija blinked as knowledge rushed at her, overwhelmed her. Drowned her in information, history coming faster than that hyperjump to Kuru. The dots were not only connecting, but fusing together the very brittle, broken shards of her life to form a whole picture. In fact, she was struggling to handle her own truth. One her brain rejected so violently, it felt as if it gripped her stomach, squeezed hard, and threatened to rip it out. Connections to people, places lit through her mind, fulfilling and completing. Filling in the gaps and heartaches she had long felt and wondered about.

And wings! Who knew? Feeling as if she had spiders tickling up and down her spine, she resisted the urge to shift and look over her shoulder.

"Origin," Reef repeated quietly, his expression mixed with uncertainty, respect . . . fear.

Another thing she hated—him looking at her like that. "Faa'Cris." *Yeah, that doesn't help, Ei.*

"Yes." Meaning radiated through Qadimiy's gray eyes. "You are Faa'Cris—a race of female warriors who long ago pledged their blades to Vaqar."

"The Ladies . . ." A nervous laugh bubbled up her throat. "You're saying that's what I am?" Questions popped out microseconds before answers manifested in her thoughts. It was strange and nauseating—literally.

"Why do you think your patron—"

She sucked in a breath. "How do you know about her?"

"She has a point." Marco's anger and agitation made the air thick. "How do you know so much? You're more than some healer Blue knows. Back there in the alley, those Draegis *deferred* to you. And obviously, you had no problem getting into this facility. And . . ." Something in his gaze shifted, went dark, then his olive complexion went very pale. "No . . ."

For a moment, Qadimiy simply looked at her and Marco, then to the floor as he sighed. "Would that we had time to sort this, but we do not." He inclined his head as a haze drifted around them, encompassing herself, Daq'Ti, Marco, and Reef.

"What . . .?" She checked the other men who, though not in the bubble, weren't moving. Or talking. It was like they were trapped in a time bubble or something.

"What is this?" Marco's scowl parked on his dark brows.

"Privacy," Qadimiy said with more than a little levity. "Though the Uchuvchi will not understand what I am about to say, there are things they cannot know."

"You're not just a healer," Marco supplied.

In the space of a blink, Qadimiy was no longer old. No longer bent. No longer bearded. He was now tall, powerfully built, full of youthful vigor, and . . . bronze. Dark eyes lined with years of experience and wisdom glittered young and fierce as he stood in full authority and confidence.

Marco jerked, gaping. "It can't be."

Familiar. The old man who had been kindly but stern was now someone . . . different, familiar. Someone she had known all her life.

An old friend known since childhood waited before him with an expression of kindness but also a vehemence that demanded acknowledgment. In response, Marco felt his own heart bow. He swallowed and managed to extract the name from the cobwebs of his past. "Vaqar."

His lips quirked to one side. "Let's sit down, Marco. We have much to discuss."

Jadon intruded into the impossible moment. "Wait. So, you're . . . *God*."

"No," Vaqar countered, his tone and expression grave, fierce. "I am supernatural, immortal—a gift granted me by the Ancient centuries ago, after I pledged my own life to protect a young fire-wielder fighting a darkness he could not alone thwart." His brown eyes mirrored the solemnity of his words. "I am not the Ancient. I serve Him."

"You were the First Hunter, the first to use smell to track quarry," Marco noted quietly, flexing his scraped-up hands.

Vaqar smiled. "My descendants have become a force, and I am proud of the legacy, that my name yet inspires hunters, but much has changed through the years. I fear the Kynigos have lost their way."

"Ending up here?" Marco gave a cockeyed nod. "Definitely lost."

"Oh, in this you are not lost," Vaqar said firmly. "You are exactly where you are meant to be."

"Speaking of being somewhere," Jadon said quietly, "do you know what happened with Eija and me? How we ended up in that village? Just happened to—"

"Hold up," Marco interrupted. "I'm not done." And he had a corner on this market, since Vaqar was the man responsible for the receptors—the ones that guided Marco, the ones for which he'd been taken from his beloved and implanted in that ship.

"Eija's ability to move across time is connected to her purpose here," Vaqar said, ignoring Marco's objection. "To explain that, I must first go back centuries to Drosero, which the Faa'Cris claim as their homeworld."

"It's strange to me that supernatural beings have a homeworld," Jadon muttered.

"Were they immortal, I would understand your insinuation that I speak falsely, but I also realize what I have divulged is much for the mind to wrestle." Vaqar inclined his head. "The Faa'Cris are not restricted to one plane, but they claim Drosero as their homeworld. So it is through there that they reach Deversoria, where their kind have always existed. And just as the anaktesios is only passed to the males of my line, so the giftings of the Faa'Cris only pass to the Daughters."

Marco glanced at Eija, slowly accepting the nebulous connection.

"In the Great Sundering," Vaqar continued, "the Faa'Cris were divided.

The Corrupt decided they no longer wanted to protect mankind, but instead, they wanted power and control over the males who, in their estimation, were so much lesser. Their treatment of men became a problem, abusive. Arrogance supplanted wisdom. In the end, the name of the Ancient was so tarnished that no choice remained but to intervene. The Corrupt were banished from Deversoria, their link with the Ancient severed by their own choices." As he stared at the table for several long minutes, he seemed to bear the weight of worlds on his shoulders. "The Khatriza are the Corrupt, and here their reign of terror has gone unchecked."

"That reign of terror is no longer limited to Kuru," Marco said somberly.

"He's right." Eija shifted forward. "The Khatriza have violated the pact. Xisya returned, killed my patron, and kidnapped Marco."

"And you say they're related to the Faa'Cris? Sorry." Marco scoffed. "That creature was nothing like the Lady who visited me on Iereania when the brand prophecy was fulfilled."

Vaqar raised a hand to slow their racing thoughts. "The Corrupt were sent out from Deversoria. At first, they used Tryssinia as a staging ground for their rebellion. But their brutality continued unabated, thus they lost the right to remain in the Quadrants at all. Sadly, they had already discovered the liodence, a mineral inherent in Tryssinian ore that enabled the warriors to be swift and fierce. However, it dulled parts of the brain connected with empathy and compassion, which suited the Corrupt well, for they saw tenderness toward humanity as weakness, so they were all too glad to take the liodence. Thus, the corruption of their minds fed into their body, and through the centuries, they have become what you encountered on that ship. They thought to remain on Tryssinia, so they permanently contaminated the water supply with the liodence to make consumption consistent and easy. What you encountered on that station is the result of centuries of cellular corruption, which they—sadly—view as enhancement. However, the liodence had terrible, lasting repercussions on the native inhabitants of Tryssinia."

"Mine plague," Eija whispered.

"Yes, that is the name adopted for it. When the Corrupt were banished from the Quadrants, they took the liodence with them to the outer reaches. Here, they discovered the liodence had a much more potent effect on males of the race encountered in this system, the Draegis. It stripped their solicitude, shriveled their skin, made them incapable of compassion or kindness. This thrilled the Corrupt, so they turned the males into their own weapons and took the homeworld, Mahatur, as their breeding ground. Their native females, however, were annihilated to stop any unwarranted interbreeding or defection from their cause."

"Why allow them to go anywhere?" Marco demanded. "Why not wipe them out?"

Sadness seemed to crease Vaqar's face as he nodded to Blue. "Consider Daq'Ti. A Draegis, yet what you are discovering beneath that ashen shell is a living, breathing, compassionate man who is more human than what we have come to know as Draegis."

"Compassionate?" Marco growled. "He attacked our ship. Is trained to—"

"Would you then say he is beyond redemption? That he should not have a chance to alter his future with each decision he makes?"

Marco hesitated. "No. I . . ." He fisted his hands and stared through his knotted brow, fighting the roiling within, restraining his anger in light of who he stood before. "Xisya is in Herakles, and she's not for a reunion to make amends with the Ladies."

"Xonim," Daq'Ti chortled, motioning toward Eija.

"Why does he call me that?" Eija asked.

Vaqar smiled. "Xonim is their word for Lady, the Khatriza. He recognizes that you are one of them."

"I am *not* one of them." Eija's gaze skated to Daq'Ti.

Strange that the girl was struggling with all this, yet since Vaqar had touched her, she seemed . . . less certain. Or maybe it was *more* certain yet less vocal. As if she didn't have anything to prove now.

"My"—her eyes went as huge as planets—"parents."

Dark eyes so intent, Vaqar locked onto the girl. "My love was Eleftheria. I encountered her after I was freed from mortality, and she pledged her blade to me. Daughter of a chieftain from a tribe in the mountains north of Kardia, she had the necessary skill to back her vow. It was clear the Ancient brought me to Drosero for a reprieve, to let me know a joy that had been ripped from me during my human existence. Our love was pure and complete for each other but more so"—he paused, his gaze darting over her face—"for our daughter."

Eija seemed frozen. "You're my father."

"Wait! What the slag—"

"Guard that tongue, Eidolon," Marco growled.

"Right. Sorry." Jadon looked piqued but plowed on. "You . . . Vaqar. This—no, this doesn't make sense." He gawked at Eija. "This . . . you're not Tryssinian. You're—"

"I *am* Tryssinian," Eija said, a self-assurance filling her that he'd not seen before. "I hid my nationality from the Academy for a number of reasons, one of which is they believe Tryssinians have a short life span." Her brown eyes struck Vaqar. "But I wasn't born there, nor did I ever truly reside there, did I?"

"It was imperative you believed you were born and raised there," Vaqar said.

"Because of Xisya—"

"If she ever suspected your Faa'Cris blood, confessing you were from Tryssinia—something you were supposedly hiding—would have explained both your guilt and nerves and any trace of Faa'Cris blood she might have detected. Since, historically, Tryssinians have long mixed their blood with the Corrupt, she would not have worried about you."

Jadon shook his head, leaned against a wall, and gripped his knees. "This is . . . I can't . . ."

Things made sense to Marco, pieces falling into place. "That's why you sensed me in the ship—your Faa'Cris blood and my brand. It's why Bl—Daq'Ti has been changing, since you touched him on the ship . . ."

Vaqar inclined his head again, and Marco felt fueled for understanding, for getting some nuance that had not yet been voiced. He wanted Vaqar to be proud of him, to know that while Kynigos may have fallen from their original purpose, they were not that far gone.

"But all Eija did was try to push Blue away to save her own life," Jadon argued. "How could she be responsible for his entire DNA rewriting itself?"

Vaqar looked thoughtful before he answered. "They genetically engineered the Draegis into the bestial warriors you've encountered, but the Corrupt also interbred with the Draegis, just as Faa'Cris do with humans in the Quadrants.

The purpose there is to maintain numbers, to infuse wisdom and encourage connection with the Ancient. Here, it is for control and power. When Eija is in her truest form, she's pure, and what's in her calls to that strand of Faa'Cris DNA threaded in him to restore itself to the perfection in which the Draegis were originally created, in their natural form. In essence, her touch imbued him with healing."

"If the Corrupt"—Marco liked that term so much better than the nice-sounding Khatriza—"have ruled here, where are they? I have seen no creature like Xisya."

"Who do you think the queens rule? Just their Draegis slaves? On most planets in Kuru, the Corrupt eradicated most of native females, and though they bred themselves into a sizeable army, the Khatriza allow no females on these worlds."

"There's a remnant of women," Eija said quietly. "Reef and I saw them when I . . . transported. They're in a tundra."

Vaqar inclined his head. "Mahatur. When the Corrupt came, they reduced the Draegis line to only males—or so they believed. As you've discovered, a contingent escaped to the frozen wastes where it is difficult for the Corrupt to track and live. That's where the males—no longer altered, controlled, or corrupted by the liodence—have begun to rebuild their race and numbers with the few remaining females. In fact, it is fitting you have called them remnant, for that sect has abandoned the Draegis name altogether and now refer to themselves as just that: the Qoldiq—the Remnant. They are a people the Corrupt have long sought to silence."

"That's why they were so afraid of me, thinking I was Khatriza." Eija chewed the inside of her lower lip as she considered Daq'Ti. "So . . . I *did* change him." She squinted. "That doesn't seem right. Shouldn't he have a choice? I was just trying to stop him from killing me."

"The healing that started at your hand would not have happened if his will rejected it. In his deepest parts of his being, he wanted restoration."

"Maybe that's why you couldn't change that green on the *Yo'qiluvchi,*" Marco suggested.

That made sense. Eija nodded, recalling that encounter. "That Draegis was furious I'd even touched him." She frowned. "But why would he want to stay like that, a puppet to such cruel creatures?"

"Power," Daq'Ti spoke quietly, though it still sounded almost like thunder. "It is a powerful sensation to be Draegis, to"—he glanced at his weaponized arm—"dispense judgment on their behalf." Sorrow creased his brow. Did he realize how much clearer he talked now? "Most of my brethren both love and hate it, but we know no other life. I was . . . relieved when I sensed the change you offered. Many of us crave it, but it is frightening. And in a way, humiliating to change, to be tamed."

A knowing smile touched Vaqar's visage. "What better way to return his ability to choose than to free his will?"

"I didn't know I was doing that." Eija swallowed. "It happened when my true Faa'Cris identity was unknown to me. I didn't know how to—"

"Your adunatos has never forgotten who you are," Vaqar pronounced. "Instinct and supernatural healing imparted what was necessary to restore him. He will return to his natural form over time. Unless he is dosed again."

"The liodence," Marco muttered, glancing at his brand. "Is that why I can't smell them?"

"The Khatriza have used it to protect themselves as they built an army for their return to the Four Quadrants. When they arrived here in Kuru, there was no technology and the planets were much like their homeworld—"

"Drosero." His home. Where Isaura and their babe waited. Jaw clamped, Marco balled a fist. "All this," he said slowly, trying to quiet the tempest roiling inside him, "has been . . . orchestrated." He dared meet Vaqar's gaze. Stared at the floor. "By you."

"I see your pain and understand your anger. Neither are without purpose."

"But I *can't smell*," he ground out. "I can't hunt. *What* purpose—"

"Your gift and purpose are not tied to the anaktesios alone, Marco." Vaqar considered him for a moment. "Perhaps you place too much weight upon a thing that does not define you."

"It *does* define me! It's who I am—a hunter, a Kynigos."

"No. That is what you *do*. Who you are is Marco, born Achilus, son of Alanathina and her bound, Zarek." Vaqar seemed aggrieved. "It is with this same broken logic that you assumed Kersei was intended to be your bound because you shared the brand."

Marco's blood iced. "Isaura had an amulet with the brand etched into it. Do you suggest she—the best thing that has happened to me—was not intended for me?" Anger sparked. "Is only heartache and pain intended for me, then?" Is that why he could not detect her now?

"Before Marco gets himself turned into a crispy Kynigos, can you help a guy out?" Jadon gave a half laugh he clearly didn't feel. "I mean, I gotta be honest—I'm with Marco on this one. I don't have a brand, but this makes zed sense. Why didn't you just send the Faa'Cris to wipe out the Khatriza? I mean, if the Ladies like Eija are all-powerful, it seems you could've erased a giant headache from the universe without torturing and killing a bunch of ordinary grunts."

"I am not all-powerful," Eija said calmly. "And while I do have abilities, they are limited since I am not the Ancient. Every action we take is dependent on will. Our Guidings forbid us from acting on behalf of a sentient creature without their will. Because of this, there is not a great transformation forced upon the Draegis."

Vaqar nodded. "When the Corrupt arrived, the Draegis were a weak, dying race, ripe for exploitation. Even now, some among their number will prefer to remain as they are than to receive the healing Eija can impart—as you have already discovered."

"No disrespect, but you're kind of missing the point." Jadon rubbed the back of his neck. "You're *Vaqar*! She's Faa'Cris. You both can travel across vast distances . . ." He stared at them. "You say Ei has a purpose here, Marco too, but . . . *Why*? Why bring them all the way here, away from family and loved ones and do nothing yourself? Why put others in danger when you and the Ladies can just zip over here and take care of the evil shrews?"

"Since you are so bold as to call me out," Vaqar said with an edge, "I will return the favor. Your questions, Young Jadon, do not seek true answers. You seek a satisfaction to your frustration, anger—that *you* have been brought here. That *you* have lost friends. That things do not make sense *to you*." The First Hunter let his words hang ominously between them for a long moment. "My answers, though I could supply them in bounty, will only breed more— more questions, more frustration. They must be surrendered. You must be surrendered. When you swore your oath to Tascan Command, did you demand to know all missions and their outcomes as soon as they pinned the arcs on your chest? All motives behind orders handed down to be fed into your neuralink?"

Jadon shifted, lips flat.

"You do not expect Command to answer all your questions because you trust them, trust that they might know something you do not. Give me that same honor." Vaqar addressed Marco again. "That brand *is* the key—your key to protecting an entire civilization hanging in the balance. Do not lose sight of that while tangled up in your frustration and anger."

"The banishment." Realization slid through Eija's young features. "It was known the Corrupt would break the pact. The prophecy . . . Faa'Cris have always spoken of the Progenitor's arrival." She eyed Marco's arm speculatively. "It was written long before the Sundering, before you were born or marked." Her eyes brightened, and she touched her temples. "We are stupid. Complaining, demanding answers—we are here, are we not? You with that brand and named Progenitor—to bring war. To the Quadrants."

Marco considered her, no idea what point she was trying to make.

"Does that not tell you that we *won't* die here? That we must *return* for the great battle."

Swallowing, Marco lowered his head, a thick ball of dread washed away with what should have been obvious. "You have a point." Though ashamed, he still felt angry. Light-years yet separated him from Isaura.

"Complaint smothers effectiveness." Vaqar seemed very much the First Hunter, training an ill-mannered pup. "I grieve that you are so distracted with your hurts that you cannot see the enormous battle already erupting in the Quadrants—*threatening* those you love. All of you are meant for that battle. Let this serve as a warning to refocus yourselves." He angled toward Eija. "Once the Ovqatlanish begins widespread, you will have more than enough to guide you. For now, depend on your friends, my daughter."

Anger mounted upon anger. Frustration drowning Marco's ability to reason. *What is the point?* It made no sense. "I'm sorry." He tightened his jaw, doing his best to restrain that anger. "Forgive me, but . . . *why* am I stolen from those I love, from my wife and child? Why am I tortured and my gift blocked when it is Eija who is needed? She does not need my skills. This—"

"The *Trópos tis Fotiás*," Vaqar said quietly, "is a prophecy that marks not only the Progenitor's arrival but his incursion into Kuru."

"Incursion?" Marco balked. "I have little strength and no ability to hunt! What *incursion* could I effect?"

Though Vaqar did not move, though only his gaze touched Marco, it seemed a storm swelled between them as the First Hunter loomed in his face and shocked his senses with a fragrance that seared warning into Marco's receptors.

He lowered his head. Knew he was out of line, anger and frustration driving him. "Forgive me."

"I am not threatened by your anger, Marco, nor your doubts. I know them well, as does the Ancient. Neither are we cold to your pains or plans. Why do you think I revealed myself to you here?" Quiet bathed the room. "Let me explain a little more: you encountered Xisya, saw the breadth of her abilities and cruelty. She is but one of four Khatriza queens who were commissioned by the Corrupt to search out and rediscover the Quadrants. Two remained here to oversee operations and, worse, the nursery. Of those sent out, Xisya alone survived and succeeded—arriving in Kedalion six cycles past."

"Six cycles," Marco murmured.

"I knew there was something about her, that she wasn't just some victim as she told Symmachia." Eija bristled. "It was all too convenient and she seemed . . . twisted. Wrong."

"It is impossible when encountering one of your own kind not to recognize it in at least some small way," Vaqar agreed.

"Alestra," Eija whispered. "That's why she was killed."

Another nod by the First Hunter. "Xisya thought Alestra intended to stow away on the *Prevenire* and realized too late what you were, that she had killed the wrong woman."

"Wait—*Galt* was a Lady?" Jadon whistled. "Gotta admit, it's kinda scuzzed that Xisya is a Khatriza . . . a Lady."

"No," Eija spat. "She's not a Lady. She's *Corrupt*. Faa'Cris still lay our hearts and blades before the Ancient."

Vaqar gave Eija a long, knowing look before managing a sad smile. "You seek to elevate your Sisters, but do not be distracted. Pride has no place in this battle. It will be humbling and demoralizing, and what has happened to the Khatriza should be a lesson and warning." Those wise eyes turned to Marco. "The hyperjump marked the beginning of the great war that will, for all time, end the Corrupt. Or destroy the Quadrants, should you fail."

"Thanks. I needed a little more pressure." Marco stretched his neck, again fought that incredible sense of futility. How was he supposed to do anything when he could not even anak these creatures? Could not hunt? What good was he? How would he ever get back to Isaura?

Vaqar smirked. "Fear not, Marco. You and Kersei were chosen for a purpose. You are on that path, and unless you deliver your adunatos to the diabolus, you will succeed."

"Kersei? But she is bound to my brother—it is not her I am concerned for."

"This is all great," Jadon said, "but we're stuck here on this rock with a medium-rare Draegis, a cantankerous Kynigos who can't smell, a goddess—"

"Faa'Cris," she corrected.

"Same thing. I mean, they say men are powerless to resist Ladies, so that's probably why I've always thought of you as a goddess, right?" His eyes widened, meeting Eija's then darting away.

Something rippled through Vaqar that was a lot like anger.

Snickering, Marco arched an eyebrow at Jadon. "Mayhap be more careful what you say about an immortal's daughter." However, there was one small problem. "The Eidolon has a point, though—we have no way to get back. And I'd like to do that now. My daughter—"

"You are not yet done here."

Should he be concerned that Vaqar completely skipped over the babe? He searched the man's face, mind still at war with the fact that he was literally conversing with Vaqar himself.

"So what are we supposed to do?" Eija asked.

Within their bubble, Vaqar angled toward the Uchuvchi, but he looked a lot like he was leaving. "I seem to recall you mentioning a remnant . . . the Mahaturans."

"Tundra people," Eija replied with a nod.

"Okay, great—she can transport herself, but what about the rest of us? I can't do that, and we have light-years to travel." Conflicted, Marco did not want this time with the First Hunter to end. "We have no ship."

Vaqar stood at the edge of the haze, his expression serene. *Too blasted serene!* "That brand is more than a reminder, Marco. Let it guide and supply what is needed." Once more, the strong, timeless form of the warrior Vaqar vanished, and in its place, Qadimiy returned. "Speed your path to the Quadrants, Friends. They are depending on you."

"Vaqar." Marco's agony over Isaura and their babe, over the distance between them, coiled in the pit of his gut. "Why not do this yourself? Free the Draegis of the skin death. Return us to our own people. Help the tundra people. Save the Quadrants."

"If I did those tasks for you, what would be learned?"

"That you understand a man's love for his wife and his need to protect his family and kingdom. That you are powerful and loving."

"Until the next time you feel I should perform based on your narrow vision of what circumstances should be and what the results should look like." Qadimiy was before Marco, clasping his arm, fire crawling up into his brand and glorying between them. "If I do everything for you, how will you learn? How will you grow? Choice and free will are removed, and you become a slave." His gaze radiated empathy. "You are chosen, Marco. You, Kersei, Eija, the others—all chosen for an integral part of this war."

"But, my daughter, m—"

"You have what you need." With that, Vaqar returned to the pilots, who started away from them as if they'd been planning that all along.

Unwilling to be thwarted, Marco hurried after them and reached Vaqar before he slipped through the door. "Why do you not speak of my daughter or Isaura?"

Vaqar slowed, turned, but said nothing.

"Please. Tell me." Marco drew closer, lowering his voice. Afraid to be overheard or draw attention. Nearly cursing as a door whisked open and thrust his hair in his face again. He growled and pushed it back, holding his crown so he could see Vaqar's expression, read there what he could no longer smell. "Do you not answer because they will die?" Another terrifying thought struck him. "Am *I* to die? Is that it? You do not wish to scare me with my imminent demise?" When Vaqar still gave no answer, Marco resisted the urge to rail or curse. He knew he was out of line, questioning the Ancient's Hand, the forebear of the Brethren, the First Hunter. "Kersei was tied to this brand, and she was taken from me. Now Isaura . . ." Blessed, beautiful, beguiling Isa . . . "My heart—she is my heart." His throat felt raw. "Thoughts of her have kept me alive. I beg you—do not take me from them."

Vaqar caught his shoulder. A spear of light shot through his eyes, so bright, so powerful that Marco flung himself away. Even as he fell, an eruption of images flickered through his mind's eye: a large crescent-shaped ship hovering over a city; a desert crevasse overrun by a flood; bodies tumbling through the thrashing water; screams of innocents—children, women, machitis, Symmachians, iereas; the walls of Kardia crumbling; screams of a babe in an empty hall; a field of blood, littered with slain Faa'Cris.

"Let fall the weight of man's approval as you pursue the Ancient's course. Be not guided by the Creed or your nose, but by this." Vaqar's hand tightened around Marco's brand, which flamed. "For far too long, they have stolen and murdered His Chosen. Stand tall as Progenitor, the instigator of a great battle that will cleanse what needs to be cleansed."

"It'd be a slaughter, not a war!" His brand seared.

"Step out, Marco. Step out from the shadow of honor where you place far too great a worth on what you do and what you have, and not on *who you are*. Move boldly, decisively with the power of the Way of the Flame."

Para bellum. Para bellum.

Yes, and there was that—the Prepare for War chant that ricocheted through her brain. Forbade her from sleeping. Eija had a mission, a purpose. She must return to the tundra, to Shad and Rhinn. Bring them back here or something.

No, bringing them here was a bad idea. But they couldn't stay on Mahatur either.

She pushed her thoughts to other areas. Like how djelling psychotic it'd been to see *her father* step out of the haze and suddenly become an old man she didn't recognize. The impact of that moment hung with her hours later as they rested, hidden in a small wing of the bunkroom where the power grid was fried, leaving it dark and the berths inactive. Apparently the jumpsuited Uchuvchi had to be plugged in each night or their absence would trigger an alarm to higher-ups. Or a Khatriza.

That word alone was enough to make Eija, Reef, and Marco comply—for now—with the order to rest. Which wasn't easy—she was churning through her own metamorphosis from Lance Corporal Eija Zacdari to Eija, Daughter of Vaqar.

Para bellum. Para bellum.

Growling, Eija shifted onto her side, hugging the pillow over her head to shield her from the chant. Why could she hear it? It should be impossible to reach her Sisters back home—a frustrating and disorienting thing. Not that she'd argue for change. The disconnection had been designed to protect Deversoria from the Corrupt who left the Quadrants.

She had to admit that she relished being back in her own "skin" and history after years as someone else. She'd nearly forgotten how easy it made life to be able to detect the emotions around her. In Deversoria, the anaktesios was as common as morning prayers or sparring.

An annoying light from the commons intruded into her thoughts. Was Marco really still out there brooding? He'd been there when she'd called it a night. She sat up and peered into the commons. Despite six narrow tables with chairs available, Marco sat against the wall, head back, staring straight ahead. Forearms resting on his knees, he seemed oblivious to the illumination his brand gave off. It cast an eerie glow across his handsome but tired features. Made his silver eyes appear to have their own light.

The Faa'Cris part of her reached out to him but immediately withdrew, sensing the intrusion of the act. He needed time alone to sort the storm. Whatever Father had shown him had knocked the confidence from this brooding hunter.

Somehow, that's when she knew . . . after all he'd been through, being stuffed in the hull of the *Prev*, guiding them here, his gift . . .

It's here.

That chant—prepare for war—was wrong. It wasn't time to *prepare* for war.

It was wartime. Time to confront evil—now. Centuries spent studying, familiarizing herself with prophecies, Guidings, and sacred texts . . . and the time had finally come.

Once, she'd thought to be excited about this era, but now, considering the dark hour, the implications . . . terrible. She sighed, knowing what her role would be. Why she was here in Kuru. And she wrestled with it. Not wrestle as in she didn't want to do it. Wrestle as in . . . *How?* How would she be Vaqar's sword? Who would she set it to?

With a shudder, Eija grieved for what must happen. The enemy would not be met with a merciful hand, but a powerful, violent one. An unsettling and uncomfortable thought when so many preferred the warm, fuzzy Ancient who made them feel good and brought peace. But when one talked of violence and judgment—*Vent them!*

Irritation pushed her from the bed and she paced, thinking through the seemingly impossible situation. Wondering about the after—when it was over. Would she survive? Would the Daughters? What of her friends?

Your thoughts are too self-centered.

Guilty, she grimaced. Rubbed her forehead and heard a somber trill and found Daq'Ti standing to the side, watching her. No doubt roused by her flailing emotions. "I am well, friend."

He inclined his head but did not leave.

After a huffed laugh, she sighed. "You know that's a lie, don't you?" She wasn't really looking for a response. "It won't be pretty." Planning, she thought of this world, the dreadnought, the men with modified PICC-lines, the people on Mahatur, Shad and the chief. Somehow, she needed to go back there. But before she could—

The Khatriza—Rohilek was their breeding . . . ground. Huh. She eyed her protector, recalling something her father had mentioned. "Do you . . . Daq'Ti, where is the nursery?"

"Mahatur."

"Can you take me there?"

"It is heavily guarded, Xonim."

"Mm," Eija said, biting her lower lip. "Not surprised." Somehow, she could see it. See the pods. A revelation wove through her that stole her breath. The idea nauseated her. Correction—nauseated her more human sensibilities. Grieved her, but . . . *It must be done.*

She needed to inform Marco. Looking into the commons, this time she didn't see him against the wall, so she wandered in there. Found Reef in his bunkroom.

He rolled onto his side and propped himself on his elbow, facing her. "What's up?"

What did he think of her now that he knew the truth?

Irrelevant.

Concern creased his brow and scent as he swung his legs over the edge of the bunk. "Ei—"

"I need to figure out an expedient way to transfer the Touch to all Draegis."

He stood, disbelief coiling through his expression. "You're kidding, right?"

"If I can affect them the way I did Daq'Ti," she said, nodding to her protector, "then there's no worrying about them jumping back to the Quadrants to kill everyone."

"But there's too many of them, maybe millions—not sure anyone's taken a census. And they're not all here on Rohilek. How—"

"I don't know," she bit out, irritated with his logic, which was . . . logical. "That's why I said I need to figure it out."

He came to her, his manners annoying, like he was handling something fragile. "Daq'Ti's transformation back to whatever is normal for him is taking a long time. Nearly a month so far."

"So?" Eija glanced at her protector, also glad she did not have to guess his feelings any longer—she could sense that protectiveness rising through him.

"So how in the 'verse are we supposed to stop them from jumping if it takes a month for them to revert?"

"It won't take a month." Eija startled herself with the truth of those words.

"Neither our journey nor their transformation."

"But Daq—"

"I initiated his transformation on instinct when I was unaware of my real identity or power, but now"—she nodded—"now I know what I am."

"Yes, but Vaqar said you couldn't force the change on them—they had to be willing."

"We can't know who is or isn't willing until I try." She went to Daq'Ti and raised her hand to his chest. "*Sizni ozod qulishga ijozat bering.*"

With a trill, he straightened and ducked in deference. "*Men beraman, Xonim.*"

Eija curled her fingers, hesitating, then nodded.

"What's going on?" Reef strode to her side. "What's wrong? Why aren't your words translating?"

"I wanted to respect his privacy until I knew his feelings and answer." She sighed. "I offered to free him—completely." Eija sensed the power of the Ancient thrumming through her as she again laid her hand on that mark and let it flow. "He said he yielded to—"

Eyes flashing, Daq'Ti trapped her wrist in his large hand. "*Mening quorlim emas.*"

Eija hesitated again, glancing at his weaponized arm. "Are you sure? You'll still have pain."

"*Lekin men sizni himoya qila olaman,*" Daq'Ti trilled quietly. Then gave her a long look and more firmly said, "*Qo'l emas.*"

"What now?" Reef asked.

"He doesn't want me to heal his weapon-arm. Says he can't protect me without it." Her gaze instinctively bounced to Marco and the Draegis armor over his brand. Should she be worried about that? It was bound to affect him eventually.

"But they have other weapons." Reef shouldered closer. "Right?"

"Not as efficient or accurate," Eija said, somehow knowing the truth of what she spoke. "If I do not heal your arm, how can we convince your brothers that the change—"

"They will be convinced." Daq'Ti gave a snap of his head. "Begin."

Was it possible to heal most of him and keep this Draegis part? Would it mean he was still corrupted? Djell—did it mean Marco was corrupted?

No. She refused to believe that and focused on her task. Light and heat flowed across her fingers, across the mark, and into his chest.

Daq'Ti arched his spine, and though she expected a howl, he instead gave a low trill, almost like a purr. Relief. For his weaponized arm, she altered the light, healing only the painful parts. When it was done, she stepped back and considered him, smiling at the chiseled jaw and clear complexion. A gasp whispered out when she saw his eyes—dark-dark brown, almost black. Perfectly oval and separate from his nose. No more slits. A thick patch of hair covered only a ring like a cockeyed crown. And the muscled body that—

She looked away. "Get him a jumpsuit," she instructed Reef.

Chuckling, he jogged to a locker and returned with a blue uchuvchi uniform. "That was either really amazing or really messed up."

"A little of both." Eija turned her back so Daq'Ti could dress. "What the Khatriza did to his kind can never be forgiven, and that is why I must stop it from happening to more. I've removed as much of the pain from the augment as I could." Again her gaze strayed to Marco, wondering what it would do to him, to his character, his wisdom.

Reef had a crooked smile as he considered her, studied her with brown eyes sparkling beneath his now-shaggy brown hair.

There was a time she loved the way he looked at her, but now it just made her squirm. "What?"

"You tired?"

"Why would I be?"

"Cuz." He shrugged, way too cute for his own good. "Ya know, you healed him."

"So?"

"Well, in novids, any time a person has powers and uses them, they get a bloody nose or their hair goes white. And they're always exhausted— sometimes they pass out." He pointed to the commons. "Or their eyes change—like Marco." He shrugged. "Mahjuk has a price."

"This is not mahjuk," she chided, "and the price I pay is obedience to the Ancient as a blade of His Servant Vaqar."

Reef studied her, his left eye narrowing.

"What now?" But even as she asked, movement in a darkened pod caught her attention. "Stay here." She strolled through the commons and entered the other bunkroom.

Kneeling in the corner completely bathed in shadows, Marco now had his back to her. The glow of his brand traveled down his hand and glided across the steel of a dagger he held, the tip scritching softly against the floor. Alarm pierced her curiosity.

Fearing what she sensed in the air, Eija rushed forward. "What're you doing?" Something prickled at the back of her neck, and she searched the passages for the source. "Trouble's coming—"

"Indeed." Marco looked over his shoulder at her as he came to his feet.

With a gasp, she jerked back as his eyes registered—pure silver. A laser-thin black line separated iris from sclera. *So that's what Reef meant.* Truthfully, she had lost track of the change to his eyes because she'd been so focused on Daq'Ti's transformation. But awareness flared through her, knowing this completion of the change in his eyes was not just from his brand but likely from the armor now ensconcing it.

That, however, had nothing on what really shocked her. "*What* did you do?"

Chin tucked, neck craned forward, Marco met her gaze. No hair dangled in his eyes. In fact, no hair *dangled*—period. Gone were his curls and black, shoulder-length hair. He'd shaved it! He shrugged. "It was irritating me."

"Voids." Reef rasped as he came up behind her. "Let's hope you never feel that way about one of us."

Marco might have shaved his hair, but he still had his trademark brooding. "Inside. We need to make plans."

He felt like a new man. A new man with a draft. The cool air over his shaved head was weird as he moved into the commons to lay out their priorities.

"There's a nursery I need to destroy," Eija said in a calm, unaffected tone.

"Void's Embrace!" Jadon's efflux was rank with fear and shock. "Kill babies? Is that how far we've fallen?"

"You mistake the term 'nursery' for the one humanity uses." Eija had firmly settled into her new—old?—identity as a Faa'Cris. "The *incubation center* will contain the Corrupt, the Khatriza, but they are not babes nor children as you know them." She pulled herself up taller. "The facility where they are raised is my priority. Daq'Ti has already said it's massive, but he can get me in. That's step one."

Jadon held up a hand. "You seriously think you can singlehandedly destroy this place? It's their young! That facility is going to be *very* well guarded."

The Eidolon had a point—and a lot of fear. "Listen—"

"You don't know that," Eija snapped. "And Daq'Ti can—"

"Then why don't we ask?"

"I was just about to before—"

"Enough!" Marco took several calming breaths. Knuckling the table, he leaned forward. "You are Faa'Cris and this is how you behave?"

"*Me?*" Her eyes bulged. "He—"

"At this rate, I fear for our survival." Marco ran a hand over his shorn head, the difference distracting.

Daq'Ti trilled his agreement. Weird that he still did that when he was now more human than beast.

Marco wasn't sure he liked Blue agreeing with him, though the being before him was much changed—healed. Had more-or-less normal human features, save a slightly elongated head. "Tell us about the nursery."

Though no longer a simmering black blob of raw power, Daq'Ti was still formidable as he bent closer. "It's a level-nine facility. Ten is highest—Command."

"So, difficult to get into."

"One of the toughest. Many protocols and guards. Only officers and Khatriza enter."

"You were an officer."

"I *treri*," Daq'Ti said. "Only *claev* and above have access."

Ranks. Marco thought of the blue mark no longer on Daq'Ti's cheek and the squad of Draegis who'd boarded the *Prev*. "Silver?"

The Draegis trilled his yes.

"So we need to find and transform a Silvermark."

"I can get in."

"But you're not a Silvermark, nor do you even look Draegis anymore."

"No, I *primis* treri, but with Xonim"—he nodded to Eija—"they will not stop me." Something about his near-human visage challenged the idea.

"As simple as that?" Jadon scoffed. "They see a beautiful woman and, like every other male, lose their minds?"

"She is Xonim and they rule. Very powerful. Draegis . . ." He was somber, sad—his efflux saturated with the acrid odor.

What must it be like for him, suddenly returning to his true form? Seeing what he had been in the lavalike appearance of the others? Devastating, to be sure.

Marco considered the guy, felt bad for what he'd been through. "But you're"—he recalled the term they'd used: Ovqatlanish—"Tamed now. Your appearance is greatly changed, Daq'Ti. Won't they question you?"

Daq'Ti did a strange warbling sound. "Heat only."

Marco squinted at him, then Eija. "Is he saying what I think he's saying?"

"Their slits—eyes," she said, her efflux gloriously minty like the Lady, but also very . . . human, fragrant with some sort of frustration, "do not see the way we do, in pictures, images. They register heat patterns. So despite his physical changes, his pattern should—largely—be the same as before."

Every time they planned one thing, another problem cropped up. Heat signatures *did* change with the shape of a body, so Marco wasn't as confident as the girl and Blue about an incursion into one of the most highly protected facilities. He could be wrong—they were a species he didn't understand. But tactics were tactics.

"We should all go," he decided.

"Disagree," Daq'Ti chortled. "You go to the ship."

"What ship?" As the words left his mouth, Marco recalled the crescent-shaped ship Vaqar had shown him, a tool for the great battle.

"Shipyard," Daq'Ti said. "Here on Rohilek. Other side of city."

Marco narrowed his eyes. "And you're not talking seafaring ships." Because that would be his luck today. "Right?"

Daq'Ti stilled. "Sea? What is sea?"

Okay, then. Not seafaring. Marco targeted Jadon. "Think you could fly one of their birds off this rock?"

"I will find a way."

"No," Daq'Ti said, motioning to Marco. "Uchuvchi fly."

Eija drew in a sharp breath. "Of course . . ."

Realizing what they meant, Marco stiffened, glanced at the arcs and lines of his brand, then to the door beyond the commons. He stared out for a long time, thinking.

"What?" Eija asked.

"The Brethren." Marco started toward the door. "Vaqar called them my brethren, but I rejected it." It hissed open, and he saw pods opening along the corridors. "They're all Kynigos . . . just without the training or sigil." It'd be a colossal coup if he could convince them to jump away with him. Remove the bulk of the ships from the Draegis fleet. His heart thumped hard at the prospect, the crippling of the Khatriza effort to destroy the Quadrants.

"Marco, listen," Eija said, coming to his side. "I have to visit Shad and Rhinn again, talk to the people, then hit the facility."

"Yeah. Sure. You do that." He glanced at Daq'Ti, who was frowning at the girl, worried about her returning to the ice planet, if his efflux was any indication. "Daq'Ti, there's a crescent-shaped ship. Massive. With an orb. Know what I'm talking about?"

Excitement thrummed through the big guy. "Prototype." He inclined his head. "In shipyard."

Heart alight, Marco flicked his gaze to Eija. "Meet us there. Okay?"

"Where are you going?"

"Hopefully to bring freedom."

Things were changing. She was changing. Daq'Ti was changing. Everything was djelling changing. In shadows, Eija crouched as Marco stalked down the passage, his steps firm and confident.

"Going to stare after me that long?"

Eija rolled her eyes to Reef with a huff.

"Kiss for good luck?"

"How about a punch instead?"

"Only if it's with your lips." And he whipped in, stole that kiss, then fell into a lope after Marco, darting through the sleeping facility.

Shocked, Eija gaped. Heat filled her cheeks. She wanted to strangle that man. Break out the wings and thwack his chest a few times. See how he liked *that* kiss.

And yet, you can't stop staring . . .

It was concern. That he wouldn't survive. She had a bad feeling he and Marco were running straight into trouble.

We all are.

"Xonim," Daq'Ti trilled. "We go."

Eija pivoted, rolled her neck as she touched his arm, then arched her spine and coiled internally into her true self. Glorious warmth washed through her. Time and age fell away. In a blink, she and Daq'Ti were standing on Mahatur, just inside the city gate of the village with Shad and the chief. With a shudder, she released her span and squared her stance, ready to face the people.

Shouts echoed up and down the small hill, drawing villagers from hovels. Elders from the larger structure. Families from more homelike buildings.

Belcmeg emerged from the main facility, his face etched in hard lines. "Yeh shouldna come back here." More men formed up around him, including Grizzled from the previous encounter. Behind them, women. Beyond that line . . .

"See?" Delsi shouted. "I told you—she's marked."

"I am marked," Eija spoke, using her preternatural voice, "by the Ancient to war on His behalf."

"Why'd you come back?" Delsi shifted closer. "You were gone. Could've stayed gone."

"Because a falsehood exists that keeps you all in fear and bondage," Eija said, letting the purity roil off her in waves of light and warmth. "I am not the creature you fear." She held her arms out to the side. "Does this resemble the creatures you're familiar with?"

Murmurs rippled on the cold air, then came shouts born of fear and loathing. They had been abused too long, beaten into humiliation and subservience, losing loved ones—far too many.

"I will give you the truth of my kind and of the creatures my friend Daq'Ti"—she indicated to him—"calls Xonim."

Murmurs rose into a dull roar.

"Who is he?" someone asked.

"I will show you what he looked like when I met him." Eija lifted a hand to Daq'Ti and swiped it as if activating a vidscreen.

Humanity bathed in a mirage, Daq'Ti was once more a Lavabeast-like Draegis.

Shouts and screams spiked the air, some people running for shelter, others raising weapons. One loosed a spear on Daq'Ti. But Eija flicked her wrist, and the weapon thudded into the heavy gate behind them, missing her protector by a wide hand. Restraining her frustration, Eija addressed them again. "Fear and ignorance tell you to attack, to kill, but you are not the Khatriza, and you are not corrupted by their poison. No longer is this man." She touched his arm. "Through healing gifts granted by the Ancient, he is freed from the bondage of slavery to the whims of the Xonim, of being their weapon. In their community and in this form, he is called Ovqatlanish, Tamed. He will not harm you."

Belcmeg shifted forward, his efflux wary, unsettled. "What d'you want with us?"

"I want you to taste freedom, to not have to worry or fear for your lives."

He dismissed her with a wave. "You are *one* person—or whatever you are."

"I am Faa'Cris. The Khatriza are a sister race to my kind, but they are corrupted. Wicked and self-serving. I have been sent here to intervene on your behalf, stop what they are doing to you and in this system."

"Like he said"—Grizzled pushed through the crowd—"you're but one. They're thousands."

"Yes, I am but one—and you are but one," she said to Belcmeg, then Grizzled, and so on, until she felt the point had been made. "*Together* we are more, stronger."

Wariness parked on the lines of their cold-burned faces.

"I merely ask that you hear me out. Agreed?" Several heartbeats passed without complaint or objection. "Good, I—"

The air grew hot and pulsing, angry. She sensed what it delivered—an arrow flying true and fast.

Eija availed herself of the Faa'Cris abilities, freezing time, giving herself a few heartbeats to think it through. She was angry and thought to flick the arrow back at the one who sent it. But truth assailed her, told her they were afraid, had been hurt and attacked too often. Anger toward them was misplaced. They were not ready to hear her words. They needed her actions.

In that millisecond, she reached out for Daq'Ti, removing them both from the path of the arrow . . . and from the small city . . . along with a whispered phrase designed only for Shad and the chief: "I'll return."

Why am I here? What do you ask of me?

How many times had Darius thrown the queries at the Lady since he'd escaped the dungeon? Even now he had no answer as he crouched with Crey and Kakuzo in the tall weeds lining the river that jutted up into Vysien, providing a freshwater source and natural pool oasis. The rest of the Hirakyn resistance force waited back in the encampment while the three of them performed reconnaissance on the royal residence, Ildiron.

"Trust the admiral," the Lady had said. Was Deken's "betrayal" all a ploy to get Darius in prison so Crey could rescue him and join him to his cause? He had expected the Lady to provide more guidance.

So . . . why I am here? he wondered again. *What am I to do? Show me, Lady. Please.* Nothing scared him more than failing and hurting Kersei yet again. He had already failed her enough.

"There." Crey's low, deep voice rumbled ominously.

"A clean shot that," Kakuzo offered, the venom in his words too rancid.

Startled at their readiness to cut down the rex—in daylight and beneath the ready eye of wall sentries and archers—Darius studied the two. Wondered at their willingness to shed blood.

Was that their purpose—shedding blood? *If not, then why are we here?*

Reconnaissance, he insisted to himself. Yet was that not a fool's fancy, an idea to settle delicate sensibilities? War was neither soft nor compassionate. It was violent and cruel.

Silence hung heavily. Crey seemed to consider taking the shot, and Darius grew more uncomfortable with each empty tick of the clock. It was one thing to spy on them, to learn their routines and habits, but to outright attack without plan or contingency? Idiocy!

"When the time is right," Crey finally said, freeing the air trapped in Darius's throat. And his relief did not go unnoticed by the rightful heir of Hirakys. "Yer brother trusted me better."

Ashamed but not surprised at the barb, Darius nodded. Thought of Marco, of all he'd been through before taking the throne and how he'd stepped into that role with great aplomb. Though he loved Kersei completely, he had impugned neither his honor nor hers in his actions. To be frank, Darius was not sure *he* would have had the strength to yield as his brother had. "By all accounts, he *is* better."

A better man. Better ruler. Better son. Better friend. Better brother. Better Tyrannous.

"Never met his equal," Crey admitted but then grew somber. "It does not make yeh a bad man, princeling."

"No, but my actions have."

"What's done is done."

So was he to merely forget the harm he had perpetrated against his loved ones? *Father . . . Kersei.*

Darius tightened his jaw and looked across the way. Rex Theule and his royal entourage were spending the afternoon on the lawn around a lavish spread, tents shielding the pampered from the summer rise. This man had stolen the crown from Crey, stolen his bride. No wonder savagery marked Crey's expression as he inched closer and gave witness to what should have been his. *Would* be his, if that look was any indication.

Still locked on the royals, Crey asked, "Have yeh thought to take the throne from him?"

Not believing what he'd just heard, Darius scowled. "I beg—"

Wild eyes came to his. "He's not here." He shrugged. "Yeh are. And yer—"

"Stripped of rank and title."

Another lazy shrug. "Still a prince by birth. Still have Tyrannous blood in yer veins, and I'm sure there are those who would follow yeh." He grunted, nodding to Theule and his entourage beyond the hedgerow. "Easier to follow a man who's here than one who isn't. He did, after all, nearly steal yer woman. It'd only be fair to make sure yer country succeeds through right leadership in his absence."

Heady, shocking words. A hint of truth made them dangerous and toxic. There was something in his tone, though, that warned Darius he was not solely discussing Kalonica's sons.

Darius understood the desire and mayhap could have been tempted once, not too long ago. "I once took it upon myself to do what I felt others would not, to step boldly into risk, believing my father had become soft and unwilling to do what was necessary for the kingdom." Darius held the man's gaze, his thoughts drifting to the marks on the Hirakyn's body.

What had Crey done to earn the anger of the Ladies and their punishment?

"Jyoti," Kakuzo muttered, motioning to the lawn.

Crey's gaze snapped to the party, and he went preternaturally still. Something in his expression darkened, enlivened. A dagger glinted in his hand.

Darius peered through the foliage. His heart jammed against his ribs— the rex was walking this way, alone. Behind the royal was the queen. Crey's onetime love. That had made the decision for Crey. In a flash, it made sense— the words, the questions. Fuel for the fire of his bloodthirsty heart. He sought justification, affirmation that it was in his right to exact the vengeance for which he thirsted.

Darius caught his wrist, forcing the blade down. "No," he grunted. "Do not."

"Get off, princeling," Crey hissed in a low tone. "Yeh do not know—"

"I do!" Darius bit out, keeping his voice low to avoid discovery. At the strength of the man's resistance beneath his own fingers, he must address this. "I *do*. I know what it is to want to run a brother through, to make him pay, to take what is rightly mine." He bored into those dark eyes. "But this . . . *This* is wrong."

"It has never been more right," Crey said around bared teeth.

"*Think*," Darius rasped. "Do this and you are dead. Your people lost to the whims of that man, whose character is as soft as the woman he beds!"

Crey's blackened eyes struck his. "What know you—"

"I see it. You crave his blood. Yet that is not alone the motivation. The queen—she was to be yours, and your blood boils to see them together. Aye?"

Crey focused on the queen upon her chaise.

"Remember yourself," Darius admonished, a trace of panic leaching into his limbs. "Theule commands the armies. Theon and the Symmachians have his back. Not yours. Without hesitation, they will bleed you. Then who will save Hirakys, your people?"

Crey arched toward Darius, his eyes ablaze with rage. "He must die."

Hearing the crunch of leaves and rocks along the shore, Darius tensed, anticipating discovery. Verified they were safe. "Mayhap. But not now. This is not justified—your thirst for his blood makes this murder. Do this and we *all* die here." Though the man seemed unhinged by his anger, Darius could not waver. "I am not ready to go into the grave."

"I am," Crey growled, both stilling when they again heard the leaves of the hedges rustle, realizing the rex stood directly across from them.

Darius flared his nostrils. Shook his head. Pleaded silently, but the bloodlust seemed to have won as the dagger was lifting, despite every effort to stay him. He slapped his other hand on it, shouldering into the man to block his free hand. As they struggled silently, wills warring, Darius feared the dagger would find his own gut.

The tension eased slightly, and he saw that the rex was moving away again. "Be smart," he whispered. "If he is to die, let it not be done with bloodlust but honor."

Nostrils flaring, Crey glared at him. "What if that was my only chance—"

"It was not," Darius said with conviction, and in his mind's eye, he saw the square. Saw the royal entourage there. Wondered at the images, the clarity of them.

"Your marks," he braved, his voice barely audible as he watched through the branches as Theule's feet turned back toward the tents, "are they not conviction enough to deter you? Setting your hand against the will of the Ancient ends poorly for all involved."

"He has not seen fit to attend my grievances, so I must resolve them myself."

"Arrogance in its simplest form," Darius warned. Then nodded. "I speak from experience." He eyed the rex, now on the far edge of the garden, away from them. Beneath the watchful eyes of his guard. "The cost of your adunatos is too high a price to pay for that bloodlust."

After transporting them to the ancient city, Eija pivoted and came up facing Daq'Ti.

Bewilderment covered his features in a tangle.

"I'm sorry, for that. But they were not ready." She sighed. "We must deal with this incubation center." With a nod, which he reciprocated, she moved toward the six red-and-black hexagonal buildings that loomed over the city, built in the same strange architectural style as the buildings on Rohilek. The center, largest tower was their objective.

It took about twenty minutes to reach the facility. Her heart thumped harder with each step they took toward the security vestibule where two Draegis stood guard, both silent and still as those crimson slits trained on their approach.

Calm down. More stress means more heat.

"What happens if I'm too hot?" Eija whispered to Daq'Ti.

"Xonim, no worry."

"I *am* worried—that's why I'm asking." Less than ten meters from the vestibule jutting out from the building.

"Follow." Daq'Ti strode purposefully toward the guards.

With no choice but to trust him, Eija trailed him and wiped sweaty palms down her pants. She really wanted Reef here. And Marco. If she died here, what would happen to this system? To Marco—would he never reach his wife and unborn child? She could *not* let that happen.

No, he's the progenitor. He will go back. But . . . will I?

"*To'xta!*" a Draegis barked, advancing, his arm powering up.

At the command to stop and the heat wake radiating around his limb, Eija slowed. She'd known this was a bad idea. Why hadn't she listened to herself?

"You dare!" Daq'Ti bellowed, surging forward. "*Xonimning yo'lidan chiqing!*"

Since Daq'Ti said she was Xonim, she must act the role. And she seriously doubted a Khatriza endured any male speaking to her in such a way.

The sentry didn't yield as Daq'Ti had promised. In fact, that wake was getting larger, hotter, and his buddy had powered up as well.

"No!" With courage she did not feel, Eija marched forward—and it was as if she had stepped into a mech-suit. Felt the weight of the air shift. Felt illumination spear her body. She let it spill through every limb and digit. Let it rule her being.

The first Draegis chortled a shout. In a flash, he was on a knee, his hands behind him in a bow of subservience.

Startled it'd worked, Eija knew she must not show it. She peered down at the kneeling Lavabeasts, then slowly looked to Daq'Ti, who snapped a nod and thudded to the door. They couldn't give the guards a chance to change their minds. She rushed past them and threw herself through the opening. She skidded to a stop at the empty foyer.

Strange . . . Wrong.

After closing the main doors, Daq'Ti pointed to a row of red hexagonal shapes set into the floor. Whereas most were dull, one glowed unusually bright.

Daq'Ti reached to guide her, something she had never seen him do before. "Hurry."

Stalking in that direction, she scanned the shapes in search of a door or stairs but saw nothing. Just gray walls. Where did he want her to go?

"Stand." Daq'Ti caught her arm and drew her gently back to the brightly glowing shape. "Here."

Even as her feet hit the red hexagon, clear walls sprang up around them. The floor lifted. Thrust them upward. The unexpected ascent pitched her into the glass wall.

She yelped and braced against the clear surface, even as Daq'Ti steadied her, his demeanor calm, unaffected. Maybe a bit amused. Two things she'd never seen from him—a touch and amusement. He truly was changing.

She didn't even know what floor or level she needed. She just had to get to the nursery. As the thought struck, the lift slowed and glided to the left. Lighter gray shapes unfolded around the hexagon. Once it was fully surrounded, the pad released the glass, which slid away.

More than a little shocked and disoriented to find herself standing before a passage, Eija quickly hopped off before that thing took them elsewhere.

Daq'Ti stalked forward, then slowed when he realized she wasn't following yet. It still rattled how human he looked now, yet very much of the Draegis race. Handsome in his own right. "Time is short, Xonim."

Glancing around, she didn't like that they hadn't encountered anyone. This was too easy. There should've been a lot more opposition once they were inside. "Where's the nursery?"

Daq'Ti pointed behind her. "There."

She looked over her shoulder to a set of tall, narrow black doors. Unbelievable—the lift had actually delivered her to where she wanted to go. "How . . . how did it know where to take us?"

"Xonim only."

"I know I'm Xonim, but—"

"Shaft responds only to Xonim. None enter without Xonim."

Eija frowned as he stalked toward the doors. "You mean—the lift knew I was . . . Xonim. It brought me here because it knew I wanted to be here." That was djelling crazy.

"Xonim only," he confirmed, then deferentially caught her wrist and raised it. He pressed her palm to a matte obsidian door.

That's when she understood—only Ladies could access the doors and lifts. All of them. This place was wired for Khatriza access only. Which made sense, since they were protecting their spawn. Pale blue flashed over the length and breadth of the barrier. It hissed open.

Relief plowed through her and she smiled at Daq'Ti. "Perfect." They'd done it. They'd—

A shriek echoed across the facility.

Glancing back, Eija looked down through the ultramodern atrium—and her gaze connected with a very familiar face. Xisya.

No, not Xisya. Another Khatriza that looked eerily like the one back on the *Chryzanthe*. The creature below sprang at the lift on her unnatural legs.

Even as Eija registered the problem, the danger, Daq'Ti pulled her through the doorway and planted her hand once more on the panel. Doors whisked shut, severing their line of sight on the Khatriza and Draegis working quickly to gain upper-level access.

Daq'Ti stepped aside and, with a howl, fired his weaponized arm at the control panel. It crackled and sparked. Fried, making it impossible—she hoped—for anyone else to use. And hopefully it was the only one. "Hurry." He motioned behind her. "Destroy."

Shaken and more than a little scared, Eija turned. Froze at what she saw. "Djell."

A vast chasm filled with row upon row of lectulos. She shoved her hand into her hair and gripped the strands tight as she stared across the enormous warehouse-like facility. On Rohilek, she'd seen this place in her mind's eye, but in person, it was much larger, entirely more vast. Seemingly endless. The most daunting part? In each silvery pod lay a black form.

Eija started. Draegis! These weren't— "Where are the Khatriza spawn?" She balked, glancing around, desperate to find the brood. That was her purpose. But it needled her stomach to think of more Draegis being augmented. This couldn't be allowed.

There were so many. Not dozens, or even hundreds as her mind strained to believe, but *thousands*. Too many.

Knowing free will factored into the Taming, she would simply need to touch them and let each one decide if he would accept it. She'd wanted to find a way to translate that touch universally, but had yet to find a way. So, one at a time.

At the first pod, she palmed the instrument panel. As soon as the lid whispered open, she shoved her hand into the cooled space and touched the roughened flesh. Shot the purity of her adunatos into him, already eying the next one.

The beast chortled.

Eija jerked back and watched as he arched his spine off the lectulo, then slumped back with a groan. Didn't move. Didn't waken. She checked the panel and somehow knew the light in her had canceled the darkness . . . But the beast wasn't changing like Daq'Ti had. This one had . . . died. "I don't understand."

"Next," Daq'Ti growled.

Confused, Eija glanced around the facility. Went to the next one. An adult. She scanned the sea of pods up . . . up . . . up. So high that they were pinpricks. An empty hopelessness rushed through her. "This will never work. I can't open every one before they get in here!" There was no way to free that many pods in a quick, efficient way. And where were the spawn? Those were the priority. She didn't have time to free the Draegis, especially if it meant killing them!

"Destroy," Daq'Ti insisted.

Thunk! Thunk!

Eija flinched away from the door, which now had indentations from the Khatriza trying to get inside.

What had she been thinking? There was no way to defeat something this vast.

"Hurry. Destroy!"

Terror rushed up at her. "I *can't*!" Grating claxons rang through the facility and likely summoned every Draegis on Mahatur.

LOWER DOCKS, VYSIEN, HIRAKYS

Sheltering in an old inn, Darius and Crey washed and rested while Kakuzo went to gather the officers and food. Darius sat in the corner as they waited, staring through the threadbare curtain into the morning light. Was it not an analogy for his life? So close to the light, to success . . . yet blocked by so much. Actions, failings . . . Yet the light that did filter through was enough to warm his bones, keep his head up. Kersei and Xylander were his light. Gifts he did not deserve.

For you I do this, Darius silently promised Kersei. She had given him her love, forgiveness, and mercy. What he would not do to have more time with her, to love her as he wanted, as he should. His heart coiled hard at the thought of not seeing her again. The love he felt for her . . .

A strange light pulled his gaze to the bed. Crey was propped against the headboard, staring down at his arm where a mark writhed across his flesh. The sight made Darius's gut churn. Never had he seen any other than the Irukandji bear a mark—except Kersei and Marco. Those were different, though. The brands were meant for good.

"Yeh were right that it is not worth meh soul," Crey rasped from the bed. "Nearly a cycle ago, I killed a man—a friend—over something stupid. We had just seen the royal caravan, then Theule and Jyoti emerged in the square. Seeing her with him, as his queen"—he bared his teeth—"my anger would not be sated without blood. But I fought it. Thought I had succeeded . . . until one of my men"—he sniffed—"Lembril spoke against Theule, who had been closer than a brother. My blade cut true and fast. Almost on its own. But the thirst of steel for the blood of an enemy is a powerful force. That night, the agony of the first mark forbade me from sleep." He drew up his sleeve, revealing more marks. "And every night since, as more have joined the first, until that pain seemed better than the pain of remembering the betrayal by my own blood."

Darius pushed his gaze to the wood floor.

"Thank yeh, princeling, for the truth yeh spoke. I . . . I had lost my way."

"It is easy to do in war," Darius conceded, too aware of his own failings. He tugged at his shirt cuffs.

"It's not true, yeh know."

He waited for the answer, and when it did not come, Darius met Crey's gaze. "He is a *different* man. But not better."

He smirked. "Would that it were true."

Screams and commotion reached through the window, yanking them to their feet. They glanced at each other, then hurried to peer down into the busy square, careful not to betray themselves or their location. Down in the square, a throng had gathered on the corner and spilled into the street. Guards were shouting, weapons extended toward the people.

"Kingsguard," Crey grumbled, then nodded to the side. "The royal carriage."

Alarm sped through Darius as he spotted an overturned carriage. Saw bodies . . . "They were attacked."

Voices carried heavily in the hall, turning shadows to specters.

Crey shoved Darius to the corner. "Back." He snatched his dagger as he darted behind the door, and Darius drew his longblade.

Feet hurried toward their room.

How had someone discovered them? Would they be blamed for the attack against the rex? Crey's visage was grim as he readied himself. The knob jostled.

Calling up all his aerios training, Darius grew calm.

The door thrust inward and four men flooded in.

Crey caught one by the throat and shouldered the door shut, even as faces registered. He uttered an oath and pushed the man away. "Yer timing is poor."

Ikku glanced at Kakuzo, who grinned. "No, my timing was perfect."

Darius shifted, wondering at their lighthearted manner. "We should give care," he warned. "There was trouble in the square."

"Yeh," Ikku said. "Thanks to Kakuzo."

That's when Darius saw the men's tunics, Kakuzo's hand. Bloodied.

Oh no.

Crey must have, too. He started forward with a dark scowl. "What have yeh done?"

"Cleared yer path to the throne, my rex."

Sheathing his dagger, Crey turned away. Roughed hands over his face. Was he upset? Or relieved? Should Darius consider fleeing, so as not to get caught up in this fiasco? Once the Symmachians learned of this . . .

Hands on the rough surface of a rickety table, Crey leaned forward. "What happened?"

"We were in the market when the kingsguard rolled into the square with the rex and his queen," Ikku explained. "Before any of us knew what was happening, Kakuzo was there, scaling the carriage." He shook his head. "No idea how he moved so fast or got past all them horses."

Jaw jutted, Kakuzo stood straight and proud. No remorse. "What I had there was an opportunity, and I seized it." He inclined his head. "Yeh are the rightful heir, my rex. The crown is yers."

Crey pivoted away, his expression inscrutable. Slowly, he turned back to the men. "This is true? Yeh took the life of the rex?"

"It was there for the taking," Kakuzo said solemnly.

Preternaturally calm, Crey stood before his man. "But it was not yer right to take it. If it is so easy for yeh to set yer hands against the rex allowed by the Ancient to rule, what is to stop yeh from setting yer hand against another?"

Before Darius realized what was happening, before the others understood, Crey thrust his dagger into Kakuzo's gut and drove it upward. "Qicien . . . yeh have erred." He hugged the man's face into the crook of his shoulder. "I would have known yeh longer."

Shock riddled the warrior's face. "It was . . . for . . . yeh."

The burly Crey lowered his officer to the ground. "Theule was our brother," he gritted out, his pain palpable. "The kill was *not* honorable." He pressed his now-bloody hands over Kakuzo's bulging eyes and closed them for all time. "Rest well in Shadowsedge, my brother."

The shock of the moment raced through the room, through each man. They stared, disbelieving, at the death of their compatriot. Crey slowly unfolded from the body, staring at it. He held out his arms and rotated them, inspecting them. Was it the blood that bothered him? But then he scanned his body. His gaze flickered at something unseen, as if thinking. Then stunned, he looked at Darius. "No mark."

"Is it true?"

Marco jerked to a stop at the exit doors and wheeled around. Surprise darted through him at the line of Uchuvchi staring at him. Somehow feeling connected to them, he threw Jadon a look—they'd been heading to the shipyard as instructed. He eyed the Uchuvchi who'd asked the question. "What's that?"

"Qadimiy said you are like us. That the marks on your temples and neck were ports used to pilot a ship." The Uchuvchi moved forward, the others following in a river behind him.

"It is true," Marco conceded, not sure what the point was. Feeling time slipping away.

"That you can . . . smell."

He hesitated, then gave a nod. "True."

"Yet, you are not . . . Uchuvchi?"

"I am not. My home is elsewhere." He shifted closer, wondering if now was the time to act on the idea he'd had earlier. "You could come with me."

Many frowned, glancing at each other in confusion. "Outside?" the leader asked.

Marco smirked. "No, farther. A lot farther." His gaze rose to the many tiers of pods around them. "Away from here."

Some shook their heads and started returning to their bays, which Marco couldn't help but think of as docking bays considering the way PICC-lines linked them.

If he mentioned he was leaving Kuru, would they betray him? "I need to return to my system, but we could use Uchuvchi like you. In fact, we need pilots. A lot of them to defend ourselves against the K—" Just in time, he realized they might not appreciate mention of the Khatriza, especially as opponents, since they served them here. "Symmachians."

"We cannot leave," the leader said soberly. "Our connection is here, Kuru."

"The lines should work fine, as long as you're in the ship." At least, Marco hoped so.

"No," the leader shook his head. "Connection here. We leave, they die."

They. "Families?" Marco ventured. "You have families here?" It defied what he'd presumed about the Uchuvchi. Since they lived here in the facility, he had assumed they were bred or grown or something.

"Connections," the leader said with a nod. "We serve, they live."

"But if . . ." No, he could not ask them to sacrifice their families.

"They must come, too, Marco . . ."

The voice was unfair—Vaqar. *"How can I ask them to abandon their families to the violence that is the Draegis and Khatriza?"*

"Ask them how long they have been here."

Marco shifted, again eyed Jadon, who raised his eyebrows and signaled toward the door. Right. Time was short. But they couldn't walk away from a possible opening to recruit the Uchuvchi. He refocused on the leader. "What is your name?"

Looking as human as Marco, the man straightened. "I am called Gi'Zac."

"How long have you been here, Gi'Zac?"

"Since Revolution fifteen mark ten of Tikleg's fifth moon."

Marco stilled, his brain whiplashing around the math that he shouldn't be able to do. Math that told him something was off. Wrong.

"Slag," Jadon breathed. "That's 313 solar cycles."

"No," the leader said with a furrowed brow. "Only fifteen revolutions."

Jadon grunted. "Eija said this was 328 mark ten—"

Gi'Zac gaped. "Impossible!"

Glancing between the two men, Marco hesitated.

"It *is* 328," Jadon insisted. "Eija explained their system to me. They count revolutions as years, naming the year then the month in that year, followed by the moon of the planet they're from."

"It cannot be that long," Gi'Zac muttered, not sounding as certain now, his gaze going distant, worried.

Marco considered the other Uchuvchi. "The rest of you? How long have you been here in the facility?" Similar timelines, all more than two hundred revolutions. If it'd been that long, unless the unaltered Draegis had unusually long life spans . . .

"Our connections—they're dead?" a younger Uchuvchi balked.

"No!" Gi'Zac snapped.

"It's been too long," another said brokenly. "They cannot be alive."

"You lie!" Gi'Zac raged at Marco. "Seek to deceive to make us leave, to make us canceled." His eyes were watery now as he crumpled against the wall. "They promised. Said we serve, they live."

Grief tugged at Marco. "I am very sorry for your loss, for all of you, but this is not the end. Not for you. Leave this place. Come with us. Please."

"No, a trap. To get us to help you."

"I vow—"

"No!" Gi'Zac stepped back. "No. We reject this."

"Please—"

"Stop!"

"We gotta go before we get caught," Jadon whispered as he shouldered closer.

"Search for your families," Marco suggested as they backed toward the door. "If you can find them, then stay. But if not, you'll know my words were true. What the Draegis and Khatriza do here is not for you. They have killed your families and will kill you."

"If we listen to you!"

Frustration coiled. "I seek to free you, friends!"

Brrrt. Brrrrt. Brrt. A drilling alarm vibrated through the facility.

"What is that?" Jadon caught Marco's arm.

"The sensors know we are not in the lectulos," someone said. "Our regeneration time is not complete."

Marco considered the men, the droning alarms. The fear spiraling through their effluxes.

"If too many are out of the pods at one time, guards come." Gi'Zac nodded. "We must go."

As one, the Uchuvchi turned back toward the lectulos without a word.

"Now." Jadon tugged Marco. "Gotta jet."

Though his body complained, Marco embraced the rigor of the exercise as they ran through the city. Strange, though, having air slide over his shaved head rather than tussle his hair. But he was glad to be rid of the hassle. He felt focused, ready. They had followed Daq'Ti's map—memorized, since it was dark and reading a map without light would have been tricky. Even using the glow of his brand could draw undue attention.

He was impressed with the pup trailing him—he had kept up, despite Marco's last-minute directional changes, following the fetor of fuel. They agreed to keep a couple of meters between them so if one ran into trouble, the other could avoid capture and render aid. Jadon was the same breed of warrior as Marco—glad for the mission and purpose. Focused on getting it done.

He banked right around the last building, spied the wall ahead. With it came a painful illumination, light flinging its beams at his corneas with precise daggers. Marco cringed, blinking at the sudden change, but didn't slow because he needed the momentum to tic-tack the wall. His toe hit and he vaulted at the vertical surface. Sprang to the left and grabbed the mortar between stones.

A whistle sailed out and Marco froze. Recognized the signal he and Jadon had devised to indicate trouble. That's when the thuds of sentries reached his ears, and he hung there, his fingers scraping and digging to hold steady as the sentries passed below.

One wrong move, one pebble dribbling down . . . and he'd be exposed.

His heart pounded. He closed his eyes. Forced himself to calm. Recite the Codes to distract from the warmth slipping around his fingers—blood. It made his grip slippery. He shifted, groping for traction. A hold that wouldn't send him to his death.

Clacking rocks behind and to his left stopped the sentries. The Draegis chortled then bounded in that direction.

Seizing the distraction, Marco dragged himself up on top of the wall. Flattened on the surface, flexing his aching fingers. He slid his hand to his other sleeve and wiped the blood, hearing the Eidolon grunt and groan as he worked his way up.

"Close call." Jadon joined him.

"Too close." Marco skidded his gaze to the left and stilled at the depression that spanned out for leagues. There was no sign of water, but the expanse was so large and vast, it might as well be a seaport. Personal and personnel transports docked along the inner wall. Just beyond that, freighters were undergoing repairs. The larger, more powerful ships like dreadnoughts or battlecruisers would be in orbit. It was just more efficient that way.

But all Marco needed was one fast-attack craft to break atmo and get through the ring—and Daq'Ti had vowed there was a new one out here ready to deploy. And where was that crescent ship he'd seen in his vision?

A small craft glided through the hazy lights that scattered darkness from the shipyard, slowly diverting Marco's attention to a multisided tower jutting far up into the sky. From one of the dozens of retractable docking pads in that structure, another craft undocked and glided away, its lights blinking a path to atmo. Higher up glittered something strange that, at first, his mind refused to comprehend. Then . . . he saw it.

Glinting like a huge bronzed scythe in the blackness—the prototype. The size disappointed Marco until he realized the scale of the tower and the ships around it. The scythe's clean, smooth arc around a center orb was massive!

"Scuz me," Jadon muttered. "How in the Void are we supposed to get up there?"

KAATA SHAHAR, MAHATUR

"You fly."

Pivoting as her body assumed its Faa'Cris form, Eija frowned at Daq'Ti. Her mind caught up with her body's instinct. She had begun the change before thought or suggestion. It was second nature, shifting from Eija into the warrior with wings and armor. She exhaled as her span unfurled, riffling the air around them. Rising, she took in the central hub with her more advanced senses.

"You go," he said, pointing to the central hub. "Destroy."

In a strange way, this facility reminded her of the *Chryzanthe* with its gold petals . . . Here, the petals were nubs that held easily a hundred or more branches. Each supported a couple hundred pods. Not just thousands—there had to be hundreds of thousands of Draegis.

Overwhelmed at the task, at the potential of them going after the Quadrants should she fail, Eija tried to remind herself that she wasn't just chosen for this—she'd volunteered. And she was Vaqar and Eleftheria's daughter. Which reminded her of the obvious: this battle wasn't about her. It was about the millions in the Quadrants targeted by the Khatriza for extinction.

But . . . was it her imagination, or did these upper pods look different? Yes, they were . . . lighter. The shape of the bodies resting in them not as dark. What did that mean? Her wings kept her aloft as she hovered near one and peered in.

Ice filled her veins at the hideous glob lying there.

"Khatriza," she whispered. What she'd thought to be Draegis pods were in fact filled with the Corrupt. Hybrids? But they already were. So, why did they look so very sinister?

This creature was still young. Possibly. What did she know about Khatriza DNA? These things were so far removed from Faa'Cris, who gave birth naturally. She took in the pods around her. All spawn. Above her. Spawn. More than three-fourths of the facility contained spawn.

Djell.

"Destroy core," Daq'Ti reiterated.

"What?" Even as the word registered, Eija visually traced the umbilicals snaking throughout the facility, some crisscrossing, diving, rising. Others simply floating. But all led to one column.

Yes, the core . . . Daq'Ti was right. Intuition told her if they took that out, it'd shut down life support for the pods. Stop growing these monsters.

And again, her years living as a human invaded her thoughts, tugged at her compassion, made her rail at killing so many . . . These were Khatriza and Draegis, yes—but they hadn't lived outside the pods. So what wrong had they committed? What evil?

"Xonim," Daq'Ti trilled from a console, tapping it. "Verify."

Clang! Clang-clang-groan!

Eija shot backward. Her span snapped out instinctively as she inspected the vaultlike door. It was now bending inward with each near-deafening impact. "Out of time!" She alighted next to her protector and looked at the illuminated display. "What is it?"

"Answers," he said, motioning to it. "You read."

First glance at the unique symbols tightened her stomach. Argument perched on her tongue that she couldn't read this, but that was her humanity clouding her thoughts, her expectations of herself. Recognition flared, warming her spine and span as the lettering—no, *script*—became familiar.

"Faa'Cris." Okay, good. So she could read it—though that clanging on the door made it hard to concentrate. She tried to hurry. Crazy how the Khatriza had done away with all things Faa'Cris except the language. "Too much effort," she guessed as she scanned the text.

A screech pierced the sterile environment.

Eija flicked her hand in front of the readout, and the script blurred past, but her Faa'Cris intellect caught and absorbed the meaning. That sick knot of dread corkscrewed and tightened as she was peripherally aware of the sentries forcing their way through the opening, which was yet too small. But they reached through with their powered arms and started firing.

Still reading, still trying to find a way to shut it down, Eija shielded herself and Daq'Ti with her wings, a rippling across the span indicating direct hits to her shield. But Eija couldn't tear herself from the intel she was gathering. The daunting truth behind what the Khatriza were doing to these unwitting males.

"Go, Xonim. Go!" Daq'Ti railed as she held him fast to their spot, spinning through the intel.

A growing fury swelled over the immeasurable harm being done. It wasn't just the physical, like augmenting their arms with weapons, but the psychological harm. The Draegis in these pods weren't just inert beasts being grown into adults. They were in an artificial environment where they were being programmed, trained to fight, and—above all—protect and revere the Khatriza. These were far more advanced than Daq'Ti and his kind. Far more deadly and singularly focused.

"Djell!"

A blast slipped around the shield and knocked Eija forward. She stumbled.

Daq'Ti bellowed, his arm roiling with the weaponization. Blasts seared past her, trimmed a bit of feather. She hissed and glanced back. Three Draegis sentries formed a shield—firing on her and Daq'Ti—while two more pried open the door further, the Khatriza screeching her way through.

Daq'Ti took a pulse to the arm but remained steadfast, strategically placing himself between a steel column and Eija to protect her.

"You have breached the treaty, Faa'Cris," a voice shrieked in her mind.

Righteous indignation whipped Eija toward the Khatriza—a queen if she accurately assessed the well-developed creature clattering toward her. "Xisya's primus violation demanded a response."

An angry, violent shriek came in response.

"Thought so." Eija shouldered aside the noise, shielded her thoughts and body. This wouldn't work much longer. Across the swooping platforms that wormed through the facility, she saw another communications module. She spun, hooked an arm around Daq'Ti's waist, bent her knees, and shot into the air. Aiming high, she burst past the pods, skimming one or two as she did and hearing the lectulos rattle beneath her wake. Then she dove around a cluster and used it for cover as she descended toward the other module. They landed and took cover.

Really, they had zed time for the encyclopedic version of what was happening here. But Eija had to find out . . . *something* . . .

Something niggled at her. She glanced up at the pods. Around. Wait. She flicked her attention to the branches around her. The ones she'd skimmed. What she'd detected . . . "This doesn't make sense."

Air singed as blasts grew closer, and Daq'Ti scrambled to a strategic location to buy time. She eyed his location, appreciating the way he protected her so she could make like a data disc and download this.

But that thing . . . the one bugging her, tripping her internal alarms. What was it? What was eating at her concentration?

A blast seared past. Heat bloomed across her face. Sizzled her skin. Outrage and instinct made her pivot. Focus a burst of pure light at the source running toward Daq'Ti. Even as it volleyed out and found its target, Eija saw the

Draegis. Realized what she'd done—firing without a weapon. *What?*

Crimson slits pulsing rapidly, he raged, but her beam stunned him. Knocked him to his knees, on which he slid the last few feet to Daq'Ti. Her protector shot upward and slammed his fist into the Draegis.

In the instant before the blow landed, the Lavabeast twitched. His eyes flashed.

Blue not red.

Daq'Ti delivered the death blow, rolling out of it and taking aim at the stream of lava coming their way.

Blue not red. Blue not red.

How? Rattled but finding no answers, Eija twitched around. Tried to concentrate on the intel streaming across the panel in the archaic Faa'Cris script.

"Xonim," Daq'Ti grunted.

"Almost done." Eija hunched behind the module as she quickly wagged her fingertips in front, rushing through the intel and training regimen. They were programming the Draegis to kill. How djelling insane—beginning in the early stages of development and continuing until the Draegis reached maturity. At whatever stage these creatures emerged, adults or children, the pods would have them ready to kill. Arms weaponized as soon as they took a breath. And not just kill, but annihilate.

"Children," she murmured, slowing, her mind racing. Her gaze trekked over the thousands of pods. Around her. Behind her. In front of her. "Children!" She zapped her attention back to the deck. Checked the life cycles of the Draegis in the pods. The completion dates. None of these were Draegis *children*. "This doesn't make sense . . ."

"Xonim," Daq'Ti said, his voice strangely gurgled, closer.

"You said this was a nursery." Granted, it did have the Khatriza spawn . . .

He backed into her, heaving a breath. A wet breath.

She glanced to the side—and startled. "Daq'Ti!"

Ever her defender, he was on a knee, firing at the onslaught. Despite having lost his other arm. "Go. Must go," he wheezed.

She pressed her hand to the wound and felt the light rush into him. "I can't." She checked the still-streaming data. "Despite the programs wired into the hub, there aren't any Draegis children." Even as she voiced that, a vision swam before her eyes—Marco and Reef fighting off Draegis, nothing but air around them.

Daq'Ti glanced around, staring at the pods. "Yes, must . . ."

"No. They're all—" What was she seeing? *Reef!* And how?

He faltered. "Eija?"

Lifespeech. *What's happening?* They had to be in a bad spot for her to start receiving images of him and Marco.

"Eija, how—augh!"

She stilled, monitoring the advancing Lavabeast, but her mind, her thoughts were with— *"Reef!"* Struggling to focus on two problems at once, she found herself squinting at the Draegis while her inner Faa'Cris reached for the shipyard. Daq'Ti had stunted the influx, but only because the Draegis were now wholly focused on widening the opening for the much-larger Khatriza.

"Eija. What's going on? How can I hear you?"

"Lifespeech," she grunted, applying pressure to Daq'Ti's injury, then glancing at the module. Too much to do. *"I sensed . . . trouble."*

Why weren't there any Draegis children? Was there another facility? She had no idea, but at least it made her decision about this place a little easier. Now to figure out how to neutralize the pods and their inhabitants.

"That'd be because we're in trouble," Reef said. *"At the shipyard. Being attacked."*

Daq'Ti stumbled into her. Collapsed onto his backside. His injury was draining him. The Draegis were pulling the Khatriza through the hole, while others fired on them. Reef and Marco were under attack.

What the djell am I supposed to do? And who first?

A heavy thud reverberated through the facility. Even as she saw the Khatriza sail through the opening, bringing a flood of other Draegis, Eija noticed a cable connected to a bubbling vat. When she saw the viscous substance, her mind registered its name—*djell.*

No way.

Yes. Djell. The sacred waters used in the Faa'Cris sanitatem. The same liquid in the lectulos. Same liquid cocooning the Draegis. This probably explained why their bodies looked like lava—so used to the healing properties of the djell during their creation and programming that after they emerged their skin was literally dying as it hung on their bodies.

This . . . this was why Eija was told to come to the nursery. It had meaning. Significance. But . . . what? Eija wracked her brain, searching for answers.

"We're trying to get into the prototy—Augh! Scuzzing Draegis are going to blow it up if they aren't careful!"

A shriek punctured the air. She jerked toward the main bridge across from the elevators and saw the Khatriza flying forward.

No. Not flying . . .

She had no wings.

Well, that's interesting.

But she was moving fast. On a collision course.

Pulse blasts from the Draegis filled the air with heat and wakes that made it hard to breathe. Eija glanced at Daq'Ti, unmoving.

Djell!

She snatched him up and spun, wrapping them in her wings and slipped from this place, even as she felt the foul breath of the Khatriza sear her nostrils.

"Go go go!" Marco sprinted across the iron grate that served as a docking bridge/arm. Ahead, Jadon raced toward the orb-shaped center of the crescent prototype.

Like pecking birds, light fast-attack craft buzzed the dock, spitting pulse cannon fire at them. At the bridge.

Jadon dove, rolled up out of it, and slammed himself against the hull. "There's no door!" He pivoted and aimed the pulse rifle he'd snagged from a sentry and unloaded on the nearest ship.

Cannon fire strafed the tower, narrowly missing Marco. Another stream came from behind, the two ships driving him to his death. Dodging the fire, he dove into the iron grate. His teeth clacked and fire blazed across his shoulder. "Augh!"

Stay down and he was slag. Run and he could be turned to ash. Marco dug his toes in and threw himself across the bridge. Felt it shift. Reek! He crashed headlong into Jadon. Vision blurring, he shook it off. Focused on the hull of that titanium-looking prototype.

"It won't open," Jadon shouted as he fired, forcing another ship to veer off.

Marco scanned the sleek surface of the crescent's hull. Saw no delineation of door or access panel. Just slick and smooth. "Where's the door?"

"Exactly!" Jadon shifted around and aimed at the other craft. "Kinda hoping you'll conjure some of that Kynigos mahjuk and get us the scuz out of here."

Was this a joke? No door? There had to be one. The bridge led out here. They'd spent an hour slipping through one hatch after another, then climbing exterior fire ladders to access this thing. Treacherous, terrifying progress.

"What about Eija?" Marco slid his hand over the hull, amazed that a hard surface like this could feel satiny.

"No idea. She was in my head one second, gone the next!"

Searching the hull, Marco noted the surprisingly warm surface. His brand flared then receded. *Strange.* Recalling the way it'd responded to the facility, he frowned but moved his hand back to where the brand yet again glowed brighter. There, the heat increased and the glow swelled. As if responding to his touch. *Why is—*

Shunk!

Marco twitched. Jerked his hand back. Glanced at Jadon.

Who—of course—grinned. "Working that mahjuk again, eh?" he called over his shoulder as he continued defending their position.

"No mahjuk," Marco growled as he trailed his fingers over the hull.

Now there was a depression in the shape of an oval, and as he touched it, a whine tremored. A bigger response. As if—

The panel retracted into the hull.

Marco grabbed Jadon and hauled him backward into the ship. They stumbled into a brightly lit white and gold deck. The door hissed shut. Light vanished. They were sealed in complete darkness.

"Uh . . ." Jadon muttered.

A faint blue light emanated from the walls and left a trail of illumination, bathing the space in a dull glow.

"Better," Jadon said.

Without warning, they were tossed aside by an insane amount of gravity.

Marco stumbled, eying Jadon, who'd been thrown onto all fours. "That seems appropriate."

"Shut up." Jadon struggled to rise, but the force exerted itself again, thwarting his efforts.

"The ship's moving . . ."

"No slag," Jadon gritted out, taking in the interior hull as he struggled to stand.

Studying the schematics on static displays, Marco realized the sphere they'd entered was somehow separate from the crescent part of the ship. "No, not moving. It's floating. Like a ball on water."

Jadon turned a clumsy circle. "It was much bigger outside."

"We're in an airlock," Marco guessed.

All of a sudden, the weight severed. Orange light flared through the space, and the wall directly in front of them slid away, revealing a Command deck.

"Scuz me." Jadon took in the new area with a taut expression.

"Not quite so small now, eh?" Marco clicked his boots to activate the magnets. No idea what would happen next, but he wasn't going to remain at the mercy of shifting gravitational forces. With no central station or pilot's chair, he had to guess his way around the deck, which was about the same size as the interior of his scout. Not bigger but definitely more advanced. Circular like the outer hull, the inner sphere boasted stations along the perimeter and a few sectioned-off areas in the middle. He eyed the controls, guessing which one would give them control of the ship.

"Let's hope they want this prototype more than they want to kill us." Jadon slid past a crash couch and eyed the arrays over it. "This looks . . ."

Hope rose that the Eidolon would recognize something.

"Completely unfamiliar." Jadon clomped to the CIC deck and checked out another station, scanning dials and panels. "Slag. Same here."

Marco wandered to the center, turning a slow circle. They hadn't come this far to fail. But what were they supposed to do if they couldn't even figure out how to power up the ship, never mind fly her? Pain radiated through his shoulder, but he focused on the hull. On his sizzling brand. He glanced at it and—

Is it possible . . .?

"We better get moving," Jadon grumbled, "or we'll be Draegis fertilizer."

"They won't fire on us." Marco recalled the way that wall pattern leapt to his arm. "It's the prototype." He did not relish the idea of reinitiating contact, but what if . . .

"Which means they won't want it under *our* control, therefore—boom!" Jadon switched to yet another station. "This is all Draegis to me."

Keeping his hand out but low—he'd also like to avoid more "mahjuk" taunts—Marco shifted to the right and felt a lessening.

Wrong direction.

He angled left . . . stronger. More to the left. Steady, focused, the brand pulsed. He rotated his wrist, palm up—

Whoosh!

Something punched out the floor. Clipped the back of his knees. "Augh!" It pitched him backward, cold hard steel molding against his back and thighs. Forced onto his back, he found this too reminiscent of the lectulo on the *Prevenire.* "Reek!" But then came the warm perfection of the brand, and the Draegis armor clattered to the floor. He glanced at his arm, stunned to find some kind of liquid steel coiling around it. System arrays sprang into the air over him.

"*Xush kelibsiz, Uchuvchi,*" a static voice resonated through the sphere.

Jadon stilled, looking over his shoulder at him. "Void's Embrace!" He thudded around. "No, this isn't mahjuk at all," he taunted.

"Quiet," Marco warned, trying to extricate himself.

"It called you Uchuvchi—pilot."

Ignoring the guy, Marco dangled a leg over the edge—but the device counterbalanced, as if it interpreted the move as him falling and tipped him back onto its cold surface. "Blazing Fires of Hieropolis . . ." His brand ignited, light speeding along the molten metal.

"Scuz me," Jadon whispered, scanning the sphere, which now had maps, arrays, and star charts floating around Command.

Light flashed, a super-ignited flare against the steel. "Augh!" Marco shielded his eyes and ducked.

When the light receded, two more shapes stood on the steel deck.

Jadon leapt back with a curse. "Eija." Stared disbelieving at the feathery wingspan that ruffled the air as it folded into her spine. "How'd you . . ."

A helm shuttered away from her fierce, radiant face. "Daq'Ti needed help." She pointed to something behind them. "Power up the ship."

"We're working on it." Jadon leapt toward her. "You're injured!"

Burns marred her neck and shoulder. Scorch marks from a pulse weapon. Marco was on his feet, though he hadn't tried to or even thought to stand up. Somehow the sphere had responded—to what? His feelings, concern for Eija?—and thrust him upward. "What happened? You took fire?"

Eija stared at him, then whispered something in a foreign tongue, her eyes going wide as she did. Her expression faltered, then transformed into something akin to the armor coating her body, and she continued talking in some strange language.

The girl had always seemed a bit odd, but he owed her for finding him in the *Prev*. So he gave her the benefit of the doubt. "You're not making sense—that wasn't any language we know."

Her eyes finally seemed to focus on him. "I found the spawn. There's—" She shook her head. "The Draegis are there, too, but there aren't any children and the pods—*djell!*"

"Yeah, we've been cursing like crazy, too," Jadon said. "Well, not Marco, but he's borderline god, so—"

"No, I mean—*djell*. It's a substance the Faa'Cris use. It fills the—" Eija looked at the unconscious Draegis at her feet. "Never mind. Just need to put Daq'Ti into the medpod. You need to get out of here. *Now.*"

Her scent was a complicated, roiling concoction. Something Marco couldn't sort. There was a . . . shield around it. That didn't make sense. Not smelling Draegis was one thing but— "What's going on, Eija?"

"There aren't any children."

"I'm— *What?*"

"In the nursery," she said, shifting aside. "There are no Draegis children. There should be, if they're being augmented from infancy—programming indicates they have been. I found the Khatriza spawn, but then we were getting shot at, and the data was right there. Then—"

"Grav down, Eija." Jadon sounded condescending. "Slow and easy. You're not making sense."

Frustration rolled through her, and with that simple shudder, her true nature started unfolding, glimmering in the air, a faint aura of pure light. What? Marco had only ever seen that in people's eyes when he touched them. But here she was rippling with it. He resisted the urge to step back when armor, transparent and formidable, coalesced around her again. She was angry, defensive as she lifted Daq'Ti as if he were a babe and hurried him across the deck. The wall shimmered as it release a medpod.

Recoiling at the sight—it was too much like a lectulo—Marco wondered how Eija had known that medpod was there. More than a little unsettled at the familiarity with which she negotiated this prototype, a name that inherently meant she *shouldn't* have knowledge of it, he adjusted his stance and processed that new, spiced efflux from her. "What about children?"

After setting Daq'Ti in the pod, she accessed a panel in the pod. "A nursery by its very name implies young ones, saplings, pups. But this one doesn't have any Draegis children. Even calling it an incubation center means they don't start with full-growns. But that's all that was there. And Khatriza spawn." She scowled. "It's just wrong."

"We're not tracking," Jadon said, face a knot of confusion. "You were supposed to destroy it—"

"There aren't any children! And there were thousands of pods filled with spawn. Way too many for me to deal without planning and preparation. Then Daq'Ti was dying, so I had to get him help. We have to get this ship out of here. Now." She nodded to Marco. "Check the nav charts." She hurried toward a glass array backlit and littered with icons nobody could decipher. "I'm powering up the engines." Determined, she nodded to Jadon. "Run a systems check."

Jadon went to a console, hands hovering above it in question. "I can't—the language."

Eija grunted. Tapped furiously in the air, her fingers flying freely among the dancing icons. She flicked her wrist to the right.

"*Standard Quadrant Script accepted and enabled.*" The mechanical voice's notification preceded the transformation of images and icons across the sphere—displays, charts, 3D maps—all now in their own language. It was oddly comforting.

"Voids," Jadon hissed, sliding a wary glance at her. "How'd you—"

"She'll know where I am and send trouble." Eija reeled around and stomped toward Marco. "In the pilot chair."

Marco was still unsettled after having been unceremoniously dumped into that thing a second ago. "I won't ever *willingly* get in a lectulo again."

Her eyes sparked. "Then I'll help your unwilling self."

"Forget it."

In a blink, she was there, urging his shoulders back. She hadn't just walked to get to him—she'd *flown*. Like Xisya. If the lectulo wasn't enough of a mind game, her transformation was.

"No!" Pressure hit his calves and spine as the lectulo lifted him into position. "Get off me!" Marco barked, shoving upward.

"Merciful Mother, are you men always so much work?"

"Why are you like this? What's going on?" Marco tried to distract her. "Tell me now—"

"You must leave." Her tone was crazy-soft yet commanding, with a hint of an echo that rang in his head. "The navigational controls," she intoned again, indicating to the side. "See those dots?" The serenity of her countenance sharpened as she waved toward the digital map floating in the air above him.

"The star chart? Yeah," Jadon said.

"They're not stars," she snapped. "They're ships!"

Alarm bit at Marco's anger as he eyed the array. There had to be a thousand or more.

"And this ship—remember how I said the *Yo'qiluvchi* was the vanguard?" She went to the lectulo and, with a preternatural sweep of her fingers, drew the thing up out of the deck and into its full crash-couch position. "This ship is the *Qirolicha*—it means queen."

He didn't care what it was called.

"Besides its many other facets, it acts as a tether, if you will. A communication hub that allows smaller ships to bounce information and communication across. They're connected via a type of neural net that is similar to the neuralink used by Eidolon, a technology likely introduced by Xisya. They can operate within any system as long as the signal can reach the *Qirolicha*."

"Okay," Jadon said, hands on his belt, "but that's not much different from standard corvettes attached to a battlecruiser."

"There is *so* much." Exhaustion rimmed Eija's eyes. "I really don't have time to explain all this. Pilot this—"

"I'm *not* plugging in and *piloting* any ship again." Marco tried again to maneuver out of the crash couch.

"So, the Kynigos Code, the one that guides you, the honor by which you swore to defend innocent lives and bring justice, means nothing."

"That Code defined my life as a hunter." Marco shrugged again. "I'm no longer a hunter."

"So you no longer have the gift, the ability of the anaktesios?"

Stubbornly, he held his peace.

"My father will be disappointed you are so easily cowed from living by honor."

He swallowed. And hated himself for it. "It was your father who told me to step out from the shadow of honor."

"Then how about this, *Medora* Marco: if you do not remain in the couch, you will never return home to your wife and child. Isaura will die because when the *Qirolicha* jumps, it generates a protective shield around its drones. They travel together. If you do not pilot this thing now into a hyperjump, before the pilots and Draegis are anticipating one, they will have time to power up, connect to the hive, and reach the Quadrants with you, where there will be nothing to stop them."

"I don't understand. The Sentinel, if we destroy it—"

"The *Qirolicha* is revolutionary—an advancement in the Khatriza's technological war that will eradicate all life because this ship does not need a Sentinel to enter a jumpstream."

"Slag."

"That's impossible," Marco said. "The physics—"

"Some would say your brand is impossible. That Vaqar is impossible. Yet both exist." Eija sighed. "We have no time left. The Uchuvchi are in their regeneration pods, but if they have not been awakened yet, they will be soon. The ship must jump away before they reach the piloting pods. If the *Qirolicha* is still in orbit when they do, we have annihilated our own people."

Marco pinched the bridge of his nose and clamped his jaw. "I spent weeks in that lectulo. I can't—"

"How about days then?" Her words made Marco hesitate, and that seemed to please her.

He resented the confusion. "What?"

"With this ship—its capabilities—the journey will take three days."

"*Days?*" Jadon squawked. "You serious? In three days we can be back?"

"Curse the reek," Marco muttered, staring at the coffin around him. Thought of returning to Isaura. Instinctively, he reached out for her with his receptors. But that blasted emptiness gaped back at him, absent her Signature but still soaked with that odd minty trace. He shouldered it aside, unwilling to be distracted. He wanted Isaura, had to find her. His heart ached that he could not. Was she dead?

Mint permeated his nostrils again. He winced, the fragrance strong, persistent.

And a realization hit—he was not *reaching* out for that scent. It was pulsing itself at him. As if it wanted his notice. Insistent, like a child demanding attention.

A child . . .

Sucker punched, Marco stilled. Entertained the minty demand. *Could it be . . . ?*

The fragrance swirled around him, stronger, more powerful. As if exultant at being acknowledged. Marco nearly laughed—until his mind caught up with the truth: the minty presence was there, but not Isaura. Had she died giving birth?

No, it was too early. The babe's time was not yet upon them.

A waft struck him, minty notes undeniable and forming their own unique, potent Signature. *"Daughter . . . ?"*

Joy rushed through the scent.

More than ever, he wanted to get home. Know if that was truly his daughter reaching out to him. Find out if Isaura was safe. But that meant going back into the lectulo. His focus again landed on Eija.

He exhaled loudly and shook his head. "Holy fires . . . I can't believe I'm doing this." But he had to know. If Isaura was hurt, he would unleash his fury on Symmachia.

A strange, warm calm slid through him as Eija smiled, setting his hand to a bar and coiling his fingers around it. "My father chose well." There was again something older, wiser in her features as she assisted him in lying back. "Think on him, on how you have honed your entire life to honor him."

Marco felt movement in the lectulo. Saw the tubes snaking toward his arms and sides. He sucked in a breath through his nose and braced. Felt the sting as they punctured the almost-healed spots. He uttered an oath, heart thudding hard.

Eija touched his forehead. There wasn't much pressure, but it somehow stilled him. "I know it hurts, but you are the Progenitor. It is time to bring the war to her."

"Xisya." A pinch at his temples warned the lectulo had snapped into his cerebral cortex as well. Growling, he gritted his teeth that this was happening again. He may not be buried in the hull of the *Prev*, but he was still trapped in the lectulo. The djell, the feel of being sandwiched in, of tubes snaking across his arms, abdomen, and neck . . . "No," he gritted out, fighting it.

"Marco, peace!" Her face pushed into his awareness, broke through the clog of panic that both embarrassed and shamed him. "When you get to the other side, make sure the Sentinel there is destroyed. You must make sure."

Right. Because of Xisya. "She's a queen," he mumbled.

"If she gets control of this ship—"

"Then everything has been for naught." He swallowed, feeling his muscles relax even as the cold venom of the lectulo seeped into his veins.

Her brown eyes hit the array that danced over his head. "Once you enter the Kedalion Sentinel, she will know you are there. She will want this ship. If somehow she succeeds, you must destroy it. Use the self-destruct."

He nodded, noticing her words. Thinking through what she'd said. The recurrence of a certain word.

"Wait," Jadon frowned, turning from the array. "You keep saying 'you' . . ."

"Ship's ready." Eija hurried to a panel, glancing at the dots hovering over Marco in the digital display. "Take it to the Sentinel—"

"I thought the *Qirolicha* didn't need the ring," Marco thought aloud, focusing on the thrumming in the ship. The way it talked to him. The communication was clearer, more focused for some reason. It both relieved and scared him.

"It doesn't—I said *to* the Sentinel, not *through* it." She darted to another console, tapping icons, flipping switches. With each one, another part of the ship seemed to come alive. "Reef will need to fire the phase weapon at the ring to destroy it as you jump."

"That'll kill us all!" Jadon objected.

"This ship will be light-years away before the concussion hits."

"Scuz that. The detonation—"

"Harness in," Eija said. "No time to argue. Trust me."

Jadon narrowed his eyes. "Hold up."

"Get in your crash couch! You launch in thirty clicks."

"*You?*" Jadon demanded. "You mean 'we'? Right?" He jerked. "What the scuz, Ei?"

"You're not coming." It made sense now—the directions, the urgency, the running around giving them orders. If she were coming, there'd be no reason to explain all this right now.

Eija met his gaze evenly. And right then golden light spilled through the deck, igniting his brand, searing his corneas—but not before he saw her span. Saw the illumination of her face. Registered Jadon vaulting at her.

A screech filled Marco's ears. He sensed the ship respond. A surge hit his veins and fire seared. The *Qirolicha* launched, the movement clean and steady, though he heard thwaps and pings against the hull—the Draegis were firing upon the prototype now.

"The Sentinel." Marco gritted against the hard-g burn as they rocketed into the sky but didn't hear a response from the Eidolon. Had Jadon been injured in the launch? He strained to look at the guy's couch—empty. Marco strained to look around, gravity a powerful master, pinning him. He scanned the vids. Nowhere. Jadon was gone. He was nowhere.

That meant Marco would have to control the ship *and* the weapons. On his own.

The deafening silence once the *Qirolicha* broke atmo proved eerie. The ship vibrated, as if in objection to entering the expanse of space. Blips came and went. Reek. They were moving very fast. Faster than he could've imagined.

Marco had a terrifying thought. *Now . . . how am I supposed to jump this thing?*

Stress tightened his muscles, the strain and burn almost more than he could bear. Instinct told him to relax, but logic said, *Voids no!*

He closed his eyes, harnessed his thoughts toward jumping.

Instantly, he felt something in his veins sear. The resonance of the *Qirolicha* purred into his thoughts. A whistle shrieked through the hull. He spotted the Sentinel and his heart started.

"Ready to fire. On my mark," he said . . . to himself, since Jadon bailed. His teeth rattled. A mask slid over his face and somehow coated his teeth, protecting them from the burn—and he felt a sharp prick somewhere at the back of his brain. Remembered the tendril that linked to his piriform cortex. "Augh." He shook his head—or tried.

No go.

Countdown.

Right. "Three . . ." Amazing that he could still communicate. "Two . . ." He eyed the blip.

The ship screamed.

"Fire!"

There came an event that punched his chest and thrashed his body. Rattled his teeth. His receptors flared wide, minty and spiced at the same time. As the *Qirolicha* hurled into the jump, Marco's vision grayed, taking his hearing with it, but not before he felt the crushing destruction of the Sentinel on the other end of the slipstream.

Marco clenched his eyes, feeling the djell of the lectulo caressing his body, protecting it against the crushing speed at which the *Qirolicha* bolted through the jumpstream.

"Isaura . . . I'm coming home."

Kersei held tight to her son, tears long since dried. She feared Darius would not return, yet a knowing deep within said this was the path he had chosen. A sacrifice. An amends.

"It was his choice," Ma'ma supplied softly.

Kersei twitched. Lost in contemplation, she had not seen her approach. "He was used."

"No, he was given a choice, and he chose to see his son's birth and aid the cause."

"You used his guilt, bribed him with Xylander's birth, then thrust him out into a war that he has no defense against."

"Your grief speaks now, and it is understandable, but in earnest, Kersei, you discount him much."

"I *know* him," she argued.

Ma'ma propped her hip against the bed and smoothed a hand over Xylander's mop of sandy blond hair. "Then you know his love for you both, that he would have done anything to return you to the life you had, not just the title but the respect both you and his son deserved."

"I was at peace with what had become of our life."

"Is that why you fled in the middle of a raging storm? Because of peace?"

Her eyes stung. "He should have waited. I would have returned."

"Is it his fault again?"

"Yes! He should have known—"

"What? That the wild daughter of Xylander would yield?" Ma'ma laughed. "You have always held tight to your convictions, even when it hurts others."

"Will I *ever* be enough for you?" Kersei bit out.

Hurt washed over Ma'ma's features, but she sighed. "Anger masks, Daughter. What lies beneath that mask? Hurt? Fear?"

"I do not want him to die, and I am sure he will." Her words ended in a choked sob. "To be sure, a raider or the skycrawlers will kill him."

Ma'ma wrapped an arm around her, pulling her close. "He is a warrior and the son of a warrior. Believe in him."

Kersei's eyes burned. Her body ached. "I cannot lose him. Not when I have just found him." She cried into her mother's shoulder and let herself grieve, work through what she had been through. A healing she had not allowed herself since the night of Adara's Delta Presentation. Her heady thoughts drifted away amid Ma'ma's murmurs to let it go, release it to the Ancient. She felt into a discomfited sleep.

She shuddered and found herself on a field. A babe in her arms. She glanced down, surprised at the child there. Not Xylander with his sandy hair. But a mop of curly black hair. Pale blue eyes. A daughter. "Who are you?"

"Augh!"

At the shout from behind, she glanced over her shoulder and saw a thick, dark mist with twinkling lights. A darker form took shape and slowly emerged. "They're coming!"

Fire shot through her arm.

With a strangled scream, Kersei shot up, panting hard. Saw a glow emanating through the room. Her arm aching. Her brand churning. With a whimper, she shook it out, desperate to unsee what had come to her in the dream.

"What is it?" Ma'ma rushed into the room.

Kersei stared at her arm, rubbed the marks. "Marco." She met her mother's gaze. "He's coming, but so are *they*."

The Khatriza.

KARDIA, LAMPROS CITY, KALONICA, DROSERO

The wild thrashing of their daughter within the womb kept Isaura awake. Or mayhap it was this strange, powerful resonance that insisted she be alert. A feeling she could neither explain nor thwart. It radiated through her, across her swelling womb. Nearing her sixth month of pregnancy, the flutter of the babe was not as often as she liked, but the little one was especially active in late evenings and through the night.

"Oh, blessed babe, that you would rest," she moaned, curling onto her side, hand on her burgeoning belly, as she pressed her face into the pillow. Longed for Dusan to be here. For his hand to rest beneath hers, feeling the movement of his heir. The anchor between their hearts and the gaping distance.

"Where are you?" she wondered.

Things in Kardia needed him. She needed him. Not simply to handle political matters, but to wrap his arms around her, love her gently through the night, whisper her name. Tease away cares with those soft but demanding kisses.

"Oh, Dusan . . ."

She had not met him in the dreamspace in long, lonely weeks, so she had filled her time sending communiqués to Vorn and staying apprised of the Kalonican pilots. A shipment had been sent with stealth technology, but a Symmachian battlecruiser waylaid the ship in orbit. Following the attack in Jherako, Isaura—at the recommendation of Mavridis—commissioned the hunter Rico to undertake the strategic and secretive development of a northern airbase, along with the relocation of a fourth of their vipers and pilots from Ironesse. The apprentice Duncan made large strides with technology, installing sensors along the palace walls, as well as developing a central air-defense command center for monitoring the skies. In addition, General Sebastiano suggested the citizens of Kalonica familiarize themselves with escape routes to caves and woods as precautions.

So much. They were so overwhelmed, and the impossibility of surviving against an air assault made Isaura ache with hopelessness, yearn for Dusan. Where was he? Why had they not connected? There was much to tell him.

The birth of little Xylander nigh on two months past had been announced by Roman, who had seen the babe. He had also reported the strange vanishing of Darius. It was widely speculated that the former prince had fled to Hirakys. Roman assured Isaura that was not the truth of it but refused to give voice to what he knew, that Vorn and Aliria were in hiding from the Symmachians flooding across the southern portion of the continent, but there had been no word of late regarding their well-being. Roman also explained the duchess had been with the Ladies when she gave birth. That and her own encounter in Jherako provided the one thread of hope to which Isaura clung: Faa'Cris were actively working in the lives of the Droserans.

For the sake of safety and companionship, she invited Kersei back to Kardia, though she second-guessed that decision often, considering the state of affairs, the impending war with Symmachia. It was the least Isaura felt she could do for Marco's onetime love and the woman who had given birth to the only Tyrannous left to rule, but mayhap she would have been safer with the Faa'Cris.

There were no guarantees, Isaura knew, having lost her own mother, sister, and brother to tragedies. She would not deny little Xylander his rightful title. If Isaura or her daughter did not survive, and Marco was lost after all,

Xylander would be the only heir. Though she knew the grand duke would argue for his own succession, since Darius had been stripped of his title.

Blood and boil—she could not let that happen.

In the morning, she would draft a secret decree, only to be revealed if no other heir—besides Rhayld—existed, that would name Xylander the blood heir to the Kalonican throne. An advocate should be assigned to ensure his ascension. Mavridis? Or mayhap Roman? No matter who would be assigned the task, Kardia must be secured.

It would be so much simpler if Dusan returned, reclaimed his throne, let her . . . rest. Give birth. Support him as his bound and kyria.

"How I miss you, Dusan . . ."

Bells of the watchtower pealed.

Lightning crackled through the sky, spitting darts of thunder down at the sea that raged with all the might and fury of a true Kalonican storm. Shivers traced Isaura's spine as she curled into herself, tugging the blanket over her shoulder. Cradling her womb with one hand, her amulet with the other.

That tremor raced through her body again.

She sat up, the blanket slipping from her shoulder as she squinted at the door that led to the solar. Voices carried through the storm-ravaged night.

Trouble.

How she knew that, she could not say. Only that conviction tightened in her breast, pushing her from the bed. Her feet had no sooner touched the hand-knotted rug than the doors pushed open and light intruded upon her sanctum. She squinted.

"Beg your mercy," Mavridis grumbled, "but you must come at once."

Isaura snatched up her robe and wrapped it around herself, appreciating the way it did not fully close around the swell of her womb. "What is it?"

"Hurry. We have little time."

Heart in her throat, she shoved her feet into slippers and followed her father into the solar. There waited Roman, Rico, Theilig, and Hushak. "What is this . . .?" She shifted the ribboned braid off her shoulder and tightened her robe, feeling a strange chill as Kita hurried toward her, Mnason in her arms.

"Symmachians, my kyria," Roman said. "They're on approach."

Isaura gulped the fear that trounced her courage. "For talks? At this hour?" She knew better, but the hope . . . she would have it. Anything to think she would survive until Dusan returned. That she would once more know his arms around her. See him seated on the throne of Kardia, defending his home and realm.

"Not with fighters," Rico muttered.

"This way." Mavridis indicated to a side hall where more than a dozen regia waited, flanking the passage. Even as they departed the apartments and kept moving, the royal entourage fell into step with them.

Ahead, she saw movement, and her jangled nerves thought it a foe. Instead, Mavridis guided Kersei and her babe into their cluster. She had no sooner linked arms with the princessa than a thundering boom rattled through the stones.

"Protect your kyria!" Mavridis shouted.

Isaura felt the press of bodies, of thick shoulders and muscled arms wedge in between her and Kersei, shuttling Kita aside. "No!" She reached out, feeling the touch of Kersei's fingers pulled from her own as their cries were drowned by another impact that rattled the castle.

"Go!" Mavridis ordered. "To the dungeons!"

Swept into the mass of bodies, Isaura had no choice but to move. She could not see the steps for the darkness and the regia huddled around her. Tears of panic pricked at her eyes.

Boom-boom-boom!

Rocks rained down.

The stone steps canted.

Isaura cried out, flinging her hands to the side for balance.

Regia caught her arms. Carried her down even as rocks and boulders tumbled from walls and lofty heights. One side of her human stretcher broke and she nearly fell. Even as she looked—blood spitting in her face as a boulder smashed a regia to death—she was rushed down the last few steps.

O, Ladies—please protect us. Protect my child!

They hurried down the touchstone-lit halls, spiraling into the damp darkness of the lower keep. A large, thick machi door barred entrance, but Hushak and Thorolf hefted it aside.

"Go!" Mavridis shouted, urging her forward.

Boom! BOOM!

Isaura was thrown forward, her feet lifting from the earth. She cried out, darkness enveloping as she had one thought: she could not die without giving Dusan his heir.

The quiet, the loneliness might have only been three days long by the time Kedalion Quadrant blinked on the radar, but Marco felt as if he'd been trapped on the ship for a lifetime. Only after he had regained consciousness and settled into the slipstream did he recall Jadon had vanished with Eija, leaving him alone with the Draegis recovering in a medical lectulo. Marco had nothing but his lonely thoughts to keep him company. And an arsenal of data. Information that left him daunted—the Uchuvchi were more than pilots in the sense he knew. They did more than direct their ships. They were integrated, powerful, and synced in with the unmanned drones they controlled as well as the hive ship.

Also, he'd learned a lot about the *Qirolicha*. Three of them built, one destroyed in a failed attempt to launch, another still under construction, and this one. The section that housed the Command deck also seemed to contain several other decks, though—being the only person on the ship—he could not leave to explore. He could decipher a power core at the center and what looked like decking that hugged the inner perimeter with close to a thousand bays of some kind. Only a tenth of them were active, so it seemed they hadn't finished out this ship either. He didn't care as long as it got him back to the Quadrants in time to destroy the Sentinel and slow or prevent the incoming attack and save those he loved.

Speaking of . . . The dreamspace had locked him out, either because of the slipstream or for some more sinister reason. He'd been unable to dream of Isaura, talk with her, hear her voice, see her smile. That had been what'd nearly broken him—not being able to reach her. The last time they talked, she said the Symmachians were there.

Anger bubbled through him, thinking of harm befalling the woman he'd come to love. The woman who'd kept him sane throughout this journey. *"You are not here, and yet you have been my guiding star . . ."*

What if I'm too late?

The thought had not really occurred before now because they'd had those moments in their dreams, spoken to each other, laughed with each other . . . Her absence now was all too real and complete.

Ancient, if she has been harmed, fuel and guide my fury.

He angled the lectulo into an upright position, a clever maneuver he'd discovered in the first twenty hours of boredom, allowing him to "stand" and look around. On the Prev, they'd been able to move around, but the speed at which the *Qirolicha* moved made it impossible on his frail, human body. He scanned the displays on the deck.

Wait . . . His pulse skipped a beat, its cadence winking at him as he studied the navigational charts. This couldn't be right.

With a few twitches of his fingers, he zoomed in and re-analyzed the stars. A small laugh climbed his throat but soon faded, replaced by a slow-burning anger that heated him from head to toe, made his brand flare brightly across the deck.

"What is it?"

Marco jerked, whipping the lectulo to the left.

The Draegis stood outside the medpod, healed. In fact, more healed and more normal than ever. And he was wearing a standard black uniform—tactical pants and an armored shirt with the right sleeve cut off at the bicep. That ring of hair was thick and dark, matching his near-black eyes.

"What is the problem?" Daq'Ti frowned. Looked around. "Where is Xonim?"

"Not here." It surprised Marco how clearly the Draegis spoke now. He turned back to the arrays. "She put you in that pod, tricked me into jumping, and then left—the Eidolon leaping after her to stop her. They both vanished."

Daq'Ti looked startled. His expressions were purely human now, as if the medpod had cleared the last vestiges of the damning ore from his body. Clearly, it wasn't an ordinary nano-based medpod. "I must go back."

Marco gave a cockeyed nod of his head. "Not happening. We're only a few light-years from my system. Besides, I have a feeling Xonim will find us." Somehow, he knew that to be true. So he focused on his mission—destroying the Sentinel in Kedalion. He flung wide his receptors again, searching. But found nothing . . .

He rifled through the data, anak'ing, straining to detect—

"You are angry."

"No." Mayhap it'd been too long since he'd hunted. That's why—

"You are angry."

Irritated at being read, Marco studied the data. "I can't find her."

"Xonim?"

"My wife." He flicked a gaze to the beast, realizing this likely made no sense to a creature who had spent his adulthood among on his brethren.

"I will help. Tell me how."

Marco again eyed him. "Never mind. Weapons." He nodded to the instrumentation. "When we leave the slipstream, we have to destroy the Sentinel."

Without hesitation, Daq'Ti strode to an alcove on the side and worked some panels.

Marco returned to his search of the maps and the efflux. Why couldn't he detect her? There were Signatures to be sure, but not *hers*. Eyes closed, he homed in. Probed for Mavridis—the most logical to be near Isaura. He pinpointed the Stalker, and traced another Signature near him, this one feminine, but not Isa. It was Kita. Isaura's lady's maid. Even better. But . . . still nothing. No Isaura.

Where are you, my aetos?

Instinctively, he again searched her out with his receptors. But that minty Signature met him. Soaked him with urgency. It was still too incredible to believe. *"Daughter . . . I am coming. Tell your mother."*

He chuckled at himself. He wasn't even sure that was really his daughter signaling him. But what else could it be? The notes—

Marco jolted. The Signature notes that were familiar and reminded him of someone? It was him! They were *his* notes! Excitement hummed yet was immediately dulled by the keen emptiness he met when he searched for his love. The pain was jarring now, being this close, still unable to find Isaura.

"Where is your mother, little one?"

Amber hints pulsed faintly. A muddled pain radiated through that Signature. It yanked him out of his morose thoughts. Turned him toward anger. *What's happening?*

An eruption of acrid odor stung his receptors.

"They're here. The Symmachians."

His grip tightened on the nav bar, angling and turning, guiding them through the stream. "So help me," he muttered to Xisya, half-believing the hideous creature could somehow hear him, "if she is dead, so are you."

"Approaching Sentinel," the mechanized voice of the ship announced.

Marco reclined the crash couch, noting Daq'Ti press a palm to the hull. A bubble ensconced him and somehow—unbelievably—edged past the hull, which vanished, leaving an open but distorted view of the expanse around them. Daq'Ti slid into a reclining chair with arms—

Marco sucked in a breath.

The guy's arms melded into the console within the bubble.

"Sentinel in five . . . four . . . three . . . two . . . one . . ."

Twang-pop!

A scream lit through his ears as an entire new solar system snapped into existence around them.

Marco shouldered against the pain, chomping into the mouthpiece. He arched his spine, powering down as he flipped and fired afterburners.

Daq'Ti powered up the weapons and chortled, "Incoming!"

"Incoming what?" The array over him lit up, shoving more than a little adrenaline through Marco's veins. Instinct had him deploying evasive measures and heat-seeking countermeasures. In disbelief that they had been anticipated before they'd even left the slipstream, he piloted away from the Sentinel's defensive measures.

The ship lurched. Shuddered.

The hit reverberated up through the cables, into the ports, and vibrated along his nerves. Teeth gritted, he focused on keeping them alive.

"The pilots!" Daq'Ti shouted.

"I don't care about their pilots. Destroy that Sentinel!" Marco glanced at the array, spotting a half dozen light fighters. Symmachian corvettes. Then he saw the larger blips—battlecruisers. He expected the *Macedon* was among them.

A warning buzzed in his brain, telling him to veer off. Head to Drosero.

No, they had to destroy the Sentinel.

"Bombardment!" Daq'Ti shouted.

Remembering the way the *Qirolicha* seemed to anticipate so many of his desires before he made any effort to put them into action, Marco drove his will into the ship. Which sounded and felt psychotic, but adrenaline and desperation told him anything was worth a try. Almost as soon as he focused on sending the payload, fire zipped through his veins.

From the icon of the *Qirolicha*, a dozen tiny dots spewed across the grid and vanished into the Sentinel.

"On-screen." Was there even a screen by which to view the destruction? He had no idea. But he wanted to see with his own eyes the destruction of that accursed satellite. An image, distant and blurry, blinked into existence beside the array. Satisfaction thrummed, muting his adrenaline and sating his need for justice. The tiny explosions. The crumbling of the *Chryzanthe*.

"Interceptors." Daq'Ti commanded his gunner's bubble like a pro, swinging around and firing on the fast-attack crafts, pelting them in another bombardment.

We're going to be obliterated. Yeah, should've listened to that instinct to head to Drosero. Little too late. Still, he hit thrusters and aimed the *Qirolicha* starboard. No. No good. They'd be ripped apart.

Jump. They had to jump again. A short one—to Drosero. He made the choice. Felt the fire in his veins as he powered up the jump mechanism.

Claxons rang through the ship.

The display glowered at him.

"Taking fire," Daq'Ti shouted. "Engaging evasive navigation."

Thump-thump-thump! A series of *whoomps* thudded through the ship. They swerved and dived.

Amid the bombardment, Marco finalized the jump protocol and keyed his comms. "Baric, not a very nice welcome back."

"Surrender the ship, Marco, or we'll be forced to destroy you," said the gravelly voice. "Like we did Kardia."

Marco stilled. Threw out his receptors, searching once more for Isaura, but this time he didn't waste time looking for Ixion or Kita. Instead, he seized on that minty note, daring it to lead to Isaura . . . Emptiness still gaped.

Where the reek was she? She could not be dead, could she? How much time had passed in the Quadrants? "This isn't a war you want," he warned the captain. "I will come at you with everything I have."

That minty Signature was strong, much stronger now. Holy Fires, what did it mean?

You know what it means.

No. It was impossible. He turned from the idea, what it would mean for his beloved.

"Wait till you see what remains of your precious little kingdom. You can't win this war, Marco. You are outwitted and outgunned."

"I think your Sentinel would beg to differ." He smirked, the navigation already laid in for Drosero, the ship reading his thoughts, he guessed.

"Which one?"

Marco blinked. *What?* The Quadrants had *one* Sentinel. Didn't they?

"Fighters incoming!" Daq'Ti exclaimed.

Without another thought, Marco spun up the drive. He slammed his hand on the jump controls.

"No!" Daq'Ti's shout chased a massive jolt that rocketed through Marco's body. Pain exploded through every limb and nerve ending. Dropped him into utter blackness.

A heavy thud snapped Marco awake. His head thundered, as if it'd been used for javrod practice. He groaned and shifted.

"It is well, Uchuvchi. We've landed. I'm almost complete with repairs."

"Landed?" Marco jerked upright, and amazingly the lectulo did not stop him. "Where?"

"I did not know your planet, but I found one like you and landed as close as I could."

One like me? What did that mean?

Marco focused on his home. On Kardia. He tried not to let the panic build when he couldn't anak her Signature. *"Where are you . . .?"* Quickly, he was able to confirm they were indeed on Drosero—he could smell Mavridis and Vorn, the latter much closer. Is that what Daq'Ti meant—one like him, meaning human?

But most Quadrant planets were populated with humans.

He closed his eyes, homed in on the dreamspace. Reached out. *"Isaura? Are you there, my aetos?"*

That suffocating emptiness hung rank, though drenched in that new minty Signature.

He swallowed, worry drumming hard on his heart. The child but not her mother. Was it possible . . .? He would not accept it. The very idea drilled him. Maybe that was the problem—the panic. Distraction. He must settle. Focus. Just like in the hunt. *Let the scent guide . . .*

He pushed past the distraction, sweeping Drosero. Ash . . . chemical . . . burning . . .

Marco tensed. "I smell fire."

"Enemy ships destroyed," Daq'Ti explained. *"Qirolicha* defended herself and you."

Marco felt a sharp pain in his side and realized the umbilicals had popped from his ports. "What happened?" The nasal one released with a tingle that made him want to sneeze.

"Navigational array was struck, so the ship disengaged from you to preserve itself."

"How did we outmaneuver a battlecruiser and end up crashing against lesser ships?"

"We've been limping since the bombardment—the pilots—"

"Why did I pass out?"

"The *Qirolicha* is very powerful, and without properly powering up, its systems were forced to pull from your body. Too much for you," Daq'Ti trilled. "It is guess."

The fetor of fuel permeated the air, along with that very unique scent he'd grown to hate. "Hirakys," he hissed, eying the Symmachian hotbed on the digital arrays. By the landmarks and open square, he guessed them to be right in the heart of the beast, their capital city of Ildiron. "This is bad—these people are in league with the Khatriza."

He eyed the Draegis forearm plating that had fallen off during the piloting of the *Qirolicha*. The thing had been so foreign, so like what Daq'Ti had, that Marco did not want to put it back on. "What personal weapons do we have on board?"

"Me, sir."

"That doesn't do me any good."

"I would agree," Daq'Ti said. "But as Uchuvchi, the ship will shield you as long as you are within range."

"How far is that?"

"Unknown. I am not familiar with this prototype's range. On a class-four interstellar light raider, two klicks."

"Then it's possible there's *no* extended shielding on this."

Daq'Ti met his gaze. "Unlikely, but . . . yes."

Great. No weapon. Possibly no shield. And taking fire right in the heart of enemy territory. Had he made it all the way back from Kuru to end up getting killed on his own planet? Hopefully Jadon and Eija were faring better.

"I will remain with you." Daq'Ti's arm weaponized.

Marco didn't miss the way he grimaced or the pained scent rolling off him—it really hurt Blue to power up that arm as he clomped toward the side hatch where Marco and Jadon had entered. The door whisked open. Red laserlike blasts danced in front of them, sparking off a staticky shield.

Daq'Ti went to a knee, angled his head and aimed. He fired twice and the incoming barrage died. They exited down a ramp, Daq'Ti urging Marco behind him as they did. Shock rippled through Marco at the destruction around them. The city was in ruins—buildings blown up, smoke pluming through the alleys and streets. People and horses lay dead, among the rubble.

Whatever had happened here . . . it'd happened recently.

Marco pressed his forearm to his nose and did his best not to breathe too heavily of the death that consumed the city. It reminded him of— "Wait." He caught Daq'Ti's shirt. "Irukandji."

A shriek lobbed from the side. Two blue-marked raiders burst from an alley, blindly barreling at Marco with pulse pistols and hatchets. Their zigzag advance made it difficult to get a lock, but Daq'Ti neutralized one. Though the other took a hit, too, he careened forward.

The shrill blast of another pulse weapon—this one from the left—squawked three times, taking the raider to ground. It slid to a stop six paces away.

Warily, Marco examined the city, the crumbling government buildings, the large square blocks that had once formed the main square. The destruction was large scale.

Daq'Ti scanned. "Four males on the other side of that broken stone animal."

"Steady," Marco muttered, watching heads appear over the piles of debris.

"We are no threat," a voice shouted.

"Prove it," Marco bellowed back.

"Would yeh like a dance? Or do yeh have another pretty Moidian in that ship of yers?"

Heat singed Marco's spine. That voice! "Crey!"

"Hunter!" The burly man rose with a laugh. "Yeh going to use that big ship of yers on us?"

"Depends."

Crey sported a crooked smile as he and his men came out from behind the monument of a mounted rider—the legs of the Black missing, along with its head. "On what?"

"How long you make me stand in the open to be picked off by Irukandji or Symmachians."

"I thought to distract them with yer good looks, giving m'self a chance to catch them unawares. Inflict pain on them for a change, like we started with this one." Crey wagged his weapon at the body of the first raider, then continued to approach, with two men sticking close. "But I think we might have something of yers here on this side of the fire gorges. Maybe we should think about finding shelter in case I'm wrong."

Something wary crawled up Marco's neck. He flung out his receptors . . . and stilled. This couldn't be. He knew that scent. "What's this?" He eyed the companions as they closed the gap. "I think you have more trouble here than you realize."

"Aye, yeh could say that." Crey grinned. "But we done had some help from the north in rousting the pretender, Theule. I'll be taking back my throne and cleaning up the city and my country, yeh."

"I think we define 'cleaning up' a little differently."

Crey shrugged. "Sometimes to clean up, yeh have to tear down first."

The two men behind the leader were the same height and build, but that Signature . . . Unmistakable. "Show yourself," Marco demanded.

Crey barked a laugh. "Even banged up and flying on an alien ship, yeh still got that nose what knows."

The concealed man on the right lowered the hood and mask.

Darius. It struck Marco like a pulse blast—this is what Daq'Ti meant when he said, "one like you." Marco's brother. Same DNA. Similar scent.

"What're you doing here?" Marco growled. "Turned traitor—"

"Now go easy with those dagger words," Crey said sharply. "This boy's been helping me and mine."

"Which means he's not helping the people he was set in power to protect." Marco surged forward. "Explain yourself, Darius!"

His brother glanced down.

How he'd hoped Darius would step strongly into his rightful role, become the man Marco knew he could be. "You are a prince of Kalonica, the prince regent—"

"No," Darius said firmly, his head snapping back up. "I was stripped of those titles."

Marco considered him. Anak'd. No lies. "What do you here?"

"I pay a debt."

Hesitation guarded Marco, his anger simmering, hope rising. "Which one?"

"In exchange for seeing my son born, I have come here to help reseat Crey as rex."

"And a fine job he's done. All that's left is for me to seize the empty throne. Return order to chaos."

What did that mean—*in exchange for seeing his son born*? Why would he not see him born? And what was Darius doing helping the southern realm? "Why aren't you protecting your kyria or bound?"

Darius looked chagrined. "My bound is with the Ladies in Deversoria. Our uncle now protects Isaura."

Not good. "Rhayld is loyal to the purse—"

"Not him. Our *mother's* brother."

"She didn't have—"

"Roman."

Marco stilled. Stared. "What?"

With a sad smile, Darius nodded. "After being chased out of the Citadel, the Kynigos took up residence in the aerios quarters of Kardia's walls. He has barely left her side since." Weariness lined a face that had matured since last they met. "Much has changed since you were captured, Brother."

Kardia. The Brethren there with— "Isaura." Marco flinched, remembering only as instinct sought her Signature that he'd been unable to anak her. He moved forward, agitation growing. "What of Isaura?"

Darius held his gaze, sad. "There was an attack—"

"No," Marco breathed.

His brother planted a hand on Marco's chest, his blue eyes leaden. "Unknown, Marco. Her fate and all of Kardia's are unknown at present. Kardia was attacked two days ago, and there has been no word since."

Heart dropping into his gut, Marco turned north. Is that why he could not anak her—she was dead? He opened his mouth. Drew in a long, deep scent and held it at the back of his throat.

Nothing.

Please. Ladies—Vaqar—Ancient, please!

"I am sure she is safe," Darius offered quietly.

Morose, Marco took in Hirakys's battered capital. "I can't anak her. It terrifies me. The thought of losing her . . ."

"That fear I know well."

Their gazes locked, and he saw in his brother's similar blue eyes the truth of what he spoke, the fear, and the grief. He clapped his upper arm. "We have much to talk—"

A rank scent erupted from behind.

Marco pivoted toward the blur—an attack! Even as he did, he knew he was too late. The raider had the advantage and a weapon.

"No!" Darius shouted as a blast flashed from the muzzle.

Sensing his end, Marco heard the *tsing* of his staticky shield. Smelled singed air. Panicked, fierce effluxes. Felt a weight crash into him, knocking him to the ground. Unbelievably the shield warbled around him and held firm, stretching and crackling, preventing injury to his person.

A heavy thump registered to his right. There lay the raider, coated in blood. Eyes lifeless. Blue marks slowly fading with his life.

Marco shifted, pinned by his brother, who had protected him. Intercepted the raider and kept him from killing Marco. He caught Darius's shoulders. "We're safe." But his brother didn't move. He nudged him aside. "Get off."

Darius slid . . .

Marco shifted, saw the blood.

"Princeling!" Crey rushed forward and planted his hands to Darius's chest. Blood sluiced between his hands from a gaping wound.

"No." Marco couldn't move. Then shock tore away. "Darius!" He leapt to his brother's side.

Confused blue eyes flickered to his. Mouth agape, crimson splatters on his face, Darius stared back. His fingers dug into Marco's shirt. Tightened. "Mmmercy."

"Hang on, Darius." Gulping adrenaline, Marco snapped his gaze to Crey. "Get help!"

Darius's lip quirked up on one side. "Brother . . ."

"*Hold on.*" Saying it, Marco had the sense of the others easing back. Away. They knew. He knew. Could anak the fading Signature . . .

"Beg mercy," Darius gurgled. "I was . . . wrong."

"It's in the past." Marco's throat felt raw. Thick. What was he supposed to say? "Forget it."

"Grant mercy—ppplease." His fistful of Marco's shirt tugged.

Marco swallowed. "Stop, Darius. Just stay still. Help's coming." He looked up at Crey and his gathered men, realizing no one had gone for help. "What're you doing? Get a pharmakeia!"

"Mmmarco," Darius wheezed. "My ssson . . ."

"Save your breath. The pharmakeia will fix you."

A crooked smile pulled at his lips again. "I love . . . her. Sssorry . . ." His efflux faded into nothingness, the light in his eyes, the pale blue light . . .

"No! Darius!"

Where were Eija or Vaqar or the Lady when he needed them?

Eija.

The medpod!

Marco scooped Darius into his arms, blood drenching his sleeves and shirt. "Hang on, Brother." He staggered up into the ship and hurried to the far corner where he'd seen Eija activate the lectulo. The ship whirred, the contraption rising . . . then stopping midway.

With a growl, Marco kicked it. "C'mon!"

Daq'Ti was there. "The pilots—too damaged."

"Open it!" Marco growled.

The Draegis worked, yanking and pulling until finally the medpod rose into position.

With a grunt, Marco shouldered him out of the way and laid his brother in the pod. It sealed but wouldn't power up. He palmed the main instrument panel, leaving a bloody handprint. Waiting for the ship to respond to his brand.

Nothing happened.

"C'mon!" He slapped it, his hand slicking across the glass.

Nothing.

Shaking the thing, he growled. Kicked it. "C'mon you piece of slag!"

"The ship doesn't recognize his body because he's gone, Uchuvchi."

"Then force it to. Give it some juice. Something has to work!" He went to another panel. Searched, but the lettering wouldn't work. Wouldn't translate in his brain. He tapped pads, hoping the sequences were right. That he'd instinctively remember something just as Eija had.

He slid back to the pod. Trying the panel again. "*Please.*" Gripped the sides. "Vaqar, please!" He shook it. Growled around a raw throat. Kicked it again. It whirred . . . then hissed into silence.

"Augh!" Marco spun away. Punched the hull. Turned and ripped a digital display from where it hung suspended and pitched it, sending it clanging on the deck. He gripped his head. The stupid recreant was supposed to survive him. Dropping back against the inner hull, sliding down to the deck, he stared across the space to the pod. He felt responsible, though he hadn't done anything wrong.

Except exist. Come back.

He rammed his head back against the wall. Did it again. And again, growling.

Slumped in defeat, arms dangling over his knees as he looked at the lectulo, he cradled his head again, shredded. They'd never had a chance to be brothers, not really. He'd despised Darius after Iereania. They'd gone their separate ways. But never had he wanted his brother dead. Not really.

Roughing a hand over his face, Marco climbed to his feet. Crossed the deck and leaned over the lectulo again. "You . . . idiot . . ." He touched the sandy blond hair.

"*My ssson . . .*"

He closed his eyes. Bent forward, he rested his elbows on his knees and pressed his lips against his arm, doing his best to stem the grief. He studied his brother, forever in a deep sleep—smoother skinned, softer around the mouth and eyes.

"*I love . . . her.*"

Kersei.

"He was a good man."

On his feet, Marco resented Crey's intrusion but could not bring himself to say anything, let alone acknowledge the man's presence.

"He came down here to rectify a wrong—his wrong." Crey clomped into the sphere but maintained a safe distance from Marco's grief and anger. "We were losing. It looked hopeless. But he said yeh would find a way to turn it around. I laughed at him—yeh weren't anywhere to be seen. Many thought yeh dead. But he—he said to look for yeh and the victory in yer hand."

Marco clenched his eyes shut again. Strange how much grief he bore for a man who'd been responsible for so much heartache. For ripping Kersei from him, a painful memory dulled by the love of Isaura.

"Then out of nowhere," Crey continued, "this ship comes blazing into the heavens and guns down the Symmachian corvettes. Sends the enemy running. The princeling knew—he *knew* it was yeh."

Darius said he had been stripped of his title. Not sure how that happened, Marco knew one thing—in the Eternal Embrace, Darius would not have any worries. He recalled his brother's pleas for Kersei and his son. "They'll be provided for." Resolve firmed in him. "I swear it. On my honor."

On his brother's left pinky was a simple gold ring. Simple save the engraved aetos, the Tyrannous sigil. What was he doing with that notable piece of jewelry in enemy territory? Just couldn't give up the gold, could he? "You really were an idiot," he sniffed around a laugh. Shook his head. Hand on Darius's shoulder, he pressed the still form. "Let's go home."

"What the reek is that thing?"

Overhearing Kalonican fliers' comms chatter, Roman eyed the strange shape on the readout from the flight command deck. "Whatever it is, keep it away from Kardia." He flipped a couple switches, keeping his gaze on the display that showed the weird ship coming straight at them. There was something in the air—familiar. Fierce.

"Zeev base to Aetos base, come in."

At the voice sailing across the comms, Roman hesitated. Why was Vorn talking rather than his flight commander? "Go ahead, Zeev. This is Aetos."

"Sent you a package," Vorn reported. "Little beat up but wrapped in a steel bow of hope. Might not want to shoot this one down."

Roman's gaze hit the strange craft on the array. It had an orblike cockpit and crescent shape around it that spun so fast, it looked like a pool of honey. "What did you—" He stilled, drew in his focus, let the anaktesios massage the efflux radiating through the atmosphere. "Can't be . . ."

"I assure you," Vorn said with a small laugh, "it is. Break out the welcome mats. Your king is coming home."

Roman flung off the headset and darted out of the booth. He shot down the steps and raced to the far courtyard. Even as he leapt down the steps toward the fountain of Eleftheria, he was searching the skies for the craft that held promise of Marco.

"What is it?" Hushak shouted from behind, alarmed, no doubt, by his swift movements.

A glint sparked in the sky.

Roman held his breath. "Call the regia," he shouted over his shoulder, watching the crescent-shaped ship sail out toward the Kalonican Sea, then bank around. He almost ordered the ringing of the bells, but the less the Symmachians knew, the better. Especially with so many raiders lurking about Lampros City. "The medora returns!"

"Should I notify the kyria?"

Roman hesitated, the sound of fighting in the streets beyond the wall reaching his ears all too easily. "Not yet—keep her belowground." The Faa'Cris had shielded her, concerned the Khatriza would detect Marco's heir and come for them. A risk, considering Marco's need for her as beacon, but unavoidable. "We need to protect them until he's within the walls."

The craft came humming in, straight for him. And he felt it. Tasted it. Marco's return.

"Lower blast shield," Marco instructed, anxious for sight of Kardia. His home.

"Forward blast shields rising," the ship intoned.

Light streaked into the once-dull interior of the ship and ricocheted off the metal braces and acrylic displays. He squinted but did not take his gaze from the—

"No." He drew in a breath at the gaping hole in the southern wall. The rubble of the servants' quarters along that perimeter. Smoke rose from the city, easily thirty, maybe forty percent of the structures reduced to rubble. Kardia itself, once noble and austere, seemed to sag beneath the destruction. The towers had been destroyed, the southern portico a pile of ruins in a deep depression.

Her name struggled up his throat. "Isaura." Is this why he could not detect her? Was she dead? His breath staggered, then latched onto his anger. If she was dead, they would pay. By Vaqar, they would pay! He glanced to the sealed pod where Darius lay in the Lady's Embrace. Not both of them. He could not lose both his brother and his bound.

"Oh, Ancient, please . . ."

He aimed the *Qirolicha* toward the clearing on the cliff, he spotted a handful of men. His anak'ing made out each efflux. Roman . . . Ixion. Relief stung his eyes. That the Stalker was not with Isaura plucked at the thin thread Marco held that she yet lived.

Do not let me return to a ruined city and dead kyria. I beg You . . .

As they landed, he felt the tubes of the lectulo retracted into the ship and left him on his feet. For a moment, he stared at the door. He could not anak her Signature, the only one he wished for. The only face he wanted to greet him was not there.

Daq'Ti strode to the hatch and palmed it.

Light spliced through the crack as the door slid away, affording a glimpse of the ramp telescoping onto a bed of grass. He mustered his courage and moved toward the door. Paused. Glanced at the pod that held Darius's body.

"I will bring him," Daq'Ti promised in that still-trilling way of his. What would the Quadrants think of him once they knew what he truly was? What would they do when it became apparent he was from the same race that wanted to annihilate them?

After a nod, Marco descended onto the soil of his forebears. He resisted the urge to drop to his knees and kiss the grass, thank Vaqar for delivering him safely back to Kalonica. Instead, he angled toward the arc of regia forming, men still sprinting toward the ship.

"Vanko Kalonica!" The shouts ricocheted around the orb behind him. "Vanko Kalonica! Long live Medora Marco!"

The words resonated, painfully reminiscent of the night he'd left his father and mother, his brothers, and climbed aboard a ship for the very first time—with the master hunter . . .

His gaze hit his master's, and Marco felt the earth shift beneath him.

Roman was at his side, pulling him into a hug. Slapping his back. "Welcome home, Marco."

Easing back, he eyed the master, recalling what Darius said—*uncle*. Was it true?

Roman sent a spurt of warm cedar to him, friendly. Welcoming. He clung a little longer than necessary, clearly giving Marco the time to find his bearings and balance.

The musty air of the passages were drenched in that minty Signature, which he yet struggled to fully accept was from his daughter. But still no Isaura . . .

Braced, he breathed into the duster-clad shoulder, "Where is she?"

Roman clapped his biceps as he stepped back. "You are a sight for sore eyes. Let us get you inside." He ran a hand over Marco's shorn hair. "Much has changed since you stood on these grounds." He laughed. "Come, you are not safe in the open."

"No doubt the raiders and Symmachians saw the ship land," Ixion's voice boomed as he stepped forward, gripped Marco's forearm, and hauled him into a one-shouldered hug. "The words have breath."

The Moidian phrase jarred him—there was some reply he should provide to complete the blessing—but Marco could not be deterred from the fact that Roman had ignored his question. His rank avoidance irritated. "I would—"

Boom! Boom!

Crack-crack-crack.

Ixion and Roman hooked Marco's arms and drew him forward. "On your medora!"

"Inside—now!"

She's dead. That's why they will not speak of her. That's why the residue is minty— she wasn't just a girl from the wastelands. She was pure.

Why? Why had he fought so hard to get back? He should've realized these last few days what the absence of her voice and visage meant. What that mint implied—not his daughter at all, but his bound's departure to be with the Ladies. Was that it? Well they would pay—Symmachia would pay for killing her. And his brother—

"Wait!" Marco dug in his heels. Turned back to the ship.

Ixion faltered as his gaze hit the lone man at the ramp of the *Qirolicha* with the lectulo.

"Come, Daq'Ti," Marco called over the murmurs and uncertainty—fear— that swelled through the gathered. "We bring my brother's body home."

Daggers of scents shot through the air—anger, disgust, grief, uncertainty again.

"Darius?" Mavridis inquired, shocked. "How? He was in Hirakys—"

"We first landed there. The ship—" He motioned with a hand, anxious to see Isaura. Not interested in details. "Later. Important part is that Darius died protecting me."

The storm of Signatures calmed, though some still simmered.

"See the medora inside," Roman ordered Mavridis. "I'll bring them in."

After indicating to Daq'Ti that he could trust these men, Marco ascended the stairs and path to the east entrance, but his gaze climbed to the balcony of the royal residence he had stood on many times. But half the balcony was gone as was a good portion of the residence. He faltered. *No.*

"This way." Ixion led not to the stairs that rose to the royal apartments, but down . . .

"What is this?" Marco asked.

"All are belowground until we purge the land of raiders and Symmachians and restore the residences."

"The walls, the balcony . . ." Marco noted the state of disrepair, the destruction, still unable to inquire as to whether she yet lived. Anger roiled that he still could not anak her. It meant she was dead. Rage boiled with each step he took that did not bring him to her.

"Two nights ago, three ships attacked," Ixion explained, ushering them further into the castle. "If the Kynigos had not sheltered here in Kardia, we would have been defenseless against Symmachia. Your uncle has been a godsend."

"Roman." Marco slid a hand over his nose and mouth, only then realizing he was shielding himself from what that minty Signature meant. He resented that the menthol grew stronger, more painful the deeper he descended into palace dungeons.

"Aye, much has changed since you were last in these halls," Ixion said.

"So everyone keeps telling me."

"Darius was convicted of treason and stripped of title—"

"He said as much."

Mavridis hesitated, his gaze down.

Raw, Marco turned to him, unable to bear it any longer. "Tell me—"

Something strange hit the Stalker's expression.

Hearing the shuffling of regia around him, the rustle of their clothes, squeak of boots, Marco homed his gift around the noises. None as loud as the grief treading their nervous movements. "Tell me," he growled. Each breath a chore. Strength leached out . . .

What was life without her? He did not want it. Did not want to be here. Yet, not telling him would change nothing.

Not true. It would force him to accept it.

And that . . . that would be when he'd unleash the most violent war.

"You should not be here," Ixion hissed.

"What?" Marco scowled at him but only then saw the Stalker did not address him. His gaze had locked on a side juncture in the stone passage. Light from the far end cast its ample beam across a rosied face—Kersei. She stood clutching a babe to her shoulder.

Knowing what body he brought home, what grief he must hand her, Marco could only acknowledge her.

"I had to see for myself." Kersei's tears wrestled her words that mirrored her roiling scent. She sobbed, then nodded. "My heart soars with the aetos to see you alive."

It would not once she learned what happened in Hirakys. *I bring only bad news and sorrow.* It was too much. All the more, he simply wanted Isaura. To be in her arms. Hear her laugh, whisper love in his ear. He started moving again, searching out Isa.

"Go back." Ixion stalked toward her, pointing to her guards. "Get her to safety. You know what terror hunts us." He hustled to catch up.

Marco pivoted to the Plisiázon, unable to meet the man's gaze. "Give it to me—how did she die? Where is her body that I may send her into the Lady's Embrace?"

"My medora—"

"*Where?*" Grabbing Ixion's jerkin and yanking him forward, Marco released the fury of a lifetime and let it course through his veins, hot, volatile. "*Where. Is. She?*"

Light flickered and danced beneath movement at the far end of a musty stone passage.

Marco stopped short. The menthol that had saturated his receptors suddenly relented, faded. Startling him. In its place—

Sweet and true, strong and potent sailed the most beautiful of Signatures. It rushed upon his receptors and drowned him in its fragrance, yanked him around.

The silhouette snatched the breath from his lungs. "Isau—" A choked sob stole her name from his lips. Could it be? Dare he hope and have it dashed? He staggered forward, the shadows around her brightening, releasing her. Frozen in place, she did not need light to illuminate her, for she *was* light.

His feet moved faster, his heart thudding in cadence. The distance felt a league!

She was a vision! Long blonde hair hung over her shoulders, strands reaching toward her enlarged womb. The sight struck him hard. Gratitude to the Ladies, to Vaqar, to the Ancient overwhelmed him. Seeing her, that glorious scent at last bathing his receptors, dropped Marco to a knee. Then two. He bent at her feet. He cried, touching her slippers. His fears were eradicated. Clinging to her, sobbing. She was here. She was alive.

Gown billowing around her as she lowered herself to the cold stone, Isaura wrapped her arms around his shoulders, her chest shuddering beneath her own tears. She cradled and kissed his head. "Dusan. Oh, my love. How I have missed you," she breathed against his ear.

Her words were life. Her scent healing. He lifted his face and cupped hers. Then shifted his hand to her enlarged, glorious womb. He anak'd the babe fully then, the mint with touches of oak and amber. It *had* been her. Drawing him back. Lips pressed there, he half laughed, half cried. "Thank you. Thank you for guiding me home, little one."

EPILOGUE

Before she stepped into the natural plane, Eija felt it—the weight of another. The heavy responsibility of another's adunatos clinging to her. In the seconds before she reshaped, she saw the nursery. Felt more than saw Reef plummet past her.

She dove, air rifling her wingspan. Gritting her teeth, seeing the distance grow between them, she surged. Grabbed his arm and deployed her wings. They snapped up and Reef groaned, slowly coming back into focus.

He grabbed at her arm with his free hand, eyes wild with panic. "Do. Not. Let. Go."

"It'd serve you right." She gave three strong snaps of her span, redirecting their landing to a spot out of sight of the Draegis who were still trolling the nursery for her. It felt like days ago that she'd nearly been killed, but it'd been less than a half hour.

"Maybe," Reef conceded, glancing down the length of his body, "but I think you like me too much to—"

Eija loosened her grip.

Reef sucked in a breath and scrambled to grab her. "Okay, okay!"

She grinned, then settled him on the deck.

"Not funny."

She alighted next to him and then slapped the back of his head. "You idiot!"

"Ow! What?"

"Marco—he needed you as a co-pilot," she said, hurrying to the side and crouching in a corner as she scanned the lower levels crawling with Draegis. "He's alone."

Reef grimaced. "I didn't *mean* to fall through the continuum with you."

She scowled at him. "The what?"

His rich, dark eyes hit hers. "The . . . continuum—you know, whatever . . . That plane you Faa'Cris traverse."

When she'd been Eija Zacdari, the Tryssinian, she'd felt more than friendly things toward this Symmachian male. But now, back in her skin—as it were—as Vaqar's daughter, she saw this male in new light. He was young, arrogant, foolish, cocky . . . "You're brave."

He gave her a lopsided grin. "Think so?"

"What I meant was foolish. You take not into consideration what I am, who I am. You realize the power I wield, the purpose of my existence—"

"But you're still Eija."

Reducing her to what he could understand and accept was typical. Yet it was strange—when he said her name, an odd, giddy warmth spread through her middle. "I'm not who you think I am, and you need to focus. We have very little time and entirely too much to accomplish."

"Just like Eija would've said." He rubbed his hands and shot her that annoying cocky grin. "Where do we start?"

Moonslight stretched across the room, sneaking between the heavy curtains. Fingers steepled, Marco sat on the tufted chair watching Isaura sleep. Trying to wrap his mind around the truth that he had truly made it home. He *was* here. This *was* real. Not dreamscape.

With a start, Isaura came up with a gasp. "Dusan!"

Flooded by her panicked scent, Marco crossed the room. "Here, my aetos." He slid beneath the coverlet and pulled her into his arms. "I'm here."

She wilted against his chest and gave a long, shuddering sigh. "I feared you were still gone. That it had all been a dream."

He kissed the crown of her head. "I share your fears."

"Seeing you walk down that passage, the regia thick behind you . . . I could not move. Did not believe it. I was absolutely convinced you were yet another dream."

"I knew that same fear," he said, scooting down to lie beside her. Kiss her. "I could not detect your Signature. But hers . . ." He caressed her swollen belly. "A strange, minty Signature found me in the void of yours. Wouldn't leave me alone. Though I wondered if it was our child, it terrified me that I could anak her and not you. Feared you had died giving birth early or some other tragedy. I so feared you gone that I could scarce speak when I saw your silhouette in the passage."

"The Ladies protected me, shielded my scent," she whispered. "I argued it, but they believed the creature Xisya would find me—and, in turn, you. I thought you might believe me dead, but then . . . there you were! Yet, when you bowed before me—I knew it could not be real. It must be a dream. No medora bows to his kyria."

He chuckled. "I do, and would again."

Silence cocooned them as they lay in the dark. The very real threat of attack kept his receptors open, his body ready to jump in an instant. And yet, the exhaustion of the jump, the toll piloting the *Qirolicha* took on his body—

"What are these?" Isaura said, tracing a port scar.

It was too beastly to explain. Somehow it made him ashamed. Made him feel weird. "Port scars. It's how they plugged me into the ship."

Isaura propped up, looking at him. "What do you mean?" Her alarm, her anger—

He cupped her face. Kissed her. Did not want to talk about all this right now. He was tired. Drained. Numb.

Alarm spiked through the hall, drawing Marco up, away from Isaura. He looked to the door and slid from bed, snagging his tunic.

"What is it?" she asked.

"Stay here." Threading his arms through the tunic, he moved toward the door. Searched for a weapon. Before there were even knocks on the door, he anak'd Mavridis and his regia roiling with fear. Marco threw open the door, stilling them. "What trouble?"

Mavridis shook off his startlement. "You need to come."

With a nod, Marco glanced to Isaura, who rushed to his side, entwining their hands.

"She should stay behind," Mavridis said.

"Never again," Isaura countered.

Shouts erupted amid screams, pulling them all forward. They raced down a passage, then up rough-hewn stone steps to a small bailey. Dozens of aerios and regia were staring up at the night sky.

Daq'Ti strode toward him. "The pilots—"

"What is it?" someone shouted. "What do they want?"

Marco strode out from the shelter of the home and stopped short. Gaped. His blood ran cold. "No . . ."

Dozens—no, *hundreds* of small ships dotted the inky expanse, blotting out the moonslight.

The Draegis had come to Drosero.

ACKNOWLEDGEMENTS

Readers—a million thanks for all your loyalty, cool hashtags, reels, and graphics you have created related to the Droseran Saga, but more than that—thank you for journeying with me and Marco through these books. Love having you along for the jump!

Sincere thanks to Jamie Foley, author extraordinaire and Enclave's Girl Wonder, for the amazing maps you find in the front matter. You got mad skillz, Lady!

Special thanks to Kim Gradeless, Jane Farrelly, and Rosalyn Schlabach for your last-minute eagle eyes on the galley. So grateful!

When life turned upside down and got insane, a handful of special friends stepped in and had my six—Deepest Gratitude to Narelle Mollet, Kim Gradeless, Jane Farrelly, Mikal Hermanns, and Beth K. Vogt. You ladies are gorgeous!!

ABOUT THE AUTHOR

Ronie Kendig is a bestselling, award-winning author of over thirty books. She grew up an Army brat, and now she and her Army-veteran husband have returned to their beloved Texas after a ten-year stint in the Northeast. They survive on Sonic & Starbucks runs, barbecue, and peach cobbler that they share—sometimes—with Benning the Stealth Golden. Ronie's degree in psychology has helped her pen novels of intense, raw characters.

Ronie can be found at: www.roniekendig.com

Facebook: www.facebook.com/RapidFireFiction
Twitter: @RonieKendig
Goodreads: www.goodreads.com/RonieK
Instagram: @KendigRonie

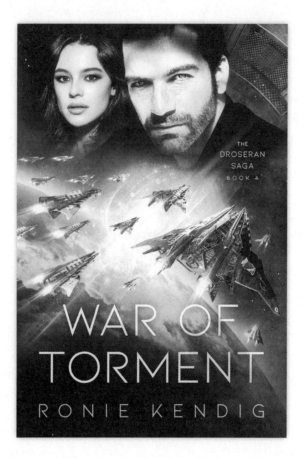

THE
DROSERAN
SAGA
BOOK 4

WAR OF
TORMENT

RONIE KENDIG